Critical acclaim for David Baldacci's novels

'Already among the world's bestselling writers, Baldacci hardly needs to prove himself but he's created one of the most intriguing, complex anti-heroes . . . Impossible to put down, especially because of Decker, who weaves a powerful spell'
Daily Mail

'A typically twisty plot never flags, and benefits from having the likeably offbeat sleuth (whose gifts include synaesthesia and photographic memory) as its pivot'
Sunday Times

'Alternately chilling, poignant, and always heart-poundingly suspenseful'
Scott Turow, *New York Times* bestselling author

'A mile-a-minute read that proves once again why David Baldacci has readers the world over flocking for more'
Jane Harper, *New York Times* bestselling author of *The Dry*

'As ever, Baldacci keeps things moving at express-train speed . . . this one will whet appetites for the next appearance of his agent hero'
Daily Express

'A plot strong enough to make the bath go cold around you'
Independent on Sunday

The Amos Decker thrillers
by David Baldacci

Memory Man

Amos Decker's photographic memory means he forgets nothing and sees what others miss. Struggling with his own traumatic past, his life is changed forever when he's pulled into a tragedy at a local high school.

The Last Mile

Newly appointed FBI special agent Amos Decker's infallible memory is put to the test to prove the innocence of a man who awaits his sentence on death row.

The Fix

Amos Decker – the FBI's most unique special agent – witnesses a cold-blooded murder outside the world's biggest crime fighting agency in Washington D. C. It proves to be the catalyst for an investigation which exposes a plot to blow apart the nation's security.

The Fallen

What was supposed to be a relaxing vacation for special agent Amos Decker and his FBI partner, Alex Jamison, turns into a murder investigation in Baronville.

Redemption

FBI consultant Amos Decker discovers that he may have made a fatal mistake when he was a rookie homicide detective. Back in his home town, he's now compelled to discover the truth . . .

Walk the Wire

Amos Decker and his colleague, Alex Jamison, investigate a brutal killing in London, North Dakota, which sits at the heart of the fracking industry. Enriched with oil money, jealousy and a deep-set rivalry in the town lie beneath a veneer of glitz and opulence.

Walk the Wire

David Baldacci is one of the world's bestselling and favourite thriller writers and author of *Long Road to Mercy*, *Redemption* and *One Good Deed*. With over 130 million copies in print, his books are published in over eighty territories and forty-five languages, and have been adapted for both feature-film and television. David is also the co-founder, along with his wife, of the Wish You Well Foundation®, a non-profit organization dedicated to supporting literacy efforts across the US.

Trust him to take you to the action.

DAVID BALDACCI

Walk the Wire

PAN BOOKS

First published 2020 by Grand Central Publishing, USA

First published in the UK 2020 by Macmillan

This paperback edition published 2020 by Pan Books
an imprint of Pan Macmillan
The Smithson, 6 Briset Street, London EC1M 5NR
Associated companies throughout the world
www.panmacmillan.com

ISBN 978-1-5098-7454-5

1 3 5 7 9 8 6 4 2

A CIP catalogue record for this book is available from the British Library.

Typeset in Bembo by Jouve (UK), Milton Keynes
Printed and bound by CPI Group (UK) Ltd, Croydon, CR0 4YY

MIX
Paper from
responsible sources
FSC® C116313

Visit www.panmacmillan.com to read more about all our books
and to buy them. You will also find features, author interviews and
news of any author events, and you can sign up for e-newsletters
so that you're always first to hear about our new releases.

To Mike and Monica Rao,
for all you've done for VCU

FBI Agent Profile

Name: Amos Decker

Date of Birth: Early forties, looks at least ten years older but feels at least a century older than that.

Place of Birth: Burlington, Ohio

Marital Status: Widowed - his wife and daughter were brutally murdered.

Physical characteristics: A big man, six-five, and about halfway between three and four hundred pounds - the exact number depends on how much he eats at a particular meal. He was a college football player with a truncated stint in the NFL, where a vicious blindside hit altered his mind and gave him pretty much a perfect memory.

Relatives: Cassandra Decker (wife), Molly Decker (daughter), Johnny Sacks (brother-in-law) - Amos discovered all three murdered in his family home.

Career: College football star, then NFL with Cleveland Browns, where he met his wife Cassie. Destined to be a professional football player, his career was cut short following a devastating injury that permanently damaged his brain. Used to be a cop and then a detective and now works as an FBI Special Agent.

Notable Abilities: His football injury gave him one of the most exceptional brains in the world. His cognitive sensory pathways got melded from the hit resulting in an infallible, photographic memory also known as hyperthymesia. Also has synesthesia, the ability to see colours where others don't. In numbers, in places and objects. Extraordinary strength and speed for such a big man. Possesses a turbocharged brain that has somehow unlocked what we all have but never use.

Favourite film: *The Usual Suspects*. With his prodigious memory he would have caught Keyser Söze in the first act.

Favourite song: 'I Will Remember You', by Sarah McLachlan. A close second would be 'Thanks for the Memory' by Frank Sinatra.

Dislikes: Doesn't like being touched. Jokes; they don't really register with him anymore. People who waste his time, which seems to be most people he runs in to. Exercise. Head injuries.

Likes: The truth. Large portions of food. Substantial legroom in a moving vehicle.

Walk the Wire

1

Hal Parker was resolutely closing in on his prey, and he felt his blood pressure amp up with every firm step he placed into the dirt. He could tell he was nearing his target by the frequency and volume of blood that had fallen onto the darkened ground, like dulled rubies scattered in the rich soil. He had obviously wounded rather than killed his quarry.

A carcass delivered was part of the deal if he was to earn his fee. He was heartened by the blood loss. It evidenced the inevitable, especially in an unforgiving climate like this.

He moved slowly and methodically forward. Fall was nearly here, but summer was still hanging on, dragging its heat-flamed and moisture-rich knuckles across the stark tundra. Right now, he felt like an egg in a heated skillet. If it were winter, he would be encased in special clothing, and Parker would never, under any circumstances, start to run after his prey. If you ran when it was fifty degrees below zero, your lungs would hemorrhage and you'd drown in your own engorged corpuscles.

Yet when it was this hot and humid, dehydration could kill you just as quickly, and you'd never feel it coming until it was too late.

Parker wore a bright tactical headlamp that literally turned night into day, at least on his narrow path. He figured he might be the only living person within many square miles. Clouds scudded across the sky, all bloated with moisture and surrounded by unsettled air. He was hoping the rain would hold off just long enough for him to finish the job.

He looked to his left, where Canada sat not too far away. Over an hour south was the town of Williston, which was the very center of the fracking universe here in North Dakota. But the Bakken shale region was so enormous that the land under Parker's feet held hundreds of millions of barrels of oil along with hundreds of billions of cubic feet of natural gas. Maybe more, he thought, because who the hell could really know the extent of it?

Parker squatted as he assessed his next move.

He gazed ahead, rotating a hundred and eighty degrees on the compass, calculating time and distance based on the size of the blood splotches. He rose and moved forward, picking up his pace slightly. He wore a hydration pack with a large camel bladder and a feed line next to his mouth. His clothing was lightweight, yet sturdy, constructed from self-wicking material. But he was still hot and sweaty at eleven o'clock at night. And each intake of air felt like he was popping habaneros. Mother Nature always had the upper hand over man, he knew, no matter how much fancy equipment they put on.

He wasn't certain how his quarry, a wolf that had already killed two cows from his employer's herd, had even gotten away. He'd had a decent sight line on it from about four hundred yards away. The thing had just been sitting there, still as a deer, sensing trouble. His rifle round had entered the upper torso, he was sure of that. It had barely moved with the violent impact, so he was sure it had been a kill shot. But when he'd gotten to that spot, it was gone and the blood trail he was now following had commenced.

He cleared a slight rise in the ground. The area he was in was known as the Great Plains, which was somewhat of a misnomer, since the land could be quite hilly. But then the bumpy fringes of the northern Badlands crept up here, like the trickles of river water forming finger coves. But drab buttes and flat grasslands coexisted just fine for the most part. A night fog was sweeping in, eroding his visuals. He frowned, and though he was a veteran at this, he felt his adrenaline spike.

He heard the far-off rumble and then the whistle of a train probably carrying a column of tanker cars loaded with oil, and also with natural gas, which after being pulled out of the earth was then liquified for transport. The whistle sounded sad and hopeful to him at the same time.

Then another rumble came. This time it was from up in the sky. A storm was racing in, as storms often did around here. He had to pick up the pace.

He gripped his Winchester rifle tightly, ready to raise the night scope to his eye in an instant and to deliver, he hoped, the true kill shot this time. The next moment Parker saw something. Fifty feet and to his left. A shadow, a shade darker than its surroundings. He looked down at the ground, shining his light there. Now he was surprised and then puzzled. The bloody marks distinctly went off to the *right*. How could that be? His quarry hadn't suddenly developed the ability to fly. Yet maybe it had sharply changed direction up ahead, wobbling on weakened legs before collapsing.

He trudged forward, wary of a trap. He drew within fifteen feet of the spot and stopped. He squatted down again, and under the brilliant beam of his tac light, he took a long look around at the vast space in front of him. He even gave a behind-the-back look just in case his quarry had managed to outflank him and was sneaking up from the rear. Parker had fought in the first Gulf War. He had seen the crazy shit that sometimes took place when living things were trying to kill each other. He wondered if this was one of those times.

Still squatting, he crab-walked forward to within ten feet of the spot. Then five.

He felt his gut tighten. He must be seeing things.

He sucked on his water line to increase his hydration. But the thing was still there. It was no mirage. It was . . .

He gingerly rose and carefully treaded the final few feet to the spot and looked down, his powerful light illuminating every detail of the nightmare he had just discovered.

It was a woman. At least he thought it was. Yes, as he leaned closer, he saw the plump breasts. She was naked, and she had also been butchered. Yet there wasn't a drop of blood to mar the pristine ground around her.

The skin covering her face had been cut from the back and then pulled down, coming to rest on the exposed bone of her chin. Her skull had been sawed open and the top part removed and laid to the side of her head. The revealed cavity was empty.

Where the hell was her brain?

And her chest. It had been apparently cut open and then sewn back together.

He glanced at the compact dirt around the body. His brow screwed up when he saw the distinct marks on the ground there. They seemed familiar to him. Next moment he forgot about these traces and slowly sank to his knees as it occurred to him where he had seen such suture patterns on a human chest before.

It was called a Y-incision. He had seen it in numerous TV cop shows and movies. It was the proverbial cut-up body on the slab in the morgue, only he wasn't in a morgue. He was in the middle of expansive, unblemished North Dakota without a coroner or TV show in sight.

A postmortem had been performed on this unfortunate woman.

Hal Parker turned to the side and threw up mostly bile.

The soil was no longer pristine as the skies opened up and the rain began to pour down.

2

"North Dakota," murmured Amos Decker.

He was sitting next to Alex Jamison on a small Embraer regional jet. They had taken a jumbo 787 to Denver, where they'd had an hour layover before boarding the far smaller aircraft. It was like going from a stretch limo to a clown car.

Decker, who was six-foot-five and weighed nearly three hundred pounds, had groaned when he'd watched the small jet maneuvering to their gate, and groaned even more when he'd glimpsed the tiny seats inside. He'd had to wedge into his allotted space so tightly that he doubted he would need his lap belt to keep him safe in case of turbulence.

"Ever been there?" asked Jamison. She was in her early thirties, tall, superbly fit, with long brown hair, and pretty enough to be repeatedly stared at by men. A former journalist, she was now an FBI special agent. She and Decker were assigned to a task force at the Bureau.

"No, but we played North Dakota State in football

once while I was at Ohio State. They came to Columbus for the game."

Decker had played college ball for the Buckeyes and then had an abbreviated professional career with the Cleveland Browns before a devastating injury on the field had left him with two conditions: hyperthymesia, or perfect recall, and synesthesia, meaning his sensory pathways had comingled. Now he could forget nothing and saw things such as numbers in certain colors and, far more dramatically, dead bodies in an unsettling shade of electric blue.

"Who won?" asked Jamison.

Decker gave her a heavy-lidded glance. "You trying to be funny?"

"No."

He shifted about a millimeter in his seat. "It used to be called D-I and D-II when I played. Now it's FBS and FCS." When Jamison looked puzzled he added, "Football Bowl Subdivision and Football Championship Subdivision. Ohio State, Alabama, Clemson, Michigan, LSU, they're all FBS schools, the top tier, the big boys. Schools like North Dakota State, James Madison, Grambling, Florida A&M, they're FCS schools, or the second tier. Now, North Dakota State has gotten really good as of late. But usually, when they play each other it's a rout for the FBS schools."

"So why schedule them?"

"It's an easy win for the top tier and a big payday and TV exposure for the other squad."

"But it's not a particularly good game to watch?"

"It's always a good game when you win. And if the score is a runaway, the starters get to sit the bench after the third quarter or maybe even the first half. When I was a freshman that's how I got to play. When I was a starter, I appreciated the extra rest a blow-out got me."

"Doesn't make sense to me. One team slaughtering another for money."

"It really only made sense to the school boosters and the NCAA bean counters."

Jamison shook her head and gazed out the window as they descended beneath the dark, thick clouds. "Looks stormy down there."

"It's basically hot with humidity through the roof for the next couple of days, with a bad thunderstorm, falling temps, and wicked wind pretty much guaranteed every evening. But then it won't be long before the blizzard season sets in and this place looks like Antarctica."

"Great," said Jamison sarcastically.

"But look on the bright side."

"What's that?"

"You won't have to do your daily workout for the next couple days. You'll lose two pounds of water just walking to the car. But after that you'll have to fatten up for the winter."

The plane shed more altitude. Working against heavy headwinds and unruly patches of air, the jet felt like it was a pebble skipping across rough water. Jamison gripped her armrests and tried to breathe deeply as her stomach lurched up and down. When the plane's tires finally hit the asphalt and bounced to a landing on the runway, she slowly released her grip and pressed a hand against her belly. A jagged spear of lightning appeared off in the distance.

"Okay, that was fun," she said breathlessly before eyeing Decker, who looked, if anything, sleepy. "That didn't bother you?" she asked.

"What?"

"The turbulence!"

"It wasn't a big deal," he said offhandedly.

"What's your secret then? Because it looked like everyone else on the plane was praying, flight attendants included."

"I survived a crash landing when I was in college. Engine went out on takeoff. Pilot circled back around, dumped some fuel, then the other engine died and he had to go in for an immediate landing. Found out later it was a twin bird strike. We hit hard enough to take out the landing gear and crack the fuselage. Everybody got off before the jet fuel ignited and fire ate the plane. I did lose my duffel of clothes," he added casually.

"My God," said a pale Jamison. "Then I'm surprised you're not more nervous than I am."

"I looked up the odds. They're about a billion to

one for my having a second incident. I feel like I'm golden now."

They deplaned, signed the documents for their rental SUV, and headed out from Williston Basin International Airport.

"Wow," said Jamison when they got outside and the wind slammed into them. Even the giant Decker was buffeted. "I don't think I packed the right clothes," she noted miserably. "I should have brought more layers."

"What more do you need than pants and a shirt and a badge and gun?"

"It's different for women, Decker."

Jamison drove while Decker punched the directions into his phone navigation. Then he settled back and watched the road zip by. It was six o'clock in the evening and they were headed right into a gathering storm. Nasty black cumulus clouds reared up ahead of them like a towering serpent about to do some serious business over this patch of the upper Midwest.

"Irene Cramer," said Decker softly as they drove along.

Jamison nodded and her features turned grim. "Found dead in the middle of nowhere by a guy tracking a wolf."

"Most notably she was apparently autopsied," added Decker.

"That's a first, at least for me. How about you?"

"I've seen cut-up bodies, but not like the photos

I saw. The crime scene was pretty clean except for the guy's vomit."

"Serial murderer? Is that why we got the call? Bogart didn't really say."

Ross Bogart was the head of their small task force. He was the one who had ordered the pair to North Dakota after the briefest of briefings.

"Maybe."

"Did Ross sound strange when he talked to you?" asked Jamison. "He did to me."

Decker nodded. "He couldn't tell us something that he wanted to tell us."

"How do you know that?"

"He's a straight shooter who has to answer to political types."

"I don't like mysteries at both ends of a case," groused Jamison.

"I don't think this is necessarily a serial murderer."

"Why not?"

"I could find nothing to match it in the databases. I checked before we flew out."

"Could be a new player."

"New players aren't usually this sophisticated."

"He might be trying to make a name for himself," pointed out Jamison.

"They're all trying to make a name for themselves," replied Decker.

"But they don't call the Bureau in for a local murder."

"I think we need to look at the *victim* and not the killer for that reason."

"You believe Irene Cramer was important to the Feds for some reason?"

"And it may also explain Bogart's reticence."

"Regardless, we're clearly looking at a killer with forensic skills."

"That could apply to quite a few people, including people on our side of the field."

"An ME gone bad, maybe?" suggested Jamison.

Decker looked uncertain. "You can probably find a YouTube video of someone cutting up a mannequin. But the report said the cuts were professionally done."

"You think this guy has had . . . what, practice?"

"I don't think anything, at least right now."

"Did you notice the highway here is all concrete?" said Jamison, glancing out the window.

"Asphalt apparently doesn't hold up well in the extreme elements they have up here," noted Decker. "Although I'm not sure how durable the concrete is, either."

"Well, aren't you a wealth of information."

"I can Google stuff just like anybody else."

"How much longer do we have to go?" asked Jamison.

Decker glanced at his phone screen. "Says forty-five minutes, nearly to the Canadian border."

"So I guess that was the closest airport back there."

"I think that was the *only* airport back there."

"This has already been a long, exhausting day."

"And it promises to be a longer night."

"You're going to start the investigation tonight?" she said, a little incredulously.

Decker gave her a stern look. "Never hurts to hit the ground running, Alex. Particularly when someone is dead who shouldn't be."

3

"What are those?" asked Jamison as they neared their destination.

She indicated fiery gold plumes that winked in the darkness like ghoulish holiday lights as they zipped past.

"Gas flares," said Decker. "Coming off the oil wells. Natural gas is found with oil. They drill for both up here. But they sometimes vent the gas off and ignite it at the end of the oil wellhead. I guess it costs too much to do anything else with it in certain situations and they don't necessarily have the infrastructure to pipe it out of here."

Jamison looked stunned. "Do you know how much gas we're talking about?"

"One stat I read said each month the gas they burn off could heat four million homes."

"Four million homes, are you serious?"

"It's what I read."

"But isn't that bad for the environment? I mean, they're burning pure methane, right?"

"I don't know about that. But it probably is bad."

"All those flames are eerie. I'm conjuring images of zombies marching with torches."

"Better get used to them. They're everywhere, apparently."

And as they drove along, they did indeed appear to be everywhere. The landscape was like an enormous sheet cake with hundreds of candles.

They passed by large neighborhoods of trailer homes, along with paved streets, road signs, and playgrounds. Vehicles, most of them jacked-up, mud-stained pickup trucks or stout SUVs, were parked under metal carports in front of the trailers.

They also drove past large parcels of land on which sat the flame-tipped oil and gas wells along with metal containers and equipment with imposing security fences around them. Hard-hatted men in flame-resistant orange vests drove or rushed around performing myriad tasks. From a distance, they looked like giant ants on a crucial mission.

"This is a fracking town," said Decker. "Only reason there still is a town. Thousands of workers have migrated to this part of North Dakota to suck up the shale oil and gas found in the area. 'Bakken' shale rock, to be more specific. I read there's about a hundred years' worth of fossil fuel in the ground here."

"Okay, but haven't they heard of climate change?"

"Hey, it's a job."

"Yeah, a job today, no planet to live on tomorrow."

"Preaching to the choir. But when you're trying

to put food on the table today? And people can make six-figure salaries here working the energy fields? They've had booms and busts before, but they seem to have things in better shape now."

"Google again?"

He shrugged. "I'm a curious guy. Plus both my brothers-in-law work in the oil and gas fields. I guess I picked some stuff up because of that."

They passed a fifteen-gas-pump truck stop that had a restaurant attached and also showers, a Laundromat, and a store that multiple signs said sold hot pizzas, propane, diesel exhaust fluid, truck driving logs, fans, and antifreeze, among many other listed items. On one sign were enormous photos of alluring waitresses in short shorts and low-cut tops. Another sign proclaimed the facility had the best adult entertainment DVDs in the entire state of North Dakota. The parking lot was packed with semis of every size, color, and style, with emphasis on chrome fittings, spike wheel caps, and spray-painted murals on the cabs. They ranged from dragons and firearms to American flags and busty, nude women.

"Well, I guess we know what's popular up here," said Jamison.

"It's not just up here where that stuff is popular," replied Decker drily.

They next passed RV parks that were packed and a shopping mall that looked freshly risen from the dirt. The mall had a BBQ restaurant with a sign promising the best southern pulled pork around; then there was a Subway, a China Express, a twenty-four-hour gym, a bar and grill, and even a sushi bar. There was an electronic marquee mounted on one wall that set forth the current prices for oil and natural gas. Next to the mall was a large brick church. On the front of its outdoor sign someone had arranged black letters to read, GOD CREATED THE HEAVENS AND THE EARTH AND THE OIL AND THE GAS. SHARE THE WEALTH. DONATE TO GOD. WE DO VENMO. BIBLE STUDY CLASS EVERY NIGHT AT 7.

Jamison glanced in the rearview mirror. "There's a column of semis and dump trucks right on my butt, and they have been for the last half hour." She glanced at the oncoming traffic. "And an army of them heading the other way. And the whole place smells of diesel fuel."

"They're bringing in equipment and supplies, including the chemicals they inject into the ground. Apparently it goes on 24/7."

"And the trucks heading the other way?"

"Taking the oil and gas out, I guess." He pointed ahead. "We have to get off this road soon. They built a loop around the town so the trucks wouldn't have to drive through downtown with their loads."

Jamison took the next exit, and they shortly saw a cluster of lights in the distance. "I take it that's the town we're headed to."

"Yep. London, North Dakota."

"I wonder how it got that name," said Jamison.

"Maybe some guy from England came here and planted a flag. Right in the middle of a sea of oil and gas. Population's around fifteen thousand, and over half of them work in the oil fields and the other half service them. And that's about triple what it was just three years ago. And it'll triple again in half that time if things keep going as they are."

"Boy, you really did read up on this," commented Jamison.

"I like to know what I'm getting into."

She looked at him curiously. "And what do you think that is, apart from a murder investigation?"

"This is the Wild West, Alex. It's like the California Gold Rush of 1849, only on steroids."

"So what exactly are you saying?"

"That the ordinary rules of civilization don't necessarily apply up here."

"You're serious, aren't you?"

"Very."

They drove down the main street that was bustling with people despite the coming storm, and reached a dead end when the first drops of chilly rain began to fall.

"Directions, please."

"Next left," said Decker.

They pulled to a stop in front of what turned out to be a funeral home.

Now Decker shot Jamison a curious glance.

19

"North Dakota is a coroner state, not a medical examiner state. The local guy here also runs this funeral home, crematorium, and mortuary. Full service."

"You read up on it?" he asked.

She smiled impishly. "I'm a curious *gal*."

"Is he at least trained in forensics?"

Jamison shrugged. "We can only hope."

They barely beat the sheets of driving rain as they sprinted for the front door to see a dead person.

4

They introduced themselves to Walt Southern, the coroner and owner of the funeral home. He was medium height and in his midforties with thinning sandy-colored hair and a runner's lean physique. He wore tortoise-shell glasses, his dark slacks were cuffed and pleated, and his sparkling white shirt seemed to glow under the recessed ceiling lights.

He looked at them in surprise. "But why is the FBI interested in this case?"

"Wait, didn't you know we were coming?" asked Jamison.

"No, nobody told me."

She said, "Well we're here and we've been assigned to investigate this murder. We've read your post report. Now we need to see the body."

"Now hold on. I can't let you folks do that without checking with the detective on the case."

Decker said, "Then call him. Now."

"He might not be in."

"You won't know till you try."

Southern moved off to a corner of the room, took

21

out his cell phone, and made a call. He spoke with someone and then rejoined Decker and Jamison, not looking thrilled.

"Okay, I guess you Feds always get your way."

"You'd be surprised," said Decker.

"Well, let's get to it. I've still got a body to prepare for a viewing tomorrow, and the family was real particular on her clothing and makeup."

"Do you bury people here during the winter?" asked Decker.

"We prefer not to. Have to dig through the snow, and then the ground is iron hard. Hassle even with a backhoe. And who wants to stand outside saying good-bye to a dearly departed when it's sixty below? Funny how quickly tears dry and people beat a retreat when their fingers, toes, and ears are getting frostbite. But most people these days opt for the quick-fried route anyway over a plot of dirt."

"'Quick-fried'?" asked Jamison.

"Cremation." He chuckled. "I mean, doesn't that mean they're opting for Hell in a way?"

"Can we see the body?" said Decker with a frown.

Southern led them down a short hall, and they passed through into a small utilitarian room smelling strongly of antiseptic, formaldehyde, and decomposing flesh.

In the middle of the room was a metal gurney. The bulge under the sheet was what they had come for. Hopefully, the body would tell them a story about who had killed its owner.

Jamison glanced at Decker, who was already seeing the room in electric blue. It was a testament to how many dead bodies he saw that this no longer bothered him. Well, almost.

"This is the first time I've done a postmortem on a victim who'd already been autopsied," noted Southern.

"You've been trained to do this, I assume?" asked Decker bluntly.

"I'm properly credentialed," replied Southern, who seemed to take no offense at the question. "Just because it's not my main business doesn't mean I don't take pride in it."

"That's good to know," said Decker curtly.

Southern lifted the sheet off the corpse, and they all three stared down at what was left of Irene Cramer.

"Cause, manner, and time of death?" asked Jamison.

"The cause and manner are pretty straightforward." He pointed to a wound in the middle of the chest, appearing a few inches above the bottom intersection of the Y-incision. "Long, sharp, serrated knife penetrated here and bisected the heart. The manner was homicide, of course."

"Killer was pretty accurate with the knife strike," noted Jamison as she leaned in for a closer look. "Clean and efficient. Only one stab did the deal."

"My thinking, too."

"So, unemotional. No savagery or lack of control," opined Decker. "Killer might not have known the victim. Or at least had no personal relationship with her."

"Maybe not," said Southern.

"And the time of death?" asked Decker.

"Okay, there we get into the speculation zone," conceded Southern. "Based on what I found out, she's been dead maybe about a week to ten days."

Decker did not look pleased by this. "That's a pretty big range. You can't narrow it down more than that?"

"Afraid not," said Southern, looking unhappy. "If this comes down to whether an alibi gets someone off or not, well, my report's not going to be a bit of help on that. I'm sorry."

"Insect infestation?" asked Jamison.

"A lot. That allowed me to gauge the week or so. After that, it gets dicey. At least for me. Again, I know what I'm doing, but this isn't exactly the FBI lab here."

"Had she been lying out there long, then?" asked Jamison.

"That's both a hard and simple question."

"Come again?" said Jamison.

"If she'd been out there too long, the animals clearly would have gotten to her. They hadn't."

"That's the simple part, so what's the hard?" asked

Decker. "The insect infestation doesn't reconcile with that?"

"Bingo. Lots of bugs, but no animal bite marks. And another thing, the lividity was fixed. Shows that after death she was in a prone position."

"The report I read says she was found *supine*," noted Decker.

"Right, but you can see that the lividity discoloration does not jibe with that. Blood won't collect around parts of the body that are in contact with the ground. But once lividity is fixed, meaning when the heart stops beating and the large red blood cells sink via gravity into the interstitial tissues, the cells don't move again. The discoloration stays where it was."

"So she was obviously killed and laid on her face. But then the body was at some point turned on its back because that's how she was found," said Jamison.

"Right. *After* lividity was fixed."

"Bleed-out would have been minimal, since the heart would have stopped shortly after the knife strike," said Decker. "But there would have been some, and none was found at the crime scene. That means she was killed elsewhere and placed there, which would also explain the lividity discrepancy."

Southern nodded. "But with such major insect infestation you would expect animal intrusion as well. I mean, if she'd been lying outside all this time, the critters we have around here would have gnawed her to bone in far less than a week, which is the bare minimum I put her TOD at." He paused and added matter-of-factly, "Other than that she was in excellent condition. Very healthy. Heart, lungs, other organs, shipshape."

"Yeah, the woman's in great shape, except she's dead," said Decker grimly.

"How much skill are we talking about with the killer doing his own postmortem?" asked Jamison.

"The incisions were first-rate. I'd say the person had some medical training. And he, if it was a he, knew the forensic protocols. What was the source of that knowledge and training, I couldn't venture to say."

Decker pointed to the Y-incision. "How about the tools he used? Regular knife or medical grade?"

"I'd say he had some hospital scalpels *and* a Stryker saw or something like it to cut open the skull. And the thread he used to suture the Y-incision is surgical grade."

Decker looked the body over and had the coroner help him turn the woman.

"No tats or distinguishing marks," noted Decker.

"No liver spots or sun damage. She was too young for age spots, but her skin was not tanned, either. She wasn't out in the sun much."

They turned her back over and Decker ran his gaze over her once more.

How many bodies had he stared at in precisely

these circumstances? The answer was easy. *Too damn many.* But if he didn't want to look at bodies, he'd have to change careers.

"Anything of interest in her system?" asked Jamison.

"Almost nothing in her stomach, so she hadn't eaten recently. No obvious signs of drug use. No needle marks, that sort of thing. Tox reports haven't come back yet."

"Anything else out of the ordinary?" asked Decker.

"I think her having a postmortem done on her before she got to me is enough out of the ordinary for any case." Southern tacked on a grin.

"So your answer is no?" persisted Decker.

The smile fell away. "Right, my answer is no."

"Is she from around here? Who made the ID?"

Southern placed his arms over his chest. "Once I put her face back on somebody from the police department recognized her."

The door opened at that moment and a man around Jamison's age walked in. He wore jeans, scuffed tasseled loafers, a checkered shirt, and a navy blue sport coat. He was about six feet tall, lean and wiry with a knot of an Adam's apple and a classic lantern jaw. His hair was dark brown and thick, and a cowlick stuck up in the back like a periscope.

He looked first at Decker and then at Jamison.

"Lieutenant Joe Kelly with the London Police Department," he said by way of introduction.

"He's the one I called," said Southern.

Kelly nodded. "I'm with the Detective Division. Sounds impressive until you understand I'm the only one."

"The only one working *homicide*, you mean?" said Decker.

"Homicide, burglary, armed robbery, domestic abuse, human trafficking, drugs, and I forget the others."

"Quite the one-man show," remarked a wide-eyed Jamison.

"It's not by choice. It's by budget dollars. We doubled the size of the force after the last oil bust went boom again, but it hasn't caught up to detective level yet. Just uniformed bodies on the streets and in the police cruisers. They'll get around to promoting a uniform to detective about the time the next bust comes along and we all get fired." He stared up at Decker. "They grow all of them as big as you at the FBI?"

"Yeah, sure. But the other guys wear shiny armor. I like my denim."

Kelly took a moment to show them his credentials, and they reciprocated. Then Kelly glanced at Southern. "Sorry I didn't come straight over, Walt. Little bit of trouble at the OK Corral. Was driving by when it happened and heard the ruckus from outside."

"Another fight?"

"Another something. Stupid name for a bar anyway. Too much testosterone, money, and liquor. I'm not a fan of that combo."

"He said someone at the department recognized the victim once she was put back together," said Decker.

"That someone would be me," replied Kelly.

Decker hiked an eyebrow. "How's that?"

"I left out one of the other things I'm responsible for here in London. Prostitution."

"So Cramer was a hooker?" said Decker.

Surprisingly, Kelly shrugged. "I don't know for sure."

"Why not?" asked Jamison. "Seems to be pretty easy to tell whether someone is or isn't."

"You'd think. Now, the term 'streetwalker' is pretty outdated these days, but up here, we still have them. The guys drive by in certain sections of town and the ladies hook up with them right then and there. With that said, a lot of the arrangements are made online so as to avoid doing any direct soliciting in public."

"So was Cramer arranging things online?" asked Decker.

"I'm on the computer all the time looking for sites that offer this stuff. I know where to look, at least for the sorts of things that go on here. I found one site advertising 'consulting services' for men in the oil and gas field here in London. Even though the site took pains to make it look legit, because these folks know cops are looking, there was one picture that looked really familiar to me. I mean, don't get me wrong, she looked really different, makeup, hair, clothing, but I recognized Cramer. I'd seen her around town," he added hastily. "So at the very least, it seemed that she was in the 'escort' business in some way. She called herself Mindy on the site, for what that's worth."

"So it wasn't a shock when you found out she was dead?" said Jamison. "I mean, prostitution is a high-risk occupation."

"Well, it *was* surprising, actually, because murders are rare, at least around here, even for prostitutes. And it *was* a shock *how* she was found."

"I can see that," replied Decker evenly, watching Kelly closely.

"But what I don't really get is why you folks were even called in for this. After Walt called me I went to talk to my chief. It was only then that I found out the autopsy and police reports had been sent to DC after a request came in from the Feds. I mean, it's a weird-ass murder, sure, but there are lots of weird-ass murders, and the locals handle them by and large."

Decker said, "Why do *you* think we were called in? You must have a theory."

"Why should I have a theory?"

"You strike me as the type."

In answer Kelly pointed to the table and the body on it. "She's got some connection to something that has you Feds interested. I just don't know what that is, but I'd sure like to."

"Wouldn't we all," muttered Decker.

5

"The paint in my room smells fresh and the carpet looks like they just laid it today," said Jamison.

They had checked into their hotel on the main street of London and were having dinner in the restaurant off the lobby. Despite the late hour, it was pretty full.

"Comes with the cycle of booms and busts," responded Decker as he glanced over his menu and frowned. "They have tofu here? In rural North Dakota?"

"Why not?" asked Jamison. "I'm sure people here eat tofu."

"Yeah, maybe with their bacon and sausage. And elk."

They ordered, and Decker sat back in his chair cradling the bottle of Corona with a lime wedge the waitress had brought him while Jamison sipped on some iced tea.

"So what do you think of Detective Kelly?" she said.

"I think his talents might be wasted in a place like

this. But then again, this might be a hotbed of crime for all I know."

"Men with too much money," mused Jamison. "Like he said."

Decker nodded absently. "Kelly wants to know why we're here. And so do I. I called and left a message with Bogart but I've heard nothing back yet."

"I did too, with the same result. What do you think after looking at the body?"

"It could be some psycho with a forensic fetish, or someone is leaving a message of some sort."

"What sort of message?"

"If Cramer was killed because of something she knew, and others knew it as well, then it's a warning not to talk or the same will happen to them."

"What could she have known?"

"Well, if I knew that, we could make an arrest and fly home," said Decker.

"Point taken."

Decker's expression grew dark. "I don't think this is a one-off, Alex."

"Meaning?"

"You heard what Walt Southern said. Medical-grade incisions and tools. You don't walk into a Home Depot and buy a Stryker saw. And the body was cut up before it was laid out there, otherwise there would have been traces of the procedure and at least some blood. And he had to transport her out there. He evidently picked the spot with care."

"So that shows he knows the area. Or at least scoped out that particular location beforehand."

Decker nodded. "That takes planning and patience." He looked over her shoulder and his eyes widened in surprise. He blinked twice as though to clear his vision and make sure he was seeing correctly.

"Stan?"

The big man who had just come into the dining area glanced sharply over at them when he heard the name. His look of astonishment mirrored Decker's.

"Amos?"

The man named Stan came over and Decker stood to shake his hand as Jamison looked on, puzzled.

"What the hell are you doing here?" asked Decker.

"Could ask the same of you," said Stan.

He was nearly as tall and broad as Decker, with reddish hair going gray at the edges, a florid face, and twinkly green eyes. His short, trimmed beard matched the color of his hair.

"Hello," interjected Jamison as she rose and extended her hand. "I'm Alex Jamison. I work with Decker at the FBI."

"I'm sorry," said Decker. "Alex, this big lug is Stan Baker, my brother-in-law. He's married to my sister Renee. They live in California." He glanced curiously at Baker. "You're a long way from home."

Baker rubbed his thick, muscular fingers, his expression suddenly nervous. "I, uh, I live here now.

And soon, well, I'm going to be your *ex*-brother-in-law."

"What?" snapped a visibly stunned Decker as he took a step back.

"Renee hasn't talked to you?"

"About what?"

"We're getting divorced."

Decker stared at him in disbelief. "Divorced? Why?"

"Lots of reasons. Blame on both sides."

"And the kids?"

"They'll stay with their mom."

"Are they still in California?"

"Yeah," Baker said uncomfortably. "The younger kids are in school and all. And Renee has a good job."

"But you're here in North Dakota, Stan. How exactly does that work?" he demanded.

"I moved to Alaska and worked there for a while, but that's slowing down. You know Tim was an oil exec up there. He got me the job."

"What do you mean Tim *was* an oil executive?"

"Who's Tim?" interjected Jamison.

"Our other brother-in-law," replied Baker. "He's married to Amos's sister Diane."

"What about Tim?" said Decker.

"He got canned and last I heard drives an Uber and does some accounting for small businesses. And then my position got cut, too. I wanted a fresh start. This place is booming. They needed experienced field hands. Been here over a year now. And you can't beat the money."

"And your kids?" said Decker again.

"I Skype with them most every day," Baker said defensively.

"You can't Skype a hug or teach your son to swing a bat from thousands of miles away. You were in the Army when the first two were born. You were gone a lot."

"I was fighting for my country, Amos!"

"I'm just saying kids need their dad."

Baker said in an annoyed tone, "Yeah, well, it's the way it is for me. I mean people *do* get divorced. And we did try to work it out. Counseling and all that."

"Maybe you could have worked harder," said Decker. "It's family, Stan. They're not supposed to be disposable."

Now Baker's green eyes flashed angrily. "Look, I know what you're getting at. We all know what happened to Cassie and her brother, and . . . Molly. It was awful. Never cried that hard in my life as when I was at their funerals. But . . . but that's you, not me. It's way different. And I wasn't looking for this to happen, neither of us was, but it just did. That's life."

Decker glanced at Jamison and then looked down. "Yeah, okay. I . . . I guess I should call Renee. I . . . I haven't been all that good about keeping in touch."

"Well, if you didn't know your sister was getting divorced or your other brother-in-law lost his job, I'd say you're spot-on with that observation," chimed in a disbelieving Jamison.

"So what are you doing here?" asked Baker.

"Investigating a murder."

"A murder!?"

"You have murders up here, don't you?" said Decker sullenly.

"Yeah, it's usually two drunk knuckleheads going at it, or some gang boys fighting over drug turf. Meth, coke, and heroin are like candy up here. Who got killed?"

"We can't go into that with you," said Jamison quickly. "But you'll probably hear about it on the news."

"Damn. And the FBI got called in for it? Why can't the locals handle it?"

Decker said, "We just go where we're told to go, Stan."

"Would you like to join us for dinner?" asked Jamison.

Baker blanched and took a step back, glancing at Decker. "What? No. I, um, I already ate my dinner."

"What are you doing here, then?" asked Decker, who was now clearly curious about Baker's discomfort. "If you've been here over a year, surely you're not staying here."

"No, I got my own place. I'm here to meet, uh . . ." he mumbled.

"Meet *who*?" said Decker sharply.

"Stan?"

They all turned to see a woman in her early thirties saunter into the room. At least *saunter* was the verb that came to Decker's mind as he watched her move. She was quite beautiful, and he could see many of the men in the room, even those there with other women, turn to stare at her.

"Caroline, hey," said Baker rigidly, glancing nervously at Decker. "This is Caroline Dawson," he said to Decker.

"Yeah, I got that," replied Decker, gazing sternly at his soon-to-be ex-brother-in-law.

"Um, Caroline, this is Amos Decker, and his partner, Alex. Amos is—"

"I'm Stan's friend," interjected Decker. "Neither of us knew the other was in town."

Caroline smiled. "Cool, what a nice surprise. You ready?" she asked Baker before glancing at Alex. "Hey, you guys want to join us? We're going clubbing."

"There are clubs *here*?" said an incredulous Jamison.

Caroline smiled and did an eye roll. "I know. You wouldn't think, but yeah, there are maybe three good places. Well, they're more bars than clubs. But not all of them play just country music, which Stan loves and I can't stand."

"We're good," said Decker. "We just flew in. Pretty beat."

"Okay, we'll do a rain check, then."

"Right."

Caroline gripped Baker's hand. "Let's roll. First stop, the OK Corral Saloon."

"Do you live in London?" asked Decker suddenly.

She grinned. "Yeah. I'd prefer to live in London, *England*. Maybe someday. My dad owns this hotel, and a bunch of other businesses. I help him run them. He lives in a big place way outside of town. I sometimes stay there, but I also have a condo in town."

"Okay."

"See ya," said Caroline, and she led Baker from the room.

Jamison looked at Decker. "What a coincidence, huh?"

Decker sat back down and stared dully at the wooden-topped table.

"Sorry about your sister," she said.

"She should have called me," said an obviously stricken Decker.

"Are you sure she didn't try to contact you?" said Jamison in a suspicious tone.

Decker suddenly looked guilty. "I think there might have been some voice mails I forgot to return."

"Wow, for a guy who can't forget anything *that* is remarkable."

"I know, I know," he said miserably. "I'm bad about that."

"You need to talk to her. Be supportive. Let her tell her story without being judgmental."

"People work stuff out all the time. And Stan has already found someone else."

"I'm not sure he's looking for a permanent companion in this relationship, Decker. And by the looks of it neither is Caroline. I think they're just two people having fun."

When their food finally came Decker only took a few bites before mumbling to Jamison, "Sorry, I . . . I lost my appetite. I'll see you in the morning."

He headed out without further explanation.

6

The OK Corral Saloon.

It was big, loud, and assuredly hopping.

The lights blazed from every window and Decker could hear the music blasting out of the place. It was country, with a dash of rock and roll, at least to his ear. It shot through the air like a sound cannon.

He stood outside and felt his skin slowly begin to pucker with the humidity that had returned after the storm.

After he cleared the outside bouncer checking IDs, Decker opened the door, and the heat and co-mingled smells of sweat and spilled alcohol hit him like a tank round. Either they had no AC or it was having a struggle to keep up with the warmth thrown off by the waves of swaying people. And from what Decker could see, he might have been the only sober customer in the joint.

He edged around a knot of young people near the front entrance. They seemed to be holding each other up, though it was not yet ten o'clock. He didn't want to be around these folks at midnight.

There was a live band, four guys, and a gal as the lead singer. Her hair was Dolly Parton big and swirled around her head as she danced while crooning a Faith Hill ballad to pitch perfection. The band looked like petrified wood next to her steamy gyrations. She started her next set, and from what Decker could hear, the lyrics focused principally on guys, gals, dogs, and guns, with a Chevy pickup thrown in for good measure. There was a quartet of ninety-inch TV screens on the walls, all tuned to sports channels. In one corner behind a waist-high partition was a mechanical bull, but it didn't seem to be in operation. It just sat there looking pissed off.

He stood near the back and took his time surveying the room. On one wall was a sign with very large letters that read, BAR RULES: YOU PULL ANY CRAP IN HERE PARTICULARLY FIGHTING AND YOUR ASS IS GONE FOR GOOD. WHEN YOU ARE CUT OFF, YOU ARE DONE. ZERO TOLERANCE. HAVE A GOOD TIME.

A minute later he spotted the pair. Caroline was on the parquet dance floor flitting around a flat-footed Baker, like a hummingbird to a very large, very stiff flower. *Or cactus, more like it.* Baker moved his feet an inch or two from side to side, stuck his hands up, and tried to look like he was enjoying himself.

Why is she with him?

Someone nudged Decker. It was a man even larger than he was who started speaking to him in a low but menacing voice.

"Look, bud, you want to stay here you need to buy something, food or drink or preferably both," the man said. He weighed in at about three-fifty, bald as a cue ball, and his flabby gut was overshadowed only by the muscular breadth of his shoulders. "Otherwise, you need to go. Somebody's got to pay to keep the lights on and the booze flowing."

Decker moved up to the bar, which spanned one entire wall. The bar stools were all occupied. He wedged next to a couple doing a lip-lock and somehow still managing to chug beer, and a well-dressed woman in her early forties who held a cocktail with about a pound of fruit in it.

The bar sported a hundred beers on tap and a similar number in bottle, many of them IPAs that Decker had never heard of. He opted for Budweiser in the can that set him back five bucks and stood with his back to the bar so he could keep watching his brother-in-law make a fool of himself.

Correction, soon-to-be ex-brother-in-law.

Caroline was now hanging off Baker, looking dreamily up into the man's face before planting a kiss on his lips. In this stark image all Decker could see was his sister Renee and her four kids, and he had to look away before anger got the better of him. Then he caught himself. What business was it of his anyway? Why was he even here?

"You're the Fed, right?"

Decker looked to his left. The person speaking was

the fruit-chugging lady. She was slender and fit, the line of her triceps showing against the fabric of her tight blouse. She had on a wedding ring and a gold-plated pinky ring. Her hair was light brown with blond highlights and hung down to her shoulders. She wore a pair of jade earrings shaped as miniature Buddhist temples. Her features were finely chiseled and quite attractive, her eyes a light blue.

"And why do you think that?" asked Decker.

"I'm Liz Southern. My husband, Walt, just did the post on your victim. He told me you were in town."

"But again, how'd you know it was me out of all the people here?"

"He said watch out for a guy in his forties who looks like an ex-NFL offensive lineman."

"That would fit about ten of the guys here, maybe more."

"You didn't let me finish. He also said you had brooding, intelligent, hard-to-read features. That definitely does not match any of the ten or so guys in this room you were probably referring to. They're as easy to read as a Dr. Seuss book."

Decker put out his hand for her to shake. "Amos Decker."

"Not a name you hear much anymore," Southern said as she shook his hand.

"Did your husband tell you details about the case?"

"He did not breach confidences, if that's what you

were asking. But I manage the funeral home, so I am there quite a bit. Rest assured, whatever I *might* have learned will go no further."

Decker took a sip of his beer and eyed the unused mechanical bull. "What's the story with that thing? Thought it'd be popular with this crowd."

"It was. *Too* popular."

"Come again?"

"It came down to legal liability issues. You get a fracker on that thing and he breaks his leg, arm, or neck, you got a lawsuit from him or his family and another from the company that desperately needed him out in the field. I guess it costs too much to remove, so now people just throw beer cans and bottles at it from time to time."

As she said this, one drunk young man in a Stetson wound up and hurled his empty glass beer bottle at the bull. It hit the bull's hard hide and broke apart, its shards collecting on the floor underneath along with a small mountain of other debris while he high-fived his buds.

"They clean it up every night and the next night it just fills up. But if they're taking their hostility out on that instead of someone's face? That's anger management, North Dakota style."

Decker nodded. "So did you know the victim?"

"No. But I understand that Joe Kelly did."

"Do you know *him* well?"

"Well enough. London's booming right now, but

that wasn't always the case. Everybody knew every-body else. That all changed with the fracking. Now we have folks from all over, even different countries. Think I heard Russian spoken at the grocery store last week." She paused and added, "But that hasn't always been the case. We almost had to shut down our business during the last bust."

"Surely people were still dying, even if the good times had gone."

"Oh, they absolutely were. Some by their own hands out of despair at having lost everything. Only their families didn't have the money to pay for our services. They'd offer to barter and such, and we did what we could, but we had our own bills to pay. Luckily, we held on and now things are fine. For now. Who knows about tomorrow?" She looked around. "Your partner isn't with you? Walt told me you were with another agent."

"We parted company back at the hotel."

"Will there be more agents coming?"

Decker sipped his beer and didn't answer. Caroline Dawson had now hung herself around Baker and was using him as what looked to be a dance pole.

"Do you know those people?" asked Southern as she glanced where he was looking.

"Sort of, yeah."

"Any leads yet?"

"I can't get into that."

"I'll take that as a no."

Decker focused on her. "You have any ideas on who might have done it?"

"Me?" she said, although she didn't really look surprised at his query. "Well, I can tell you that we do have violent crime here. Not as bad as the last boom cycle. Before we just got all guys, transients with problem backgrounds looking for a quick payoff and then they'd move on. Now we're still getting some guys with shady backgrounds, but we're also getting more families. People are putting down roots. They want a nice, safe community."

"I sense a *but* coming."

She smiled demurely. "*But* we have places like this where young, single guys in particular come to spend their money and blow off steam. And sometimes that turns out badly."

"Kelly mentioned an incident earlier here today."

"I heard it was a fistfight between a bunch of guys that turned into something more. Joe apparently de-escalated it. But some people went to jail and some went to the hospital."

"The guy I'm looking for is probably not in the 'dumbass bar fight' category."

"I saw the body when it came in," said Southern softly. "So I understand what you mean."

"Not a pretty sight."

"We've had some bad ones here. Not murders. Accidents. Explosions and fires from fracking gone wrong. Those were . . . challenges from a cosmetic perspective. We had to do a closed casket with a picture of the deceased in . . . happier times on top."

"I can see that."

She finished her drink and put the empty on the bar. "Something like this could be a real drag on the town, just when things are going so well."

"And Irene Cramer probably deserves some justice, too," said Decker bluntly.

She bowed her head slightly. "I never thought otherwise. Good night, Agent Decker."

She left and walked up the stairs leading to the second story of the bar. Decker turned back to see that Stan Baker and Caroline Dawson were no longer on the dance floor. He looked around the bar space but didn't see them anywhere. He finished his beer, braced himself, and headed back out into the heat, though he found it was cooler outside than in.

A bolt of lightning far to the west speared downward, and something seemed to explode at the spot where the slash of electricity had stabbed the earth. The sound reached them even here, and a plume of flames shot upward and lit the sky for miles around. The other people on the streets kept on walking, or staggering, as though detonations like that were routine.

London, North Dakota, was getting more interesting by the minute, thought Decker as he trudged on.

7

Six a.m.

Decker flicked open his eyes and rose without the need of the set alarm on his phone. He trudged to the bathroom, showered, and changed into a fresh set of clothes. He looked out his hotel window. The sky was dark and still clogged with clouds, but he could see a seam of dawn starting to build, like a sleepy eye about to open. He looked at the weather app on his phone. It was only sixty-eight degrees but with a dew point that would make Louisiana proud. Decker thought he could actually see the air outside, it was so thick with moisture.

He sat on the edge of his bed for a couple extra seconds as he awoke more fully. Another town, another case to solve. His life. And welcome to it.

He went down to breakfast to find Jamison already sitting at a table with Joe Kelly in the hotel's restaurant. The local detective was dressed in a dark two-piece suit, white-collared shirt, and no tie. His shoes were black scuffed boots with worn heels.

Decker sat at the table. "I thought I'd be the first one down," he said.

"I'm a borderline insomniac, so I'm usually up by four having my first of too many cups of coffee," said Kelly.

"And we gained an hour coming out," said Jamison, who was looking over her menu. "So it's actually a little late for me."

Decker eyed Kelly. "I was out walking last night and a bolt of lightning hit something in the far distance. And there was an explosion."

"I heard that, too," chimed in Jamison. "Wondered what the hell it was. But nobody in the hotel seemed bothered by it."

Kelly nodded. "It was probably just lightning hitting a saltwater disposal pond. The lightning is sort of drawn to those things, and also to the metal freshwater tanks and piping stations. The bolt hits it, it blows up, and they come and repair it. Cost of doing business up here."

"Okay," said Decker. He shot Jamison a quizzical look.

After they ordered and their coffees were delivered Kelly said, "Any updates on why Irene Cramer was important to you guys?"

Jamison glanced at Decker, who said, "Not yet."

"So Feds keep things from other Feds?" asked Kelly, looking disappointed.

"These days everybody keeps things from everybody else," noted Decker. "Anything on your end?"

"I've got an interview lined up for us with Cramer's landlady. I was going to go see her when I found out you were coming to town. So I held off."

"We appreciate that. Did Cramer have a job other than being an 'escort'?" asked Jamison.

"She did actually, a pretty important one," replied Kelly. He paused and said somewhat haltingly, "She worked as a teacher with the Brothers."

"The who?" said Jamison.

"The Brothers. They're a religious group. Branch of the Anabaptists."

"Care to elaborate?" said Decker.

"They're sort of like the Amish, only they can drive cars and use heavy machinery and stuff. They're farmers and also do some manufacturing. Communal living is their standard. They take it straight from the scriptures. Good people, but they keep to themselves."

"So an escort was employed as a teacher by a religious group?" asked Decker with a pair of hiked eyebrows. "How the hell does that work? And why didn't you tell us that last night?"

"Well, they obviously didn't know that she was also an escort. Plus, she was apparently a really good teacher and got along well with the kids. They're going to be devastated by her death. I've already talked to Peter Gunther, the minister, though I didn't tell him about Irene's 'other' job *or* what had happened to her. And I was working up to tell you. I just couldn't find the words last night. You Feds coming to town was a little bit of a surprise. I hadn't decided how to handle it."

"Minister? Like a preacher?" said Jamison curiously.

"No, as in the leader of the organization." He eyed Jamison. "The Anabaptists are a male-led sect. The women do a lot of the work, including all of the butchering, cooking, cleaning, and sewing. But the men are the leaders."

"Welcome back to the 1950s," said Jamison drily.

"They're good people, like I said," replied Kelly defensively.

"How do you know so much about them?" asked Decker.

"My grandparents used to belong to the sect when I was a kid" was Kelly's surprising reply.

"And they got tired of communal living in an age of male dominance?" retorted Jamison.

"No, but my parents did, apparently. They left after my grandparents passed on, when my sister and I were still kids."

"Do your parents live here?"

"Nope. They retired to Florida about three years ago."

"And your sister?" asked Jamison.

"She passed away a few years ago."

"I'm so sorry. She was really young then?"

"Yeah. She had a rough life."

"What else can you tell us about the Brothers?" asked Decker after a few moments of silence.

"They're antiwar pacifists. Some of the Hutterites, the largest branch of Anabaptists in the country, were persecuted for that stance during World War II."

Decker nodded. "So that covers her place of lodging and her work as a teacher. What about her work as an escort? You said you weren't sure if she actually was one, even though you recognized her from the website. But are you sure it *was* her?"

"I am."

"How?"

"I contacted her through the site. I made arrangements to meet with her. It was at a flophouse on the other side of town. I got there before her. Badged her when she showed up."

"Did you arrest her?" asked Jamison.

"No."

"Why not?" asked Decker. "You're a cop. She broke the law. Seems pretty simple."

"Look, I was trying to help her out. She didn't need a prison sentence. She just needed some positive reinforcement and guidance. Only it looks like I failed on both counts."

"But when you met with her did she confirm that she was selling sex?" said Decker. "Because earlier you intimated that you weren't sure what she was up to."

"She never admitted to being a prostitute, or an

escort. She did say she was lonely and that while she admitted to arranging to meet men from the website, she never took any money from them. And they didn't always have sex. Sometimes they just talked."

"Right," said Decker skeptically. "I'm sure they did."

"And she wasn't dressed like most hookers I've run into. Her outfit was pretty normal."

Their meals came and they ate fast, with a lot of work ahead of them.

As they prepared to leave Decker said, "You ran her prints through IAFIS, right? To see if she had a record?" He was referring to the FBI's Integrated Automated Fingerprint Identification System.

"I did, but how'd you know that?"

"It's the only reason we're here. When her print came through it obviously dinged some pretty high-up corridors at the Bureau. You said it was a request from the Feds that sent your reports to DC. That had to be how they knew."

"So she *was* important?" said Kelly.

"They're all important," retorted Decker.

"But we didn't get any hit on our submission," said Kelly. "As far as the FBI was concerned, they had no criminal record of Irene Cramer."

"Well, maybe they didn't under that name," replied Decker.

"But if they had another name in that database with those prints, they should have let us know that," said Kelly a bit angrily. "You sure you're not with-holding anything from me?"

"Scout's honor," said Decker.

"Didn't figure you for a Boy Scout."

"I wasn't. Now let's go. Busy day and I'm not get-ting any younger. And Irene Cramer's not getting any older. And somebody has to answer for that."

Decker headed out.

Kelly looked thoughtfully after the departed Decker before glancing at Jamison. "Anything I need to know about your partner?"

Jamison managed a smile. "Oh, it will become readily apparent all on its own."

8

A few drops of rain hit them as they trudged to their rental SUV. Kelly rode next to Jamison while Decker took up most of the back seat.

"So Cramer had no family in the area?" asked Jamison.

"None that I know of or could find."

"How'd she end up here?"

"She arrived a little over a year ago. No record of her before, that I can find, other than she went to Amherst. And I only found that out from the Brothers. It's like she had no past. Now, we do run into that up here from time to time. I mean we have lots of folks who are trying to escape from their pasts and whatnot. But this was the first time I could find absolutely nothing on somebody like that."

"That is weird," noted Jamison.

Kelly looked at her. "Well, maybe not all that weird, when it comes to people like you. I thought that might be the connection to you guys."

"What, you mean WITSEC?" said Jamison, referring to the Witness Protection Program run by the U.S. Marshals Service.

"To tell the truth, it was the only thing I could think of. I mean what else would explain my not being able to find anything on the lady?"

"But if that were the case, the Marshals would be all over this and the Bureau would not be leading the investigation," said Decker. "And they're not and we are. So it can't be WITSEC. We have to keep digging."

Kelly's eyes narrowed. "So what could it be, then?"

"Tell us what you do know about Cramer."

"She was pretty. Very pretty. Tall and carried herself well. Almost like a model. And she was educated. I could tell that just by talking to her. She didn't get that teaching job based on her looks. Amherst is a top-notch school."

"If she actually went there," noted Decker. "What about her personality? Give us a take on that."

"Quiet, but confident. You could tell she believed in her ability to handle any situation. I think that's why my pitch to her to quit what she was doing fell flat. She thought she could manage it. For some reason, little things she said led me to think she'd traveled around some. She seemed pretty sophisticated."

"But you also said she denied being a prostitute," pointed out Jamison. "So she may not have felt there was any reason to stop what she was doing."

"That's true," conceded Kelly.

"Any signs of her being in the money?" asked Jamison. "With the clothes she wore, or other possessions she might have had? Something she said?"

"No. She drove a used Honda. The apartment building we're going to is no great shakes. I highly doubt we'll find a Rembrandt on the walls there. I guess her pay as a teacher was enough to cover her expenses. But finding a decent place to stay for an affordable price is tough."

"Cost of living really that high around here?" asked Jamison.

"Some of the rents here would rival what you would pay in a lot of metro areas. When people first move here they usually sleep in their cars or a friend of a friend's spare room in a trailer, or someone's couch for a month or longer. Fracking crews coming in are usually housed initially in old shipping containers set up as tiny studio apartments with a bed, a toilet and a shower, and a fridge and a microwave, with one door in and the same door out. They're building homes as fast as they can, but they can't keep up. Everybody's chasing the dollars this place throws off. The result is we're growing way too fast and the cracks are showing."

"Did you believe her when she said she didn't charge for sex?" asked Decker.

"Thing is, we've been all over her place, and we've checked her bank records. Other than her teacher salary there is no sign of any other money."

Decker seemed taken aback by this. "Okay, that is odd. Most hookers have evidence of cash flow somewhere."

"She show any signs of drug use?" asked Jamison. "The coroner couldn't find any trace of it in her system."

"Nothing that I observed, and I know what to look for."

"So why'd you pick her out of all the escorts out there to have a 'come to Jesus' talk?" asked Decker.

"She wasn't the only one I had that chat with," replied Kelly.

"Who else?" asked Jamison.

He restlessly tapped his fingers against the window. "Look, in the interest of full disclosure, my sister had some of those same issues. Only she got trapped on drugs, and hooking was the only way out, or so she thought. She overdosed and they couldn't bring her back. It was a tragedy all around."

"That's so awful, Joe. I'm sorry," said Jamison.

"So that's why you don't arrest escorts?" said Decker.

"All I know is, prostitution is not a victimless crime. And if I can do something to help people who need help, then I will. It's why I signed up to be a cop. I have no problem putting people away who deserve it, but that's not all I want to do."

"How'd you find out about her connection

with the Brothers?" said Jamison. "Was that widely known?"

"I'm one of the few people here that know the Brothers well. I've been out to the Colony—that's what they call their collective home—many times. Just part of being a local cop, get to know the people in your community. I'd seen her there, in fact. That's how I recognized her picture from the website. And I highly doubt anyone from the Brothers would be surfing the web for sex services. So I think her secret was safe with me. And I never told anyone."

"Including anyone at the Brothers, or else she would have been dismissed, I imagine," noted Jamison.

He nodded. "Especially not them. She seemed troubled in a way. I didn't want to add to those troubles." He paused and added. "And I've dealt with a lot of hookers. Most come from shitty backgrounds and situations. Vulnerable and lost. But Cramer didn't fit that pattern. There was something about her that seemed, well, focused and intent. Like she was on a mission or something. So, to tell the truth, part of me believed there was something else going on with her."

"Well, since we were called up, we know there *was* something else going on with her," observed Jamison.

Decker said, "The killer might have dumped the body right before it was found."

Jamison and Kelly glanced sharply at Decker and

his abrupt segue, but then Kelly nodded. "I thought about that, too. A body lying out there in the open? Well, you wouldn't expect to see it in such good shape with all the critters we have up here." He looked at Jamison. "But to kill someone and then cut up the body like that? That's pretty damn perverted."

"We don't usually hunt anybody who's not," noted Decker.

9

Following Kelly's directions, Jamison parked at the curb in front of a four-story brick run-down building that was in an area where no construction cranes and work crews had come to roost. Yet.

They climbed out, and Kelly led them quickly inside because the wind had picked up to a nasty howl and it had started to rain as well.

The landlady's conjoined apartment and office were on the first floor just off the front entrance. The apartment's walls were painted a faded green, and the furnishings were old and frayed and looked straight out of the seventies. But the TV parked on one wall was a sixty-inch curved Samsung 4K without a set of rabbit ears in sight.

The landlady's name was Ida Simms. She was in her seventies, with thinning gray hair tied back in a severe bun. The woman was nearly as wide as she was tall. She greeted them politely, though Decker noted the tremble in her voice and the crumpled tissue clutched in her hand. She had on a large burgundy

T-shirt and faded corduroy pants with pale green Crocs below.

They sat in her small front room after declining Simms's offer of coffee.

She slumped back in her faded recliner and gazed around at them. "Irene, dead? I . . . I can't believe it." She shot Decker a terrified look. "And the FBI called in on top of it? I feel like I'm in a movie."

"That's perfectly understandable," said Jamison kindly. "We're just here to ask you some questions."

"I'll tell you whatever I can if it will help you catch whoever did this," the woman said earnestly. She blew her nose with authority into the tissue.

"When did she move in here?" asked Decker.

"About a month ago."

"Do you know where she lived before that?"

"I think at the Dawson Towers complex. It's about a mile from here. Nicer part of town. Pretty luxurious."

"Dawson?" said Decker. "Like in Caroline Dawson?"

"Yes. She has a condo there, I believe. And her father, Hugh, owns the Towers, along with about three-quarters of the businesses in London. This building here is one of the few he doesn't own. Probably wouldn't make enough money for him," she added dismissively.

"So he's the local business tycoon?" said Jamison.

"But a man named Stuart McClellan is even richer."

"How so?" asked Decker.

Kelly answered. "He owns pretty much all of the oil and gas fracking operations in this area."

"So do the two men get along?" asked Jamison.

It was Kelly again who answered. "They do business together. But I wouldn't call them best friends."

Simms said huffily. "They're men, and rich men to boot, which means they're in a lifelong pissing contest—pardon my French—to see who's the bigger dog in the fight." She shook her head. "Boys never really grow up, don't care how much cash they have."

"Did you know Ms. Cramer very well?" asked Jamison.

Simms said, "I guess as well as anyone in the building. She worked as a teacher out at the Brothers' school."

"So we heard. What can you tell us about her?"

"She was quiet. Kept to herself. I mean she was an attractive young woman, but she never had anyone over to her place, least that I know of."

"Why'd she move here from Dawson Towers? Is it cheaper here?"

"Oh, yes, much cheaper. The Towers is far nicer, like I said. But our rooms are clean and we include trash service and cable TV."

"Did you ever see her go out at night?"

"No. I get up very early and go to bed the same. If it was after nine o'clock I wouldn't see her leaving."

Jamison said, "Did she ever talk about her personal history? How she came to be here?"

Simms sat back and thought about this for a few moments. "Come to think, not really. For some reason I had the feeling that she was from the West Coast. But that's just a guess."

Decker looked out the window, where the rain was continuing to pour down. "Did she say why she had come to London in the first place? Did she have a job lined up?"

"Not that she ever said, no. But she did work at the Brothers' as the teacher, like I said. So maybe that's what brought her up here."

Jamison added, "Or was she coming here to be with someone? Maybe followed a boyfriend?"

"Not that I know of."

"When was the last time you saw her?" asked Kelly.

Simms looked pensive once more. "I believe it was a week ago today."

Decker glanced at Kelly. "That tightens the coroner's outside TOD from ten days to five, since her body was found two days ago."

"But weren't you concerned that you hadn't seen her for a week?" asked Jamison.

"No, because she said she was going on a little vacation."

"Vacation where?" asked Jamison, shooting a glance at Kelly, who looked equally surprised by this revelation.

"She didn't tell me."

"She didn't say if she was meeting someone or traveling with them?" interjected Kelly.

"No, again, we didn't really discuss it."

"Did she have any friends who lived here?" asked Jamison.

"Not that she mentioned to me."

"Not to sound like a cliché, Ida," said Kelly, "but have you seen any strangers lurking around? Or did Irene mention she was having a problem with anyone?"

"No, nothing like that," replied Simms, looking alarmed. "This is a good town. Safe for the most part. Oh, I know some of those bozos lose their tempers and get in fights and somebody ends up dead, but, well, people don't go around murdering each other on purpose."

"Until now," said Decker. "I think it's time we went over her room."

The apartment was neat, perhaps too much so, thought Decker. The furnishings looked like they had come with the apartment, a fact that Simms had confirmed for them. The tiny kitchen was utilitarian and appeared as though it had never been used. The bedroom held a bed and not much else. There were no books, photos, or mementos. No desktop or laptop computer. And no power cords showing she had such devices.

Decker eyed Kelly. "Simms said that she never saw Cramer go out at night, presumably because she went to bed too early."

"She would have hit the streets long after Simms was in bed."

"Simms also said that she wasn't aware of Cramer's having any friends in the building. But she could be wrong about that, too," remarked Jamison.

Kelly said, "But would she bring her clients back here or sleep with someone in her own building? The jig would be up."

Decker shook his head. "But what if she just had someone over for consensual sex?"

Kelly looked intrigued. "Maybe she had a boy-friend that Simms didn't know about."

"She ever mention anyone like that to you?" asked Jamison.

He shook his head. "But it's not like she would have."

Decker said, "Has this place been dusted for prints?"

"No, because it wasn't the crime scene."

"It needs to be done," said Decker sharply.

"We've got one tech, and he rides the circuit for a few other police forces around the area. I'll get him to make this a priority for us."

Decker said, "What about her car? I didn't see a Honda parked on the street."

"We've got a BOLO out on it, but nothing yet."

"If she was working through a website she probably had a laptop. And she had to have a phone," said Jamison.

"I'm sure she did but we haven't found either one," replied Kelly.

"Where would she typically meet up with the men? You mentioned you met her at a flophouse?"

"Yeah. We can go there next."

Decker said, "And we'll need to talk to the Brothers, obviously."

"I don't believe they could have had anything to do with this. They're a pacifist group."

"Pacifists or not, it only takes one bad apple in the bunch. And there's almost always one bad apple in every bunch."

10

"I take it this is the really, really seedy side of town," said Jamison as they pulled up in front of a dilapi- dated, wooden-clad three-story building that looked around a century old. It was about a quarter of a mile from Cramer's apartment, but in an even less desir- able part of London.

"You could say that."

"Who owns the building?" asked Decker.

"Hugh Dawson, or one of his companies. In fact, like Ida Simms mentioned, he owns pretty much all of London, the good and bad parts."

The man at the front desk was about forty and looked like he would rather be anywhere else on earth than where he currently was. He put down his iPhone, took off his black rimmed specs, wiped them on the sleeve of his shirt, and replaced them as they strode up to him. He barely glanced at Decker or Jamison.

"Hi, Joe," said the man, nodding at Kelly with a wary look.

"Ernie, these folks are with the FBI out of

Washington," replied Kelly, indicating Decker and Jamison.

Ernie's prominent Adam's apple bobbed up and down like an out-of-whack elevator car.

"Okay," he said suspiciously. "Never met any FBI agents before. You look pretty normal. Thought you'd be scarier."

"We can be very scary, if the situation calls for it," said Jamison brightly.

"We want to ask you some questions and have a look around," said Kelly. "I'm sure you have no problem with that, right?"

"Yeah, I do. What kind of questions? And I don't know if you can look around without a warrant."

Kelly leaned in close to Ernie. "You surprise me, Ernie. That doesn't sound too helpful or friendly."

"I'm not paid to be either one."

"Fact is, we're investigating a murder."

"Who got killed?"

"You would probably know her as *Mindy*."

Ernie's features screwed up tight. "Mindy? I don't know nobody by that name. Would've remembered that one."

"Sure you do, Ernie," said Kelly. "I met her here one night. You saw me with her and I saw you."

Ernie shook his head. "Your memory must be a lot better than mine."

Kelly glanced past him. "What do we have here? An ex-con drug dealer with a bottle of pills on that shelf back there that doesn't look like prescription drugs? That would be a serious violation of your parole. You don't want to go back inside, do you?"

Ernie glanced nervously at the bottle. "Those ain't mine. Just holding 'em for a buddy."

"You have no objection to me seeing what they are." Kelly started to walk behind the reception desk to get the bottle.

"Okay, I know Mindy," he blurted out. "Are we done here?"

"When was the last time you saw her?"

"I forget."

Kelly started to reach for the pill bottle.

"Okay, okay, it was last week."

"Be more precise than that," said Decker.

Ernie rubbed his lower lip and did the calculation in head. "Six days ago."

Decker looked at Kelly. "Now our TOD is down to four days. That alone made it worth talking to this guy."

"Did you speak with her?" asked Kelly.

"No."

"Was she with anyone?" interjected Jamison.

"She doesn't come here unless she's with someone," replied Ernie flatly. "That's sort of the point of the, um, line of work she was in."

"The guy's name?" asked Kelly.

"They don't tell me. They pay me cash and they

get the room. And I don't ask no questions and nobody shows ID."

"Description, then," demanded Decker.

"Short, muscular, blond, young, stupid, horny."

"Male or female?" asked Jamison.

"Are you serious?" Ernie snapped. "It was a *guy.*"

"Fracker?" asked Kelly.

"He looked it. Hands all chewed up and skin sunburnt and a wallet full of cash nearly as big as he was."

"How long were they here?" asked Decker.

"About forty-five minutes. They usually all take about that much time. I don't imagine there's much chitchat that goes on."

"Did they leave together or separate?" asked Decker.

"Guy left first, then Mindy."

"How'd the guy seem?"

"How do you think? He was smiling ear to ear with a spring in his step. Hell, it was like he'd won the lottery or something."

"She seem okay?" asked Kelly.

"She didn't seem not okay."

"Be more specific," prompted Jamison.

"Well, she seemed happy, actually. Maybe the sex was good, I don't know."

Jamison said, "You must have other women come in here with men, to . . . have a good time."

"Look, I don't know what you mean," blustered Ernie.

"We're not looking to bust you over this," said Jamison. "I just want to know was Mindy different from the other ladies?"

Decker glanced at her and then stared at Ernie, awaiting his answer.

"Different how?"

"I think you know how," said Jamison.

Ernie let out a long breath. "Look, the other gals come down still counting their money, if they do take cash. Some insist on Venmo because it's safer. But it's all business with them. It's not like they enjoy getting strangers off over and over."

"Very perceptive of you. And Mindy?"

"Well, she . . . she didn't seem that way. Never saw her with any money, in fact. And she wasn't like the other gals. Over half of them are strung out all the time. To my eye, I doubt the lady ever popped a pill or even smoked a joint."

"Well, you're the expert on that, Ernie," noted Kelly.

"Would you recognize this guy again if you saw him?" asked Jamison.

"Doubtful. They all look the same to me. And I see enough of them."

Kelly eyed the stairs. "Take us to the room they were using."

"Okay, but there have been other people in there since then."

Ernie grabbed a key from a box on the front desk

and led them up a flight of steps to the top floor and then down the hall. He unlocked the door and motioned them in. "Have at it."

He left them there and scurried back down the stairs like a rat abandoning a ship.

Decker wasn't even sure the man would still be there when they came back down.

11

"This is beyond disgusting," observed Jamison. "Do they even clean these rooms?"

The carpet was tattered and stained. The small bed was unmade. The smell in the air was fuggy and foul. The paint on the walls was chipped and peeling. The few bits of other furniture looked decades old and badly in need of repair. There was a single bare light bulb clinging to the ceiling like a barnacle on a ship's hull.

Jamison's gaze dropped to the floor, where sat an opened plastic condom package.

"Okay, I'm getting a tetanus booster as soon as we get out of here."

Decker was walking around the room taking everything in. His observations were being placed on mental slides and uploaded to the cloud that constituted his largely infallible memory. "We'll at least need to check all the prints here and try to do an elimination run."

Kelly said, "Well, from what Ernie told us, it

seems like Cramer and the young buck had sex that night."

"Yeah, it does," said Jamison. "And maybe the guy was so happy because she didn't charge him for it."

"And Ernie said Cramer was happy, too. I wonder why?"

Decker said, "We have to retrace her steps, every minute of every day. Now, Simms told us that Cramer was planning to go on a trip." He eyed Kelly. "It's early September, so I assume school has just started. Unless the Brothers have a different schedule."

"No, they pretty much follow a traditional schedule when it comes to that."

"Is she the only teacher there?"

"Except for the woman who lives out there and is a member of the Brothers' Colony. Cramer taught the subjects the state requires under compulsory education, English, Social Studies, math, that sort of thing."

"So what were they going to do while she was gone?" asked Jamison.

"Probably just have the kids taught by the other teacher. The Brothers only go to school until they're fifteen. A week isn't going to matter much one way or another."

Decker said, "Let's go talk to the Brothers, then."

"We'll have to make an appointment."

Decker frowned. "Why, are they that busy?"

"It's just common courtesy."

"Fine. Then call them and tell them we're on the way."

"Decker, they might not like us barging in like that."

Decker stared down at Kelly. "I doubt Irene Cramer 'liked' being butchered. So I'll take finding her killer as fast as possible over somebody else's possible hurt feelings over a *visit*." He eyed the local cop severely. "This is a murder investigation, Kelly. Nothing takes precedence over that, at least in my book. If you think differently, we might have a problem working together."

Kelly shot Jamison a glance and then looked back at Decker. "I have no problem with that."

"Glad to hear it. Let's go."

"What the hell is that thing?" asked Jamison.

They were in the rental SUV heading east. They had cleared a slight rise in the otherwise flat plains and spied what appeared to be an Egyptian pyramid with its top chopped off and what looked like an enormous golf ball set atop this flat space. It was about a hundred and fifty feet high and made of what looked to be stone. It dwarfed the other buildings set behind it, all enclosed by double perimeter fencing with razor wire toppers.

"That's the Douglas S. George Defense Complex, otherwise known as London Air Force Station," replied Kelly, who was riding next to Jamison.

She said, "Air Force station? I don't see any planes or runways."

"It's not an air base. It's an air *station*. Although they *do* have a runway for planes and a helipad. And a super-duper radar array is housed in that blob. It can see into space. It's part of the early warning system in case somebody fires nukes at North America."

"Stuck way out here?" commented Jamison.

"I guess some politician from North Dakota lobbied hard for it. But it's pretty ugly, so would you want something like that in your backyard? Anyway, it's been here since the fifties, long before I was alive." He pointed to an upcoming road. "Hang a right there, Alex."

She did so and they found themselves passing fairly close to the Air Force station.

"Not too far now," said Kelly. "Just up ahead we turn left and then we're there."

Decker looked puzzled. "But it looks like we're still on the Air Force property."

Kelly smiled. "About ten years ago most of the property went up for auction and the Brothers bought it. And then frackers recently leased some of it from them."

"The Brothers bought land from the federal government that has an Air Force installation on it?" said Jamison, looking surprised.

"I guess Uncle Sam is trying to cut costs, or they didn't need all of the acreage. And they didn't buy the Air Force station, of course, just the spare acreage. Now, the Brothers *did* need that land. They've spun off a few new colonies and they needed the space for those folks to set up their farms and other operations."

"Just so I've got this straight, you have a religious sect plowing fields right next to a government eye in the sky looking for nukes coming our way?"

"It would make for a great skit on *Saturday Night Live*," observed Kelly.

Jamison hung the next left, and another quarter mile down a freshly paved road, they arrived at the Brothers' compound.

Kelly had phoned ahead, and there were two men waiting by a large metal farm gate. Even in the heat and humidity they were both dressed in heavy, dark clothing and wore battered black fedoras with silk gray bands. Full beards covered their jaws and chins. One wore a pair of old-fashioned pince-nez glasses. The other one, younger by about ten years than his late-fiftyish companion, gazed at them curiously through horn-rimmed spectacles. About a hundred feet behind them was a tall woman in her late forties with brown hair flecked with silver, wearing a long dress with colorful stripes and a kerchief with white polka dots. She, too, was watching them closely.

In the distance, Decker could see low-slung cinderblock buildings fronted either by well-tended lawns or crushed gravel. There were large corrugated-metal buildings, some grain silos, fenced crop fields, and many pieces of neatly arranged heavy farming equipment along with some other machinery that, to Decker's eye, looked like they would be used in a building or manufacturing process. Everything was laid out with thought and precision, he concluded.

"Like I said before, it's all communal living here," said Kelly as the SUV came to a stop. "No personal property, really, except your clothes and what's in your house."

"The big buildings?" asked Jamison.

"They sell eggs and vegetables, and other things that they grow. They also make furniture and some parts for manufacturing, and they also do metal fabrication. The fracking people buy from them. They have their own truck fleet to deliver everything. It's a fairly large-scale operation when all is said and done. They're very self-sufficient. Their English is excellent, though their first language is German."

"And you haven't told them why we're here?" said Jamison.

Kelly's look darkened. "No, not over the phone. It's going to come as a shock."

"I'm surprised they have phones," she said.

"Well, they don't allow TV or the internet, strictly speaking. But younger members do use Facebook and Instagram and email to keep in touch with friends, though that's closely regulated. And cell phones are necessary for business and personal tasks, so they have those too. There's only one central hard line phone. They worry that the outside world will try to encroach on them."

"And maybe convince some of the younger members to leave?" said Jamison.

"The outside world can be enticing, for all the wrong reasons," conceded Kelly.

They climbed out of the vehicle and approached the two men, who came forward and extended their hands in greeting. They all introduced themselves to one another.

The older man was Peter Gunther, who was the minister of this particular colony, and his companion was Milton Ames, the secretary. The woman, who had remained standing back, was Ames's wife, Susan, her husband told them. She was the tailor of the colony, Gunther said.

"And what does that mean?" asked Jamison curiously.

"She picks all the clothes or at least the fabric and is in charge of the making of the clothes," offered Ames.

Jamison turned and waved at the woman, but she simply stared back and didn't return the gesture.

Gunther warily looked at Decker. "So the FBI? Joe didn't say why you wanted to meet with us."

Kelly said, "Can we go inside? We're going to

tell you why we're here, but it's not going to be pleasant."

Gunther and Ames exchanged a startled glance. Gunther turned and led them toward one of the buildings.

It was a startlingly clean communal kitchen with two long picnic-style tables down each wall and a similar table in the middle of the room. The appliances were commercial grade. A woman in a dress similar to Susan Ames's was unpacking some supplies and placing them neatly in overhead cabinets.

"Excuse us, Martha," said Gunther. "We need to talk to these folks about some important matters."

Martha glanced suspiciously at Decker and Jamison and hurried into another room.

They sat down at the table in the middle of the space. Gunther clasped his hands in front of him.

"Now, why are you here?" Gunther asked Kelly.

"Irene Cramer."

Gunther kept his surprised gaze on Kelly. "Irene? What about her?"

Decker interjected. "We understand that she was going on a trip?"

Ames spoke up. "That's right. Our school had just started back up. But we saw no reason not to let her go. She coordinated with Doris, the Colony teacher. It was only a week or so. She should be back soon."

"When did she tell you about the trip?" asked Jamison.

Gunther said, "Why all the questions about Irene?"

Kelly glanced at Decker, who nodded. "Irene was found dead," Kelly said to Gunther.

"Dead?" exclaimed a horrified Gunther. "Where? How?"

"The 'where' was out in the middle of nowhere. She was found by a hunter. The 'how' was that she was murdered."

"Well, I'm not surprised."

They all turned to see Susan Ames standing in the doorway where Martha had earlier walked through.

"Susan?" exclaimed Ames. "What in heaven's name do you mean you're not surprised?"

"Mindy? It was only a matter of time."

12

"Okay, I admit that one hit me out of left field," said Kelly. They were outside in the heat, and he was smoking a cigarette. Decker stood there looking back at the building they'd left a few minutes ago. Jamison was standing a little away from Kelly's cigarette smoke.

Gunther and Milton Ames had apparently been so taken aback by Susan Ames's statement that they had quickly ushered Decker and company out of the building, while they "discussed" things among themselves.

"She knew about Cramer's other life," noted Decker. "Which begs the question of why she continued to allow her to teach their kids. And there's something else."

"What?" Kelly asked as he tossed his spent smoke on the gravel.

"If Susan Ames knew, who else did here?"

"You really think one of the Brothers butchered Cramer like that?"

"Locals can come here. Cramer *worked* here and she was an outsider. Any other non-Brothers around?"

Kelly looked shrewdly at him. "Yeah, they hire

contractors to help with the manufacturing stuff and some of the farming operations."

"Okay." Decker glanced toward the dining hall. "If they keep us out here much longer I'm just going to kick the door down before heatstroke fully sets in."

"They might not like that," warned Kelly.

"They're pacifists. So what are they gonna do about it?"

Kelly grinned and then pointed. "Well, you just got your wish."

Decker looked over to see Peter Gunther standing at the open door and waving for them to rejoin him.

Inside, Susan and Milton Ames were sitting side by side at the center table. He appeared upset and she looked somewhat contrite.

Milton said, "Um, Susan wants to explain her earlier *remark*."

"Okay," said Kelly, sitting down opposite them while Decker and Jamison hovered behind. Kelly said to Susan, "So you knew about Irene?"

Susan wouldn't look up. "Yes. And . . . it was very cruel what I said before. I don't know what I was thinking. I guess . . . I suppose I was upset." Now she did look up and her eyes were watery. "But I did fear for her. And it seems that those fears were unfortunately justified."

"How did you know about her other life?" asked Decker.

"This past spring our oldest son had gone to visit

my sister and her family in Pennsylvania. They're not part of us. But we do visit and keep in touch. He traveled by bus. I went into town to pick him up at the depot. He was late coming in, it must've been after midnight. I was waiting in my truck when I saw her walking down the street with some man."

"Irene, you mean?" said Kelly.

"I had to look three times before I recognized her. It was more the way she walked, really, and how she would tilt her head. I would see her do that at the school all the time."

"Then you're a careful observer," noted Decker.

Susan glanced nervously at her husband, who still stared down at the table. "I . . . I am someone who notices things. My duties here require that attention to detail."

"Go on," prompted Kelly.

"Well, the man was obviously drunk and had his hands all over her. I thought she might be in trouble. So I got out of the truck and called out to her. She was horrified to see me, I could tell. She started trying to get rid of the man who was with her. But he said the name Mindy, which is how I knew about that. Anyway, the man yelled that he'd pay her an extra hundred dollars if she, well, if she performed a certain *act* on him." Susan blushed deeply as she said this, and Milton and Gunther looked like they might be ill. She noticed this and hurried on. "That's when I realized it was more than some date that got out of hand. The man finally left and we sat in my truck and talked. She could tell I was very shocked and she explained at length about what was going on."

"Take your time and tell us everything you can remember," said Jamison.

"She said her mother had cancer, had no insurance, and she was sending all the money she made by, well, by being with men—"

Here Gunther made a clucking sound.

"—so as to help her mother," finished Susan hurriedly.

"So just to be clear, she told you she was selling sex for money?" said Kelly.

"I know nothing about it, of course, but isn't that the point? To do it for money?"

Kelly glanced at Decker and didn't answer.

"Did you believe her about her mother?" asked Decker.

"I was so stunned I didn't know what to believe. But she seemed incredibly sincere, and so, against my better judgment, I promised I wouldn't tell anyone about what I had seen. She would have been instantly dismissed from working here if I had."

"Of course she would have," bellowed Gunther. "And you *should* have told us, Susan. To think that our children were being taught by someone who . . . who engaged in such immoral behavior."

Susan glanced up at him defiantly. "And would it be moral to let her mother die?"

"I'm sure there were other ways," said Gunther. "Do you not agree, Milton?"

Milton looked startled, as though he were a student hiding in the back of the room when the teacher called on him for an answer he didn't have.

"Yes, yes, of course. I'm sure there were other pathways." He brightened. "She could have come to us. We would have helped her."

"Exactly," said Gunther.

"Maybe she didn't want anyone's help," said Susan dismissively.

"Well, then she alone should be accountable for it," said Gunther firmly.

"It looks like she was," said Decker, drawing all their attention back to him. "Someone took her life, very brutally." He scrutinized Susan. "What else did she tell you? Was she afraid of anyone? Had she received threats of some kind? Was anyone stalking her?"

"Nothing like that." She paused. "But there was something. Something she said. It was about two weeks ago. She was here working on lesson plans when I popped in."

"What did she say?" interjected Jamison. "As detailed as you can be, please."

"She was looking upset. I asked her why. She told me she had gotten a note or letter that had disturbed her."

"But you said she hadn't been threatened," noted Kelly.

"Well, she didn't say that the note was threatening. Just that it had *disturbed* her."

"Did she say who it was from?" asked Decker.

"No. But it was shortly thereafter that she mentioned taking a trip." She eyed her husband. "You were there, too, when she asked for permission to miss a week of school."

"Yes, yes, that's right. She said she was going to visit her mother."

"And where did her mother live?"

"She never said," replied Susan. "In fact, I know little about her background."

"But surely if she was teaching here you needed to know about her background," said Jamison. "She had to have appropriate credentials and experience and all that. Kelly said he learned from you that she had graduated from Amherst?"

Milton chimed in, "Oh, yes. She brought her credentials and teaching certificate with her when she interviewed for the job."

"Do you have copies of those documents?" asked Decker.

Milton said, "No, I looked at them but didn't make copies."

"Did you do a background check on her?" asked Jamison.

Milton shook his head. "No, we . . . no, we didn't

do that. She didn't seem like a person who would have a criminal record. She was a young woman, nice, presentable with a college degree from an excellent school." He glanced at Gunther. "It didn't occur to us that there might be a problem in her past. She worked here for a year without any issues at all."

"And she was a very good teacher," added Susan. "She was lively and engaging, and her curriculum was interesting and never crossed the bounds of what, well, what we value here. And the children loved her. They're going to be devastated by this."

"We'll find another teacher," said Gunther firmly.

"I'm sure you will," said Decker. "And let's hope nothing happens to that person."

"This has absolutely nothing to do with us," said Gunther indignantly. "This woman was a prostitute. I can only imagine the unsavory and dangerous people she would run into doing that sort of thing. I'm sure one of them is responsible for her death."

"I wish I was as sure as you are," replied Decker before looking over at Susan. "When was the last time you saw Cramer?"

She considered this question, her lips moving as though she were counting off days in her head. "Eight days ago."

"Here, at the school?" asked Jamison.

Susan shook her head. "I was in town. We needed some . . . supplies. There's a shop we use. They normally deliver out here, but they had two people out sick, so I drove into town."

"So where did you see her?" asked Decker.

"She was coming out of a building."

"Did you talk to her?" asked Kelly.

"I asked her when she was leaving on her trip to see her mother. I thought she would have already left, actually. She said she had been delayed but that she was leaving the next day, and she would be back to teach when she had originally said she would."

Decker asked, "Did she say *how* she was getting to wherever she was going?"

"She had a car. An old Honda. I know that because she drove it to our school. But she didn't tell me how she would be traveling to her mother's."

Jamison said, "How did she look? Nervous? Happy?"

Susan thought about this for a moment. "Resigned. Yes, she seemed . . . resigned."

Decker said, "As though her fate was already decided, you mean?"

"Well, I didn't think that at the time, because I didn't know she was going to be murdered. But now that I know, I would say yes."

Kelly said, "So maybe she saw her own death coming?"

Decker glanced at him. "Well, she saw right, didn't she?"

13

"Do you happen to know a guy named Stan Baker?" Decker asked Kelly on the drive back.

Kelly said, "Stan Baker? Name doesn't ring a bell. *Should* I know him?"

"He works for a fracking company. He's, um, he's my brother-in-law."

"Brother-in-law? So you knew he was here, then?"

"No, it was a surprise. He's a big guy, almost as big as me. Reddish hair, with the same color beard. Rugged in appearance. Ring any bells now?"

Kelly smiled. "Hell, you just described half the guys here, Decker."

"Yeah, I guess so," said Decker absently.

Jamison said, "We didn't find any note or letter at Cramer's apartment. She might have taken it with her, or she might have destroyed it."

"At least it shows she was concerned about something," said Decker. "And it might also account for the air of resignation Susan Ames alluded to."

"What can you tell us about Caroline Dawson?"

asked Jamison suddenly as she glanced briefly at Decker.

"Caroline?" said Kelly. "Why? Did you meet her?"

"Just for a minute. She's apparently dating Decker's brother-in-law."

Kelly looked at her oddly. "Really? Okay. Well, she's Hugh Dawson's only child. Well, his only living child."

"What do you mean?" asked Jamison.

"There was a brother, Hugh Jr. He was older than Caroline."

"What happened to him?"

"He, uh, he killed himself. This was a number of years ago."

"My God. Do you know why?"

"His father and him didn't see eye to eye on some things and it just got out of hand. I guess depression set in and that . . . was that."

"Care to elaborate?" asked Decker.

"Not really, no. I don't like telling stories out of school, and it has nothing to do with the case."

"And Dawson's wife?"

"She died a few years ago. In an accident."

"Caroline mentioned being involved in her father's businesses," said Jamison.

He nodded. "Hugh's training her to take over one day. She's really smart. Went to college out of state. And then came back here to begin her 'apprenticeship.'"

"She seemed more of a party girl when we met her," noted Jamison.

"She works hard and she's ambitious. She *was* a right little hellion in her teens. But she knows she has the golden egg in front of her and she's not about to screw that up. Then again, Hugh's only sixty and in good health, far as I know. He won't be retiring anytime soon."

"It sounds like you know her well," observed Decker.

Kelly looked thoughtful. "We grew up together, were pretty close all the way through high school. But I don't think anyone really knows Caroline. She can be fun on the outside, but most never get to see her inner core. At least that's my observation."

"And her father?" asked Jamison.

"Hugh Dawson is a big, gregarious man who likes to come across as just a regular guy despite his wealth. He'll make you laugh. But if you cross him he'll make you cry instead. Not a man you want to get on the wrong side of."

"So what's the deal with this military complex?" interjected Decker. "Who works there?"

"It used to be a mix of folks. Military and contractors. But a year or so ago the military outsourced all the operations to a contractor. They have their own fire station, bowling alley, and even a bar. An Air Force colonel still commands the installation—Mark Sumter."

"Ever had any problems over there?"

"Nothing serious."

"You know this Sumter guy?"

"Yeah. He's been here about a year. But why all the questions about that place?"

"Woman gets butchered and there's a sensitive government facility nearby? It's at least worth a look." He glanced at Jamison, who said, "And it might explain why the FBI got called in."

"And Cramer came here about a year ago, too, same as this Colonel Sumter," added Decker.

Kelly nodded slowly. "Okay, yeah, I can see that. Maybe."

"So *maybe* you can arrange an interview and visit," said Decker.

"I'll make a call, sure."

They dropped Kelly off, and Decker and Jamison returned to their hotel. As they walked in, Decker's phone buzzed. He looked spooked as he stared at the screen.

"Who is it?" asked Jamison, noting his expression. "Bogart?"

"No, it's my sister, Renee."

When Decker made no move to answer the call Jamison said, "Well? You wanted to talk to her. Here's your chance."

Decker moved over to a corner of the room and put the phone to his ear. "Hey, Renee."

"Stan called me, Amos."

"Yeah, I figured. Look, he told me about . . . you two."

"We're getting divorced. We're not terminally ill. So don't sound so morbid. It's not the end of the world. And it's not like you kept in touch. You've never even visited me here."

"Well, it's a long way."

"And it was a long way every time I came to visit you. But I didn't call to argue."

"Why did you call then?"

"I wanted to just let you know that despite Stan and I going our separate ways, we're doing okay. The kids understand. They're fine with it."

"Why didn't you call and tell me?"

"I left two messages for you. And what would you have done? I figured that you'd find out at some point. Diane knows, of course. She's already been down to see me."

"Stan said you tried to work it out."

"And I imagine you think we didn't try hard enough. But we did, Amos. We just couldn't make it work. I'm not getting any younger and I've got two kids still at home, and one in college. And Danny just graduated from college and he's moving back here. I didn't have time for endless counseling when it became clear it was going nowhere."

"Are you going to be okay financially?"

"Stan makes good money, and he's helping with all of the kids' expenses. And we had college funds set up. And I've got a good job that pays well and has excellent health benefits."

"So what happened? You both seemed so happy."

"How would you know? I haven't seen you since the funerals. And if you call more than once a year, well, you called the wrong number. I almost had a heart attack when you picked up just now."

"I . . . I guess I have been sort of AWOL lately."

"I invited you to live with us after Cassie and Molly died. When you turned that down, I offered to move the whole family to Ohio to be close to you."

"I couldn't let you do that, Renee. That would have disrupted all of your lives."

"I would've done it in a heartbeat. You *are* my only brother, after all."

"I got through it. I'm okay."

"I know you found the person who did it, though you never talked to me about it. I read it in the newspaper," she added in a hurt tone.

"Yeah, well, it's not something I really wanted to talk about."

"But it must've offered you some closure."

"Not as much as you might think."

She didn't say anything for a long moment. "So how was Stan?"

"He looked okay. He . . . when I saw him, he . . ." Decker could not bring himself to tell her.

"It's okay, Amos. I know he's seeing someone. It's okay. We *are* divorcing."

Relieved, he said, "So are *you* seeing anyone?"

"Yeah, my four kids. Motherhood is sort of a full-time gig. But once I have some time getting to know myself again, and actually taking care of some of my needs, I intend to find some companionship. Don't know if I'll ever take the plunge again. How about you?"

"How about me what?"

"Are you seeing anyone?"

"I keep pretty busy, too. Look, I gotta go. Something's come up."

"Good *talking* to you, little brother," said Renee sarcastically.

Decker clicked off and rejoined Jamison.

"How'd it go?" she asked anxiously.

Decker started to say something but then shut his mouth, turned, and walked off.

Jamison watched him go and then said under her breath, "That good, huh?"

14

Decker and Jamison grabbed an early dinner at the hotel.

"I checked the weather outside. It's down to eighty-one with a thousand percent humidity. Winter is clearly upon us," added Jamison, attempting a smile.

Decker put down his menu. "It's like Mark Twain said, everybody complains about the weather, but no one ever does a damn thing about it."

After the waitress took their orders and departed Jamison said, "So why don't you tell me how it went with your sister?" She gave him a look. "If you *remember,* you just walked off without a word."

Decker sighed. "She said she's doing fine financially. Her focus is on the kids and she said they're handling it okay. When things slow down a bit she's going to concentrate on her own well-being."

"Well, that's smart. And Stan?"

"She said it was amicable and he's been very supportive."

"I guess not all divorces are that easy. So, good for them."

Decker said, "Did you ever consider getting married again?"

"If you can believe it, I never ran into Mr. Right, which includes my ex-husband."

"I'm sure you had suitors."

"How very old-fashioned of you. I had men who were *pursuing* me, yes. What they were pursuing me for, well, I don't think it was marriage."

Decker held up a hand. "Okay, sorry I asked."

"I speak my mind. I'm independent. And some guys find that a turn-off." She paused. "Although I seem to have no problem playing second fiddle to you."

Decker looked surprised at her statement. "I wouldn't describe it that way. I rub people the wrong way. Sometimes that works, other times not. You're good at rebalancing things."

"So we make a good team, you think?"

He seemed startled by the query. "Yes. Don't you?"

She patted his hand. "Don't worry, I'm not looking to get a new partner. I'm just now breaking you in."

"Can anybody join the party or is it totally private?"

They looked up to see Caroline Dawson standing next to their table. She was dressed far more conservatively than the last time they had seen her. A modest white blouse buttoned to her neck, black slacks, low pumps, and her hair pulled back. Her makeup was minimal but her personality was as effervescent as the first time they had met.

Jamison indicated a seat. "Help yourself. We're just grabbing a quick bite."

Dawson sat down. "Stan told me about you, Decker. Said you're a crackerjack detective, the FBI's finest."

"Did he?" said Decker, not looking pleased.

"And here I was asking you to go clubbing. I'm really sorry about that."

"You had no way of knowing why we were here," interjected Jamison.

She glanced at Jamison. "He didn't really know you, but if you're an FBI agent, you must be great, too. And I love it that they have women in the ranks doing the job and not just guys."

"I agree with you there," replied Jamison.

"Well, it's nice that tiny London, North Dakota, gets so much firepower. You should finish solving it in no time. Stan said it was a murder?"

"That's right."

"Irene Cramer?"

"How'd you know that?"

"Hal Parker. He works for my father sometimes as a hunter. He was tracking down a wolf that was doing damage to some of my dad's livestock when he found the body."

"You keep livestock out in this heat?" said Jamison.

"The winter is actually harder on them than the

summer. And when it's fifty below out we provide dry bedding, which is important. Their coats will adapt to the cold, but when they're penned inside, you have to keep an eye on the ventilation. Too much nitrogen, moisture, or odor in the air, and other factors like that can lead to respiratory infections. With the heat it's important to make sure they have water and shade and enough to eat. My dad's been doing this a long time, and he gets the balance just right."

"And it sounds like he taught you well," commented Jamison.

Dawson brightened. "He *has* taught me well. Sometimes too well, such that I'm sitting in a restaurant with two strangers talking about cow pens and nitrogen levels."

Jamison said, "The closest I've ever gotten to livestock is at a petting zoo."

"What else did Hal Parker tell you about finding the body?" asked Decker.

"That he threw up. That he'd never seen anything that awful in his life. And he fought in the Middle East."

"But he couldn't have known it was Irene Cramer. She was identified *after* she was brought in."

Dawson sat back and looked at Decker in a new, perhaps sobering light.

"I'm good friends with Liz Southern. She told me. But I don't want her to get into trouble. I was just curious after Hal told me he'd found a body of a woman."

"That's okay," said Jamison. "It's a small town and news was bound to get around."

"Got any suspects?"

"None that we can talk about," advised Decker quickly. "Did you know Ms. Cramer?"

"No. But I knew that she taught school over at the Brothers' Colony."

"Do you know the folks there?"

"I can't say I really know them all that well." She glanced at Decker. "So, Stan also told me that you're his brother-in-law."

"Soon to be ex-brother-in-law, as I'm sure he also told you."

"I wouldn't be seeing him if he were still happily married," she said firmly.

"That's good to know," replied Decker. "I have to admit that I went to the OK Corral Saloon and watched you two dancing. Frankly, I don't think I've ever seen him more uncomfortable."

Dawson smiled. "He *is* very awkward in his own skin when it comes to things like that. But it's also very endearing." She glanced up at Decker. "But I've found that I like showing him there's more to life, you know."

"I can see that," said Jamison appreciatively. "Sometimes guys need a little helping hand in that regard."

"He's nice and there's something about him, I

don't know, this naïve quality, that really appeals to me. Plus, he's quite the gentleman. And he fought for his country. I mean, I definitely feel safe when I'm around him."

"Did he talk about his combat days?" asked Decker.

"Never, and I've asked."

Decker said, "He was Special Forces. Fought in the Middle East. Got a bunch of medals. Was even wounded. But the ones who do the most in war don't talk about it. That's why Stan keeps quiet about it. He's a straight-up guy."

"Wow, that's impressive."

"I'm not sure he can keep up with you, though," said Decker.

"We're not looking to get married. We're just having fun." Dawson's smile faded as she looked over Jamison's shoulder.

Jamison and Decker turned to see what she was staring at. A short man, barely five-two, in his early sixties had come into the dining room. Despite the heat he was dressed in an expensive woolen three-piece suit and blue paisley tie with a matching pocket handkerchief. Decker thought he had never seen a pair of more intense eyes. Next to him was a good-looking, tall, well-built man about Caroline Dawson's age.

"Let me take a wild guess," said Jamison. "Is that Stuart McClellan?"

Dawson said, "Yes. And his son, Shane. I wonder what they're doing here."

"Do they not frequent places like this?" asked Decker, studying the two men.

"They don't frequent any place owned by my father. At least Stuart doesn't."

"Well, from what we learned, that severely limits their options," said Decker.

"Something my father takes delight in."

Stuart McClellan spotted Dawson and headed over with his son in tow.

"Hello, Caroline," said McClellan, his voice surprisingly low and baritone. So much so that Decker wondered if it was affected.

"Stuart." She glanced at his son. "Hi, Shane."

Shane broke into a grin and drew closer to the table. "Hey, Caroline. What's up?"

His father aggressively elbowed him aside. "And these two are the FBI agents?"

"Yes," said Jamison after glancing at Decker.

"Nasty business. I'm Stuart *McClellan,* by the way. You probably passed some of my fracking wells when you were coming in."

"We did," replied Jamison. "And I guess we also saw some of the neighborhoods where your workers live."

"I had Shane oversee some of their construction, and for once he didn't . . . I mean to say, he did a pretty good job."

"Thanks, Pop," said Shane, seemingly oblivious to the underlying meaning in his father's "praise." He seemed to have eyes only for Caroline, who would not meet his gaze.

Decker said, "Did either of you know Irene Cramer?"

Stuart shook his head. "Shane?"

He finally managed to draw his gaze from Caroline and said, "Nope. Didn't know her."

"Why is the FBI here?" asked Stuart. "I mean, don't you people have anything better to do than investigate local murders? We have police to do that. Shouldn't you be going after terrorists and the like?"

"We cover a lot of ground," said Decker. "And we go where we're told to go. So nothing else you can tell us about Cramer?"

Caroline Dawson said, "She lived in an apartment building. It wasn't one of the nicer ones, but it was affordable."

"But it's also one of the few that your father doesn't own, or at least we were told that," Jamison pointed out. "So how did you know that she lived there?"

"I went there to drop off an offer to purchase the building this morning. Ida Simms, the manager, told me that she'd lived there."

"So you're looking to buy that building, huh?" said Stuart. "Why's that? Your daddy's been building like crazy the last two years."

"Well, he can't build fast enough to support all the people moving in to work at *your* fracking operations," retorted Dawson. "So we want to buy that building, rehab it, and then rent it out. It needs a lot of work."

"And you'll charge a nice premium for it when all is said and done," commented Stuart.

"That's sort of the point," Dawson said. "But it's also not cheap to rehab, and it's really hard to find workers. Everyone wants to frack. It pays a lot."

"That's not my problem," said Stuart.

"We built those other tract neighborhoods for your workers as fast as we could."

Stuart laughed, pulled a short cigarillo from his pocket, and stuck it in his mouth unlit. "Your old man went cheap on the materials like he always does. I've had complaints from my workers. That's why I'm starting to build my own."

Dawson looked at him sternly. "If they have complaints, they should take them up with us, not you. We have an entire department that focuses solely on matters like that."

Stuart rolled his eyes. "Sure, sure, I bet that's a priority for you all."

Dawson apparently had had enough. She looked at Decker and Jamison. "Well, I hope you find who you're looking for. If you'll excuse me."

As she turned to leave, Shane called out, "Bye, Caroline. Maybe I'll see you around."

She didn't look back but merely waved.

Decker noted that Stuart McClellan eyed her every step of the way.

After she was gone, Stuart said, "That girl has some issues. Anger issues."

"She seemed perfectly reasonable to me," said Jamison.

Shane said, "She works hard, Dad, you have to admit that."

"I *do* admit that. And I wish you worked just as hard."

"Well, work's not everything in life." Shane turned and gazed in the direction where Caroline had gone.

Stuart followed this and then stuck a finger in his son's broad chest. "You work for your family. You work for me. Your loyalties lie there, son, no room for anything else. And if you make work everything in your life for a long enough time then you'll find you have the means to do what you want when your work is done." He glanced at Decker. "Do you not agree?"

"I think everybody's different. So one-size advice doesn't fit all."

"Well, with that perspective it's a wonder we ever liberated ourselves from the British or won World War II. I wish you luck with your investigation, and with that attitude I think you're going to need all the luck you can get."

He turned and strode off.

Shane looked at them sheepishly. "He . . . gets on his soapbox a lot."

"I'm sure," said Jamison.

"Nice meeting you," said Shane, and then he hurried after his father.

Jamison looked at Decker. "I couldn't stand being around his father for five seconds."

When Decker didn't answer she looked at him. He was staring pensively at the ceiling.

"What *are* the McClellans doing here?" he said.

"Why is that our concern?"

"Because you never know how things will pan out, Alex, that's why."

15

"That is one of the most unusual buildings I think I've ever seen, especially in a place like this," said Jamison as she, Decker, and Kelly drew closer to the chopped-off pyramid representing the centerpiece of the Douglas S. George Defense Complex. They could see now that it was surrounded by other far-more-ordinary-looking buildings.

Kelly said, "I remember as a kid seeing it and imagining all sorts of things going on inside there. We pretended that it was a castle with a damsel in distress inside that we were going to rescue. We would charge it on our bicycles and minibikes."

Jamison glanced at him with an amused look. "And did you ever rescue her?"

Kelly grinned sheepishly. "Only in our dreams. The fact was you couldn't get near this place. As kids we did come close sometimes. Even once ran into a soldier carrying a big-ass gun. I think we all wet our pants when he suddenly appeared out of nowhere. But he was nice. Didn't give us a hard time. We were just dumb boys messing around. He gave us some gum and a warning and sent us on our way."

"You said there were some incidents here before?" noted Decker.

"Just stupid stuff. Couple of drunken fights."

"Anything else?" Decker persisted.

"Not really."

"Okay," said Decker, looking thoughtful.

They were cleared through a security post manned by a quartet of very serious looking men wearing Level 2 body armor and holding combat weapons. They were dressed all in black with security stenciled on the backs of their vests.

"Vector?" said Decker, reading this name off the label on one of the guard's sleeves.

Kelly said, "Vector is the contractor that runs this place. They're the subsidiary of some big player in the arena. Least that's what I heard."

They drove to a one-story brick building. It was within walking distance of the pyramid.

Decker eyed the line of ambulances parked in a row next to the pyramid.

They were escorted inside by a uniformed guard and led down a short corridor to a large office. The guard left and Kelly introduced them to Colonel Mark Sumter. He was medium height, about fifty, trim with a bald head and intense blue eyes. He was dressed in an ABU, or Airman Battle Uniform, that carried a camouflage design.

He invited them to sit down across from his desk in three straight-back chairs. "Good to see you, Joe." He looked at Decker and Jamison. "So you're the FBI? How can I help?"

Decker said, "There's been a murder. A young woman named Irene Cramer."

"Yes, I heard about that."

"She taught school at the Brothers' Colony," added Kelly.

"Did she?" Sumter looked interested. "Do you suspect someone from there might have been involved? They're very religious folks, from what I understand. Pacifists, in fact."

Decker shrugged. "We're just gathering facts, conducting interviews, nailing down timelines."

Jamison interjected, "I guess it's unusual to be sharing property lines with a religious organization."

Sumter bristled a bit. "The DoD, with all its money, somehow found it imperative to sell off most of the land surrounding this installation. Now, I have no problem with the Brothers. I'm just not used to being on base and seeing a tractor plowing a field in the distance. Or oil rigs pumping up crude from the earth. I'm one who likes more buffer, particularly with what we do here."

"And what is that?" asked Decker. "Kelly just gave us a thumbnail sketch."

Sumter instantly adopted a more guarded look. "Much of what we do is classified."

"Just the nonclassified parts then," said Decker. "Kelly here said you watch the sky for nukes?"

"In part. Have you ever heard of PARCS?"

"As in like parks people visit?" said Jamison.

Sumter smiled. "No. It's an acronym, just like everything else in the military. It stands for Perimeter Acquisition Radar Attack Characterization System."

"Long name."

"And it's justified. Along with watching for nuclear weapons, we also track earth-orbiting objects."

"Why's that?" asked Decker.

"We're sort of like air traffic control for outer space. We analyze and track about twenty thousand objects per day, from giant satellites to small space debris. We can spot something the size of a soccer ball at a distance of two thousand miles."

"Expensive pair of binoculars," commented Decker, drawing a sharp and somewhat unfriendly glance from Sumter.

Jamison said in a more casual tone, "I understand you have a bar and even a bowling alley on-site."

Sumter smiled. "Yes. Drinking and bowling, not the best of combinations, but still, it allows people to wind down."

"How long has Vector been running this place?" asked Decker.

"The United States Air Force *runs* this place," said Sumter firmly. "But Vector's involvement is fairly recent. I can't give you the exact date because that's classified."

"So getting back to Irene Cramer. Has she ever been here?" asked Decker.

"No. And she wouldn't have the clearance to get on the installation."

"Would she know any of the people who worked here?"

"I don't see why."

"Well, she worked right next door," said Jamison.

"Yes, but no one from the Brothers can just stroll over here."

"Cramer had a second occupation," said Decker.

"What was that?"

"An old-fashioned way of terming it would be a 'lady of the night.'"

"She was a hooker?" said Sumter, sitting upright. Decker just stared at him.

Now Sumter looked more guarded. "And you think one of the men here . . . ?"

"I just want to acquire the facts. It's sort of like your radar here, always sucking up information."

Sumter eyed Decker in a new light. "I, uh, I can make inquiries."

Decker said, "Actually, we would prefer to do that. I doubt that anyone here will volunteer that they paid a hooker. Wouldn't that land them in trouble?"

"It could. But we're experienced with ferreting out the truth."

Kelly said, "Why don't you make a first sweep, narrow it down, and then we can interview those folks?"

"I'll have to think about that."

"This is a murder investigation," said Decker. "A young woman was badly butchered."

"And this is a U.S. military installation," retorted Sumter. "And we do things a certain way. Now, if that's all, I can get on with my duties and you all can do the same."

As they were leaving Decker turned back. "You have many accidents here?"

"No. It's not really a dangerous place to be stationed. Beats the hell out of Iraq or Afghanistan," he added with a forced grin.

"That's great. Keep up the good work."

As they were walking to their truck, Jamison said, "Why did you ask him that?"

"Because I wanted to know the answer," Decker said bluntly. "And that answer has led to another question."

"What's that?" asked Kelly.

Decker pointed to the ambulances. "If this is such a safe place, what the hell are all those for?"

16

When Decker got back to his hotel room he ended up taking Jamison's advice and called his sister, but probably not for the reason his partner had intended.

Renee exclaimed, "Okay, I'm going to stroke out, Amos Decker calls his big sister. Stop the presses."

"Growing up, I never really realized how funny you were, Renee."

"Disappointed how our last conversation went? Want to make amends?"

"Right now, I just want Stan's cell phone number."

"You didn't get it from him when you saw him?"

"It didn't seem appropriate under the circumstances."

She gave him the number and he put it in his contacts. "Thanks. Stan said Diane's husband lost his job?"

"That was a year ago. Tim's back on his feet and Diane has a good job. They're doing okay. And I guess it's a good thing they don't have any kids they have to support. Now, don't call me for another year."

"What, why?"

"I need time to recover from the shock of talking to you *twice* in such a short time."

He next called his brother-in-law. Baker was at work but got off at five thirty. Decker arranged to meet up with him at the OK Corral Saloon at seven thirty.

He had some time to kill and decided to put it to good use.

He pulled out a copy of the pathology report from the postmortem that Walt Southern had performed on Irene Cramer's remains. He went over it, page by page, line by line. When he got to one sentence, buried in the middle of a long paragraph near the end of the report, he sat up.

Son of a bitch.

He headed out. The rain had stopped falling, but the humidity level was off the charts. He turned left and reached the funeral home a few minutes later. A young man outfitted all in black except for his dazzling white shirt rose from behind a small desk and greeted him. Decker asked for Walt Southern, who wasn't there. But his wife Liz was.

She came out a minute later. Liz Southern was not dressed in black but rather in lavender. She stood out like a pink flamingo in a desert, and it occurred to Decker even more forcefully how strikingly attractive the woman was. He wondered how happy she was working with dead people. But then again, someone had to do it.

117

"What can I do for you, Agent Decker?"

"I was hoping to talk to your husband."

"He's out of town. Be back tomorrow. Is there anything I can help you with?"

In answer Decker held up the autopsy report. "Had some questions about this."

She looked at him in surprise. "Questions about the report Walt did?"

"It's not unusual for detectives to have follow-up questions about a postmortem report."

"Well, is it something I can help you with? I've picked up a lot just being around Walt, and also with the business we're in."

He flipped to a page of the report and pointed at one long section.

"Buried in the middle of this it says that her intestines and stomach were *sliced* open."

She stiffened. "But isn't it standard procedure to take out the stomach and slice it open to analyze its contents?"

"Yes it is, only these cuts were not done by your husband. Which is why I need to see her remains. Now."

She led him into a room where the thermostat was set very low. It felt great after all the heat outside.

Out of the fryer and into the fridge.

Set against one wall were columns of small doors behind which corpses were kept in refrigerated climates.

Southern opened one of the drawers and slid the gurney out.

"There she is," she said.

Decker nodded and glanced at her when the woman made no sign of leaving. "Thanks, I'll let you know when I'm done."

She seemed unsure about this but withdrew from the room.

Decker turned to the body when something suddenly occurred to him.

The room's not electric blue.

It wasn't that he missed experiencing this phenomenon. But Decker's brain had begun to change recently; his memory had hiccups and he had momentarily forgotten some things he thought he never would. And he didn't enjoy change like that.

Decker lifted the sheet off the corpse and looked down at Cramer.

The first time he had viewed her body, he had known nothing of the woman's past. Now he knew that she was a teacher and possibly a prostitute/escort, although the jury was still out on that. And he also knew that her past beyond her time here was a mystery.

But what he had *always* known was that someone had murdered her.

Decker turned to the pages in the report that contained photos of the deceased's remains. There were pictures of every organ. But Decker focused on the images of the small and large intestines and the stomach. The slices referenced in the report had not been photographed, which was why Decker was here.

He was about to do something he had never done before, something he had never even thought of doing before, but under the circumstances he could see no way around it.

After finding them in a locker, Decker put on gloves, donned a long apron, and settled a surgical mask over his mouth and nose, and a pair of goggles over his eyes. He grabbed short-handled forceps off a tray and pulled out the Y-incision sutures, often called the "baseball stitch" because of its resemblance to that threading. Inside the revealed cavity the woman's organs had been placed in bags to prevent leakage.

He took out the stomach and looked at it from every angle he could. It *had* been sliced open on the bottom, revealing the inside of the organ, like a slit balloon. Southern had apparently used this opening to examine the stomach's contents because Decker could see no other incision. Whoever had made this cut had saved him the trouble. He used an over-head light to peer into the chest cavity once more and opened the bag containing the intestines. They lay coiled inside like a snake sleeping. He saw where sections of them had also been sliced open in mul-tiple locations. He hit these spots as best he could with the light. The slits were large enough to get a hand into them. Decker knew that for sure, because he did so himself. The cuts were jagged and seemed hurried, as though the killer had either been rushed while doing it, or—

Had he gotten frustrated?

Decker took pictures of everything with his smartphone. He bagged the organs, closed the cavity, redid the sutures, covered the body once more, and slid it back into the drawer. Then he disposed of the gloves, apron, and mask in a metal container marked medical waste. He put the used goggles on a metal table. He then washed up in the sink. He let the warm water and soap flood his face and then stared at himself in the mirror attached to the wall above the sink.

I can't fucking believe I just did that.

He closed his eyes. He felt like he might be sick, but he managed to keep what was in his stomach right where it was.

Too bad Irene Cramer hadn't been able to do the same.

He left without speaking to Liz Southern. He had nothing to say to the woman and he wanted to get outside. His legs felt wobbly and he was again feeling nauseous.

The heat hit him as he opened the exterior door and, surprisingly, his sick feeling began to dissipate. His body was now probably focused on dealing with the hot environment.

He slowly and gingerly walked back to the hotel.

Decker went up to his room, pulled out his phone, and looked at the pictures he'd taken. They were far sharper with a higher res than the grainy ones provided by Walt Southern.

Decker might have just made a significant stride in the investigation, but the discovery had also led to a great many more questions.

The stomach and intestines shared an attribute that none of the other organs in the body did. If you swallowed something the object would eventually travel to those two destinations. Irene Cramer had been carrying something in her belly or intestines.

And whoever had killed her had taken it from the woman.

17

"Oh my God. You did *what*?"

Jamison was sitting in the driver's seat of their rental SUV staring at Decker like he had just told her that he'd been the one who'd murdered Irene Cramer.

"Didn't you hear me the first time?" he said, looking slightly embarrassed. "The killer was obviously attempting to get something back that Cramer had ingested."

"Look, despite what you found, that theory seems a little far-fetched."

"Drug mules do that all the time. They either stuff plastic bags of drugs up their anuses, or else they swallow them."

"And very often the bags burst and the person dies when all those drugs enter their body." She glanced sharply at him. "Is that what you think? That she was a drug runner?"

"That would be the easy answer, but I'm not sure it would be the right one," he replied. "And there's something else."

"What?"

"Why didn't Walt Southern highlight this fact for us? It was literally buried in his report. And there were no pictures of the cuts to those organs. And when I asked him if there was anything out of the ordinary, he replied in the negative."

"You think he didn't believe it was important?"

"Any pathologist worth his or her salt knows about contraband being carried in the body."

"I guess that is odd. So what do you think?"

"Did he intentionally not highlight it, or take pictures, thinking we would just take his word and not look too closely at the pathology report?"

"But why would he do that? Wait, do you think he killed her? That would explain the way she was cut up. He would have just performed *two* autopsies on her."

"Southern cutting her up like that would be really the *only* way we would suspect someone like him. So why would he do it that way, unless he wants to be caught?"

"No, I don't see that happening, either," commented Jamison.

"So let's go back to the question of what she might have been carrying inside her."

"I guess we could hearken back to the days of the Cold War. She could be a spy and swallowed a microfiche dot loaded with government secrets."

When Decker didn't respond to this, she added,

"I'm just kidding. She's too young to have been part of the Cold War."

"But why *wouldn't* that be plausible? We have a pretty sensitive government facility right in the neighborhood."

Jamison said slowly, "Since we don't know her past, it could be she *was* a spy."

"And maybe the reason she came here was to spy on the Douglas S. George Defense Complex. But she's been here a year," he added, looking puzzled.

"Meaning what took her so long?" said Jamison.

Decker nodded.

"How . . . was doing what . . . what you did?" she asked.

"I never want to do it again."

"So what now?"

"Bogart hasn't gotten back to me. If we can't get at her past from the Bureau's side, we need to try from another angle. She was here a year. Someone might have seen or heard something suspicious about the lady."

"So, we talk to people? But we already did that."

"I think some of the people we've talked to have been less than forthcoming. And Colonel Sumter was stonewalling us the whole way."

"But how do we get him to talk? He has the DoD behind him. He has to follow orders."

"I'm not sure. So for now we keep pushing ahead

on other paths. We met one local titan with Stuart McClellan. Maybe we should meet the other."

"Caroline's dad? I guess he might know something useful."

"Well, for one thing, he was the one to hire Hal Parker to get the wolf that had killed his cattle. So the body was presumably found on *his* property."

"Do you think he knew Irene Cramer?"

"That's one of the first things I'm going to ask him."

They got Kelly to join them and he gave directions to Hugh Dawson's estate.

Kelly eyed Decker, who sat in the front seat next to Jamison. "So why the interest in Dawson? You never said."

"We're just trying to get the lay of the land at this point."

"Okay, that really tells me nothing."

Jamison added, "We're not trying to play coy, Joe. We're looking around for some traction on this case. We've talked to the military and the Brothers and people who knew Cramer. We talked to Caroline Dawson and we ran into the McClellans, so we're rounding it out with Hugh Dawson."

"When did you see the McClellans?"

"At the restaurant at our hotel," replied Jamison.

"Both of them?"

He sounded so puzzled that Decker turned to look at him. "Yeah. Why? Is that unusual?"

Kelly shrugged. "Stuart, as a rule, doesn't frequent places owned by Hugh Dawson."

"And the son?" asked Jamison. "Shane McClellan looked to me like he was head over heels for Caroline."

"Shane's a nice guy. Not what you would call an intellectual, but he's got a good heart." He added in a more subdued tone, "And you're right, he's got it bad for Caroline. Has since we were kids."

"But that would be a problem, considering the fathers are business rivals," noted Decker.

"Sounds like Romeo and Juliet," interjected Jamison.

"Or the Hatfields and McCoys," replied Decker.

"I think you might be closer to the mark with that one," said Kelly. "But though they don't get along, and they are sort of in a pissing contest like Ida Simms said, they're not exactly true rivals either. Hugh's businesses service Stuart's workers. That actually helps both of them."

"And what about Shane's mother?" asked Jamison.

"Katherine McClellan died a while back. Cancer. She and Shane were really close. A lot closer than he and his old man. After that, it was just Shane and his father. Not the best of situations. Katherine acted as a buffer between the two. After she was gone, well, it wasn't pretty."

"Sounds complicated," said Jamison.

Kelly nodded. "It is."

"I take it you and Shane are friends. You're close to the same age."

"We all went to high school together. Caroline too. Yeah, we were all good friends. Pretty much inseparable."

"Getting back to the case, Hal Parker was hired by Hugh Dawson," said Decker. "To hunt down a wolf?"

"Yep."

"Wolves are a problem around here?"

"They certainly can be. Them and wild dogs. Coyotes, mountain lions. They can devastate a herd."

"What else can you tell us about Hugh Dawson?" asked Decker. "You said he was big and gregarious but could take your head off if need be."

"That's pretty much all you need to know about the man. I'll leave it to you to form your own impression when you meet him."

"And you said his wife died in an accident?" said Jamison.

Kelly nodded. "It was really tragic. The worst sort of accident, because it was like a perfect storm of connected events. Maddie Dawson was caught in her car in a blizzard and died from carbon monoxide poisoning." Kelly shook his head. "Fortunately, she probably would have gone unconscious before she knew what was happening. Still a helluva way to go."

"Yeah," said Decker. "But a lot better than what happened to Irene Cramer."

18

"It looks like the house on the TV show *Dallas*, only twice the size."

Jamison made this comment as she drove them up a long cobblestone driveway that was bracketed by two rows of large trees with full, leafy canopies.

"Where does Stuart McClellan live?" asked Decker.

"He has an apartment in a building in downtown London."

"An apartment?" said Jamison. "Isn't he richer than Dawson?"

"He's been through so many booms and busts that I think he now hedges his bets."

"And his son?"

"Shane has a little farmhouse and some land on the western edge of the county. Bought the place right after he came back."

"Came back from where?" asked Jamison.

"Fighting overseas. He was in the army. Joined up right after he graduated from high school. He likes it simple. Hunts during the season, drinks his beer, works for his old man, gets yelled at for not doing it well enough, and tries to enjoy life. It's no secret the father doesn't think the son is up to taking over his fracking operations."

"And what do you think?" said Jamison.

"Shane's no dummy and he works hard. We've hunted together a lot. He's sharp, methodical, and knowledgeable about stuff he cares about. He just doesn't care for business. It's not how he's wired."

They parked in front of the house and got out. Kelly led the way up the steps to the double front door.

"So what will it be for us?" asked Decker. "Gregarious, or do we get a knife in the back?"

"All depends on what and how you ask him, I guess."

"Well, knowing Decker's tact, let's prepare for the shiv to the spine," said Jamison, with a sly smile at her partner.

The door was answered by a woman in a maid's uniform. After Kelly showed his badge, she stepped back so they could pass through. She led them down a hall with ash plank flooring to a set of oak double doors.

Inside the room, the man who rose from behind a large desk was nearly as tall as Decker, but far thinner with narrow hips. His brown, wavy hair had a thick shock of gray in the front. He was clean-shaven, with a nose that had been broken and healed slightly off center. He was dressed in an untucked white shirt and black jeans. When he moved around the desk with his hand outstretched to Kelly, Decker noted the dark blue slippers on the man's feet with a *D* monogrammed on them. The walls were festooned with the heads of unfortunate creatures who had had their mortal remains fashioned into showpieces.

"Joe, how the hell are you? Been a while."

Kelly shook his hand and then introduced Decker and Jamison to Hugh Dawson.

They all sat in front of an empty stone fireplace and Kelly said, "Thanks for meeting with us. Guess you'll be heading out of the country in a month or so."

Dawson looked at Decker and Jamison. "I used to laugh at the snowbirds who would head south for the winter. Then a number of years ago, Maddie suggested we start spending the winters in Australia when it's their summer. We rented a place near the water. After she passed, I kept going. We had some really wonderful times down there."

"Memories like that are important," said Jamison. "Like therapy."

"Yes they are. Now, I understand a woman was murdered. And Hal Parker found her."

"He was out looking for a wolf," said Jamison.

"That damn thing had already killed two of my cows. Hired Hal to get rid of it."

"How do you know it was a wolf?" asked Decker.

"They finally found the carcass with Hal's bullet in it. So who was it that got killed again?"

"A woman named Irene Cramer," said Kelly. "Thought you would have known that. We released her name."

In answer Dawson pointed to his desk that was stacked with three-ring binders. "I'm up to my eyeballs in financial stuff. Working on some big deals. I haven't watched or listened to the news for a while."

"But you knew of the murder, obviously," said Decker.

"I knew because Hal told me."

"So you didn't know her?" asked Decker.

He shook his head. "Used to be I knew everybody around these parts. Now, too many people coming in. I'm not complaining. It's good for business."

"Irene Cramer worked as the teacher at the Brothers' school," said Kelly.

"The Brothers? I do business with them. Their word is their bond."

"What about the military installation?" asked Decker.

Dawson's eyes narrowed. "London Air Force Station? What about it?"

"Do you do business with them, too?"

"Sure. Their folks come to town and frequent my places, and we provide some of their supplies. Why?"

Decker shrugged. "It's a murder investigation. We ask questions about everybody."

Dawson glanced at Kelly. "But why do the Feds get called in on a local murder?"

Kelly said, "We always appreciate the help."

Dawson eyed him skeptically. "And I can sell you the Brooklyn Bridge."

"We met your daughter," interjected Jamison. "You must be very proud of her."

Dawson grinned. "She's gonna be running the world before long. She'll leave what I did in the dust when all is said and done."

"She's dating a man named Stan Baker," said Decker. "We met him, too."

The light seemed to dim in Dawson's eyes. "Is that right? Well, I keep out of that. She's grown and can make her own decisions, especially when it comes to *men*."

Jamison said, "Wow, I wish my father would be as enlightened. I'm in my thirties and I still get detailed emails and phone calls about my personal relationships."

Dawson grinned. "Oh, I tried to poke my nose in here and there. The fourth time it got chopped off, I said, okay, I'm done here. Not worth it." His expression darkened. "Then after Maddie died . . ." An awkward silence persisted until he said, "Anything else you folks want to ask me?" He glanced at the papers on his desk.

"We understand that your son committed suicide," said Decker.

Dawson immediately tightened. "He took the coward's way out, yeah. But what the hell does that have to do with anything," he snapped, glowering at Kelly, who looked taken aback by Decker's comment.

Decker said, "We also understand that you and Stuart McClellan are best friends."

Dawson looked wildly at Decker for a few moments, and then burst out laughing. "Okay, I didn't figure you for having a sense of humor. Fact is, that's been blown way out of proportion. I'm not saying the guy and I will be going on vacation together anytime soon. But the town is booming and we're both making money hand over fist. And we don't compete. We're more complementary." His tone became more businesslike. "But this has nothing to do with a gal being murdered, right?"

"Like I said, we ask lots of questions in the hope of finding a path forward."

"Sounds to me like you're trying to dig through mud to get to the gold."

"It always seems that way right before you hit the mother lode," replied Decker.

Jamison said, "We met Stuart McClellan and his son, Shane. Your daughter was there, too. At the hotel where we're staying. It's one of your places."

"Okay, so?" said Dawson.

"Any idea why the McClellans would be there?" asked Jamison. "Caroline seemed surprised that they were."

"It's a free country. They can go where they want." He grinned. "And, hell, I don't mind old Stuart putting some cash in my pocket."

"Shane seemed quite smitten with Caroline," pointed out Jamison.

Dawson stood. "Well, it was nice meeting you. Maybe I'll see you around."

The others stood, too, but Decker remained seated.

"Your daughter was making an offer to buy the apartment building where Irene Cramer lived. Did you know about that?"

"Caroline doesn't have to come to me for every little thing. We *are* trying to acquire properties. And now's a good time to do it. Stuff is still relatively cheap."

"But you'd think prices would be going up in a boom," said Jamison.

"It was booming last time, too. And then in a few years everything went to hell." He paused and rubbed his chin. "What do you folks know about fracking?"

Jamison said, "Just what we read in the papers, so not much."

"We produce more oil than any other state except Texas. But with fracking there are *two* downsides.

First is, you get overwhelmed by the people coming in for the good-paying jobs, and drugs, prostitution, and other crime and shit like that goes through the roof. And you can't build the homes, schools, roads, and stores and all the other stuff people want fast enough. Then there's the second downside. You get busts. Last time oil prices went through the floor overnight and stayed there because OPEC increased production to drive the frackers out of business. Then everything around here shut down, and I mean everything. I got close to losing every nickel I had. But that's also how McClellan really solidified his hold on the shale land around here."

"What do you mean?" asked Jamison.

"When the fracking industry really came into vogue a while back, the big boys came up here loaded for bear. And they gobbled up all the available leases and paid top dollar for them. But with the bust cycle, they fell by the wayside and McClellan bought up their leases for pennies on the dollar. And he has his business model all squared away, so apparently no more booms and busts for him."

Jamison said, "That still doesn't answer my question about the prices around here now."

"Well, despite McClellan's operations being in good shape, people are getting damn nervous, waiting for the rug to get pulled out again. So it creates opportunities for those with a healthier appetite for risk."

"But you almost pulled out a few years ago," commented Kelly.

Dawson glared at him. "Maddie didn't want to live here anymore. She'd been through hell and back with me. The last bust came, but then things started picking up again. But she'd had enough by then. She wanted out come hell or high water. We had a few dollars left. So we were going to buy a little villa in France and spend our golden years there. But then—"

"We understand she died in an accident," said Jamison.

He nodded. "I was out of the country and she ran off the road during a blizzard. She didn't realize that the rear of the car had run up against a berm. It had bent her tailpipe and clogged it," said Dawson, the misery clear in his eyes. "She breathed in all that crap. And . . . died."

"Why were you out of the country?" asked Decker.

"I was buying the place in France. Caroline was with me."

"So she was going to live there with you?"

"She was tired of this place, too. Fresh start all around. And it's what Maddie wanted." He glanced at Decker. "But, again, why would any of that be relevant to your investigation?"

Decker rose. "I take the position that everything is relevant until it isn't."

"And you didn't answer my question from before. I still don't know why you Feds got called in on a local killing."

"Well, on that one, you can join the club," said Decker as he headed for the door.

19

As they drove back to town, Jamison glanced at Decker and said, "You should fill Kelly in on what you found."

Decker proceeded to tell Kelly about what he had done with Cramer's corpse.

The local detective's eyes kept widening the longer that Decker talked.

"Okay, I thought I had heard it all, but you just took it to another level."

"Wasn't on my wish list, I can tell you that."

Kelly said, "You really think she was carrying something inside her?"

"It would explain why her intestines and belly were sliced open. I think the rest of the 'autopsy' done by whoever killed her was just to cover that part up."

"It would have to be a lot of drugs to justify killing someone."

Jamison shook her head. "But these days you don't need mules to transport drugs. The U.S. Postal Service unwittingly does it. Or FedEx. Or UPS."

"Which is why I don't think it was drugs," replied Decker, causing Jamison to gape.

"Well, thanks for sharing, Decker," she groused.

He looked back at Kelly. "Tell me something. How well do you know Walt Southern?"

"Pretty well. Why?"

"Just wondering."

Jamison caught a look from him that said not to comment further.

"And now, let's head out and do something we should have already done," said Decker.

"What's that?" asked Kelly.

"Go to the scene of the crime," answered Jamison.

It was a breathtakingly beautiful view, made ugly only by the purpose of the visit.

Decker was staring out over the spot where Cramer's body had been found. In the distance one could see the humps of the Badlands. The sky was the clearest it had been since they had arrived. To the north was Saskatchewan, to the west the vast footprint of Montana.

Decker was interested in neither. His sole focus was this little patch of North Dakota soil where someone had dumped Irene Cramer's body. As he gazed around, his mind was analyzing a million different factors. Only one of them might hold any importance for the investigation, but you had to go through all of them to get there. It seemed both a likely and an unlikely place to find a dead body. Likely in that it was isolated and remote, and that was good for getting rid of unwanted dead bodies without being seen. But unlikely in that such wide-open spaces allowed no cover for anyone disposing of said dead bodies. One could literally see for miles. But at night, it would have been a different story.

"What's near here?" he asked Kelly, who was leaning next to the SUV. Jamison was hovering to the right of Decker and staring at the spot where Cramer had been found.

"Hugh Dawson's cattle ranch is that way." Kelly pointed west. "About two miles. It's a big place. He has a lot of land. But we have an abundance of that around here."

"Dawson said they found the wolf. Where?"

"About three hundred yards from here. With Parker's round still in it, like Hugh said. Dang thing was pretty big. If Hal had arrived much later, that critter would have torn up Cramer's remains. We lucked out there."

"Did he say why he was hunting in this particular area?" asked Jamison, who was now kneeling down and more closely examining the ground where the body had lain.

"He told me he'd been tracking it the last three nights. He drew up a range of places to check, based on the animal's hunting pattern. I hunt too, but not like Hal. He's a real pro. Can track anything anywhere. He said this quadrant was a likely spot to pick the wolf up based on that analysis. He'd been at it about two hours before he caught sight of the thing and took his kill shot."

"Are we sure it was the same wolf that had attacked the cattle?"

"Yeah, they found some of the remains of the animals in its belly."

"Were there any tracks around Cramer's body? Foot or car tire or anything like that?"

"We did check for that but the problem was a heavy rain had started up right when Hal found the body. If there were any tracks, they got washed away when that happened."

"And Parker didn't mention seeing any before the rain hit?" asked Decker.

"No. And that's the other reason I don't think there were any. The guy's a seasoned hunter and tracker. If there had been any, he would have spotted them and told us."

"So the fact that the body was untouched by animals could be because it was dumped here shortly before Parker found it, like you suggested previously, Decker," said Jamison. "So we might have lucked out there."

"And the wolf might have been in this area *because* it caught the scent of the dead body," added Kelly. "But that doesn't explain the insect infestation."

Decker said, "She could have been *kept* somewhere else, where flies and insects could have gotten to her but animals couldn't have."

"But why would the killer bother doing that?" asked Kelly.

"He might want to screw with the timing of death, which would make our job harder. And if there was something inside her that he wanted to get, that would have taken time and he couldn't cut her open while she was alive. At least I hope he didn't."

Jamison said, "Was anyone else around to see or hear anything?"

Kelly shook his head. "No, just Hal. Doubt there was another living person anywhere near here at that time of night."

"How far away does Parker live?" asked Decker.

"About forty-five minutes from here."

"Well, let's go hear his story."

20

The road was long, dusty, and wide open to the waves of heat shimmering under a sun that seemed closer to the earth than it should have been.

In the distance they could see oil rigs pumping and a sea of gas flares burning off straight into the atmosphere. They passed one tanker truck that had gone off the road and was driving through what looked like farmland.

"What the hell is he doing?" asked Jamison, who was driving the SUV.

"Dumping his saltwater waste," Kelly replied, looking angry. "Some of what comes back up the pipe after it goes down it to fracture the shale. What that trucker is doing is against the law. He'll ruin that land for farming forever because the salt permanently burns the soil to nothing. They pull that shit all the time just to save themselves time and trouble. We fine the crap out of them and they still keep doing it."

"How much farther?" asked Decker.

"It's right up ahead, on the left."

They rounded a curve and a modest ranch house

came into view. An old and battered gray pickup truck was parked outside.

"Parker have any family?" asked Jamison.

"No. His wife died. His kids are grown and gone."

As they climbed out of the SUV Decker glanced down at the bumper sticker on the rear of Parker's truck.

GUN CONTROL MEANS USING BOTH HANDS.

Kelly led the way up the plank steps.

The front door was standing partially open. Seeing that, all three instinctively pulled their weapons.

Kelly called out through the opening, "Hal? It's Joe Kelly. You in there? You okay? We want to ask you some questions."

There were sounds coming from inside but they were unintelligible.

"Hal? You okay?" Kelly cried out again. He looked at Decker. "What the hell is going on here?"

Decker looked at him. "Your call. Do we go in?"

"You bet we do." Kelly took the lead, pushed the door fully open with the palm of his free hand, and they all charged inside.

The front room was plainly furnished with a Remington shotgun and Winchester rifle on a rack on one wall and two fishing rods leaning in a corner. An open beer can was on a table next to a recliner. But there was no sign of Parker.

"Hal?" called out Kelly again.

Decker took in the space, top to bottom, left to

right. It looked like Parker had just stood and walked out of the room. The TV was still on. Those were obviously the sounds they had heard.

On one wall was a series of photos. Decker ran his gaze over each of them. They were pictures of Parker and members of various hunting parties next to the carcasses of large, dead animals.

"That's Shane in that one," said Decker.

Kelly nodded. "Yeah, they hunt a lot together. I'm in that one over there. Got an eight-point buck on that trip," he added, indicating another photo. He looked around. "I don't like this one bit. He wouldn't leave his door open like that."

"Does he have a vehicle other than the truck?" asked Jamison.

"He has an ATV. Keeps it in the shed out back."

They quickly searched the house including the small bedroom but found no one there.

"Bed is still made," noted Kelly.

Decker walked back into the front room and touched the beer on the table. "Warm. Would he be drinking during the day?"

"Not the Hal Parker I know."

Decker went into the kitchen, slapped on a pair of latex gloves he'd pulled from his pocket, and opened the dishwasher. There was one plate, a set of utensils, and a water glass inside. He eyed Jamison, who had followed him. "Dinner last night. Beer while watching the TV. Whatever happened, I think it took place last night."

Next, he eyed the two wineglasses and a half-empty bottle of wine on the counter. "One beer can but two wineglasses. How does *that* figure in?"

"Somebody showed up while he was drinking beer and watching TV, maybe?" speculated Kelly. "They crack open some wine and drink it. Then either that person takes Hal, or somebody else comes in here and takes him and the other person. But I don't know who that could be."

"He have any enemies?" asked Jamison.

"Never heard anyone say a word against him. Everybody liked Hal."

"Let's check the shed," said Decker.

They trooped outside to the small plank shed. It had an overhead garage door that wasn't locked. With his latex gloves still on, Decker carefully lifted the door and it rolled up on well-oiled tracks while the other two stood ready, their guns pointed at the emerging opening ready for whatever might be revealed.

There was a Honda ATV parked right inside the small space.

Decker had half expected to see the body of Hal Parker in here.

Parker wasn't inside.

But another dead body was.

She was on the ATV, lying forward on her front

side so her torso and head were resting against the handlebars with her legs splayed out behind her. She was dressed in a short tight skirt, a low-cut body-hugging midriff top, thigh-high black stockings, and spiky shoes.

On the right side of the woman's head was a bloody hole where a bullet had ended her life.

They all just stared at the body for a few moments.

"She's young, looks to be in her early twenties," noted Decker as he gazed at the body. He glanced at Kelly. "Do you know who she is?"

Kelly nodded, looking grim. "She's Pamela Ames, Susan and Milton's oldest daughter, from the Colony."

"But she's not dressed like the other women there," pointed out Jamison. "She's dressed, well, pretty alluringly."

"And I wonder why," said Decker.

21

As Decker stared across the width of the London Police Station's main room, he had a sense of déjà vu, and for a horrible reason. Milton and Susan Ames were sitting in two straight-back chairs after having been told of the murder of their daughter and having viewed and identified her remains at the funeral home.

Years ago, Decker had found the bodies of his wife, daughter, and brother-in-law in their home in Burlington, Ohio. He had called the cops and then sat on the bathroom floor staring at his daughter. Molly Decker had been bound to the toilet using the belt of her bathrobe after her killer had used that very same belt to strangle her to death. Decker had sat there with his service pistol in hand. He had finally stuck it into his mouth and was seriously contemplating eating a round and dying with them. But something, he wasn't exactly sure what, had stopped him.

After his brain injury his personality had also changed. Thus, he was no longer adept in moments like this, that called for delicacy and empathy. He usually said the wrong thing or made the wrong gesture. It was just a disconnect he often could not control.

He refocused on the grieving Ameses. He would ordinarily leave this sort of thing to Jamison. She was now sitting next to him and studying the Ameses as well. She touched his hand and started to say something, but at that moment Decker got up and walked over to the stricken people. He knelt down in front of them.

Jamison looked on fearfully, no doubt thinking her partner would not be up to dealing with the bereaved parents.

Susan Ames had aged a decade since he had last seen her. The woman's face was fallen in, her eyes bloodshot, her hands shaking, her thin chest heaving unevenly. Her scarf had fallen off, and she hadn't seemed to have noticed.

Milton simply stared down at his hands, his eyes reddened from the tears shed.

Susan focused on Decker when he picked up the scarf and held it out to her.

As her fingers closed around it, he said, "I'm so very sorry."

Susan nodded. "She . . . she was very smart. She could have . . ." She shook her head, unable to finish.

Decker cleared his throat and said, "I had a daughter. She was smart and could've been anything, too. But somebody took that opportunity away from her."

Now Milton looked at Decker, as though he were just now seeing him for the first time.

Decker continued. "And I caught that person. And I will do the same for your daughter because she deserves nothing less."

Susan slowly nodded and murmured, "Thank you."

Jamison sat there transfixed by what she was seeing. When Decker turned to her she tried to assume a normal expression, but she wasn't quick enough. He showed no reaction to this.

He rose and said to the Ameses, "I know this is a really hard time, but the sooner we can get some information from you, the faster we can catch whoever did this."

Milton just sat there, but Susan nodded. "We understand."

Kelly appeared in the doorway having overheard this last part. "If you're ready, then?" he said quietly.

The Ameses rose as though roped together and followed them down the hall to a small, windowless room with one rectangular table and four chairs, two on either side. They all sat except Decker. He leaned against the wall, his thick arms folded over his broad chest.

"Okay, the most obvious question: was there any connection between Hal Parker and your daughter?" asked Kelly, his small notepad open and his pen hovering.

"None that I know of," said Susan. "There would

be no reason, you see. He never worked for us. We didn't require his services. He never came to the Colony. She never mentioned him."

"Okay," said Kelly. "When was the last time you saw Pamela?"

At this, Susan glanced nervously at her husband.

Decker said, "We found her at about one in the afternoon. Prelim on the time of death was around nine o'clock last night. So there's a long gap of time unaccounted for."

Milton looked up, his eyes watery. "She had left the Colony. Pammie had left *us.*"

"When did this happen?" said a clearly surprised Kelly. "I hadn't heard anything about that."

"Well, we don't broadcast when people leave us," said Susan, assuming a more measured and prim manner. "It's not something we like to dwell upon."

"And it happens very infrequently," Milton hastened to add. "But we can't keep someone against their will, not when they're of age. We would never do that."

"But we did counsel her, we tried to show her how bad it would be," said Susan.

"Let's get back to what happened to your daughter," said Decker.

At this comment, both Milton's and Susan's eyes filled with fresh tears.

Jamison handed them both Kleenexes, which they used to wipe their eyes.

"Pammie was . . . bored with life at the Colony," began Milton. "And because of that we let her go and stay with my cousin's family in San Antonio last year. She got a taste of . . . life outside. She apparently liked it very much. When she got back she told us she wanted to leave, go back to San Antonio and enroll in some classes, find a job and—"

"—start living her life," finished Susan.

"But then you tried to talk her out of it," said Jamison. "Like you said."

"And we were unsuccessful, as we also told you," replied Susan stiffly.

"When exactly did she leave the Colony?" asked Kelly.

"A month ago," answered Milton brusquely.

"But she didn't go to San Antonio?" Decker pointed out. "She was still here. Unless she went out there and came back."

"She . . . she hadn't gone yet," said Milton in a small voice.

"What was she waiting for?" asked Jamison.

Milton was about to answer when Susan cleared her throat. He glanced at his wife, who was staring at him with such a rigid expression that it was like she had been transformed from flesh to wood.

Milton shut his mouth and looked away while Decker watched this interaction closely.

She said, "We . . . we live a communal life here, and have no personal resources, but we could have asked the community to provide her with some means to travel to San Antonio and given her a bit of a cushion until she became self-sustaining."

"But you didn't," said Jamison.

Susan could only shake her head.

Milton said, "We thought it would be a way to make her come . . . home." He broke down entirely now and rested his forehead on the table, his body quaking. His wife didn't look at him, but she did pat him gently on the back.

Decker eyed Kelly and said, "We'll need to check her movements, friends, whether she had a job. Where she was staying and what if any connection she had to Hal Parker." He stopped and stared over at Susan. "Before, you said that Parker never came to the Colony. But then you said that you had never required his services, which implies that you knew what he did for a living. Did you know Hal Parker, Ms. Ames?"

She glanced at her husband, who was still bent over, weeping quietly.

"I . . . I knew him, yes. Unlike Milton I . . . I have not always been here at the Colony. When I was younger, much younger, I lived in London with my parents. Hal was older than I was, but our families were neighbors, so I would see him a good deal when I was a child. I've . . . I know what he does for a living."

Jamison said, "So did Pamela know him? Might she have gone to him for help when she left here?"

"It's possible," said Susan. "I don't know for sure."

Jamison frowned. "You didn't keep in touch with her?"

Susan said defensively, "She didn't have a cell phone."

"I find that hard to believe," said Jamison. "Even if she wasn't used to having access to one at the Colony, it would be hard to do without one once she had left there."

Kelly added, "And London's not that big. Surely you could have gone to see her."

"I chose *not* to see her," snapped Susan. "She had made her choice. She didn't want to be a part of our world anymore."

Decker pushed off the wall, came forward, and said offhandedly, "So she might have been staying with Parker. And if someone came there to take him away and she was there, she might have just been in the wrong place at the wrong time."

Kelly nodded in agreement. "That could be, yes."

Jamison said, "But, Decker, it's a one-bedroom house. And we didn't find any clothing or other things that would indicate that Pamela Ames was living there. And there was no vehicle other than Parker's." She gazed up at him, puzzled. "You know all that."

Decker kept his gaze on Milton. "That's right, Alex. So now maybe Milton can tell us what his wife doesn't want us to know."

All eyes turned to Milton as he slowly sat back

against his chair. He rubbed his eyes and would not look at his wife this time.

"Unlike Susan, I *did* keep in touch with Pammie."

"And?" said Decker.

"And she was working as a waitress at the big truck stop on the main road coming into town."

"She told you this?"

"No. I heard it from someone else. A trucker who makes deliveries here. He knew Pammie. He told me she was there. I . . . I went there to see her. But when I saw . . ."

"I'm sorry, but I'm not sure what you're getting at," said Jamison. "When you saw what?"

"Well, what she was wearing! What all the waitresses wore in that place. They were barely clothed. And all the men ogling them. It was . . . I just couldn't believe that my daughter—"

Susan made a clucking sound and glanced at her husband with a scathing look.

Milton swallowed nervously and looked down.

"And you told her what you thought about it?" said Jamison.

He nodded, still looking down. "I . . . I told her I was ashamed of her and never wanted to see her again."

On that, Milton broke into sobs and couldn't answer another question.

22

Decker looked out the window of his hotel room onto a street that was bustling with people and traffic. This fracking stuff, he thought, had really transformed parts of North Dakota from a flyover state to one of the world's great economic booms.

He still didn't know why Pamela Ames had been at Hal Parker's. If she'd had a purse it had also been taken. Ditto for her cell phone. The gun that had killed Pamela was nowhere to be found. They had also found no trace of Ames having been in Parker's truck, so how she had gotten out there was still unknown. Walt Southern would be doing the postmortem, and Decker was hoping something would pop from that.

They had spoken with the truck stop people. Ames had been working there. She had missed her shift that night. They had tried to call her phone, which they confirmed she had, but had gotten no answer. Kelly had tried to trace the phone's location but gotten nothing. They were also trying to trace where Ames had been living but so far had gotten zip, and the truck stop people hadn't known that, either. The company didn't mail out paychecks, they just handed them out at the end of the week, her manager had told them. If she had moved around or lived in abandoned premises as some did here, it might be impossible to pinpoint exactly where she had been on any given day.

Decker checked his watch. He was due to meet Baker at the OK Corral Saloon in thirty minutes. He called Bogart's personal cell, got the man's voice mail, and left a message. How and whether Cramer's death coincided with Pamela Ames's murder and Hal Parker's disappearance he didn't know. And had Parker been abducted? Or had he killed Ames for some reason and then run for it?

He washed up, changed into clean clothes, and headed out.

He met Baker as the big man was walking up to the bar.

"How's the investigation going?"

"It's going. How's the fracking?"

He grinned. "Hot, and I'm not talking temperature wise."

They went inside, miraculously found an empty table, and ordered two beers on draft.

When the drinks came, they each drained about half their mugs.

"I spoke to Renee again," said Decker.

"Yeah, she told me. I hope you feel better about things."

"Look, Stan, you don't have to worry about whether I feel better or not. If you two are good with it and the kids are taken care of, then that's great."

Baker looked surprised but also pleased by this statement. "Thanks, Amos. I still care for Renee and she does for me. Guess it'll always be that way. We were together a long time and then we got the kids, of course. That's the glue that really holds a family together regardless. The kids." Baker paled a bit with this last part. "Um, I mean . . ."

"I know exactly what you mean, Stan," Decker said, taking a sip of his beer. "So you like it here, you said?"

"Oh, yeah. Some of the younger guys, they think it's too isolated. Hell, I've lived in Alaska. 'Isolated' takes on a whole other meaning up there."

"So tell me about this fracking business," said Decker.

Baker looked surprised. "Why does that matter to you?"

"I'm investigating a murder. People get killed for lots of reasons, like money and power. The money-and-power thing here is tied to fracking, right?"

"Right. Otherwise, pretty much nobody would be here. So what do you want to know?"

"Basically how it works."

"There's oil and gas in the ground. And folks pull it out and sell it for a lot of money."

"That part I get. Only I understand it wasn't always that easy to get out of the ground."

"That's right. So before I came here I read up on it. I'm not a young punk with no obligations. I needed to make this work, so I wanted to know whether this thing had legs. North Dakota has gone boom and bust before."

"Understood. Go on."

"Well, the first bit of oil in North Dakota was discovered in a small town called Tioga back in the early fifties. But drilling up here, in the Bakken region, was considered a no-go because the oil was too hard to get out. All the big boys had given it a try over the decades and failed. They just assumed that it would be stuck down there forever. So by the end of the nineties, drilling was done here. Then, it turned out the oil companies were drilling in the *wrong* direction. Vertical doesn't work here like it does pretty much everywhere else. You had to drill *horizontally* after you've drilled vertically down far enough to reach the shale region. And you had to do that in combination with fracking, or piping water and mud and chemicals down into the deposits. That's done both to keep the drill going and to break up the shale. And you send sand down too in order to keep the breaks in the shale from resealing."

"You mean like stents a surgeon puts in to open up a blocked artery?"

"Exactly. And on the extraction end think of a straw inserted into a cup of water. You pour more liquid and other stuff through the straw and into the water. With no place else to go, the water down below has to come up through the straw. Here, after fracking a deposit, the oil starts to flow to the surface."

"How far down do you go?"

"About two miles vertically, and then you move sideways, or horizontally in a series of carefully monitored stages. That could be quite a few more miles. All told, you're talking about twenty thousand feet or more of drilling and piping."

"Then all these rigs I see around are over deposits of oil and gas?"

"Yeah. You pretty much always find one with the other. It takes anywhere from one to five million gallons of fresh water to frack a single well. And a couple thousand truckloads of sand. Each well from site prep to readiness for production takes about three to six months. But then the well could be productive for twenty, thirty, or forty years. When all the oil and gas have been gotten out, they plug everything, clean up the surface, and the owner who leased the land goes back to using the property."

"What's your job in all this?"

"When I first came here I was just a run-of-the-mill oil field hand. I ran pipe and worked drilling rigs with all the youngsters. Then, when they found out I had real experience, they put me in charge of monitoring operations at some of the rigs. I get to sit in a trailer and watch computer screens. I'll show you sometime if you want."

"That'll be great, Stan. I appreciate that."

Baker smiled.

"What?" asked Decker.

"This is the most I've seen and talked to you since you graduated from college and went pro."

"Right," said Decker. "So tell me about Caroline Dawson."

Baker looked embarrassed. "I know, you're thinking what is a rich, smart, beautiful, young gal doing with a big old lug like me?"

"That wasn't what I was thinking."

"You're a bad liar."

"So?"

"So I came into this bar one day and there she was. Hell, she was mixing drinks. I thought she was just a bartender earning her daily bread here."

"Why would she be mixing drinks?"

"Her father owns the bar."

"I didn't know that, but I guess it makes sense. But surely, she doesn't need the money."

"She likes to get her hands dirty with all the lines of work they're involved in. She's done maid service at some of the hotels and apartment buildings, cashiering at some of the stores, even drove a semi. She has her CDL," added Baker, referring to a commercial driver's license.

Decker looked impressed. "Okay. That speaks well of her."

"Anyway, I ordered a beer from her, not even knowing who she was. Of course, all these young, drunk punks were hitting on her all night, but she kept her cool. She seemed interested in me, maybe because I wasn't hitting on her. And also because I knew some of the punks and told them to back off. She asked questions and I told her a little bit about myself. Showed her pictures of the kids. Then she told me what time her shift ended."

"Why did she do that? Did she want to meet up with you later?"

"No. And she only told me because *I* asked. She seemed a little put off by that, like I *was* hitting on her. But then I told her I just wanted to make sure she got home okay because those punks were not leaving well enough alone. She told me she had her car outside. It's a sweet ride. A Porsche SUV with these special wide tires and fancy tread. Her father bought it for her birthday. Of course, I only found out about that later."

"Okay, what happened?"

"I was waiting across the street from the bar when she came out. Just to be sure. Two of the punks who'd been harassing her followed her out. She told them to get lost but they were drunk and wouldn't listen.

It started to get dicey. Them pawing her, and I was afraid it might move on to something really bad. So I ran across and . . . well, persuaded them to leave her alone."

Decker smiled. "And how exactly did you do that, Stan?"

"Mostly by knocking them out cold. I don't think they expected that from a guy my age. Anyway, Caroline was really grateful, and . . . and, well, *she* asked *me* out. Couldn't believe it. Never had a gal do that, not even Renee and she's no shrinking violet. So we see each other from time to time. I'm not in her league, but, well, she makes me feel good about myself, I guess. And she's fun. I guess everybody deserves to have some fun, right?"

"Absolutely. Have you met her father?"

"No. And we've never, I mean we haven't, you know."

"Slept together?"

"Right. We're just friends."

"Full disclosure, I followed you here that first night. She was hanging all over you."

"The gal likes to have fun. But I'm in my fifties. Hell, I could be her father."

"Hasn't stopped people in the past."

"Yeah, well." Baker hunkered down over his drink.

"You both disappeared when I wasn't looking. Thought you might have, well . . ."

"Nah. Caroline keeps a room over the bar. She

went up there. She had a headache, she said. I went home."

"Okay."

Decker pulled out a picture of Irene Cramer that Kelly had provided and slid it across. "You know her or ever seen her?"

Baker picked up the photo and studied it. "She the gal that got killed?"

Decker nodded. "Irene Cramer. She taught over at the Brothers' Colony."

"Schoolteacher, huh? Who'd want to kill a schoolteacher?"

"She also had a sideline. An escort. Went by the name Mindy."

"Okay," exclaimed Baker, sliding the photo back. "I've never seen her. And I don't mess with 'escorts.' I've got four kids. I don't want any more by accident. I'd rather just drink my beer and watch movies."

"Know any young punks that might have seen things differently?"

"Oh, yeah, more than a few."

Decker slid the photo back across. "Then show this around and see what comes up. Now, what do you know about the Air Force station?"

"I pass by it every day going to and coming from work."

"I went out there and spoke with the commander of the place. Tight-lipped."

"Yeah, they take things seriously over there, or so I've heard. Lots of security."

"He told me it was a pretty safe place to work, no accidents. But they had a line of ambulances there, so it didn't make sense."

Baker took this in, and his features slowly clouded.

"What is it?" asked Decker, who had noted this.

"Well, some of the guys from there used to come into the bars from time to time. I wore the uniform, so we speak the same language. They're Air Force and I was Army, but still, I did enough joint ops and training to get along with them."

"Okay."

"Well, I was drinking with some of them one night. And one fella, think his name was Ben, said something odd. Stuck with me, see? Memorable what he said."

"So what the hell *did* he say?"

Before answering, Baker finished his beer and then looked directly at Decker. "That we were all sitting on a fucking time bomb."

23

Decker and Baker each had another beer and split a plate of chili, chips, and jalapeños, and then headed out of the saloon. Neither one had noticed the knot of young men who had been closely watching them at the bar. It was dark now, and the streets were emptier than they had been, not only because of the late hour but also because of the fine rain that had begun falling.

They hadn't gone more than a block down a side street where Baker had parked his truck, and which was also a shortcut to Decker's hotel, when Decker slowed.

"What's up?" said Baker, noting this.

"We have some company. And I don't think they're friendly. Look."

Baker gazed ahead where three young men stood, blocking their path.

Then Decker looked behind them.

Three more men barred the way they had come.

"Buddies of yours?" asked Decker.

As the men came closer on both sides, Baker said

quietly, "I recognize a couple. Guys I busted up for going after Caroline that time."

"Thought it might be that. Guess they're here for payback."

"This isn't your fight, Amos. I can see if they'll let you pass."

Decker gave him an incredulous look. "You really think I'm leaving you here to face this alone, Stan?"

Baker grinned. "Well, this won't be the first fight we've been in together."

"And probably won't be the last."

"See any weapons?"

"I think one of them might have a knife." Decker looked behind him. "And one has a baseball bat."

"You have your gun?"

"Unfortunately, I left it in my room. Didn't think I'd need it to have a beer with you. I can flash my creds at them."

"Hell, those idiots probably can't even read."

"Okay."

"Looks like we're going to have to do this the old-fashioned way. I'm not thrilled about that because I'm wearing my good clothes and don't want to mess them up with their blood and stuff."

"I don't see a way around it, Stan."

Decker looked to his left and saw a row of garbage cans. "You want the guy with the knife or the bat?"

"I'm actually partial to the knife guys. Hey, I

remember that game against Michigan your senior year. What'd you do again?"

"The center spit in my face after I sacked the QB, so I pile-drove him into the turf. Got a fifteen-yard personal foul call but it was worth it. And we won, so hey."

"That's right, now I remember. Okay, you might want to pull that one out of your playbook 'cause here they come."

The six men rushed forward, the bat and the knife leading the way.

Neither Decker nor Baker moved until the very last possible second.

When the bat guy was within a foot of Decker, he grabbed a garbage can lid, swung it around, and caught the man flush in the face. He dropped the bat and fell backward with blood streaming down his features and two teeth missing.

Baker stepped up to the knife wielder. When the man began his downward thrust, Baker used his forearm to block it. Then he deftly gripped the man's wrist, ripped the arm behind him, and cranked the elbow upward past all breaking points, and the man's shoulder separated cleanly and painfully. He dropped to the ground screaming and cursing.

Decker had picked up the baseball bat and used it to club the knee of one man, then used the wood to stroke a kidney punch on the third fellow. When the second man came at him again, Decker dropped the bat, flipped him around, heaved him into the air by the waist, and slammed him into the ground.

The man let out a long groan, closed his eyes, and fell unconscious.

Meanwhile, Baker drove his hammy fist into one man's face, breaking his nose, which spewed blood, and knocking him up against the brick wall. He slumped down, senseless. The last man was the smartest of them all. He took to his heels and sprinted off before either Decker or Baker could get to him.

Baker looked at the fallen men, then reached down and took out the wallet of the guy he'd knocked out.

"What are you doing?" asked Decker, as he watched Baker extract twenty bucks from the wallet before dropping it on the man's chest.

In answer, his brother-in-law pointed to his shirt where it was heavily stained. "His blood got on my new shirt. I'm not paying for that." He nudged the man's arm with his boot. "Idiot." He folded the cash and put it in his pocket.

Decker looked down at the fallen men who were still conscious and flashed his badge. "I could arrest all of you for being stupid, but I don't want to fill out the paperwork. Now, those of you who need medical attention, can you get there or get your buddies there without us calling anybody? Because if you leave it to us, it could take a while and then all of you morons are going to jail."

"Bullshit, man," yelled one of them. "Who the hell do you think you are?"

Decker took out his official creds and pointed to them. "This says *F-B-I*. It stands for 'Federal Bureau of Investigation,' in case you didn't know. So if I press charges, you guys are going to a federal lockup a long way from here to spend about ten years contemplating your evil ways. And the guys you'll be spending that time with won't be nearly as nice as me and my friend are."

The man who Decker had clubbed in the knee looked up and nodded. "We can take care of each other," he said quickly. "No need for you to stick around, sir."

"Fuck you," screamed the man whose shoulder Baker had separated.

"Did you think of that one all by yourself?" said Decker drily.

He and Baker walked down the street to the next block over and parted company there.

"I'll call you tomorrow about coming out to the worksite," said Decker.

"I'm usually there six in the morning until six in the evening. And thanks for helping me back there. Wasn't your fight."

"I'm not sure you needed me," replied Decker.

He left Baker there and continued on his way. The street he was on was even emptier than the previous ones. The rain was falling harder now, and Decker picked up his pace. He calculated that if he took a shortcut down the alley coming up he would shave his time in half.

He ducked into the alley as the rain picked up. He was about halfway down it when something hit him from the side. It was as hard as a Mack truck and took Decker right off his feet. It reminded him of the blindside tackle he'd taken that had led to his brain trauma.

An instant later a gun was fired and the bullet hit the brick wall opposite right where Decker would have been. It punched a two-inch hole in the wall, and as soon as it did a mini explosion happened and flames licked the brick. If it had struck him, he'd have been a dead man.

The person who had hit him was lying on top of Decker. He whispered into Decker's ear, "Stay down and stay safe. I'll be right back."

The next moment Decker was all alone.

24

The man who had fired the shot at Decker was now sprinting from his concealed position. He had followed Decker to the alley after shadowing him most of the evening. When Decker and his friend had been attacked by the group of thugs the man thought his work might be done by them.

He wasn't thrilled with having missed, but for some reason Decker had gone down right as he had fired.

As though someone had . . . Shit. The mission's been compromised.

He picked up his pace as the rain soaked him. He did this for a living, and his paranoia antennae were kicking into high gear. His weapon was a custom-built .44-caliber pistol with a special long barrel to give it more range. He had the big man right in the crosshairs, pulled the trigger, and gotten zip for all his troubles.

He was irritated. Not only would he not get paid, *he* might get killed for missing his target. It was just that sort of high-level gig. He had no idea who had hired him, but he'd been doing this long enough to know the presence of heavy hitters.

Yes, one crappy night this is turning out to be.

He reached the rental car. The long-barreled pistol went under the front seat. He climbed into the driver's side and hit the button to start the engine.

Only it wasn't there. The button was gone. He was just looking at the mechanical innards behind it. What the hell was—

He stopped wondering when the passenger's-side door opened and the man who had knocked Decker down and saved his life stood there, his pistol trained on him.

His gaze flicked up and down over this new man on the scene. The eyes were cold, colder than his had ever been, and somehow he didn't think this was the man's top range of ice. He was about six feet, lean, wiry, probably strong as an ox without all the muscle mass. Nimble, alert, quick in his ways, a pro. That could be read in the calm features as the rain poured down on him.

"Should I even bother to ask who you are?" he said.

The other man shook his head one time and one time only.

"You fouled my shot back there."

One curt nod was the response to this statement.

"Full disclosure. I've got a lot of juice behind me. You can walk away from this or go down under the wheels. I'm not the only one out there. It's a good deal. Take it."

Another brief shake of the head.

"Then what do you want?"

It was then that the man spotted the suppressor on the end of the gun barrel pointing at him.

"You're making a huge mistake," he said. "This is a lot bigger than both of us."

"First thing you've said that makes sense," said the other man.

He pulled the trigger once and drilled a hole in the other man's forehead. Dum-dum round, it stayed inside. The man slumped forward over the steering wheel.

The other man had a comm bud in his ear and spoke into a mic tagged to his jacket.

He gave the location and situation. He received an affirmative that "cleanup" would commence right away. He put the starter button back from where he had earlier taken it. Then he closed the door without looking at the man he had just shot dead.

He slipped his pistol into a holster that rode on the back of his waistband and sprinted back to the spot where he had left Decker.

Decker was still there lying on his belly in the middle of the alley. With the falling rain he was as soaked as though he had jumped, fully clothed, into a pool.

When Decker saw the man heading down the alley, he called out, "Hey, can I get up?"

"Affirmative." The man hustled over and helped him up. Decker could feel the strength in the other man's grip.

"Someone just tried to kill me," said Decker.

The man pointed to the hole punched in the brick. "Forty-four-caliber steel jacketed with an incendiary, mini-explosive kicker. Someone really wanted to make sure that you would be joining the ranks of the dearly departed."

"But you saved my ass. Why?"

"It's my job."

"Why?"

"That's it."

"What happened to the other guy?"

"He was my job, too."

"And what happened to him?"

"That's it."

Decker looked flustered by this odd response. "What's going on?"

"We're counting on you to get us there, Mr. Decker."

"Who's *us*?"

"I won't insult your intelligence."

"And if I can't get us there?"

"Not an option. That's *your* job."

"I'm here to investigate a murder. I don't know about the rest of this. I don't know about whatever element you're attached to."

"We're on the same team, just a different division."

Decker looked him up and down. "When did you get into town?"

"Just in time for you, it seems."

"How long have you been following me?"

"Not long enough to really give you any answers. How did it go tonight other than the shitheads, and the shooter?"

"So you saw the shitheads, too?"

The man nodded. "I would have intervened, but you and your buddy seemed to have it covered, and revealing myself for the JV team was not an ideal use of my time. It would have spooked the guy who took the shot."

"The shitheads had everything to do with my 'buddy' and not with me."

"But not the shooter. He had everything to do with *you*."

"Someone doesn't want the truth to come out?"

"There's always somebody who doesn't want the truth to come out. So what did you learn tonight?"

"I learned about fracking," answered Decker.

The man studied him. "You consider that a good use of your time?"

"If you've got a reason why's it's not, I'm listening."

"Not enough for you *not* to cover that angle."

"You obviously know something is going on in this place."

"I just don't know the something. I'm not a detective. My talents lie elsewhere."

"Did you get the shooter?"

"He won't be bothering you again."

"We can question him," suggested Decker.

"He won't be bothering you again."

"Are you telling me he's dead? He could have led us somewhere."

"He would have led us nowhere. Probably at least four layers between him and where we need to go. Waste of time, and we don't have time to waste."

"Did you just kill him?" said Decker.

"Does it matter to you?"

"I'm a cop. Shit like that *does* matter to me."

"You let me worry about that. You do what you do. We're counting on you."

"If this is such a big deal, how come we don't have more federal assets here?"

"Stealth, Mr. Decker."

"Why do I think you didn't fly commercial into North Dakota?"

"It's a free country. You can think what you want. I won't stop you."

"How do I get in touch with you, then? And you with me?"

"We'll figure a way."

"Can you tell me your name, at least?"

The man hesitated, the first instance of indecision Decker had glimpsed in the fellow.

"It's Robie. Will Robie."

25

"Will Robie? He told you his freaking name?"

Jamison was staring across at a soaked Decker, who was leaning against the wall of her hotel room dripping water on her carpet. Decker had come directly back to the hotel, knocked on her door, and woken her up, and now she was sitting on her bed in sweatpants and a long-sleeved T-shirt staring at him incredulously.

"Yeah, he did."

"So let me get this straight. First you got attacked by a bunch of morons and you and Baker beat them up?"

"They were after Stan, not me."

"Then someone tries to shoot you with an exploding bullet, only this Robie guy saves your butt. After that he runs off and takes out the guy who was trying to kill you. And then he comes back and intimates to you that there's something big going down in this town and we're expected to find out what it is really quickly with no other assets coming our way."

"That's actually a pretty good summary."

Jamison slumped against the headboard. "And this Will Robie actually said he was on our side?"

"Different division, same team, he said. But the most interesting thing I found out tonight was what Stan told me the guy from the air station said."

"That we're sitting on a time bomb? Yeah, that's comforting," she said sarcastically.

"Stan thought his name was Ben. And he was in uniform, so it was before Vector took over out there."

"And he didn't follow up with what the guy said?"

"Stan isn't a cop. And they were drinking at a bar at the time. Stan probably thought he was bull-shitting."

"But what the guy said obviously stuck with him."

"Yeah, it did," conceded Decker. "In retrospect."

"So this Robie, what is he? Your guardian angel?"

"He was tonight. I'd be on a slab with my head literally blown off but for him."

This comment drew a shiver from Jamison. "I'm never going to let you go out alone again. You always get into trouble. I mean *always.*"

"I just went to have a beer and talk with Stan. I wasn't looking for any trouble."

"Well, it always seems to *find* you," she retorted. In a calmer tone she said, "So how does this change our investigation?"

"There's no concrete proof that what happened tonight and Robie's appearance on the scene are tied to Irene Cramer's murder."

"Can a place like London, North Dakota, support two simultaneous dark conspiracies?"

Decker swiped his wet hair with his hand. "Let's look at this logically. Cramer was thirty. She came here a year ago, and had a college degree."

"We just have the people at the Colony's word for that. And they said they didn't have any record of that other than what Cramer showed them."

"That's true. But if she *did* earn her college degree, then from the age of eighteen to twenty-two or so she was in school. Then she comes here about eight years later and we can find no record of her before that? And the FBI's alarm bells go off when her prints come through their system?"

"And your point?"

"Cramer didn't have all that much time to establish herself as some international spy, like we were speculating before. In fact, she didn't have much time to do anything so remarkable that the Bureau would be hopping when her prints came through. But that's exactly what happened. And that's why I seriously doubt she was the catalyst for whatever had happened in her past. So we need to find out what was the actual catalyst."

"But if not WITSEC, what then?" asked Jamison, her brow furrowed. "Because I can't think of anything else."

"Well, I thought of one thing."

"What was that?"

181

He gazed at her with a pensive expression. "The sins of the *parents* can carry over to their children, Alex."

Jamison's puzzled look turned to one of understanding. "Cramer's parents? So it might have been something *they* did that led Irene to go underground? And maybe change her name?"

"I'm sure she changed her name. We just have to find out who she really was."

"We don't have a lot to go on."

"We usually don't."

"And we don't know that what happened to Cramer is tied to this 'ticking time bomb' comment."

"No, we don't. But we will figure it out."

"I wish I were as confident as you."

"Now, get some sleep."

"Wait, will you tell Kelly about what happened tonight?"

"For now, let's keep it between you and me."

"Are you sure? He *is* a local cop."

"I'm not sure, but I'm trusting my gut."

He headed to the door.

"Decker, promise me you're not going back out," she said imploringly.

"I'm going to slide the bureau up against my door, and sleep with one eye open and my gun in my hand."

26

Decker didn't go to sleep, at least not right away.

He sat fully dressed in his wet clothes on the floor.

From his wallet he took out two pictures. They were of his wife and daughter. Each had been taken shortly before their deaths.

Tonight, he had come as close to dying as he ever had, he supposed. If this Robie fellow had been a second slower, or not there at all?

I'd be dead. Like Cassie and Molly.

He peered down at their images. He hadn't looked at these pictures in quite a while. On the day of their funerals, he had been unable to speak, unable to really function. Tearful, devastated people kept coming up to him and saying how sorry they were. And he couldn't comprehend at the time what they were even trying to communicate. He felt as dead as his wife and daughter were. He had actually *wanted* to be dead, because he had no desire to keep on living while they could not.

But then time passed, he grieved, mightily at first, too mightily because he came close to losing everything, including his own life. Then more time passed and his days and nights were taken up with doing his job, interacting with others, even making new friends. The loss was still there, it would always be there, but the phrase "Life goes on" appeared to be an accurate one.

And from time to time Decker would feel guilty that he was becoming so absorbed in his work that the memories of his family were receding into a little box in his head, only to be taken out from time to time and wept over. And for him that equated with forgetting about his wife and daughter, or at least allowing other priorities in life to supersede what they had meant to him while alive. And this after he had promised them faithfully, while standing over their graves, that they would be the center of his life until he joined them. A sense of betrayal steadily crept over him.

A tear from his right eye fell onto Molly's photo. He very carefully brushed it away from the picture, fearful that it would mar her final captured image.

He had told himself back in Burlington when he had been visiting their graves that he could live in the past or live in the present, only he couldn't do both. Although part of him desperately wanted to.

So what's it going to be, Amos?

He supposed all who had suffered such a loss struggled just as he did. That notion didn't console him at all.

We all feel alone. We all feel unique in our pain.

He slid the photos back into his wallet and put it away.

It was then that he noticed the bulge in his jacket pocket.

He slowly put his hand in there and pulled out . . . a phone?

The answer hit him a second later.

Robie.

The man had slipped this phone into his jacket when he had helped Decker up in that alley. He had said he would figure out a way for them to communicate, and this must be it. He looked more closely at the device. It both looked and did not look like a typical mobile phone.

He punched in the number of his own cell phone to see if it would go through. It didn't.

He looked down at the phone, then simply pushed the green talk button.

The phone made a small buzzing sound and then the voice came on.

"I expected you to be a little quicker on the uptake," said Robie. "I've been waiting for your call for an hour."

"I just found the phone and figured out how to work it."

"Anything up or are you just checking in?"

"The latter. So if I push the green button you come running?"

"No. If you push the *red* button I do. But I don't have a cape and superpowers, so don't expect me to be there in seconds."

"So it's like a panic button, then?"

"And only use it when you are indeed panicked. Now if there's nothing else, I'm going to get some shut-eye."

"Sorry to bother you," said Decker brusquely.

"I don't mean to sound like an asshole, Decker. But this is a job. A critical one. We're not here to make friends."

"I wouldn't have it any other way."

"Good."

"One more thing."

"Yeah?"

"Thanks for saving my butt tonight."

"You're welcome." Robie clicked off.

Decker stood, put the phone on the nightstand, stripped off his wet clothes, and changed into dry skivvies. He lay back on the bed, suddenly wanting to be anywhere other than here. That was surprising, shocking even, because normally he wanted to be wherever there was a crime that needed solving. And right now that was squarely in London, North Dakota.

The first victim, Irene Cramer, had a mysterious past and might not have been who everyone thought she was. She was a teacher by day, and doing something else entirely at night. She had been murdered and a postmortem performed on her body, presumably by her killer. Something had perhaps been taken from her stomach or intestines.

The man who had found her, Hal Parker, was looking for a wolf that had killed some cattle owned by Hugh Dawson. And now Parker was missing. And Pamela Ames was dead. Had Parker killed Cramer and Ames? But if he had, why pretend to find the body and call the cops? That put him right in the middle of the investigation, which made no sense.

Now Decker came to Will Robie's involvement. He only had Robie's word for it that he worked for the federal government. But Robie *had* saved his life. And the man who had tried to kill Decker? Where had he come from?

And finally, Decker came back to what his brother-in-law had said the man from the Air Force station had told him about sitting atop a time bomb. Did it tie into the row of ambulances at the facility, and did it explain the reluctance of the station's commander, Colonel Sumter, to cooperate with them? They had to find the man who had uttered those words. And he would need Baker's help in learning more about this fracking business. In Decker's experience, when there was money to be made, big money as here, that provided an excellent motive to kill.

As if humans really needed a reason to hurt other humans.

With that thought, he fell into a troubled sleep.

27

"This looks like a command center," said Jamison.

She and Decker were inside a roomy trailer staring at a series of computer screens set atop a long, laminated desk. They were at an oil rig site that was in the process of being fracked. Baker sat in a swivel chair in front of the desktop units, his gaze flicking alertly over each screen. The trailer had a bathroom and an AC window unit and was quite comfortable inside.

"That's exactly what it is," said Baker. "We actually call it the *data* center because that's what all this is," he added, pointing to the screens. "Data."

Jamison indicated a Maxwell House coffee can sitting on a table with its plastic lid on. "You've got a Keurig over there, so what's that for?"

"Don't open that top," warned a grinning Baker. "It's the other supervisor's spit can. You can't smoke anywhere around a rig, so nicotine addicts *chew* tobacco instead."

"Great, thanks for the heads-up," said Jamison, looking disgusted.

Baker pointed to one screen. "This monitors the

barrels of fracking fluid we pump in the hole by the second."

"Is it important to monitor it that closely?" asked Jamison.

"Oh, yeah, because things can go sideways fast and people might get hurt, and you could end up wrecking a wellhead site. Nobody wants that to happen. Now, we're just beginning to frack this well. The drilling and piping have all been done by a separate crew."

"How does all that work?" asked Decker.

"The initial well bore is drilled. After that's done the drill pipe and bit are taken out. Then a steel tube, which we refer to as a surface casing, is put in the hole. That makes the sides of the well rigid and stable and also prevents stuff from leaking out. Then cement is poured in to secure the casing tube. We pressurize the shaft to make sure it's holding okay, sort of like testing a plane fuselage. Then the drill pipe and bit goes back in and the drilling continues vertically. When that's completed the horizontal drilling starts up. We continuously lower in more casing and cement to make sure everything is secure. When that's all said and done, then comes the insertion of the fracking fluid. It's all done in *stages*. And each one takes about two hours."

"How many stages?" asked Decker.

"Nearly a hundred," said Baker.

"Good God," said Jamison. "Why so many?"

"We're going down a long way, and we have to break up the rock in just the right manner and direction." He went to the small window and pointed out. "Those trucks will pump the fluid mix into the wellhead through all those connected pipes. Now, we've also got an artillery van where they prep the necessary explosives and attach the detonating gun to the perforating gun."

"An artillery van," exclaimed Jamison. "Sounds like you're going to war."

"We are in a way, against some really tough subterranean rock that's a zillion years old and has never been disturbed before. We pump the gun down to blast fractures in the rock. Then the perforation device extends fissures or cracks that reach into the oil deposits, sort of like fingers poking in to get something. Then we drop a ball down and seat it in a plug. That isolates the area we're interested in, and that's when we start blasting fracking fluids into the rock cracks and fissures."

"What do the fluids consist of?" asked Decker.

He led them back over to the screens. "It's a pretty well mapped-out mixology of stuff. Sand and fresh water make up ninety-nine-point-five percent of what we put down the hole. The rest are chemicals— biocide to kill bacteria in the water so it can't foul the product, then other chemicals to provide viscosity to the liquid. Guar gum, magnesium chloride, barite, hydrochloric and citric acid, ethanol and methanol, sodium erythorbate. All this stuff has different purposes. Some help with gelling, others with iron control, corrosion counteractor, clay stabilization, friction reducer, crosslinker, and the list goes on and on." He grinned. "Hell, some days I feel like I've got my degree in chemistry three times over. These graphs over here chart the PSI in the pipe. We use regular sand, which we refer to as the proppant, to start with, and then change over to ceramic sand, which holds the fractures open longer." He glanced at Decker. "Like your 'stent' analogy to unblock an artery. We use about two hundred fifty thousand pounds of proppant per stage."

"That's a lot more than a sandbox full," noted Decker.

"Which is why you see all those trucks hauling it in," replied Baker. "Without sand none of this works. Natural sand comes from Wisconsin. The ceramic stuff is imported from China."

"So the Bakken region is chock full of oil and gas?" said Decker.

"Northwest corner of North Dakota hit the jackpot for fossil fuels. All told the state is pumping about two million barrels of oil a day. To give you some perspective, the Saudis alone do around twelve million barrels a day. The Middle East in total has about half the world's total proven oil reserves. And over forty percent of the natural gas."

"Which is why everyone pays attention to what goes on there," noted Decker.

"So most of the oil is trucked out?" said Jamison.

"No, a lot of the oil captured here actually gets transported out via the Dakota Access Pipeline, which is a lot cheaper than trucking it to a train. But that pipeline is filling up fast, so they're building another one."

Jamison said, "And this is one of Stuart McClellan's operations?"

"That's right."

Decker said, "The Air Force station is close to here. And the Brothers' Colony."

"Yep. McClellan's rigs are the only ones hereabouts except for one company also located near the Air Force station."

"What about all the gas flares?" said Jamison. "Isn't that wasteful?"

"It is," conceded Baker. "But there aren't enough pipelines here to transport the gas. And even if there were, the gas up here has a high percentage of hydrocarbons. Pipeline operators hate that because it can clog the pipe."

"What's the solution?" asked Decker.

"They're coming up with a technology to separate the methane from the hydrocarbons right onsite."

"Do any problems come up with fracking?" asked Decker.

He nodded. "Something called a 'screen-out' is

fairly common. That happens when the sand plugs up the perforations. The pump automatically shuts down when that happens because the PSI spikes and the warning bells go off."

"What do you do to fix it?" asked Jamison.

"We open the well and force up lots of barrels of fluid that we just sent down to clean up the blockage. If there are more serious issues, like a well needs some type of invasive intervention because it's deteriorating, equipment has corroded, or the reservoir conditions have changed, then we call in a workover rig. They'll drop in a wireline to lower both measurement and testing equipment to see what the issue is and arrive at a solution. They can usually find an answer and get it back online."

Decker looked impressed. "And here I always thought you were just a guy digging holes with a shovel."

Baker grinned. "Well, I did my share of that too, back in the old days. Now it's all technology and science and engineering. But, hey, I'll take working inside a trailer with my own toilet and AC in the summer and heat in the winter any day."

"Quite the operation," noted Jamison.

"How long do you see yourself here, Stan?" asked Decker.

"Long enough to save up what I need to retire and to help out the kids and their education. Then I'm heading to Florida, chucking my cell phone into the ocean, and I'm going fishing. And I'm not going to stop till I croak."

"Now, tell me what you remember about this guy who talked about the time bomb," said Decker. "His name was Ben?"

"Yeah, least that's what he said."

"Last name?"

Baker rubbed his face and sat back in his chair. "I'm not sure. It was over a year ago and there were a lot of people around and I'd been drinking."

"And you're sure he was in the Air Force?"

"Yeah, he was in his official cammies and he told me he was assigned there."

Decker said, "What if we can show you pictures of people who worked there? Would that help?"

"It might, yeah. But how are you going to do that? I was in the military. They don't like giving out info to nobody."

Decker glanced at Jamison. "We'll think of something."

28

"How *are* we going to get Colonel Sumter to give up his list of personnel?" said Jamison on the drive back. "He hasn't even gotten back to Kelly on his earlier request. And I don't see us getting a search warrant. We have no probable cause. And on top of that, this Ben guy was military; he's not there anymore anyway. It's all Vector personnel now."

"So let's dial up some help." Decker pulled out the device Robie had given him.

"What's that?" she asked.

"Apparently, a hotline to Batman."

He hit the green button. Within two seconds, Robie answered.

"Yes?"

"Need some help. Wondering if you could provide it?"

"Tell me what it is and I'll see what I can do."

"We're looking for a guy who used to work at the Air Force station here. First name Ben, last name unknown."

"Is he military?"

"Yes. We learned that the DoD pulled out the military component and outsourced the work to a firm named Vector. You know them?"

"Why is this guy important?" said Robie, ignoring the query.

"He told a guy I trust that we were sitting on a ticking time bomb here. So I want to talk to him."

"I'll see what I can do."

"One more thing."

"Yeah?"

"Irene Cramer. Any idea why the Feds are interested in her?"

The line went dead.

Jamison glanced at Decker. "Well?"

"Not sure. I might have just said something I shouldn't have."

They drove past the western edge of the Brothers' Colony, where they saw colorful oil rigs erected along the way with trailers and trucks and lots of activity.

Decker read the sign erected in front of one rig nearest the Air Force property: the all-american energy company. Two large Stars and Stripes were suspended from tall flagpoles and flapping in the breeze. Decker said drily, "Well, that's patriotic."

"What could be more American than drilling for oil?" quipped Jamison.

★

Kelly said, "We've had a BOLO out on Parker from the minute we found him missing. There's been no sign of the guy."

They were walking to the room where the post-mortem had been performed by Walt Southern on Pamela Ames.

"I guess around here there are lots of places to get rid of a body," said Jamison.

"Yep. We got landfills full of crap that they add to every day, including some radioactive stuff that comes naturally out of the drilling process."

"Radioactive," said Jamison. "And they can just dump that in a landfill?"

"Well, they're not supposed to. But people aren't supposed to do lots of things and they still do."

"That's why we have a job," grumbled Decker.

As they entered the room Southern was finishing up some notes in a paper file.

He eyed Decker warily. "Heard you came by to look at Cramer's body while I was out of town."

"I did."

"It looks like you opened her up again."

"I did," Decker said again.

"Why?" he said sharply.

"Because I had to. Now, I'd prefer to talk about Ames's post."

Southern started to say something but then seemed to catch himself. "Okay. Not much to tell. Dead about fourteen hours when you found her.

Single contact GSW to the right temple. Dum-dum round." He held up a baggie with the round inside. "All beaten to hell. No striations, lands, or grooves visible. Did what it's designed to do. Won't get a ballistic match off it."

"Fourteen hours," said Kelly. "So around ten o'clock at night?"

Southern glanced at his notes. "About, yes."

"Stomach contents?"

"Some dinner, half digested. That's it. Tox screens have been sent out. I found no obvious signs of drug use. No sign of a sexual assault or recent sexual intercourse."

Kelly nodded but said nothing. He was watching Decker.

Decker said, "Did you confirm that nobody cut her up, like they did Cramer? We didn't look under her clothing. Just noted the gunshot wound and bagged her for the post."

Jamison looked at her partner in surprise, because this was an unusual thing to say. But from the look on Decker's face, the man had a reason.

Southern slowly put down his file. "Do I have to read between those lines or are you going to come to the point?"

"You noted that Cramer's stomach and small intestines were sliced open. *Sliced*. I don't need to tell you those places are pretty popular to hide contraband. When I asked you if there was anything unusual in the post you never mentioned either of those things. Now I'd like an explanation for that."

"They *were* in my report."

"But they were not *highlighted*. They were buried, in fact. A single sentence for both organs. And you took no photos of them. You should have drawn our attention to them. That's standard protocol."

To this, Southern shrugged. "But you found out about them. So what's the problem? No harm, no foul."

"If you have to ask a question like that I'm not sure you're in the job you need to be in."

Southern scowled. "I do this out of a sense of public duty. It's not like they pay much."

Decker glanced at Kelly, who didn't look inclined to say anything.

Southern said, "So you think she might have had something inside her?"

"Did you find any trace of that?" said Jamison.

"Because if you did it wasn't in your report," noted Decker.

"That's because I found no trace of any foreign substance inside her stomach or intestines."

"And you specifically looked?" asked Decker.

"I checked the organs."

"Did you give the stomach and intestines a more focused look because of the way in which they had been sliced open?" Decker wanted to know.

"I was thorough. And that's all I'm going to say on

the matter. If you got a problem with that, you can take it up with Joe. Now, if we're done here? I'll have my very *thorough* report ready for you later today."

And with that Southern walked out.

Decker stood there for a minute and then walked over to the body of Pamela Ames and lifted the sheet. The Y-incision stared back at him along with the dead woman's pale face.

No electric blue light again, thought Decker. *My brain keeps me guessing and I don't much care for it. No, I hate it.*

"Decker?" Jamison said, coming to stand next to him. "You okay?"

Decker curtly nodded.

Kelly said, "I wish you could have given me a heads-up on all that."

"What are you going to do about it now that you know?"

"What can I do? It was in the report, right?"

"Not where it optimally should have been."

"*Optimally*? I can't take that and run with it. Hell, without Walt we don't have anyone here who can do posts. I don't see that I have many options."

"I would think that you have options for some-body like *that*."

"You can't believe that Walt would have intentionally—"

Decker cut him off. "I don't believe or disbelieve anything until I can prove it. Just so we're straight on that."

He put the cover back on Ames's remains, then walked out of the room and slammed the door behind him.

"I take it he's pissed," said Kelly.

"And I think he has every right to be," retorted Jamison.

And with that Jamison left, leaving Joe Kelly alone with a corpse.

29

Will Robie was on the move. It was night, and a warm rain was falling. He was on foot, dressed in a camouflaged ghillie suit, with a pair of night optics, and a GPS tracker mounted on his forearm. Under the ghillie was Level 3A body armor along with rifle plates that could stop and disperse all handgun rounds and most rifle rounds. They offered superb stab and spike protection as well. Unless someone got a head or femoral artery shot on him, then it was over.

He took up position on a slight rise of earth and surveyed the area in front of him through the optics. To the left were the lights of the Brothers' Colony, and to the right those of the Air Force station. And then there were the oil rigs surrounding these two facilities like a hostile army ringing an enemy.

There was movement at the oil rigs as people and trucks came and went. He could see the lights of vehicles moving across the land owned by the Brothers. The radar array sat high above all this activity as it scanned the night skies for incoming nukes and other space traffic.

Amos Decker had been described to him in three precise words: brilliant, quirky, relentless. After meeting the man he hadn't gotten to see the quirky part so much, but Decker certainly seemed intelligent enough. And he hoped the relentless part was spot on because the man was going to need it. His partner, Alex Jamison, had an excellent rep at the Bureau. Partners were important, Robie knew. He was missing *his* partner on this assignment. Jessica Reel was currently in a different and far more dangerous part of the world. Although this area of North Dakota certainly seemed to have its share of violence.

He got up from his position and moved forward with efficient strides of his long legs.

The outer perimeter of the Air Force station loomed in front of him.

Robie's people had tried to do this the nice way and had gotten zip for their politeness.

Now Robie had been sent here to do it the impolite way.

He had brought some tools with him in case he came across any opposition but had been instructed to use them judiciously. His orders were also to not kill anyone in his path tonight. Of course, those on the other side would have no compunction about doing that to him, since they would see him as only an intruder. An intruder looking for the truth, but an intruder, nonetheless.

He had a map of the facility downloaded on his

phone, and he stopped to take a brief scan of the outer perimeter. It was sophisticated and had been thoughtfully implemented by people who knew what they were doing.

Yet he had been told about a sliver of a blind spot in the facility's defenses. It took him ten seconds to scale the first perimeter fence. His gloves with metal mesh palms allowed him to easily circumvent the concertina wire atop the fence. He dropped down to the other side and eyed the ground in front of him. Fortunately, he knew that pressure plates aligned at two-foot intervals and set at forty-five-degree angles ran off the support posts for the fence. Best-case scenario, if he stepped on one an alarm would go off. Worst-case scenario, Robie would be blown to nothing.

He picked his steps carefully and safely reached the interior perimeter fence. This had double rows of razor wire toppers, and it took him longer to get over it than he ideally wanted. He dropped silently to the ground and squatted there, watching and listening. This endeavor made up three-quarters of most of his missions; this was the part that allowed him to live. So he paid attention to it, gave it the due it deserved. He wanted to walk out of here, not be carried out in a body bag.

Now the easy part was over.

The one unknown for him was whether they deployed dogs here. His intel had been sketchy on that. Dogs were almost impossible to defeat, at least for long. But if they were present, he had brought something that would help him overcome this obstacle.

There were surveillance cameras along the pedestrian routes, but he also knew where each of them was, and he stayed out of their lines of sight.

He saw the first sentry up ahead dressed in black with body armor and carrying a sub gun with a thirty-round extended mag and a walkie-talkie attached by Velcro to his shirtfront. A sweep light mounted on a tower was making its rounds over the ground. Robie watched its routine and then moved forward, avoiding its glare.

He drew to a stop about fifteen feet later and waited for the guard to finish his walk. When he disappeared around the corner of one building, Robie crept forward, his gaze moving across the area in front of him, side to side, then a look backward to check his full rear flank.

Two more guards appeared on the scene and they were joined by another—not an armed guard, but a woman dressed in civilian clothes. They all shared a smoke and talked. Robie strained to hear what they were saying but couldn't quite make it out.

The woman finally left and the guards moved on, one going right and the other left.

Robie skirted along the shadows, occasionally looking down at his GPS tracker and the facility map on his phone. The building he wanted was up on the right. He reached the door but, after looking at it, decided not to make his entry that way.

He crept around the corner and eyed the window there. Basic snip lock, blinds half drawn. He risked hitting the window with his light to check the inside edge for signs of an alarm port. He saw none.

That was when he heard someone coming.

With his knife he flipped the lock, raised the window, slipped inside, and closed it a few seconds before a figure passed by. As he gazed out the window in the direction of the pyramid building he saw something extraordinary. Three guards came out of a side door pushing two gurneys with two men lying on them. They hurried over to the ambulances parked there and loaded the gurneys into the back of one of them, and two guards climbed into the rear. A driver must have already been in the vehicle because it started up, geared into reverse, and pulled out, its taillights winking as it drove away.

Robie had taken pictures of all this with his phone. He lowered the blinds, turned away from the window, and looked around the small office he was in. There was a desk with large American and U.S. Air Force flags resting in stands behind it. Gunmetal-gray file cabinets were parked against one wall. That was his target. In the digital world the military could still be counted on to also deal in good, old-fashioned paper products.

He slid open each drawer until he found the one he wanted.

Personnel files.

He went through them as quickly as possible, holding a penlight in his mouth and shining its light into the drawer to keep as much of the illumination as possible hidden. Twenty minutes later his hand closed around the file he wanted, after he made sure there were no others that fit the bill. He took pictures of each page with his phone camera, put the file back, closed up the drawer, and turned to leave. Right as someone walked up to the door and he heard a key being inserted into the lock.

30

It was the same woman. Up close, she was around thirty, with straight blond hair that fell to her shoulders, an athletic build, and resolute, focused, intelligent features. She shut the door, clicked on the light, and moved over to a desk by the window. She sat down, opened the desk drawer after unlocking it, and pulled out some files.

As she sat at her desk she was intently focused on the documents in front of her. So much so that she didn't notice it at first. The sound, that is. Or sounds.

But the collective noises outside finally made her glance that way. She stiffened and then, as the sounds became more recognizable, she relaxed. She was about to turn back when the woman tensed again as she looked at the window. Now it wasn't simply the noise that had jarred her. It was something else far more tangible. Literally staring her in the face. Her hand immediately went to the phone on the desk. She had barely picked up the receiver when she collapsed forward.

Robie stood next to her, having come out from

his hiding place behind the flags. He had on a small gas mask and was holding a bottle in his hand. The knockout spray had an amnesiac component to it. When she woke up she would remember nothing. He glanced at the window. She had no doubt seen that the blinds had been fully lowered. She might have been in the office earlier and could have even been the one to raise the blinds. She had probably been about to call security when Robie had stopped her. He darted to the window, edged the blinds aside, and peered out. There definitely appeared to be more activity out there. The sounds had lessened somewhat, but they were still there.

He waited three beats for the noises to move away and then took his opportunity to escape.

Outside he reversed his course and made his way to the inner security fence. Before he got there he heard the sound above and looked up. Maybe that was the source of all the ruckus going on here.

The small jet was coming in for a landing on the runway that ran east to west behind the buildings that constituted the Air Force station. The landing gear hit the asphalt and the pilots applied the brakes along with the thrust reversers, and the small jet rolled to a stop. As it did so, several people hurried over to the plane and a golf cart drove up and parked next to the aircraft.

Someone of importance was clearly arriving.

For Robie, the temptation to see who was getting

off the ride was too strong, overriding his good sense. But in Robie's line of work one's personal safety was not paramount. His focus was mission-centric. He had come to gather intel, and this alone might be well worth the clandestine visit. In fact, this might be just as important as what he had found in the file cabinet.

He reversed course and edged along the side of a building, until he gained a sight line to the runway as the plane's airstairs came down. Robie moved closer still as a few moments later the passengers began to deplane.

The first person off was a tall man around fifty with broad shoulders. He was not in uniform but rather in a trim, dark suit with no tie. The second person off was a woman, also around fifty, dressed in a gray pantsuit. She clutched a soft-sided leather brief-case. The last person off was another woman, younger, dressed in a dark skirt with a matching jacket. She was checking something on her phone.

Robie watched all of this and even managed to snap pictures using the camera built into his optics. He followed their movements as they walked over and climbed into the golf cart. As soon as they were in their seats, the vehicle zipped off. Robie took some more pictures before the cart turned and disappeared between two buildings.

The next moment Robie was off and running.

Because it was clear to him now that they did

indeed have dogs here. And they had picked up on his presence.

As he ran he took three items from his pocket and tossed them behind him in a triangle-shaped pattern, each about five feet apart from the other.

He glanced back; the beasts were running free. Luckily their handlers were nowhere in sight because while Robie had a chance with the canines, he had no chance against a fired bullet. There were two of them: one a German shepherd that looked big enough and vicious enough to rip his arm off, the other a smaller Rottweiler who looked even meaner. Robie had it on good authority that the surprises he had left behind would do the trick and that even the best trained dogs would not be able to resist, even when in full chase mode. He hoped the authority was really that good.

Both dogs skidded to a halt and attacked what he had left behind. As soon as they took a bite of what he had dropped, they wobbled and fell over. They would be super attack dogs again, but only long after Robie was gone.

He scaled the fence twice as fast as he had coming in and successfully avoided the pressure plates.

The fired round came out of nowhere and hit him on the lower right side of his back. The plate absorbed the kinetic energy and flung it across the face of the vest. Robie wasn't dead, but he felt like he'd been kicked by a seriously pissed-off thousand-pound mule.

The second fence was climbed even faster than the first. He dropped onto the other side as the search-light began its sweep and alarms blared throughout the complex.

He immediately hoofed it into the darkness.

But then his life got even more complicated.

Will Robie would have expected nothing less.

31

The chopper lifted off a helipad and swiftly moved west, hot on the trail of the intruder. A searchlight sparked to life on the starboard side of the aircraft. Its beam bore down over the countryside, dramatically illuminating the flat dark land as though it were suddenly aflame.

A few moments later the beam caught and held on its target.

A second later the SUV roared to life and its headlights came on. Before it could drive off, though, the chopper was hovering in front of the vehicle, its .50-caliber nose cannon pointed right at the windshield. One rumble from the weapon, and the SUV would be shredded and the occupant dead in a non-survivable field of fire.

Over the PA system the pilot ordered the driver to step out of the vehicle.

The driver did not comply with this order.

The chopper hovered there for another minute while the pilot communicated with the higher-ups on what they wanted done with the situation.

A minute later the chopper landed, and four heavily armed and armored men climbed from it and surrounded the SUV. When their orders to come out were not obeyed, they were about to force the issue when the SUV horn started blaring loudly. The men took a step back as the driver's-side window started to come down. Every man pointed his assault rifle at this spot, ready to open fire the moment a weapon appeared.

The glass hit the bottom and stopped. The blaring horn ceased. And the truck's engine cut off. The men looked at one another before charging forward.

They reached the side of the truck and peered inside. The front seats were empty. The back seats the same. The rear cargo area held nothing.

The curses could be heard over all their collective comm packs when this was relayed back up the chain of command.

Will Robie kept the throttle on the electric scooter wound as far as it could go, as the little bike, its headlight off, moved nearly silently over the quiet roads. He was already miles away from the site of where he'd parked the truck in which he'd carried the scooter. He'd programmed in the truck starting, horn blaring, lights coming on, window coming down, and engine cutting off, then executed all of those commands through his phone app. He had watched the chopper and strike team approach the vehicle through a camera built into the grille of the truck, with the video feed going directly to his phone.

He veered down a side road and ditched the scooter in an abandoned shed, as prearranged. He drove off in a pickup truck that had been left there for his use after stripping off his gear, underneath which he wore jeans, a corduroy shirt, and boots. A Stetson hat completed his disguise. He could be a local coming home from either a bar or a job.

He made it back to town in three-quarters of the time it had taken him to drive out.

He parked the truck behind the hotel where Decker and Jamison were staying.

Decker was sound asleep in his bed when he heard a slight noise that made him sit up.

"Piece of advice: you might want to become a lighter sleeper."

Decker clicked on the nightstand light and looked over at Robie sitting in a chair with a placid expression.

Robie held up his phone. "I just sent you some documents and pictures. I'm here to provide context."

"What do the pictures and docs concern?"

"Ben *Purdy*, who used to work at London AFS."

"Used to. When did he leave?"

"Around the time they transitioned to Vector."

"Where is he now?"

"Don't know. And his papers don't say. That's a

puzzler because they would normally list what his next deployment was. The files I looked at for other personnel all did."

Decker picked up the phone off the nightstand and opened the email. He took a minute to scan down the pages that Robie had photographed.

"How'd you get these?"

Robie just looked at him.

"Do they know someone was there tonight?" asked Decker.

This comment drew a look of respect from Robie.

"Or was it clean?" added Decker.

"My exit was not as clean as I would have liked. But they won't know what my area of interest was, that I can guarantee."

"That's good to know."

"What are you going to do now?"

"Show the picture to someone to make sure it's the right guy."

"We don't need you showing this picture all around."

"I'm only going to show it to one guy. A person I trust implicitly."

"I hope your trust is well placed."

"It is. That I can guarantee you."

"And if it is the right guy?" asked Robie.

"Then we need to track down this Ben Purdy."

"And if you can't?"

Decker looked at him. "Why would that be a

problem? Even if his current assignment wasn't in the file. He's in the Air Force, not in hiding."

"He *was* in the Air Force. We don't know if he still is. And *if* you find him he may not talk. For a number of reasons," he added grimly.

"You think it goes that deep?"

Robie ran his fingers along the chair's armrest. "FYI, I wouldn't be here otherwise."

"That's also good to know."

"Anything else?"

"When I asked you about Irene Cramer, you hung up on me. Why?"

"I had nothing to contribute to that discussion."

"You have a funny way of not answering questions."

"Goes with the territory I call home."

"I can deal with half-assed answers and even outright lies, because pretty much everybody lies to me at some point. But to solve the case, I have to get to the truth. And *FYI,* I will."

Robie eyed the phone. "Those are the facts. Do with them what you think is best." He rose from the chair, a bit stiffly.

This was not missed by Decker. "I take it the non-clean exit was also painful?"

"They almost always are."

Robie was at the door when Decker said, "I know getting this wasn't easy. Thanks."

Robie turned back long enough to say, "It's my job. Now do yours."

32

"That's the guy," said Baker.

He, Decker, and Jamison were having coffee the next morning at a café down the street from their hotel. Decker had shown him the picture of Ben Purdy that Robie had sent him.

"You're sure?"

"Oh, yeah. That's him. He still around? Haven't seen him since that night."

"All the military guys are gone except for the man who runs the place, Colonel Sumter. The rest are private contractors."

Baker shook his head. "Never liked those guys. They were paid three times what us grunts got and did a quarter of the work we did." He eyed Decker. "Where'd you get that picture?"

Jamison glanced at her partner. Decker had already told her about the encounter with Robie.

"Just good, old-fashioned police work, Stan," said Decker, taking his phone with the photo on it back as Jamison hiked her eyebrows at this comment.

"If he's gone, how are you gonna talk to him?"

"Have to think of a way. Did he say anything else to you? Talk about his family? Friends? Anything that might help us track him down?"

"Well, he said his family was from Montana. Just over the border."

Decker sat up. "Did he mention a town?"

"No. Just that it was small and rural. I guess most of Montana is rural." He checked his watch. "I got to get going. I'm normally at work by now, but we had some repairs to make and we don't start staging for another two hours."

"Thanks, Stan, see you later."

"Hey, um, Caroline wanted me to ask if you two wanted to join us for dinner tonight."

"Dinner?" said Decker. "I don't—"

But Jamison interjected, "That would be great, Stan."

Baker grinned. "I'll email you with the details. You'll love the restaurant. It's a pretty special place."

Before they could comment on this, Baker hurried off.

Decker whirled on Jamison, who put up her hand.

"He's your brother-in-law."

"Soon to be ex."

"Is he your friend? Do you like him?"

"Well, yes. He's a nice guy, solid as a rock."

"And didn't you two just fight off a bunch of guys together?"

"Well, yeah."

"The point is, he invited us to dinner. We should accept. At the very least we might learn something that could be helpful."

Decker fingered his coffee, looking uncertain.

"What?" she said.

"If you want the truth, I guess I'm pissed that he seems so happy. Without my sister. I know that's stupid and petty, but . . ."

Jamison put a hand on his shoulder. "And it's also normal to feel that way after something like this happens to a family member. But you have to let it go. It's his life to live, not yours. Don't judge him, Decker, just support him. Like you just said, he's a good guy."

He refocused and said, "If Purdy's family lives in Montana just over the border we should be able to find them."

"It's a long border, Decker. What about Robie? Could he help?"

"He got us the photo and the name. He did his job. His forte is not running stuff down in a database or interviewing witnesses. We should be able to do that."

"In a normal case, yes. But this is apparently not a normal case."

Decker thought about this for a long moment, took out his phone, and punched in a number.

"Who are you calling?" she asked.

"A professional colleague . . . Hello, Bernie, it's

Amos Decker. Yeah, it has been a long time. Yeah, still doing PI. Look, I'm on a job for a client who's trying to track a deadbeat dad. Name's Ben Purdy. He's in the Air Force, but I think he might be AWOL, so he's got bigger problems than alimony and child support. We tried to garnish, but the guy's gone all cash and the military's not been very helpful. Right, I know. Same old story. Now we got a lead on some of his family being in Montana, near the North Dakota border. I remember you know a guy out that way who was pretty good. Any chance you dial him up and get some intel for me on Purdy and his family? An address for them because I happen to be out that way?" Decker paused and listened. "Yeah, that's right, that'll work. Give him my number so you don't have to be caught in the middle. Right, thanks, Bernie. Beers on me next time and I'll cover the guy's hourly."

He clicked off and looked at Jamison. She stared back at him incredulously.

"You just called in a favor from, what, your private PI boys' club? I thought that only happened in the movies."

"Bernie Hoffman used to be a homicide detective in Cincinnati. We got to know and trust each other working some joint cases. About the time I went private so did he. We helped each other back then, too. I remembered he had a really good guy in South Dakota. Bernie will put him on the case and we'll see what pops. And it's not a favor. I'm paying the guy."

When she kept staring at him, he said, "What?"

"Well, you handled that so deftly over the phone. I mean, you weren't, um . . ." Her voice trailed off and she looked a little embarrassed.

"I get tongue-tied in social situations, Alex. Put me in the middle of a dinner, or a party or anything like that, I'm not your guy for eloquence or even stringing a few words together. But when it comes to what I do for a living, I don't have that problem. I thought you would have remembered that from our first few encounters back in Ohio."

She smiled, shamefaced. "You're right about that. Okay. So what do you think Purdy meant when he said they were all sitting on a time bomb here?"

"He could have been speaking metaphorically. Or literally."

"The latter gives me the chills."

"Robie got the photo by breaking into the military facility."

A wide-eyed Jamison said, "You didn't tell me that part. Did he actually say that?"

"He didn't have to. But it was a close call for the guy, and he strikes me as the sort who can pretty much go where he wants. So the security there must be tough."

"Well, it *is* a secret government facility," said Jamison.

"Yeah, I just wonder what the *secret* is."

"What do you mean?"

In response Decker brought up some photos on his phone. "Robie didn't tell me about these. I guess he thought the photos would speak for themselves, and they sort of do."

He showed Jamison shots of the men on the gurney being taken to the ambulance, and the man and two women getting off the jet.

"I wonder who they are," said Jamison. "And I wonder what happened to the men on the gurneys? Sumter said the place was really safe. No accidents."

"Well, maybe what happened to them was no accident," replied Decker.

33

The room was dark. Any illumination appeared to be coming from a lamp in another area. A man sat in a comfortable upholstered chair. He was dressed in a suit, crisp white shirt, and a tie. His winged loafers were polished. His hair was salt and pepper. His face was creased with decades' worth of worry, all honestly earned while serving on behalf of his country. His demeanor was calm; he was used to projecting such a façade in times of extreme peril.

This was one of those times.

His code name was Blue Man, which denoted the sky-high ring of seniority of which he was a member in America's intelligence apparatus.

Will Robie sat opposite him.

"Amos Decker has the information?" asked Blue Man.

"He does. Plus the photos."

"Good fortune shone on you last night, Robie."

"It didn't feel like it at the time. How's Jess?"

"Busy" was all that Blue Man would say on that. "Now, I take it from your overall demeanor that you wonder why we are not performing a full frontal assault on this particular problem?"

"I do what I'm tasked to do," said Robie evenly.

"But still."

"Yes," said Robie. "But still."

Blue Man held up one of his hands. "Unfortunately, we have one of these tied behind our back, Robie. Very tightly, in fact."

"Is that so?"

"Powerful interests are arrayed all over this situation. The problem is, while they are arrayed, they are not *aligned* with our interests."

"Money?"

"And power. Now if we knew for sure, with demonstrable proof, what is going on, it would be different. Without that, I can't even get a meeting. I can't even get an email returned. People would rather ignore a potential problem in the hope that it will go away."

"And when it doesn't?"

Blue Man looked dubiously at him. "You've been in this game long enough to know that when it *doesn't*, those who ducked their responsibilities will point fingers at others. That apparently qualifies as leadership in certain places."

"Don't you get tired of this shit, sir?"

"I became tired of it my first day on the job." Blue Man leaned forward. "But if all of us who hate the status quo were to leave, then the status quo would not only remain, it would become intractable."

"Meaning evil only wins—"

"—when good men and women do nothing. I choose to do something."

"So what now?" asked Robie.

"Do you think he can find Ben Purdy?"

"If anyone can, I think Decker can."

"I have a good friend at the Bureau. He speaks very highly of Decker. In fact, he told me Decker is the best pure investigator that the FBI has. He also said that Decker has some quirks."

Robie nodded. "I read the file. The man's entitled to some quirks after what happened to him."

"Agreed."

"Vector?" said Robie.

"A recently created company but already embedded throughout the DoD's operations with a cavalry of powerful political allies whom they have bought and paid for."

"But there's something going on out there that doesn't jibe with their mission."

"For various reasons, I have been concerned with the Douglas S. George Defense Complex ever since Vector was given the contract to take over operations."

"But with an Air Force colonel, Mark Sumter, in charge."

Blue Man waved this off. "He's a titular placeholder. A career soldier who, unfortunately, will follow any order he's given without gauging the moral or legal virtue of it."

"Which may be one of the reasons why he got the assignment."

"I think it's the *only* reason he got the assignment."

"Radar array. Eye in the sky," said Robie.

"Officially, yes."

"Unofficially?"

Blue Man settled more deeply in his seat. "The walls of secrecy have always existed within the American IC," he said, referring to the intelligence community. "But I have never seen it so compartmentalized. Secrets are being kept everywhere. DOJ, DHS, DoD, and all their related platforms. Members of both parties in Congress have made inquiries and met a stone wall in response."

"Meaning something might be going on there other than what we think is?"

Blue Man said, "It actually might be fortunate that Irene Cramer turned up dead here."

"Not so fortunate for her."

"I'm only talking about the bigger, strategic picture. Her murder has engaged the official machinery of the FBI. They might be able to make some headway where we could not. You know that we have no authority to operate domestically."

"They already tried to kill Decker."

"Which is why you were sent out, to prevent that from happening. And you did."

"The body was disposed of?" inquired Robie.

"Yes. He was a gun for hire with no possible route back to who hired him."

"Any guesses?"

"We can't guess, Robie. We don't have time for it."

Robie cocked his head. "And why *were* the FBI called in? It has to do with Cramer. Decker asked me about her. I had nothing to tell him."

"And I have nothing to tell *you* on that subject. Perhaps at a later time."

Robie took this in stride. He was used to not having the full story on any op for which he was called in. "Okay. But she must have been important to us."

"She may be more important to us in death than she was in life. But I for one believe that every death such as she suffered must lead to justice, and punishment."

Blue Man gave him a curt nod, and Robie rose to go back to work.

"Look out for Decker and his partner with the greatest care, Robie."

Will Robie didn't say anything. He didn't have to.

34

"Sumter hasn't gotten back to me," said Kelly as he joined Decker and Jamison by prearrangement in the lobby of their hotel. He had on a gray two-piece suit and white shirt, but instead of scuffed boots he wore black loafers.

"That's telling," said Decker.

"The DoD works like a glacier, at least that's been my experience."

"Sumter came here about a year ago?"

"That's right, when the operation of the facility transitioned."

"What do you know about Vector?"

"Not much. But they got a lot of people over there. And most of them carry weapons. The very serious kind."

"Got a question," said Decker.

"Shoot."

"Why all the ambulances over at the Air Force station? Sumter said it was a really safe place, no accidents, so I don't see the need."

Kelly looked at him shrewdly. "You asked that when we were over there."

"And I didn't get an answer. Thought I'd tee it up again."

"You think *I'm* supposed to know?"

"I *think* you might have an opinion."

"Well, the easiest answer is all military facilities prepare for worst case, so having ambulances there might just be for that reason."

"And it might not. Lot of security there for a radar array. I mean, it's not like someone can go in and steal that pyramid."

"But they can *sabotage* it," countered Kelly.

"Okay, I'll give you that one," conceded Decker.

"Why do you care about any of that?" asked Kelly.

"I care if there's something going on over there that might be tied to Irene Cramer."

"I don't see a connection."

"It's our job to find one, if there is one."

"Well, like I said, I've heard nothing back."

"Then we have to move forward in other directions."

"And where would that be?" asked Kelly.

"I'd like to go back to the Brothers' Colony."

"What do you expect to get there?"

"Irene Cramer worked there. We might have missed something. At the very least we can talk to other people. A lead might shake out from that."

"I'll give them a heads-up that we're coming. But let's tread carefully. They've all been hit hard by this."

"I'm sure they have. And the sooner we solve this, the sooner they can get on with their lives. The not knowing probably isn't good for them."

"That's a fair point," conceded Kelly. He suddenly gave Decker a hard stare. "Some young punks went to the hospital the other night with assorted injuries. Nothing too serious. You know anything about that?"

"Why would I?"

"They didn't file a police report, but one of my guys was over there interviewing some other dumbbells who got into an altercation. That's how he hooked up with them. They said it was a couple of really big, rough-looking guys who took them out. Six against two, and the two kicked some serious ass. Surprised they admitted to that, but I think even they were impressed. Sure you don't know anything about that?"

"Lot of really big, rough-looking guys in this town."

"Yeah, there are," said Kelly, not looking convinced.

"You want to call the Brothers so we can head out?" said Decker. "I'll go bring the SUV around."

He left Kelly and Jamison there.

Kelly eyed her. "So what exactly is going on?"

"I don't know what you mean."

231

"You going down the obfuscation road, too?"

"Wow, that's an SAT word if ever I heard one."

"Where do you think I got it?" replied Kelly.

On the drive out to the Colony they passed the All-American Energy Company's oil well site, which bordered both the Brothers' land and the Air Force station.

"Colonel Sumter really hates all this stuff right next to his installation," said Jamison. "I guess I can understand that. I mean, what if there's an accident with one of those oil rigs, a fire or something? It could affect what he's doing over there."

Kelly stuck an unlighted cigarette in his mouth. "Like shooting fish in a barrel."

"What is?" asked Jamison.

"Drilling for oil around here."

"You ever think about getting into the fracking business?" asked Jamison.

He shook his head. "I prefer steadier work. It's not like crime is ever going to go away." Kelly glanced at Decker. "If you weren't a cop, what would you be?"

"Unemployed," answered Decker quite truthfully.

35

Milton Ames and Peter Gunther were waiting for them in the dining hall. They were dressed the same as before, but each man seemed paler, with Ames looking feeble and disoriented.

He mumbled, "When can we have Pammie's remains? We have to bury her properly."

"I'll let you know as soon as possible, Milton," said Kelly in a gentle tone. "It shouldn't be too much longer."

"Do they . . . did they have to, you know?"

"They had to perform an autopsy, yes," said Jamison quietly. "It's legally required under the circumstances."

"I . . . I guess so. Susan keeps asking. She . . . we . . . want to . . ."

Kelly said, "We're doing all we can, please believe that."

"I do, Joe. Thank you."

Decker said, "I know you didn't keep a file on Cramer's documents, but after she gave you the information about her undergraduate degree, did you check with Amherst to see if she actually went there?"

Ames said firmly, "No, we didn't. Why would she lie about that?"

Gunther chimed in, "And why would someone come all the way out here with a made-up story? We can't pay a lot. What would be her motive to lie to us about her past? I just don't see it."

"Well, if she wanted to disappear but needed a job to support herself?" said Jamison. "That would be one motive."

Gunther's expression showed clearly that he did not believe this to be a plausible explanation.

Jamison said, "Did she give you references from past places of work that you could check out? She'd been out of school for about eight years. She had to have held other jobs in the meantime."

Gunther and Ames exchanged a glance.

Decker said, "During job interviews, you always ask about a potential hire's experience. You check references."

Gunther placed his hands together and said quietly, "We needed a teacher and . . . and she was the only one to apply for the job. It's not like we could be choosy."

"Teaching is a lot of work," added Ames. "And a person could come here and make twice what we were offering just to be a cashier at a truck stop. So when she applied for the position we were thrilled."

"In fact, I imagine you were desperate for someone?" said Jamison.

"Yes."

"How'd she find out you needed a teacher in the first place?" asked Decker.

Gunther answered. "We placed an ad online and also in the local paper. She apparently saw it and came in. She interviewed very well. She brought model lesson plans with her, seemed very well prepared to teach our children, and appeared happy and well-adjusted. And she had done a very good job for the time that she was here. Susan told you that herself, if you recall."

Ames said, "But why all these questions about Irene's past? How is that relevant to what happened to her? She was a prostitute. Don't a lot of them have bad things happen to them? I mean, it's just the nature of the beast, isn't it?"

"It can be, yes," said Jamison. "But we have to follow up other angles as well."

"We're just trying to trace her past. It might have an impact on what happened to her," explained Kelly. "At least we can't discount that yet."

"Meaning it might be someone from her past who killed her?"

"Could be."

Gunther nodded. "Well, that is a little comforting. At least it might not be anyone from London. I would hate to think that we might have a brutal killer running around here."

"You'd be surprised how many places have brutal killers running around," said Decker, drawing a sharp look from Gunther.

Ames said, "I know that you have to look into what happened to Irene, but do you have any clue as to who killed my daughter?"

Decker looked at Ames. "As Detective Kelly said, we're working hard on it. Both these cases are a priority for us."

"Do you think they might be connected?" asked Gunther.

"How so?" asked Kelly.

"Well, both women had ties to this place. Both were killed when they were off our property. Do you think it might be someone who had a grudge against our lifestyle and beliefs? These things do happen. Religious persecution."

"Yes they do," said Jamison. "And we will look at that angle, although Cramer was not a member of the Colony."

"Someone might have held it against her that she taught here or had a mistaken belief that she was a member somehow."

"Again, we will look into that," said Jamison, glancing at Decker.

Kelly added, "Do you have any idea where Pamela might have been living in London?"

"She never told me," said Ames. He paused and his expression grew uncomfortable.

Jamison was quick to pick up on this and said, "Is there something on your mind?"

"The way she was dressed when she was found? I saw the clothing. I . . . she never had clothing like that when she lived here. I saw how she dressed at the truck stop but this . . . this was far more . . . What was going on there? I would like to know. And Susan asked me about it, too. She was deeply worried."

Kelly said, "She might have just been, you know, trying out a new style."

Ames said, "You . . . you don't think she was? I mean . . . s-sex? With Hal Parker? She wouldn't have done that because she found him . . . attractive. He was older than we were!" He looked down. "But she might have . . ." He stopped and shook his head. "No, I cannot believe something like that about my daughter. She would not have done that. Never."

Decker said, "The postmortem showed that they didn't have sex, if that makes you feel better."

Ames put his head in his hands, moaned, and looked like he might retch right there on the flowery tablecloth.

Decker reached out and put his hand on Ames's shoulder. "I'm sorry, Mr. Ames. I just wanted you to know that whatever she went there for, that particular act didn't happen with Hal Parker, okay? Just put that right out of your mind. And tell your wife that, too."

Ames lifted his head, rubbed his eyes dry, and nodded. "Okay. Right. Thank you."

When Decker glanced at Jamison, she was gaping. She quickly said to Gunther, "We understand that you bought some land from the Air Force? And then leased some of it to frackers?"

Gunther nodded. "Yes. The lease payments have come in very handy. It was one of the best invest-ments we made, winning that auction."

"I'm sure," said Jamison.

Decker said, "Did you ever notice anything odd at the Air Force facility?"

"Odd? I haven't. But I don't really pay attention to it." Gunther looked at Ames. "What about you, Milton?"

"My home is not near there. But there are others who do live closer to the facility. I can ask them."

"Do you mind if we do that, and if we could meet with them now?" said Decker.

Gunther said, "All right. But what is all this about?"

"I wish I could tell you," said Decker. "But I'm not sure myself."

36

Judith and Robert White sat across the table from Decker, Jamison, and Kelly in the dining hall. They were young, having been married for less than three years, but she was already pregnant with her second child. Her scarf was colorful, his clothes were dark and nondescript. He looked nervous; she looked intrigued.

They had been asked to come here because their small farm was closest to the Air Force's outer perimeter fencing.

Robert fiddled with his hat and looked at his feet while Decker scrutinized the pair.

"Anything you can tell us," he said, now looking directly at Judith. "Whether it seems important or not."

Robert shrugged and glanced up. "I don't know nothing."

His wife elbowed him in the arm. "Bobby, tell them."

"Shush, Judy, this is no business of ours."

"Two women have been killed," said Jamison.

"One of them lived here and the other worked here. That *makes* it our business."

Judith started to tear up. "Bobby, tell them. It's important. Oh, poor Pammie and Ms. Cramer."

Robert straightened, resignation clear on his features. "Okay, there were odd noises at night."

"Odd? Like what?" asked Decker.

"Planes coming and going. Choppers doing the same. Seen the lights going over our house."

"And the dogs, tell them about the dogs," implored his wife.

Robert sat up straighter and his expression became somber. "They got guard dogs there. Fierce things. We got a puppy. Went over to the outer fence one time. Just curious. Well, thank God there were two fences between it and them. Thought they were going to tear right through both to get our little pup."

"And tell them about the you-know-what," prompted Judith.

Robert screwed up his mouth and shook his head. Decker leaned in. "The 'you-know-what'?"

"The man!" said Judith. "Bobby, if you won't tell them I will."

"Good Lord, woman, don't you see what you're getting us into talking like that?"

"The truth is always better," said Decker. "You tell the truth, you won't get in any trouble."

"Says you," retorted Robert.

"Bobby!" exclaimed his wife.

He sighed again. "It was about a month ago. Late. I couldn't sleep. I was out in my little workshop repairing some tools. It's about a hundred yards from the fence. That's when I heard a commotion outside. Around two in the morning. We've never had any problems around here, but, well, this sounded not good. I picked up an ax from my workbench and went outside. I could hear the sounds of someone running. And there were shouts and then I heard those dogs barking. They were in a frenzy, seemed like. I ran over toward the fence but stopped before I got there because I could see lights. They were wobbling around because the people holding them were running."

"Go on," said Kelly.

"I got scared, so I dropped to the ground, but I kept watching. It was a pretty full moon that night. And then out of the darkness this man jumps up on the inner fence and he's trying to climb to the top."

"What did he look like?" asked Decker.

"He had a beard, and his hair was all wild and thick like. Tall and he looked skinny, but he was climbing that fence for all he was worth."

"Clothing?"

"Like overalls and his feet were bare."

"What happened next?" asked Jamison.

"He was halfway to the top when a dog got to him. Jumped up and grabbed a hold of his pants leg. He was screaming."

"Could you understand anything he said?"

"No, I was too far away and it sounded like gibberish to me. I think he was crazy or on drugs or something. But I would've been doing the same thing if a dog had a hold of me like that. Then the men came running up and they called the dog off and pulled him down from the fence. He just gave up and went limp. A truck pulled up and they put him in that, and it drove off. Then the others left. By the time I got back to the house I was shaking like a leaf."

"He was," said Judith. "I made him some tea to help him calm down. That's when he told me what happened."

Decker eyed Kelly, who looked both concerned and confused.

"Did you tell anybody else about this?" asked Jamison.

"No," said Robert. "Look, it's the government. I don't want to get mixed up in any of that. I'm just a farmer. We want to be left alone, that's all."

Judith said excitedly, "Do you think this has anything to do with Ms. Cramer and Pammie?"

"It might," said Kelly, while Decker sat back and stared at the ceiling, lost in thought.

Jamison said, "Did you know Pamela and Irene Cramer?"

Judith nodded. "I knew Pammie pretty well. She didn't like it here. Our son is only one, so he's not in school, but I helped out Ms. Cramer some in the schoolroom. I helped the last teacher we had, too."

"Did Cramer ever say anything to you that seemed odd? Did she mention the Air Force facility?"

"No, never." Judith paused. "She did ask me where in the Colony I lived."

"And you told her?" said Jamison.

"Yes. It was funny, though."

"What was?" Jamison said quickly.

"Well, we practice communal living here. And with a lot of Anabaptist colonies, everyone usually lives in little houses next to each other or attached. I know this because my second cousin is a Hutterite, lives in North Dakota, too, only not near here."

Decker was now eyeing her steadily. "And your point?" he said.

"Well, here there's enough land for all of us to have our own place, and we each grow some of our own crops. We contribute most of it to the Colony, but we get to keep some for our own use. And folks can grow different things that they might like, that the Colony doesn't grow collectively."

"And your point?" Decker said again.

"I told Ms. Cramer about that. And it was just funny what she said. She said to maybe not do that. To maybe not grow our own food."

"Why would she say that?" asked Jamison, glancing at Decker.

"I don't know. She never said."

Decker said urgently, "Where did she teach class here?"

"In the little schoolhouse next to the building where we have the egg production," said Robert.

"Did she have an office there?"

Judith nodded. "In a room in the back."

Decker rose. "Can you show us? Now?"

37

Doris, the Colony teacher, answered their knock. She was in her fifties and dressed like the other women at the Colony but with a different color and pattern for her skirt and scarf. Behind her they could see students ranging in age from six to teens, sitting in separate clusters in the middle of the large room. They all looked at the visitors with both interest and puzzlement.

After Judith introduced Kelly, Decker, and Jamison, Doris explained she was filling in for Cramer.

"It was so terrible about Irene," she said in a low voice.

"Yeah," said Decker distractedly. "Look, we need to see Cramer's office."

"Oh, all right. It's this way."

She led them past the students. Several of the younger boys looked up at the giant Decker in awe, while several of the teenaged boys watched the pretty Jamison every step of the way.

Doris opened the door to a small room and ushered them in.

It was ten-by-ten with one window. A small desk sat in the middle of the room with a straight-back chair slid into the kneehole. Two metal file cabinets were set against one wall.

On the desk was an ink blotter, a Rolodex, a stack of books, and what looked to be some student journals.

Doris and Judith left them there to look around.

"What are we looking for?" asked Kelly.

"Anything that will help us," replied Decker.

"Well, that's kind of vague."

"Decker thinks that Cramer's murder might be tied to something in her past. Before she came here." Jamison glanced at Decker. "Old sins cast long shadows, or something to that effect."

Kelly looked intrigued by that. "So, before she came here, then? Which is maybe why the Feds are interested?"

Decker nodded. "Yes. I think finding out the reason she came here in the first place will go a long way toward helping find who killed her."

"So are you thinking her murder had something to do with her past?"

"It's certainly possible," noted Jamison.

"Works for me." Kelly slid open the desk drawers and looked through them, even checking underneath each one. Jamison started going through the books and journals, while Decker popped open one of the file cabinet drawers and began searching.

"Nothing here," said Kelly, a while later.

"Same here," said Jamison as she put down the last journal, while Decker was still poring through the file cabinets.

Jamison sat down at the desk and pulled the Rolodex toward her.

"Funny thing to have these days, especially for a young person."

Decker looked up from the cabinet drawer. "Anything in there?"

Jamison flipped through some of the cards starting with the letter A. "They look to be all empty," she said. "Why have an empty Rolodex on your desk?"

Decker walked over, took it from her, and started going through each card. Finally, near the end he pulled one out that had some writing on it.

"What letter was that under?" asked Kelly.

Decker said, "I think Cramer was trying to be cute. It was under X, as in 'X marks the spot.' And I guess she was counting on the fact that almost no one would search every card."

"Well, she didn't *count* on you," quipped Jamison.

"What does it say?" asked Kelly.

Decker read off the card. "Lesson Plan C dated December 15th of last year."

"Any idea what that might mean?" asked Jamison.

In answer, Decker raced back over to the file cabinet, quickly searched through the material there, and pulled out a scheduling binder. He flipped it open to December.

"Okay, on December fifteenth, she's written the name 'Bud,' Green Hills Nursing Home, Williston, North Dakota." He looked up. "And there's an address and phone number."

"Why would she have that written down in a lesson plan?" asked Kelly.

"Well, considering the subterfuge with the Rolodex, she probably didn't want it listed on her phone but still wanted it around to refer to."

"Williston isn't that far from here," said Kelly. "You want to go check it out?"

"Yes, but call first and see if they have anyone named Bud there."

Kelly took out his phone, looked at the number on the page, and made the call.

He spoke into the phone for a bit and then waited for about a minute. "They're checking," he said. Someone came back on the line and he listened for a few moments. He clicked off and looked at them. "They don't have anyone named Bud living there. Nor anyone who lived there recently with that name."

"It might be a nickname," said Jamison.

"Which means we need to take a trip to Williston," said Decker.

They left and climbed into the SUV.

"You think this might finally be a break?" said Kelly.

"From your lips to God's ear," replied Decker.

"I'll take a little divine intervention about now," chimed in Jamison.

"Looks like a nice enough place," said Jamison as a little over an hour later she steered the SUV into the parking lot of the Green Hills Nursing Home.

They climbed out and went inside. At the front desk was a young woman dressed in blue scrubs.

"May I help you?"

Kelly showed his credentials, as did Decker and Jamison. That got them referred to the supervisor on duty, a woman in her fifties with short, white hair, a portly frame, and a disagreeable look on her face.

"I spoke to you earlier," she said to Kelly when he explained what they wanted. "We don't have anyone here named Bud."

"That's probably a nickname," said Kelly.

"So what's his full name?" she said.

"Well, if we knew that, I would have given it to you already."

"Did you ever have an Irene Cramer work here?" asked Decker.

"Cramer? Irene Cramer, no I don't believe so. Look, what is this all about?"

Kelly took out a copy of Cramer's driver's license and showed it to the woman. "This is Irene Cramer."

The woman put on a pair of glasses and looked closely at the photo. "Why, that's Mary Rice. At least that was her name when she worked here."

"When was that?" asked Decker.

"Come to my office."

They followed her down the hall to a small, windowless room with drab furniture. She sat down at her desk and logged on to her desktop computer.

"Her last paycheck was issued about fourteen months ago."

"What did she do here?" asked Jamison.

"She worked with our residents. She did physical therapy with them."

"And she was certified to do that?" asked Decker.

"Yes, she had all the proper paperwork."

"And you checked on all that, her references and all?"

"Yes, that's our proper procedure. Everything was aboveboard."

"Can we get copies of all that?" asked Kelly.

"Not without a warrant. I'm not looking to bring a lawsuit down on this place. Now, I don't know what she's involved in, but if Mary were to find out—"

"Mary is dead," said Decker. "So she won't be doing any suing."

"Dead!"

"She was murdered. Which is the reason we're here."

"Oh my God."

"And you're sure you don't have anyone here named Bud?" said Jamison.

"Quite sure. I know all the residents. There's no one here with that name or nickname."

Decker interjected, "But what about with those *initials*, B-U-D?"

The woman started to peck on the computer keyboard. A few minutes passed as she scrolled through some screens. Then she stopped and smiled. "It's Brad. Bradley Unger Daniels. That's B-U-D, right?"

"Yes it is," said Decker.

38

"Mary?" said Brad Daniels. He was old and shrunken and seated in a wheelchair in the tiny, antiseptic room he would call home for the remainder of his life.

Decker, Jamison, and Kelly were seated across from him, pretty much filling up the small space.

Jamison nodded. "Yes, Mary Rice. She worked here a little over a year ago as a physical therapist."

Daniels's arthritic fingers clutched the head of his cane. "Mary, okay, yeah. I knew her."

They had been told that Daniels was in his nineties and had been at the facility for ten years. His wife was dead; he had outlived his siblings and even both his children. His grandchildren lived out of state and came once a year at Christmas to visit him.

Kelly had tried to show him the picture of Cramer but Daniels shook his head. "Can't really see no more."

Decker looked around the room. Next to the bed on a small shelf were some pictures of little kids, and what looked to be birthday cards. On the nightstand was a ballcap. It was one worn by people who had served in World War II and denoted their branch of service.

"You were in the Air Force in World War II?" said Decker, glancing at the hat.

"Called it the Army Air Forces back then," said Daniels, smiling feebly. "Was the Army Air Corps before that. Didn't come to be the U.S. Air Force till later."

"Were you a pilot?" asked Jamison.

"No. A navigator." He perked up. "Flew on the B-17, -24, and the big boy, the B-29 Superfortress. Boy, those were some exciting times."

"Navigator, huh?" said Kelly.

Daniels slowly nodded. "Always liked that stuff. Signals, radio waves. Radar, which was new back then. Got us where we were going and then got us back. Did a lot of bombing runs. Thought I was gonna die every time. Never managed to." He chuckled softly.

"What'd you do after the war? Did you leave the service?" asked Decker.

"No, I stuck around and worked for the government."

"What did you do?" asked Jamison.

Now the man's weakened eyes narrowed. "Why do you want to know?" he said, his tone suddenly sharp.

Decker squatted down in front of the man. "Did

you talk to Mary about some of the things you'd done?"

"You haven't answered my question yet, so why should I answer yours?"

"You liked Mary?"

"She was a nice gal. Patient. Pushed me to do my therapy, but she did it in a way that wasn't too overbearing like some of them can be here. I liked her. Too bad when she left. Where'd she get to?"

"Would it surprise you to learn that she moved to London, North Dakota?"

The old man flinched. "London?"

"Yes. It's where the Douglas S. George Defense Complex is located."

"Well, I know that."

"Because you worked there? A long time ago?" said Decker.

"Maybe I did and maybe I didn't. But if I did, it's classified," said Daniels. He closed his eyes and gripped the head of his cane tighter.

"But you talked to Mary about it?"

"How do you know that?" said Daniels. "Did she say I did?"

"No. But why else would she have moved up there? I mean, otherwise it's a really big coincidence."

"I got nothing to say on the subject."

"Did you know that the Air Force sold most of the land around the radar facility?"

"Sold the land?" said Daniels sharply. "To who?"

"A religious organization called the Brothers. Ever heard of them?"

Daniels shook his head.

"And they in turn leased some of the land to frackers."

"Frackers?"

"Companies that drill down for oil and gas."

"They're drilling on that land?" asked Daniels.

"Yes." Decker glanced at Kelly and then Jamison. He turned back to Daniels. The old man was staring directly at him. "The thing is, we unfortunately can't talk to Mary."

"Don't know where she is, then?" Daniels said.

"No, we do."

"So what's the problem?"

"Someone murdered her."

The old man seized up. For a moment Decker thought he might be having a stroke.

"Get out of here," he suddenly roared, blinking away tears. "You just get out of here, right now. Leave me alone. Leave me the hell alone."

A uniformed nurse rushed into the room.

"Mr. Daniels?" she said frantically. "What's wrong?"

He pointed at the others. "These people are harassing me. I want them to leave."

The nurse looked sternly at the three.

Jamison held out her FBI badge and said, "We had

to ask him some difficult questions because of a police investigation."

"Oh, I see. But he's upset now. I . . . I think you should leave. He's not in the best of health."

Jamison tugged on Decker's arm. "I think you're right. We're going."

They left the room.

As they walked down the hall Decker said, "He knows. He told Cramer something that made her quit her job here, change her name, and move to London."

"We just don't know what," said Kelly.

"He worked at the Air Force station," said Jamison. "That has to be the connection. He said he was a navigator and was into radar and radio waves and all. That's what they do up in London."

"We need to find out when he was there, exactly," said Decker. "It's been around since the fifties, you said?"

"That's right," said Kelly. "I don't know the exact date when it opened."

"I can get Bogart to check on that," said Jamison.

Decker said, "And when we find out when he was there and what he was doing, we're going to come back here and have it out with that guy."

"But he's a really old man, Decker," said Jamison.

"Yeah, I know. And right now, he's also the best shot we have to solve this case."

As they walked outside, Kelly said, "What the hell is going on here?"

"I don't know," said Decker. "But we're getting closer to them."

"Okay, but let's just hope they don't get us before we get them," said Jamison ominously.

39

"And Bogart said he was on it?" asked Decker.

He and Jamison were walking to a restaurant where they were having dinner with Baker and Caroline Dawson.

Decker had changed into another pair of pants, a clean white shirt, and his worn corduroy jacket with elbow patches, which constituted his most elegant set of clothes. The weather had changed; the temps had dipped into the sixties and the humidity had vanished.

Jamison had on a dark skirt that hit at her knee, ankle boots with zippers on the side and chunky heels, and a white blouse with a jean jacket over it.

"Yes. I talked to him just a bit ago. And since it has to do with the military he was going to call Harper Brown."

Harper Brown was with the DIA, or Defense Intelligence Agency, and she had worked with them on a previous case.

"Good. Anything on Cramer and why she's important to the Feds?"

"No. I asked him and he said he had come up empty. Boy, the wind really makes it chilly," said Jamison as she pulled her jean jacket tighter.

"Two days ago you were complaining about the heat."

"As I recall, it wasn't just me complaining."

As they drew closer to the restaurant, Decker said, "So dinner tonight. What am I supposed to do?"

She looked at him, not in surprise, because she had more or less expected this query.

"Well, first of all try to enjoy yourself. It's been an intense few days, and even you need to recharge your batteries. Next, be supportive of Stan and Caroline. Don't go in there thinking that she's trying to replace your sister."

"And if I say something stupid?"

"Just think about what you're going to say *before* you say it."

"Easy for you to *say*," muttered Decker.

An etched bronze sign next to the front door of the restaurant read MADDIE'S. "That's her mother's name," said Jamison.

"No coincidence there, obviously," replied Decker.

Maddie's was on the first floor of a restored brick building with a pair of flickering gas lanterns on either side of the polished wood door.

Jamison glanced at the fiery lanterns and quipped, "Great, more methane."

Dawson and Baker were at the bar having a drink.

Baker was dressed like Decker: khakis, white shirt, and a jacket that had seen better days. Dawson was glammed up in a turquoise dress with a leather belt, black tights, and low heels. Her hair was down around her shoulders. They moved over to their table and sat down.

Jamison looked around at the interior space that appeared both brand-new and very old but was fleshed out with thought and in spots even artistry. "Wow, this is really beautiful. Didn't expect to see something like this here." She shot Dawson an embarrassed glance. "I didn't mean it that way, sorry."

Decker gave her a funny look, leaned over, and whispered, "Think before you say something."

Dawson smiled in understanding at Jamison's remark. "No, I get that. This is actually my baby."

"What?" exclaimed Jamison.

Baker grinned and said, "She runs the whole place, not her dad."

"We spoke to your father," said Decker.

"Why did you need to talk to him?"

"Just routine questioning."

"So this is really your restaurant?" said Jamison, deftly changing the subject.

"My dad technically owns it but I worked out the financials, did the planning, the build-out, the hiring, everything from the utensil choices to the drapes to the types of gin in the bar. The place has a website and a social media platform, and we also cater and do special events."

Jamison stared around the crowded space. "Well, if this is any indication, you've got a real winner."

"We're booked up for the next three months, in fact. It's pretty much the only fine dining choice in town. I got the chef from Napa Valley."

Baker added with a chuckle, "We only got a table tonight because she owns the place."

She laughed and gripped his big hand. "Thing is, my dad thought I was crazy. He said don't try to make this town into something it's not."

"Meaning?" said Decker.

"My father will always see London as a one-horse place that will never rise above that status. Even with all the wealth being generated by the fracking. But I see things differently. I think we're past the boom and bust cycles. People aren't just coming here to work and get rich and then get out. They're coming to stay. I know the weather can be a real challenge, but it is in lots of places. And warmer spots are a short flight away. The point is, if you have nice things here people will want to stay and put down roots. And North Dakotans are nice people. Salt-of-the-earth types."

"I'm a Midwesterner," said Decker. "So I agree with that."

"And with the money that's here now, people can

both afford and appreciate the amenities and service like I've tried to offer here."

"I think it's terrific," said Jamison.

Baker raised his glass. "To terrific things." He nodded at Dawson. "And terrific people."

After they ordered their dinners Dawson asked about the investigation. "I heard there was another murder and that Hal Parker went missing."

"That's right. Pamela Ames. She used to live at the Brothers' Colony," said Jamison.

"But why would someone have wanted to kill her?" asked Baker.

"Could be wrong place, wrong time, if Parker was the target."

"But why would *he* be a target?" asked Dawson.

Decker said, "Did either of you know Pamela Ames?"

Baker shook his head, but Dawson said, "I worked with Milton Ames on some business matters. I knew Pamela was his daughter, but I wasn't friends with her."

"But why was Ames at Hal Parker's in the first place?" asked Baker.

"They might have known each other," said Jamison vaguely, shooting a glance at Decker. Shifting gears, she said to Dawson, "We went to see your father at his home. It's beautiful."

"After Mom died, we both needed something to occupy our minds. Since we weren't moving to

France without her, I decided building a new home for Dad would be a good thing. Give him something to focus on. He loves getting into the details. He just finished it. Took nearly two years with crews working around the clock."

"And how did you cope?" asked Decker.

She smiled sadly. "I buried myself in work, too."

"Your mother died in a blizzard, I understand," said Decker.

Dawson nodded and rubbed at a ring on her pinky. "From carbon monoxide poisoning in her car," she said in a low, halting voice.

"What was she doing out in a blizzard in the first place?" asked Decker.

"Alice Pritchard, an elderly neighbor, had called. Her power was out and she was in trouble. She had health problems."

"Why didn't she just call 911?" asked Decker.

"My mom would have gotten there faster than the 911 folks. And we had a backup generator, so Alice would have been fine at our house. It had happened before, and each time Alice would call us."

"But your mother never made it to Alice's?" said Decker.

"No, and Alice died, too."

"My God," said Jamison.

Decker said, "If the neighbor died, how'd you know she had called your mom and that was the reason she was out in the blizzard?"

"My mom had texted me when Alice called. But with the time difference I didn't see the text until the following morning. The first I knew about it was when they found her in the car after the blizzard had passed."

"I'm very sorry," said Jamison as Baker tenderly patted Dawson's shoulder.

There was a moment of silence until Decker said awkwardly, "Um, your dad said you'll be running the world before long."

Jamison eyed Decker nervously, but before she could say anything, Baker chimed in. "Daddy's perfect little girl."

Decker noted that Dawson did not seem happy about this remark. "And we understand you had a brother?" he asked, drawing another stern look from Jamison.

She said, "I'm sure Caroline would rather talk about something else."

Dawson coughed and took a drink of her water. "No, it's okay. Yes, my brother, Hugh. We called him Junior. He . . . died."

Decker said, "Joe Kelly told us he and your father didn't see eye to eye on things. But he wouldn't elaborate."

Dawson gazed at Decker with an intensity that made him feel uncomfortable. "Good old Joe. He does like to keep things close to the vest."

"Was that wrong of him?" asked Jamison.

"No, I suppose he was just trying to shield the family from undue attention. Joe's always been loyal that way. The fact is, my brother was gay and my father had a big problem with that. He cut him out of the will, out of the business, out of his life. In the end, Junior couldn't live with it, I guess. So he decided to end his life. He took a bunch of pills. I was the one who found him." She dabbed at her eyes with her napkin.

"Damn, Caroline, I had no idea," said Baker.

"No reason you should have known. I cared deeply for my brother. We were very close."

"That . . . that must've made things difficult between you and your father," said Decker.

"We didn't speak for about a year after Junior died. But then we lost Mom, and . . . and we decided as the only family left we needed to seek a truce. So we did."

"Do you think the truce will hold?" asked Decker.

She tapped her ring against the wood, as though for luck. "I don't think I have a choice," she replied.

Decker said, "Well, like Stan said, I think your father does see you as his perfect little girl."

Dawson said firmly, "I don't think there's any such thing."

40

When Decker and Jamison returned to the hotel, they found someone waiting for them.

Shane McClellan rose from a seat in the lobby and came over to them. He was dressed in jeans and an untucked gray shirt. His hair was slicked back and he had a few days' worth of stubble on his face.

He gazed anxiously from one to the other. "Hal Parker?" he began.

"What about him?" said Decker.

"Heard somebody took him and left a gal dead in his shed."

"What's it to you?" asked Decker.

"Hal was one of my best buddies. We would go hunting all the time."

"We actually saw a picture of you with him at his house on one of those hunting trips," said Jamison.

"Do you know what happened to him?"

Decker said, "We're working on it. Mind if we ask you some questions now that we know you two were friends?"

"Sure, whatever I can do to help."

Decker led them over to a seating area next to the lobby. When they were settled in he said, "When was the last time you saw him?"

"Two days after he found that woman's body. I went out to his place to pick up some stuff and he told me about it. It shook him up bad."

"Did he tell you about the wolf he was tracking?"

"Yeah. He was hunting it when he found the lady."

"Did Parker know a woman named Pamela Ames?"

Shane's brow furrowed. "No, not that I know of. Is she the gal they found dead there?"

"She was. Now, what we found *might* point to Ames having been there for paid sex. Knowing Parker, do you think that's plausible?"

"Hal? A hooker? No way. Why the hell would you even think that?"

"We found some evidence that suggests it might have been the case," said Decker vaguely.

Shane folded his arms over his chest and looked at them stubbornly. "Well, I'll never believe that. Hal liked to hunt and fish and drink his beer. And that was about it."

"When you saw Hal, was he worried about anything?"

"Not that he mentioned. He was upset about the lady and all, but that was it. We were planning on doing some hunting soon. He was excited about that."

"I'm surprised you have time considering all the things you're doing with your father," interjected Jamison. "He seems to keep you pretty busy."

"He'd keep me busy every minute of the day if I let him, but I got a secret weapon."

"What's that?" asked Jamison.

"I don't give a shit about what he really cares about, which is making money from pulling oil out of the dirt."

"You have a farm?" said Decker. "Near the Air Force station?"

"That's right."

"You know the Brothers?"

"Yeah, good folks."

"You go out there at all?"

"Sure. They do metal fabrication. We use some of what they make in our fracking operations. Plus they have a lot of trucks, and we pay them to haul stuff for us."

"Did you know Irene Cramer?"

"No, I didn't."

Jamison said, "Are you and Caroline friends?"

"We grew up together, me, her, and Joe Kelly. Went to high school together. We were sort of insep-arable back then."

"Right, Kelly told us some of that."

"Joe and I were on the football team. He was the starting QB and I was his best receiver." A grin slowly spread over Shane's features. "I caught forty-five touchdown passes from him over two seasons and we won the state title both years. And not to sound boastful or anything, but we were really popular in high school. Best times of my life. Got up every day with a smile."

"And now?" said Jamison.

"Now we don't see each other much. Caroline's busy with running all her dad's stuff. And Joe being a cop, he doesn't keep regular hours." He added wistfully, "Sort of miss those days. Long gone now."

"But you like Caroline?" said Jamison.

He looked down. "Hell, everybody likes Caroline. Used to have these fantasies that we got hitched and had a bunch of kids." He paused. "She and Joe even dated in high school. Thought for a while that they were going to get married." He grinned weakly. "Only thing I ever hated about the guy. Caroline seemed to like him more than me." He paused. "Me and Joe used to be best friends, together all the time."

"What happened?" asked Jamison.

"Life . . . life happened," said Shane sadly. "We're still buds. Just not like before. Nothing's like it was before," he added wistfully.

"That tends to be the case with everybody," opined Decker.

"We just came from dinner with Caroline," said Jamison.

"Is that right? At her newfangled place?"

"Yes, Maddie's, named after her mom."

269

"Damn shame what happened to her."

"Yes, it was a real tragedy," noted Jamison.

"So Joe became a cop, Caroline went to college, and you joined the Army," said Decker.

"That's right."

"How long were you in?"

"Long enough to do and see things I'll remember till the day I die," Shane said sharply. "Don't get me wrong. I was proud to do my duty, but I was glad to put it behind me. I had buddies who died or lost limbs. After that, I came back here."

"You ever see any strange activity over at the Air Force complex?"

"Strange?"

"Just anything out of the ordinary."

"Not really. They got a lot of security over there. Locals call the radar over there the eye in the sky. Used to look for nukes, so I heard. Thing's been there since before my dad was born."

"You ever been over there?"

"Nope. Why all the questions about them?"

"Just routine."

"So what can I do to help find Hal?"

"You've helped us by telling us what you did."

"So that's it? Nothing more I can do?"

"Not unless you have any information about who might have killed Irene Cramer and Pamela Ames."

Shane shook his head. "I guess I can see why not a damn thing gets done in DC."

Jamison said, "We're working hard on this, Shane. But it's not easy."

"Yeah, okay, I guess," he said offhandedly. "Well, see you around."

He walked off.

Decker said. "He was pretty certain that Hal Parker would never hire a prostitute. But I think that—"

Decker had stopped so abruptly and looked so out of sorts that Jamison snapped, "Decker, what is it?"

"We've got to go." He turned and started hustling to the door.

"Go? Go where?"

He called over his shoulder, "To see a body."

41

The doors to the funeral home were locked, and Decker had to pound on the wood for a full thirty seconds until they saw someone cautiously approach the front entrance. It was a thin, young man dressed as a custodian and holding a mop.

"Yes?" he said from behind the door glass, his features anxious.

Jamison laid her federal badge against the glass and said, "FBI, open this door. Now!"

The man dropped his mop and nearly fell over. He fumbled with the door lock and then jumped back as Decker bulled past him.

"What's this all about?" cried out the man. "This . . . this is a funeral home, for Pete's sake. Show some respect. Hey, where are you going?"

Neither of them answered him.

Decker quickly led Jamison to the morgue room and opened the door. He looked at the wall of drawers where the bodies were kept until he saw the name "Ames" on a notecard taped to one of them. He opened the door and slid out the gurney. Decker lifted off the sheet, revealing the naked body of Pamela Ames.

"What are we looking for, Decker?" said Jamison anxiously.

"Where do you think her clothes are?" he said distractedly.

"I would imagine back at the police station in the evidence locker. I know that Kelly collected them for analysis."

"Call Kelly up and tell him to bring all that over here."

"Okay, but I'd like to tell him a reason."

"Tell him that Ames and not Parker may have been the real target."

Jamison had worked with Decker long enough not to question a statement like that. She went off to a corner to make the call.

Decker looked over the body and then glanced around and spotted a file folder on another table. He picked it up and leafed through it, quickly finding that it contained Walt Southern's preliminary notes on the postmortem he'd performed on Ames.

He read through all the notes and then walked back to the body, carrying the folder with him.

Jamison joined him. "He's getting the clothes and heading over. He was at the station, so it won't be long."

Decker nodded absently as Jamison looked down at the body.

"So what did you mean by Ames being the target?"

"Look at the body, Alex. Lividity sets as quickly as thirty minutes after death, and then permanently after about two hours. Southern gave us that speech before with respect to Cramer's postmortem, not that we didn't already know that."

"Right, he did."

Decker pointed to the body's waist, chest, and thigh areas. "Once livor mortis is completed, and the blood settles, if the body comes into contact with a mechanical pressure of any kind, blood can't collect there and the skin remains pale. Now, we found Ames facing forward in a prone position over the handlebars of the ATV. After she died gravity would have forced the blood in *that* direction once her heart stopped. But even before lividity was fixed, the tight clothes she was wearing would act as multiple pressure cuffs. But do you see any paleness in those areas because the blood couldn't get there?"

"No, they're purplish and red." She glanced sharply up at him. "Which means she was killed and then, sometime later, she was dressed in the clothes she was found in. Did Southern note any of that in his report?"

"No, he didn't."

"Then Ames *wasn't* a hooker?"

"They tried to fool us by clothing her like that."

"How does that connect to Cramer?" asked Jamison.

"She certainly would have known Cramer from the Colony. What if when she left the Colony she went to Cramer for help? A place to stay, to get some money? And what if Cramer confided in her, something that disturbed Ames? Then Cramer ends up dead and is found by Parker. What would Ames have likely done in that situation?"

Understanding broke over Jamison's features. "You mean Ames might have gone out there to ask Parker about his finding the body? Maybe hoping he could tell her something that would help her figure out what had happened? Especially if, like you said, Cramer had already told Ames something disturbing."

"Only someone got wind of it and went there to stop it. And as we saw, they obviously succeeded." He glanced at the report again. "And you remember the bottle of wine and two glasses?"

"What about them?"

"Ames's stomach contents show no signs of any wine. So how could that be if she had been drinking wine with Parker?"

"So that was staged."

"It was *all* staged."

"But why kill her and take Parker?"

"To make us think exactly what we did. That *he* was the target and she wasn't. That she was wrong place, wrong time only. And they couldn't let Parker go after that. Not if he saw what they did to Ames."

Jamison let out a breath. "Damn. So where's Parker then?"

"I really wouldn't count on us ever finding him alive."

"God, Decker, this is really spiraling out of control."

"They're trying to tie up loose ends, Alex. But that cuts both ways. Every time they do stuff like this, they risk leaving something behind that will allow us to catch them."

"But how many more people have to die before we *do* catch them?"

Decker stared down at Ames's body and didn't answer, because he had no answer to give.

42

Kelly showed up with the clothes and lots of questions.

While Jamison filled him in on Decker's deductions, Decker took the clothes and laid them over Ames's body in the exact same manner in which she had worn them.

When Jamison was finished giving Kelly the rundown, Decker said, "Look at where the clothes drop on her."

They clustered around the body as Decker methodically pointed out the different strike points. "Here, here, and here. Lividity's fixed. There's no way the skin and blood pool presents like what we're seeing right now if she were wearing those clothes when she was killed. They were so tight they actually cut into her skin, there and there."

Kelly nodded enthusiastically. "She *was* dressed in something else, then they changed her into these clothes to make it look like the encounter was paid sex."

"Then they took her real clothes and deposited her in the shed on the ATV."

"And took Parker. You think he's dead?" asked Kelly.

Decker shrugged. "I wouldn't bet against it. Did Walt Southern have access to these clothes?"

"Of course. He had to examine them for trace and then for purposes of the postmortem. You know that."

"Yeah, *I* know that. I just wonder if he does."

Decker picked up the skirt and one of the shoes. He eyed the sizes on both and then eyeballed Ames's body. "Alex, help me out here. Would these sizes be right for someone like Ames?"

Jamison looked at the skirt and shoe sizes and then tried to put one of the shoes on Ames's foot. "This is two sizes too big. No way she's walking around in these. And I'd say the skirt and top are at least two sizes too *small*. I get that she might have wanted it tight, but not *that* tight."

"I thought that when I noted how deeply they had cut into her body," said Decker. "That would not have been too comfortable."

"They might have killed her before they even got to Parker's," suggested Jamison. "Then drove her out there and then dressed her."

"Which would explain the lividity being fixed and also the absence of blood on the ATV and in the shed. Whoever was behind this knew something about forensics—look at Cramer's postmortem—but not the finer points, like livor mortis."

"Are you folks going to make a habit of barging in here at all hours?"

They turned to see Walt Southern standing at the door. His wife was beside him.

Decker turned to face them and said, "I take it the guy who let us in called you."

Southern entered the room and his wife followed. He saw the clothes draped over Ames's corpse.

"What's going on?" he asked. "Why are those things on the body?"

"Just verifying some details that *weren't* in your report," said Decker.

"You saying I missed something?"

"There was nothing in your report about the lividity presentation."

Southern came forward and picked up the report Decker had set on a table.

"I hadn't finished it yet."

"Regardless, it should have been in the preliminary report."

"Okay, what about the lividity?"

"It was off. She was killed earlier than you said, and then after lividity was set, she was dressed in those clothes and placed in the shed on the ATV."

"That's only speculation on your part."

"It's a conclusion based on the evidence."

Liz spoke up. "Anything else that struck you?"

"Well, if there is, there's no need for you to know," said Decker bluntly. "Your husband provides us information based on the forensics of the body. We don't keep him apprised of our investigation. Even if you trust the person doing the post." Decker fell silent and stared Southern down.

Southern dropped the file on the table and gazed pointedly at Decker. "I really don't like your attitude."

"I've never felt the need to be liked by anybody."

"We're all on the same team." This came from Liz Southern, who had advanced farther into the room and now stood, in solidarity it seemed, next to her husband.

"My confidence has been shaken in my 'team-mate.'" Decker moved closer to the couple and leaned down. "Maybe you can help me out on that."

"If you're accusing me of some sort of negligence—" began Southern in a loud voice.

"No, I'm not accusing you of negligence."

"Well, that's something."

"Because negligence implies a mistake was *unwittingly* made."

Liz Southern sucked in a breath while her husband glowered at Decker.

"What exactly are you saying, Decker?" asked Kelly.

"You want to tell us, *Walt*?" asked Decker. "I mean one big mistake, okay, that happens, if rarely. But two? Now that's what I call a pattern."

"I'm not going to stand around and listen to this

garbage," exclaimed Southern. "You can talk to my lawyer." But then he took a provocative step toward Decker, his face flushed and his features angry.

Kelly quickly stepped between the two men.

"Now, just hold on. This is getting way out of hand." He turned to Southern. "But, Walt, there are some weird things going on here. Now, I'm not directly accusing you—"

"Oh, shut the hell up," roared Southern. He turned and stalked out of the room.

All eyes turned to his wife, who looked wobbly on her feet.

"Liz?" said Kelly. "What is going on here?"

"Walt is upset, naturally." She flashed an angry look at Decker. "Who could blame him with all the foul things this big jerk is implying?"

"I'm *implying* nothing," said Decker. "I'm saying that your husband intentionally misstated the postmortem results in order to interfere with our investigation."

"That is a damnable lie."

"Who made him do it?" persisted Decker.

"I have no idea what you're talking about. My husband would never do such a thing."

They all jerked when they heard the shot, which was immediately followed by something hitting the floor.

They rushed out of the room, with Jamison in the lead.

Down the hall a door stood partially open. Jamison pushed it open all the way and hurried inside. Then she stopped as the others piled in behind her.

This was apparently Walt Southern's office, with diplomas and certificates on the wall. A desk was set by one wall. The high-back chair behind it had been pushed back against the wall.

Jamison, Kelly, and Decker peered around the corner of the desk. On the floor was Walt Southern. The gun he'd used to shoot himself in the mouth was on the carpet next to him.

"Walt!" shrieked Liz as she saw the body.

When she tried to push past them, Kelly held her back. "You can't Liz, this . . . this is a crime scene now, I'm sorry."

She punched and slapped at him until Kelly pinned her arms to her sides. She slumped against him, sobbing.

Decker looked first at Kelly and then at the dead man.

Well, I didn't see that one coming.

43

The room at the police station contained three people but was quiet other than the sounds of co-mingled breathing.

Decker, Jamison, and Kelly sat there staring at the scuffed linoleum-tile floor.

It was early in the morning, the dawn not yet broken, and Walt Southern's body was on a gurney in his funeral home. A stricken Liz Southern was at the home of friends. Another coroner from Williston was traveling to do the post, though everyone in the room knew the exact cause of the man's death.

He had scrawled a note, which they'd found on his desk: "I'm sorry for everything. I hate myself. I—"

He obviously had chosen not to finish it.

"So why?" asked Kelly. "Was he really compromised?"

Decker said, "Clearly somebody made him fudge the post results to throw us off. First, with Cramer having ingested something, and then with Ames's going out there to meet with Parker. It wasn't for sex, it was for information. They blackmailed Walt to leave out the parts of the autopsy that would have led us to know that."

"Do you think Walt really was *blackmailed*?" asked Kelly. "Maybe they just paid him off."

"People doing this sort of thing for cash don't usually blow their heads off when they're discovered. They try to cut a deal by ratting on whoever paid them. And despite what I told Southern, we had no direct proof that he did anything intentionally wrong. I just called him on it, and he reacted the way he did. It was clearly because of a guilty conscience. Just look at the suicide note. 'Sorry for everything'? 'I hate myself'?" He added, "But I didn't think he'd kill himself over it. I was clearly wrong about that."

"So what did he have a guilty conscience about?" asked Jamison.

"For that, we're going to have to talk to his wife," answered Decker.

Later that evening Liz Southern looked pale and worn as she sat up in the bed of a guest room in a house belonging to a close friend of hers. She cradled a large cup of tea, and her bloodshot eyes spoke of the misery she was enduring. She looked at Decker with an unfriendly gaze as he sat down next to the bed. Kelly and Jamison stood immediately behind him.

"You couldn't wait even one damn day?" she said harshly. "My husband killed himself!"

"If we could wait, we would. But we can't. So anything you can tell us will be much appreciated."

"I don't know why Walt did what he did."

Decker leaned forward in his chair. "Then let's work through it together. Starting with what he wrote in the note."

Southern closed her eyes and sighed.

"It's important, Liz," chimed in Kelly.

"I know that, Joe!" she snapped, her eyes now open and blazing at him.

Decker cleared his throat. "If Walt was forced to fudge the autopsy results for Cramer and Ames, we need to know how and by whom."

"I have no idea why he would do that. I still don't believe that he did intentionally mess up those reports. If it's anyone's fault he's dead, it's yours! You accused him of all those terrible things."

Decker sat back, not looking convinced. "If the guy was innocent of what I accused him, no way he's taking his own life. Before he walked out of the room he mentioned his lawyer. That's not a guy looking to off himself over what I said."

"Then why would he kill himself instead of calling his lawyer?" she shot back.

"I think he was just blustering, grasping at anything he could in the heat of the moment. I think as he walked to his office, reality set in. And that's when he made his decision."

"You really want me to provide dirt on my dead

husband? Is that what you're asking me to do?" she added shrilly.

"What I'm asking you to do is help us solve a series of murders. And whoever blackmailed your husband and drove him to kill himself deserves to be punished. We need your help to get to them."

"Well, if you hadn't accused him like you did—" she began.

"If I missed something like that, I'm in the wrong line of work," Decker interjected. "You know something of the forensic business. Do you think he could have really missed big items like that on two separate posts?"

Southern drew a deep breath and settled a shrewd gaze on him. "I think you're in the exact line of work you should be in, Agent Decker."

"Okay," he said expectantly.

Southern reached out and plunked a tissue from a box on the nightstand. She dabbed at her eyes and blew her nose before crumpling the tissue in her hand. "My husband was a good man."

"I'm not suggesting he was a bad guy," said Decker.

"But he had . . . issues."

"What sort of issues?"

The woman's eyes welled up with tears. "He . . . was into some things that others, particularly around here, might have found . . . troubling."

"What sort of things are we talking about?"

"Was it something criminal?" said Kelly.

"No, but it would have done a lot of damage to his reputation." She let out a long breath. "He was having an affair with the wife of a friend." She clutched the edge of the sheet, and her eyes filled with tears.

"How did you find out?" asked Kelly.

"Text messages. Something I saw on his computer. Late-night phone calls. And I had him followed."

"Did you . . . confront him about it?" asked Decker.

She grabbed another tissue and wiped her eyes. "Yes. At first, he denied everything. Said I was mistaken, said it was all a misunderstanding. But he finally admitted it. We talked about getting a divorce, but we hadn't gotten around to it yet."

"That must have put a strain on your marriage," said Jamison.

"I finally told myself to ignore it. He did what he wanted and so did I. We have no children. So I would get glammed up and go out and have some drinks, and if I didn't come back at night and I was in someone else's bed, so what?"

"That night I saw you at the bar?" said Decker.

"I left you to attend to just such an appointment," said Southern, avoiding their gazes.

Decker moved a bit closer to her. "So someone else might have found out about his affair. They might have sent him photos or other incriminating evidence and threatened him with exposure if he didn't do what they said."

"It's certainly possible."

Jamison said, "But people do have affairs. Would the threat of exposure be enough to make him alter postmortem reports? He had to know that whoever wanted him to do that might have had a hand in the murders."

"Walt was a very proud man. A very upstanding citizen of this town. I agree that it seems crazy that he would do the bidding of what could be a murderer in order to keep his reputation intact. But I also know that's what he did."

"Who was he having an affair with?" asked Kelly.

Southern shook her head. "No, I'm not going to tell you. It has nothing to do with the murders."

"You don't know that," said Kelly.

But Southern shook her head.

Decker took all this in and said, "Did he mention anything, even in passing, that might shed some light on who was making him do this?"

"I've been wracking my brain trying to think of just that," she said. "And I can't come up with anything."

She sank back against the pillow and closed her eyes.

44

Jamison and Decker dropped Kelly off at the police station and drove back to their hotel.

Along the way Jamison said, "We've got three people dead, two murdered and one suicide, including the coroner who did the post on the other two and screwed them both up because he was possibly being blackmailed for sexual indiscretions. And the guy who found the first body is missing and presumed dead. What a mess."

"And an old man in a nursing home who knows a lot but won't tell us anything," added Decker, gazing moodily out the window.

"I agree that Cramer came here possibly because of what Brad Daniels told her. But if he won't reveal to us what he might have told her, what do we do? We can't waterboard the guy."

"We can threaten him with obstruction and put him in prison," pointed out Decker.

"A ninety-something-year-old war veteran in a nursing home? Really? Do you see the FBI or a court doing that?"

The phone that Robie had left him started to vibrate.

He pulled it out of his pocket and hit the green button. "Yeah? Robie?"

Robie said, "Be at this address in a half hour." He gave the destination and clicked off.

Decker looked at Jamison, who said, "What?"

"Change of plan."

He punched the address into his phone, and they set off.

It was fifteen miles outside of town at what looked to be an abandoned apartment building.

"I guess this was a casualty of the last bust," said Jamison as she pulled their SUV to a stop in front of the structure and they climbed out. "So where's this Robie guy?"

Robie stepped out from the shadows of the front entrance and called out softly to them. "Follow me."

He led them down a covered walkway that led to the rear of the building.

He opened a door there and motioned them inside.

As she passed him Jamison said, "Nice to meet you, Robie."

He simply nodded.

Inside, Robie closed and locked the door and led them past an empty, stained pool and down an interior corridor, illuminating the way with a small tac light. He opened another interior door and motioned them in.

When he closed the door behind him, a small light came on in the room, brightening it, if feebly.

In a chair sat Blue Man, dressed in a regulation suit and tie that would have allowed him to blend in at most any event in Washington, DC, but made him stick out conspicuously in London, North Dakota.

"Mr. Decker, Agent Jamison, please sit," said Blue Man.

"Who the hell are you?" said Decker.

"A wise question. Your phone should be buzzing any moment, ah."

Decker lifted out his vibrating cell phone and hit the answer button.

"Ross? What's going—? What?" Decker glanced at Blue Man. "Yeah. We are. Okay. You're sure? Right. Thanks."

He clicked off and looked at Jamison. "Bogart says this guy is on the up-and-up, and we should listen to him."

Jamison nodded and noted that Robie stood with his back to the door they had come through. "I don't think we have a choice anyway," she said, studying Robie's granite expression.

Blue Man motioned to the two chairs in front of him. "Please."

They sat.

Blue Man said, "I understand there have been developments?"

"If you call the coroner on the case offing himself a development, then, yes, there have been developments," said Decker curtly.

"And the reason?" said Blue Man.

"His wife thought it possible that he was being blackmailed for sexual indiscretions," said Jamison.

"And you believe her?" said Blue Man.

"I don't believe anybody just because they tell me something," said Decker. "And I'm not sure if present company is excluded or not."

"I would have been disappointed had you answered otherwise," said Blue Man benignly. "Any other developments?"

"I've got somebody tracking down Ben Purdy. He has family in Montana."

"The 'ticking time bomb,' as you told my colleague?"

"Yes."

"Any thoughts on that?"

"Yeah, all of them apocalyptic." Decker paused and studied Blue Man. "And you're involved in this why? Because you don't strike me as the law enforcement type."

"I have no authority whatsoever to do anything in this country. Neither does Robie."

"Well, you've run right over that rule."

"That certainly is one interpretation. Anything else?"

"We think Pamela Ames was the target, not Hal Parker."

"Why?"

"They tried to make it seem that she was there servicing Parker as a hooker, but I believe that was fabricated."

"Why would they do that?" asked Robie.

"To explain away why Ames was at Parker's house. If it wasn't for sex, then why? She lived at the Colony. She would have known Irene Cramer. It's perfectly plausible that when Ames left the Colony she would reach out to Cramer for assistance. In fact, I think she did. And it might have been then that Cramer told Ames something that later made Ames suspicious. Whoever killed Cramer might be very worried that Ames knew something that could lead back to them. And it's also possible they might have had reason to get rid of Parker. It was a stroke of genius to get them both out of the way at the same time, and make it seem like Parker was the only target and Ames was in the wrong place at the wrong time."

"What would Parker have known that could hurt them?" asked Blue Man.

"He was a trained tracker. He found the body before the rains started. Now, the killer had to get the body out there. And it couldn't have been lying out there long at all because it hadn't been attacked by animals. So I doubt the killer carried her for miles to place her there. And the ground out there is relatively soft."

"So he would have left tracks," noted Robie.

"Yes. And if he did maybe Parker saw them."

"But why wouldn't he have told the police about that if he did?" wondered Jamison.

"Now that's an interesting question," said Decker. "Because it opens lots of possibilities."

"Interesting," said Blue Man. "Very interesting."

"Is this a two-way street?" asked Decker.

"Meaning?"

"What can you tell us?"

Blue Man nodded slowly and looked thoughtful. "I think some quid pro quo is in order. You ask why I'm involved, and, ultimately, why you and Agent Jamison are involved in this?" He paused. "Irene Cramer is the answer, of course."

"Or Mary Rice, as she was known at a nursing home in Williston," interjected Jamison.

Blue Man said, "Or Terry Ellison or Denise Finley. I could go on and on."

"Please do," encouraged Jamison.

"Irene Cramer was collateral damage in a disastrous mission undertaken decades ago by the U.S. government."

"How so?" asked Decker.

"Her mother was a Russian agent."

Jamison shot Decker a glance. "Sins of the parent, Decker, like you said."

"Oh, so you had figured that out?" said Blue Man.

"Only to that extent. So her mother was a spy and you caught her. How is that a disaster?"

"You didn't let me finish. Her mother was a Russian agent who we thought was still working against us. She was actually a double agent and was working on behalf of a sister agency of ours that had neglected to tell us of that arrangement."

"And the FBI's involvement? Because Cramer's fingerprints set off alarm bells all over Bureau Land."

"They were the agency tasked with bringing Cramer's mother in, since we have no authority to arrest anyone."

"What happened?" asked Jamison.

"Irene Cramer was only eight at the time. I won't tell you what their real names were. The point is the mission went sideways and her mother was . . . killed. And, unfortunately, Irene saw the whole, disturbing thing."

"And her mother was working for us?" said Jamison. "Risking her life?"

"What a clusterfuck," added Decker.

"Yes, it was. We could not let her daughter go back to Russia, of course. So, for all intents and purposes, we *adopted* her. Gave her a new identity. Paid for her education and living expenses. Gave her money when she needed it as she grew up."

"You were paying for her silence?" said Jamison harshly.

"In a way, yes, though who would have believed her? But the far more important thing was to keep her safe. The Russians have a long memory. And were they to find out about her mother spying on them, which we believe they actually did, Moscow would have no compunction about using the daughter as an example. She would have died a horrible death, I can assure you."

"Did you know she was applying for a teaching job here?" asked Jamison. "She told the Brothers that she went to Amherst. And she had a teaching certificate. They apparently didn't check up on that because they needed someone badly."

"Normally, if she needed a reference for some reason, the information she provided an employer would run through one of our departments, which would handle it."

"So you would give her a bogus reference?" said Decker incredulously.

"It's not like she ever applied to be a commercial airline pilot or heart surgeon. And as a matter of fact she *had* gone to college at Amherst, and she *did* have a teaching certificate under the name Irene Cramer."

Decker looked at Blue Man. "But you knew nothing about her applying for the job here?"

Blue Man shook his head and said, "About fourteen months ago, she disappeared off our radar completely. That had never happened before. We were concerned, of course."

"That's just about the time she stopped working at the nursing home," noted Jamison.

"So when her prints and the name hit the FBI database?" said Decker.

"We knew what had become of her. But we don't know who killed her."

"Or why she was here?" said Decker.

"Precisely."

"There's an old man at that nursing home named Brad Daniels who worked at the London Air Station decades ago. Irene, under the name Mary Rice, worked as a physical therapist and met Daniels that way."

"We actually knew about her job at the nursing home," said Blue Man. "We paid for PT training for her. I think she continually changed occupations just to make us do things for her. Provide her education and money."

"She must have hated you all very much," pointed out Jamison.

"No doubt she did, as I would have if the positions were reversed. But this elderly gentleman, Daniels? Explain, please."

Decker said, "We talked to him. He clammed up when we asked him about the work he'd done here. Said it was classified."

"And when Decker told him that Mary Rice had been murdered, he lost it. Screamed at us to get out."

"You think he told her something? That's why she came here?" This comment came from Robie.

Decker and Jamison both nodded. "That's right," she said.

"And perhaps he feels guilt for what happened to her," said Blue Man. "Which might have caused his anger."

Decker looked at Blue Man. "What do you know about the Douglas S. George Defense Complex?"

"The Air Force, in theory, runs it. But it is odd."

"What is?" asked Jamison.

"There's a similar facility on the other side of North Dakota. The one here was constructed in the fifties, the other one in the sixties. The latter only operated for a very short time before being decommissioned; its original mission had fallen into disfavor and its price tag became too costly. But it still tracks the skies with its PARCS radar array."

"Just like the one here?" said Jamison.

"Yes."

"So they're redundant?" noted Decker.

"Exactly."

"In addition to the ambulances and the men Robie saw being wheeled away, we talked to a farmer who lives right next to the facility." Decker went on to explain what Robert White had seen that night.

"That is quite disturbing," said Blue Man.

"But maybe enlightening, too?" suggested Decker.

"Illuminating, at the very least," replied Blue Man. "Robie?"

"Yes, sir?"

"We'll need to check that out. Now."

"Right." Robie left.

Blue Man looked back at Decker. "This is obviously far more than a murder investigation."

"I'm just a cop doing his job."

"I have no doubt that you will do your job, Mr. Decker. And your country needs you to."

"If this sucker is that critical, why don't you call in the big boys?"

Blue Man looked at him with calm resignation. "The problem is, Mr. Decker, I strongly suspect they're already here."

45

Decker and Jamison drove back to London. When they got there they passed by a sleek six-story apartment building that looked fairly new.

"Isn't that Hugh Dawson?" said Jamison.

The man was climbing out of a late-model black Range Rover.

"Yeah, it is."

"He's out late."

They watched as Dawson looked furtively around and then strode through the front door and into the building.

"Pull over," said Decker.

Jamison parked at the curb and they got out.

Jamison followed Decker into the building. There was a concierge desk, and they heard elevator doors closing as they approached it.

A young woman was at the desk, dressed in a trim dark blue uniform with a name tag that read SARAH. She said, "May I help you?"

Decker and Jamison approached the desk. Decker said, "Sarah, we work for Mr. Dawson. We know he was scheduled to be here. I think we might have just missed him." He patted his jacket pocket. "We have some papers he needed. He forgot them and called us to bring them to him.

"You *did* just miss him. He's already gone up in the elevator. I can take them up."

Decker frowned and shook his head. "I'm sure you're perfectly reliable. But Mr. Dawson is very particular. And these documents are confidential. If he knew I gave them to an unauthorized person I'd be out of a job."

The woman looked at Jamison.

"He's not kidding," said Jamison.

"Well, all right, I guess it's okay. He went up to number five-oh-three."

"Right. That's—" He looked helplessly at Jamison. "Crap, I forgot the guy's name." He glanced apologetically at the concierge. "Mr. Dawson does so many deals. It's hard to keep them all straight."

She smiled and said, "It's Mr. McClellan's apartment."

"Exactly. I knew that's who it had to be. Good old Stuart McClellan. Well, thanks."

They got on the elevator and took it up to the fifth floor.

"Dawson is meeting secretly with McClellan?" said Jamison.

"Not so secret if the concierge knows about it," replied Decker.

"What do you think is going on?"

"Those binders he had on his desk? He told us he was working on some big deal. Maybe that deal is with McClellan."

"But I thought they didn't get along."

"Lots of people who don't get along still do deals together."

"You think this has something to do with our investigation?"

"It's possible. People have been killed and abducted. Walt Southern was blackmailed. Parker was hired by Hugh Dawson. He and McClellan are the two wealthiest men around. It wouldn't be the first time murder has been tied to money."

They got off the elevator and walked down to number 503, where Decker knocked on the door.

They could hear footsteps coming and the door opened.

Stuart McClellan's tie was unknotted and the buttons of his vest were undone. He had on a pair of reading glasses that were perched halfway down his nose. He looked up at them in confusion.

"What the hell are you doing here? How did you even get up here?"

Before Decker could say anything Jamison stepped forward. "We're federal agents investigating a murder. Do you really think a concierge is going to keep us at bay?"

Decker glanced at Jamison with admiration. Next,

he peered over McClellan's head when he heard movement in the room. "We understand that you're not alone."

"What business is that of yours?" snarled McClellan.

"Can we come in?"

"No!" barked McClellan.

Jamison said, "Fine, we'll keep eyes on the place until we get a warrant issued."

"On what grounds?" snapped McClellan.

"On the grounds that you're harboring a witness who we need to speak to right now. Did you hear that, Mr. Dawson?" Jamison added in a raised voice.

Dawson came around a corner and stood behind McClellan. He looked both pissed off and weary at the same time.

"What do you need to speak to me about?" he said.

"Do you want to do this out in the hallway?" said Decker. "I would have thought you'd want some privacy."

McClellan glanced at Dawson, who shrugged.

The apartment was spacious and luxuriously furnished. Decker had noted, as they came down the hall, that they'd passed number 509 and had not seen another door until they came to 503. So McClellan had apparently cobbled together several units into one.

He looked around and said, "Nice place."

"Why are you here?" demanded McClellan. "We're busy."

"With what?" asked Decker.

"That is none of your business," retorted McClellan. "Federal agents or not," he added, looking spitefully at Jamison.

Decker eyed Dawson. "He was at your hotel that night. You're working on this big deal, you said. You told us that McClellan finally has his business model right, which means maybe no more booms and busts for him. And you've been acquiring property on the cheap. Now you're meeting secretly?"

Jamison said to Dawson, "You're selling out to McClellan, aren't you?"

Dawson eyed McClellan. "Guess the cat's out of the bag, Stu."

"We don't care what you're doing with McClellan," said Decker. "And this will go no further," he added when McClellan looked like he was about to erupt in anger.

Dawson slipped his hands into his pants' pockets. "Then what *do* you care about?"

"I've got two murders, one suicide, and a missing person."

"Suicide?" said McClellan.

"Walt Southern ate a bullet."

McClellan looked at him goggle-eyed. "Walt? Why?"

"We don't know yet. Maybe a guilty conscience. Did you know him well?"

"I knew him. But we weren't close or anything."

Decker eyed Dawson, who changed expression when he caught Decker's gaze. "Guilty conscience?" said Dawson. "What for?"

"Can you think of a reason?"

"No. And I didn't really know the man well enough to have knowledge of any demons that might have led to his killing himself."

"Surely he would have done your wife's funeral."

Dawson's eyes narrowed at this provocative statement. "So what if he did? That wouldn't make us best friends."

"So Walt Southern did the autopsy on her?"

"Yes. And it was confirmed that she died from carbon monoxide poisoning. And—" Dawson stopped and stared at Decker. "What are you implying?"

"I'm not implying anything. And what did Alice Pritchard die of?"

"Exposure. She apparently tried to make it to her car when Maddie didn't show up. They found her outside, frozen stiff."

"And the text your wife sent you?"

"I was in France with Caroline. We didn't see it until the following morning. By then, it was too late." He looked away.

Jamison said, "That's what Caroline told us."

"How is Liz Southern?" asked Dawson slowly.

"Shaken, distraught, as you would imagine," answered Jamison.

"You know her?" asked Decker.

"Walt moved here about twenty years ago and started his business. But Liz is from London. Our families knew each other. Her parents are dead now, and she and Walt live, well, now *she* lives in town. But she still has her parents' farmhouse about ten miles outside of town. And she and Caroline have become good friends over the years. Liz is older than Caroline, of course, doesn't have any siblings, and never had any children. I think she sees Caroline as a younger sister."

McClellan interjected, "So now can you get on with your investigation and leave us to our business?"

Decker eyed Dawson. "Caroline is very proud of her new restaurant. Does that get sold to this guy, too?"

McClellan said sharply, "This is *private* business."

"Again, an answer in itself."

Dawson said, "Don't worry. Caroline will be just fine."

"I wouldn't bet the farm on it," replied Decker.

46

Long-range night optics were Will Robie's best friend. He was lying prone, sighting through one of his favorite pieces of surveillance hardware. It didn't match the "eyesight" of the radar array facility he was watching currently, but it was more than good enough for his purposes.

He'd been here for an hour and during that time had barely moved. Being able to lie motionless and intensely focused on his target for inordinately long periods of time was Robie's bread and butter. Without it, he couldn't do his job.

Vector guards continued to make their rounds. A small jet had landed about an hour before. He couldn't see who had gotten off. Before that, two choppers had lifted off the ground and one had returned. A few vehicles had left the facility through the main gate but all had returned.

He watched another car head toward the front gate. He zeroed in on Colonel Mark Sumter as the driver. Robie had been briefed on him and seen multiple photos of the man. Sumter was alone in the vehicle, and he was not in uniform.

Where might the colonel be going at this late hour?

Robie collapsed the tripod holding his scope and sprinted to his electric scooter. He timed it so he would hit the road Sumter was on about ten seconds after the man passed that spot.

He pulled in behind Sumter with his lights off. He had slipped on a pair of night-vision goggles, enabling him to see clearly without exposing himself by using his headlight. Sumter drove straight down the road, not turning off at any intersection until he was about five miles from downtown London. Then he hung a left down a windy gravel road. In the distance, as he rounded a sharp curve, Robie could see a small house with a light on. There was a large tree out front.

Robie pulled off the road and set his scooter down on its side in some tall grass. He made the rest of his way to the house on foot. He performed a sweep of the property looking for sentries but saw none. He took up a surveillance position behind the tree, which was set about ten feet from the front door. There was no other vehicle in front of the house other than Sumter's car. A minute later Robie quietly made his way to the front window where the light was shining through.

The window was closed, but the curtains were not fully shut. Through a sliver of an opening, Robie could see the profile of a man. He was in his late sixties, jowly and gray haired, and dressed in a conservative dark suit with a blue-and-red unknotted tie.

Robie took the man's picture with a thumb-sized camera and next pulled from his pocket a device that looked like an extra-long pen with a wired earbud attached to one end. He pressed the other end, which had a small suction cup attached, against the glass and inserted the bud in his ear.

Voices filtered into his ear.

"The intrusion *is* concerning, Colonel," said the older man. "It's not something that was anticipated."

Robie next heard Sumter's response. "We don't know what they wanted. The SUV was untraceable. It's not just concerning. It's my ass on the line after all."

"Don't let your nerves run away with you. It'll be fine."

"Again, my ass *is* on the line."

"*All* of our asses are on the line. But what we're doing is for the greater good. You agree with that, don't you? National security and all?"

"Yes, otherwise I wouldn't be here."

"Then we just have to redouble our security efforts and keep our heads down. I can run interference for you in Washington. You have our full backing."

"And Vector?"

"They do their job and they do it well. Enough said."

"But what if someone's found who can, well, blow everything up?"

"It's true there is not complete alignment on this issue, but I think even if the American people found out they would not be troubled."

"Jesus, we can't go take a poll. This is all classified. Maybe the most classified thing I've ever been involved in."

"The same could be said for me, although I've been in this business far longer than you. Now, the FBI came to see you with questions?"

"I'm executive-lagging that. And in the end I won't get back to them. I'll blame it on DoD security protocols."

"I think that's wise. I can help with that as well. I have high-up contacts at the Bureau. Whatever got that tail wagging, I can put the kibosh on it."

"That would be greatly appreciated." Sumter paused. "You know we could have just spoken on the phone. These late-night meetings could raise suspicion."

"No, we could not talk on the phone, no matter how secure it might be. Emails, texts, phone calls, all of that can be captured and then used against someone. These meetings, face-to-face, no record exists." The man paused. "Except in the memories of each of us."

Sumter seemed to get the man's meaning. "I'm never going to talk to anyone about this."

The man nodded. "Everything else is fine? No concerns?"

"The ones I've already told you are concerns enough for me. But the rest of the operation is fine, yes."

"Good. Well, I will put my efforts into motion and you will do what I have advised. Until next week, then. I'll let you know where and when."

Robie retreated to about fifty yards from the house and watched as Sumter came out, climbed into his car, and drove off.

When the other man did not appear, Robie drew closer to the house and waited.

He did not have to wait long.

He fell back and hunched down as the sound of the chopper came closer. He saw the blinking lights from the belly of the aircraft. Next a searchlight flitted over the house and yard as Robie quickly lay flat in the high grass, facedown.

He only lifted his head when he could tell by the sounds of the engine reducing power and the *whump-whump* of the chopper's props lessening that the aircraft was landing.

The front door of the house opened up and the older gent came out, crossed the yard quickly, and climbed into a rear door of the chopper. It immediately lifted off, as Robie shot pictures of all of it.

A minute later he was back on his scooter flying down the road toward town. He wanted to report in with Blue Man.

It would prove to be far more difficult than he had thought.

47

"But does that have anything to do with our case?" asked Jamison as they sat in the hotel lobby late that night.

"It's not a crime for Hugh Dawson to sell out to Stuart McClellan," noted Decker. "But to answer your question, I don't know if there is a connection. Yet."

"Do you think McClellan is involved in this somehow?"

"If Irene Cramer knew something that was damaging to him, it's possible. I just don't know what that might be. But I think the military installation is a more promising suspect. I think that's why she came up here."

"There's clearly something going on over there," said Jamison. "From what Robie found out and our discussion with his boss."

"We need to talk to Brad Daniels again."

"And Robie's boss seems to think that something is off there. I mean, why have two redundant facilities in North Dakota?"

"So the one here has an ulterior purpose."

"The guy running away that Robert White saw?" said Decker.

"Yeah?"

"The guy was obviously trying to escape."

"So you think there's some sort of *prison* being operated over there?"

"Maybe."

"And the ambulances?"

"It seems to be the sort of prison where people suffer injury routinely enough to require medical attention off-site."

"But if they are operating a prison over there, where would they take the injured prisoners? I mean, if they're trying to keep it secret, they can't just drive them to the local hospital."

"They have a runway. They have choppers coming and going at odd hours."

Jamison looked at him in alarm. "You think they're flying these guys out?"

"And maybe they don't come back."

"Decker, all of that sounds really illegal. I mean, you can't hurt prisoners, fly them out, and then they disappear. They have rights."

"Maybe they're not ordinary prisoners, Alex."

She gaped at him. "Meaning what?"

"It's a military facility. Maybe they're military prisoners of a sort."

"But if they are military prisoners, they still have rights."

"Maybe they're not members of the military or even American citizens. Remember White said the guy was talking gibberish?"

"He said he thought the guy was nuts or maybe on drugs."

"Or maybe speaking a foreign language."

"Are you saying what I think you're saying?"

"Maybe they're running another Guantanamo up here in North Dakota."

Jamison slumped back in her seat. "Another Gitmo, here?"

"You wouldn't want to transfer a bunch of enemy combatants or terrorists to New York City or another really populated area. And if this facility is redundant, it would be the perfect place."

"Right. And then Vector is brought in to handle security."

Decker nodded. "They show up here and the Air Force people get kicked out, leaving Sumter as the sole remaining flag bearer to give it a modicum of respect. I think Vector was brought in to watch over the people they're keeping there. And maybe interrogating them to the point of their being injured."

"But that's not allowed anymore."

"Says who?" replied Decker sharply.

Jamison started to reply but then seemed to think better of it.

He eased forward in his chair. "It would also explain why Robie is on the scene."

"But they told us why. It was because of what happened to Irene Cramer's mother."

Decker shook his head. "Robie's boss struck me as one real heavyweight. And Robie, too. Maybe they're upset that Cramer got killed after what happened to her mother under their watch, but feeling guilty isn't a reason to bring those kind of assets up here. There's something else, another reason why they're here."

Jamison snapped her fingers. "Robie's boss said that some big players may already be on the scene here. And that clearly was a problem."

"If they're running a secret prison engaging in illegal interrogation, I think that would qualify as something people would kill to keep quiet about." He tapped his fingers against the arm of his chair. "The only problem is that theory doesn't square with why Cramer came here in the first place. Daniels told her something about that facility. But that was from a long time ago, long before Vector or any potential prisoners showed up there."

"So you mean there has to be something *else* going on? Namely, whatever Daniels told Cramer that compelled her to move here?"

Decker nodded. "But if Cramer came up here to find out something about that facility based on what Daniels told her, and then stumbled onto what they're doing *now*?"

"That's a motive to kill her. But why slice open her stomach and intestines?"

"Her mother was a spy. Maybe she taught her kid to swallow secrets, or she saw her mother do it before. The people who killed Cramer might have somehow known this and cut her open to get it back. Then they tried to hide that by performing a postmortem on her and also blackmailing Walt Southern."

"But why leave the body out there like that? I mean, they could have buried it somewhere. No one would have found her and we'd never have been called in."

"Well, one explanation is that they didn't know about her past. Local murder, local cops working on it, not the FBI. If it came out she was a prostitute the local cops would have chalked it up to that. And if they had blackmailed Southern to mess with the postmortems, the cops probably wouldn't have even focused on the stomach and intestines. I had to read that report three times to find a reference to it."

"I'm surprised he even referred to it at all."

"Guy was covering his ass in case this all came out. He could say, hey, it's right there, even if I didn't highlight it or take photos of that specific region. I checked for contraband and found none. And the livor mortis miscue? He could chalk that up to not being a full-time pathologist. No, he was hedging his bets all right."

"So they would have found her body, done the post, conducted the investigation, and come up with zip."

"Which is better for them than no one finding her, and the cops keep digging and maybe call in other resources to try to find her. The fact that she was a prostitute, or at least holding herself out as one, would make for an easy answer for the cops. It's a high-risk profession. Women like that get murdered all the time and their bodies get dumped. Cops poke around and then move on to the next case."

"That does make sense."

"Well, that's something, since nothing else in this damn case makes the least bit of sense," growled Decker.

48

Robie parked the scooter outside the same abandoned apartment building where he had taken Decker and Jamison to meet Blue Man. His boss wasn't here, but Robie had secure communications inside the building to contact him. And Robie had also made this derelict place his home base for now.

The sound reached his ears a few seconds before it would have been picked up by anyone not as well trained as he was.

Seconds of warning meant he got to live another day.

Maybe.

He immediately flitted for cover near the building's front doors and pulled his pistol. There were at least five men that he could see. Where they had come from he couldn't tell. Most likely they had already been here before he arrived. Which meant his hiding place had been compromised.

In the moonlight he could see that they wore light armor and carried automatic, combat-grade weaponry. They were advancing in a diamond-shaped attack pattern. There was no way he could fire at one without revealing his location. And his cover position could not withstand concentrated counterfire.

This dilemma presented a clear tactical first step. Since his current position was indefensible, he moved. He was through the front doors and up the stairs before any of them could gain a line of sight on him to fire. Any building that Will Robie had ever occupied had been thoroughly researched by him beforehand, and this one was no exception.

He turned left and sprinted down the hall that bisected the main floor. He reached the rear doors, knelt, and peered out. Tac lights and gun muzzles were coming his way. They were smart enough to have cut off his rear exit. This op had involved some planning. He heard the front doors opening. Robie hit the stairwell, running up three flights of stairs, popped through the door, and hustled down the hall to the last room on the left.

He unlocked the door and then bolted it behind him. He raced to the window even as he heard the reverberations of multiple feet pounding up the stairs. He never thought about calling anyone for help because there really wasn't anyone *to* call—and even if there were, they would never get here in time. Robie had to rely on himself, which was nothing new for him.

He opened the window and pulled out a coil of rope that he had earlier placed behind a piece of furniture. There was also a small duffel with some things that might prove helpful, along with his comm equipment. He slung the duffel over his shoulder and tied the rope to the railing that ran around the small balcony attached to the side of the building. He looked down and now saw no tac lights or other signs of someone being down there. They must have entered the building already.

In the distance he saw the blinking lights of an aircraft as it zipped across the clear sky. The flare lights of the oil fields burned far away, looking like clusters of shiny objects.

He slipped over the side of the balcony and, using his legs around the rope as stabilizers, he methodically made his way down. As soon as his feet touched dirt, he took out his weapon, screwed a suppressor can onto the muzzle, knelt down, took aim, and shot the man who had just come around the corner. The fellow dropped silently to the ground, but the sound of the suppressed round seemed to boom across the flat, dark land like cannon fire.

What was up was now coming down, as from inside the building Robie heard the sounds of feet charging down to the first floor. He sprinted to his left even as gunfire rained down on him from above. They also had the high ground now, which was the best ground to possess. Fired rounds careened off the stucco hide of the building, and shrapnel flew off like little whirlwinds of twisted metal. Robie felt one slice into his arm, but he never slowed until he reached the man he'd killed. In one smooth motion he jerked the man up and used him as a shield while he grabbed the loaded sub gun out of his hands along with three spare thirty-round mags from ammo sleeves in his pants. As rounds slammed into the dead man, Robie waited for a pause in the firing, then dropped the body and sprinted around the corner of the building.

Reaching the front, Robie threw himself forward in a prone position and opened fire right as the group of closely massed men erupted from the front entrance.

Because of the body armor they wore, he employed only head shots, and in short order had taken out all five who had burst into his range. Those not instantly dead moaned, cried, and cursed as Robie rose and sprinted toward his scooter.

He heard another sound that caused him to change direction and then dive down, right as the bullets zipped over him. He rolled right, took aim, and strafed the field in front of him with gunfire. This would give him a few precious seconds to assess the new threat.

It was coming from two directions, ninety and two-seventy on the compass.

Looked to be six men in each group, armed and armored.

Robie felt flattered they had sent basically a platoon to take him out.

He fired off the rest of his mag to keep his enemy at bay for another few seconds, and then slammed in his next-to-last sleeve of ammo.

His scooter was out of the question now. His adversaries owned that ground.

He couldn't run for it. They would cut him down in a matter of seconds. No help was coming, he was outnumbered ten to one, and he had two thirty-round mags and seven additional shots in his pistol. They probably had thousands of rounds to expend on him. So it was just a war of attrition now with only one clear outcome.

He thought of pulling out his phone and calling Decker, if for no other reason than to tell him what was happening and to take charge of his body. But he decided against that. That was a defeatist attitude, and that was not really in Robie's DNA.

He looked left and then right, searching for options as the group of men in front of him slowly moved forward. Just to show he wasn't to be toyed with, he focused on one man, leading the pack on the right. He watched the guy through the scope on his pistol and gauged his diversionary movements for about ten seconds. He discerned the pattern and took aim with his pistol, and when the man stepped to his right, it was the last step of his life.

As the man fell dead, Robie immediately rolled to

his left and kept going as rounds poured into the location he had just occupied, his shot having given it away.

Then the others ceased firing and hunkered down. Robie could imagine them using their comm packs to assess the situation and arrive at a solution to the little problem represented by him.

Robie didn't wait to confront the result of this discussion. He rolled to his left and kept rolling until he reached a planting bed that was full of dying flowers and small bushes. Tac lights were flying all over the ground as they searched for him from a safe distance, because there were limits to the accurate range of the sub gun. It was designed to be devastating in close-quarter battle, but it was for shit at long range.

He debated whether to use the tac beams as a convenient target to take out one or two of them. But doing so would only lead to overwhelming firepower directed at him. And he couldn't keep rolling out of danger. They would figure that out and send fields of fire in every direction he could possibly take. Then it became a numbers game, and one round would eventually find him.

He assessed the situation again. It was a shitshow, to be sure. But Robie had some more cards to play.

He opened the duffel and took out two metal fist-sized canisters and a pair of headphones with a built-in battery. He put on the headphones and powered them up. He punched an engagement switch on each of the metal canisters, tossed one and then the other.

They hit the dirt about two feet from his adversaries.

The blinding flash of light was followed by an avalanche of sound, and, far more lethally, sheets of packed shrapnel traveling at speeds no person could dodge.

Two seconds later, Robie got up and fired through the smoke, emptying his mag. Then he ran to his left toward the road using an evasive zigzag movement.

He heard shots fired in his direction, but none hit their target.

When he looked back, the smoke had cleared, and he was dismayed to see that six men were barreling toward him. They must have anticipated his tactic and had kept low enough to let the shrapnel sail harmlessly over them. He turned and fired his last mag at them. Two went down, but the other four returned fire and kept charging.

Okay, the shitshow was turning into maybe his last stand.

He dropped the empty sub gun, pulled his pistol, knelt down, and took aim. He might very well get two of them before the other two got him. At this precise moment in time that might be as near to perfection as was possible.

He sighted through the scope on his Picatinny rail,

as they were no doubt doing with him. He prepared himself mentally for the impact of the rounds that would end his life.

Okay, Robie, it's been a good run, but all good runs have to come to an end.

The next instant one man dropped, then a second.

Then a third. They were all head shots, and bits of skull, flesh, and eruptions of blood covered the ground around the men as they went down.

The shots were so rapid and so precise that they almost seemed to blend together into one round fired.

The thing was, Robie had not pulled the trigger on his weapon.

As the last man stopped and gazed around, wondering where the hell the shots were coming from, the next round pierced his skull and blew out the back of his head.

He fell to the North Dakota soil without any last words.

Robie rose from the ground and looked around, his pistol at the ready. Just because someone had taken out his enemies didn't mean they were necessarily his ally.

He whirled when he heard the sounds of methodical footsteps coming across the road. He pointed his gun at the interloper.

When the person came close enough for him to

see, Robie was stunned for one of the very few times in his life. He lowered his weapon.

"What the hell are you doing here?"

Dressed all in black, Jessica Reel lowered her customized sniper rifle with her favorite scope attached. She looked him up and down, then surveyed the field of carnage behind them.

Gazing back at him she said, "What else? Saving your ass."

49

"I want to know what the hell is going on," exclaimed Joe Kelly.

It was the next day, and he was standing next to Decker and Jamison, as they surveyed the grounds in front of the abandoned apartment building. It was strewn with dead bodies with sheets over them. Hundreds of yellow markers, denoting found shell casings and bullets, covered the ground.

"Looks like quite a gun battle went on," observed Decker slowly.

"That I can see," barked Kelly. "What I want to know is why."

"How should we know?" replied Decker calmly.

"Nothing like this ever happened before you guys showed up," replied Kelly testily.

"Doesn't mean it's cause and effect," pointed out Decker.

"Have you identified any of the bodies?" asked Jamison.

"None have ID or any other traceable items. And

they don't look American to me, at least most of them don't."

Decker glanced at Jamison and said to Kelly, "Do you have photos of the dead?"

"Yeah, why?"

"I'd like to see them. Something might pop."

Kelly looked at him warily and then said, "I'll get them. Don't go away."

As soon as he moved off, Jamison said, "This is the building where Robie brought us to meet his boss."

"I'm well aware of that."

"Do you think Robie——?"

"That's why I want to see the photos."

Jamison gazed around. "It looks like a war zone."

Decker nodded. "Kelly and his team have searched the building and it's empty, but there are signs out back of another gunfight and a rope dangling from a balcony."

"Have you tried to call Robie on that phone he left you?"

"To tell the truth, I'm afraid to try."

"You'll know soon enough. Here comes Kelly."

Kelly rejoined them and handed over an iPad on which were loaded photos of all the dead men. It took about a minute to go through them. Decker and Jamison exchanged a relieved glance when they saw that Robie was not among the pictures.

"I don't recognize any of these guys, but like you

said, most of them seem foreign. Eastern Europe, the Middle East. A couple of Asians."

Kelly took the iPad back. "It's a hodgepodge all right."

"Have you spoken with Mark Sumter?" asked Decker.

"Sumter, why?"

"Well, he heads up the military presence here. This might be something the Pentagon wants to know about."

"Okay. But it's not like the people under Sumter came here and had a pitched battle and left all these dead guys."

"Well, you won't know for sure till you ask him," retorted Decker. "The government likes its secrets."

Kelly shook his head. "It'll take us weeks to process this scene. You think the Bureau will send up more agents now?"

"Maybe," said Decker. "If we can show there's a terrorist angle to this."

"Terrorists!" exclaimed Kelly. "What would they be doing in North Dakota?"

"Well, that's our job to figure out."

They left Kelly and walked back to their SUV.

"You going to call Robie? I mean, he *has* to be involved in this."

"The probabilities lie there."

"But do you think he killed all those men? I mean, that seems impossible."

"Nothing about that guy seems impossible to me."

As they reached their vehicle Decker's phone buzzed.

"It's Harper Brown," he said, checking the screen. "Hopefully, she has some news for us."

Decker answered the phone and Harper Brown, their friend at the DIA, said, "What the hell are you mixed up in out there, Decker?"

"I was hoping you could tell me. And how's Melvin?"

Melvin Mars was one of Decker's best friends. A former college football star convicted of murder and sentenced to death in Texas, Decker had proved his innocence. Mars and Brown were now dating.

"He's great. He sends his best and told me to tell you that if you need him as a bodyguard again, don't hesitate to call."

"I don't think I want him anywhere near this place. Besides, I think I have a pretty good bodyguard already."

"Don't let Alex hear you call her a bodyguard."

"I wasn't talking about her. So what do you have for us?"

"I'm thinking time is of the essence?"

"Your thinking is spot-on."

"First things first, anyone I could find with first-hand knowledge of the Douglas S. George Defense Complex provided nothing helpful. It's been under

Air Force control since the Korean War era when it was built."

"Has it been a radar array looking for missiles all that time?"

Strangely, she didn't answer right away. "Well, it's hard to tell. From what I could find out, it didn't come online as an eye in the sky until the late sixties, well into the Cold War."

"The Korean War was in the early fifties. What was it used for back then?"

"I don't know. I couldn't find out."

"How is that possible? Don't you have every security clearance they give out?"

"I thought I did, until I started asking questions about the place, particularly what it was doing back in the fifties. There I ran into a stone wall."

"I understand there's another eye in the sky around here."

"That's the other funny thing. The Stanley R. Mickelsen Safeguard Complex is on the eastern side of the state and is part of the Twenty-First Space Wing, and designated Cavalier Air Force Station. It's near Grand Forks, North Dakota, and was deactivated in 1976, but it has a PARCS radar array and keeps watch out for incoming missiles and also tracks objects in space."

"Which was how the commanding officer at the facility here described what they do. A *pair* of eyes in

North Dakota? Isn't that a bit of overkill, especially considering the Cold War is long dead?"

"You would think, Decker, you would think." She paused. "What do you believe is going on up there?"

"I think the answer to that would scare the crap out of even somebody like you."

50

"Things are accelerating," said Blue Man.

He, Robie, and Reel were sitting in Reel's black SUV on a quiet road about a mile outside of London. In the distance they could see oil rigs and crews pecking at the earth with drill bits and detonation guns.

"The police are all over the property," noted Robie.

"Well, there was no way we had the resources to clean up something like that. But that was a big loss for them, thanks to you."

Robie glanced at Reel. "Thanks to me and Jess. I thought you were on the other side of the world on assignment."

"I was." Reel was a female version of Robie, tall, lean, rock hard, with the calm and resolute features of a fighter pilot. "But then I got the call to come to wonderful North Dakota, where there were pressing matters that needed my attention."

"You were following me?" said Robie, his features troubled.

"I knew your itinerary, otherwise I would not have been able to. Don't worry, you're not losing a step."

"Your timing was impeccable, I understand," noted Blue Man.

"I'm six feet under if she was a second later," added Robie. "Jess and I checked some of the bodies out before we left the scene."

"They weren't members of our military," said Reel. "They weren't even from this country."

"Foreigners on domestic soil," murmured Blue Man.

"Which begs the question of why," said Reel.

Robie said, "Decker told us about the farmer who saw the man trying to escape. Speaking gibberish?"

"A foreign language, possibly Arabic or perhaps Farsi. I believe Mr. Decker would have already come to a similar conclusion."

"So it's a prison, then," said Robie.

Reel interjected, "It's no secret that some of the prisoners at Gitmo have been transferred to federal prisons across the country. But that Air Force facility is not a prison, at least not that anyone's told me."

"Perhaps they haven't told anyone," suggested Blue Man.

"What's going on with Gitmo now?" asked Robie.

"Past administrations either tried to keep it open or shut it down. The latter turned out to be harder than it looked. It now costs about thirteen million dollars per prisoner. Currently, there are roughly one hundred prisoners there."

"So one point three billion bucks to house them," said Reel.

"A steep price," added Blue Man. "But no one seems to know what to do about it."

"So you think they transferred some of them up here?" said Robie. "Why?"

"I didn't say that," said Blue Man. "These might be *new* prisoners. We're still fighting over there, of course. Taliban, Al-Qaeda, ISIS, even Houthian rebels and Iranian operatives, and other groups that are not as well known."

"So that Air Force station might now be Gitmo Two?" asked Reel.

"And maybe doing things to prisoners there that are no longer allowed at Gitmo One," mused Blue Man.

"Meaning torture?"

"I used to talk the company line and say, instead, 'enhanced interrogation techniques,' but things like waterboarding, well, we need to call them what they are."

"How in the world could something like that get authorized?" said Reel. "And at a military facility? The DoD has always been against that sort of thing. It violates the Geneva Conventions and opens up American soldiers held as prisoners to the same kind of treatment."

"It might *not* have been authorized, at least not through the proper channels," said Blue Man. "I think the politicians have learned their lesson on that one."

"Which brings us to this," said Robie. He took out a thumb drive and inserted it into the USB port on his laptop. He brought up the photos he had taken the previous night and turned it toward Blue Man.

"This guy was meeting with Sumter, and whatever they're doing is definitely not on the up-and-up."

Blue Man looked at the pictures of the older man.

"Recognize him?" asked Reel.

Blue Man nodded. "Patrick McIntosh, a former, obscure congressman who did little during his time in DC. He has since made his mark, first as the head of a think tank, and now as a formidable lobbyist and kingmaker with a Rolodex that would rival anyone else's, and a desire to make as much money as possible by any means possible. He is supremely well connected in all the corridors of power that matter."

"Never heard of him," said Robie. Reel nodded in agreement.

"Which he would be delighted to hear. McIntosh does what he does from the shadows. The only time he seeks the limelight is when it suits him, usually accepting some honor for philanthropy that he performs only to keep in the good company of people he needs to further his own goals."

"You sound like you know him well," said Robie.

"I've had my run-ins with him. I found him

337

prepared, methodical, ruthless, shockingly lacking in empathy, and not above lying when it advantaged him in some way. Given that, I have always been surprised he didn't rise higher in government."

Robie passed Blue Man the recorder he had used to tape the conversation of the two men. "You need to hear this."

Blue Man turned on the recorder and listened to the conversation with great interest.

When it was done, he turned the recorder off and closed his eyes for a moment. When he opened them, Robie said, "What will you do with that?"

"I will do what needs to be done. And I will move swiftly. If they are keeping a prison over there, we need to nip this in the bud as quickly and quietly as possible."

"You need any help from us on that?"

He held up the recorder. "You've given me all I need."

Reel folded her arms over her chest and gave Blue Man a stern look. "And what's *our* next move?"

"The two of you will shadow Decker and Jamison. I'll let you know when you can fill them in on what you know and have them reciprocate. Based on our comingled intelligence, we can hopefully then map out a strategy going forward."

"Do you think it wise to share what we know with them?" said Reel, looking surprised.

Robie said, "We can trust them."

"And since you saved Mr. Decker's life, I would think that he will believe he can trust you," said Blue Man. "And he can, up to a point."

"You see our agendas misaligning at some point?" queried Robie.

"I have seen that happen before, so I can't say it won't happen now. We simply need to see how it plays out."

"When do you want us to meet with them?"

"Now," said Blue Man. "Whatever is being planned up here has a short fuse. I sense we have no time to waste. And it's not just this prison business. There's something else going on here that is far worse. A 'ticking time bomb' reference does not provide for either restful sleep or dalliance. Now, drive me to the airstrip. I need to get back to DC as quickly as possible. I have many things to arrange and not much time to do so. And then, I have a meeting to attend."

Reel put the SUV in gear and they drove off.

51

"Amos Decker? Rex Manners. Heard you wanted a line on an AWOL named Ben Purdy."

Decker had answered the call while sitting in his hotel room the next day.

"That's right, Rex, thanks for getting back to me. What do you have?"

"A name and an address. Beverly Purdy. She lives in Montana, a few hours from the border with North Dakota, which I understand is where you are now."

"That's right."

Manners gave him the address. "Beverly Purdy is the mom. She's a widow, and Ben is her only kid. She lives on a farm, raises some crops and cattle. I don't know if Purdy is there or not, but it seemed like a good place for you to start."

"I appreciate the assist. Be sure to email me a bill. I can give you my address."

"Don't worry about it. PIs do each other favors. You'll be able to return it one day. Good luck."

Manners clicked off, and Decker put his phone

away. He called Jamison and filled her in. When they Googled the location of Purdy's farm, they found it was about five hours from London.

"Should we grab Kelly?" asked Jamison.

"I don't want to involve him in something that might come back to haunt him. There may come a time when we have to tell him, but now is not that time."

They met up downstairs and drove out of town heading west.

"Did you contact Robie?"

"Not yet. I was going to when the PI called. Let's check out Purdy and then we can hook up with Robie when we get back."

The long drive seemed longer than it was because there was nothing to see except landscape that never changed.

"I've never been in a car this long without seeing another car," observed Jamison as she drove along. "And I grew up in Indiana."

"This is Big Sky country."

Jamison looked out the window. "You got that right. You don't get this sort of impression in DC or New York."

Decker glanced at her wrist, where she had tatted *Iron Butterfly*. "You said your mother got you onto that band when you were a kid. After they re-formed."

She smirked. "Wow, good *memory*."

"Still listen to their music?"

"I've moved on to Janis Joplin, and the Doors."

He glanced at her hand. "When I first met you, I noticed the slight indentation on your ring finger from when you were married before."

She glanced sharply at him. "I've never known you to make small talk. What gives?"

"Maybe I'm evolving."

"Okay."

"You've never really spoken about your ex. You just told me you were married for two years and three months, then things went sideways. He wasn't the man you thought he was and maybe you weren't the woman he thought you were."

She frowned. "Sometimes your perfect recall is really irritating."

"How do you think I feel? So?"

"Nothing to really say about it other than what I already did. Dan was different when we dated. He was all things I liked. After we said our vows and started living together, he became all things I disliked. And maybe I became that way to him. Though I don't think I ever really changed."

"Amicable split?"

"We were both too young and I was too naïve. Way too naïve. He ... he took advantage of that, at least thinking back I see that."

"Where is he now?"

She shrugged. "Your guess is as good as mine." She glanced at him again with an annoyed look that she finished off with a warm smile. "Right now, I think I liked it better when you had no interest at all in personal matters."

He held up his hands in mock surrender and then stared out the window. "When I woke up from my coma in the hospital after getting wrecked on that football field, I thought everything was normal. I thought *I* was still normal. Until it happened."

"What happened?"

"You know the little monitor on the stand they have to record your vitals?"

"Yeah."

"When I looked at the numbers there, I was seeing them in all sorts of different colors. At first, I just thought my vision was still funky, or maybe I was just out of sorts. You have to understand that I still didn't know what had happened to me. But later, when I looked at the clock on the wall, same thing—weird-ass colors. Then I knew I was definitely not the same. And when I had to interact with people, well, it was a brave new world. I'm sure the doctors and nurses were glad to be rid of me. I was a royal pain in the ass. I was somebody else but only in the same body. My way of coping was just to . . . not cope. Just move on as though I'd always been that way."

"But you seem to understand it a lot better than when we first met. Back then you were really aloof, and impossible to read. And you had absolutely no—"

She stopped and looked nervous.

He glanced at her. "No filter? You're right. And I'm not *that* much better now."

"You don't walk out of rooms while people are still talking to you nearly as much as you used to," she said encouragingly.

"I guess progress is measured in baby steps."

"I know we've talked about this before, but what is it really like not to forget anything?"

"My personal cloud, you mean?" he said, tapping his temple. "It's probably a lot like your memory, only mine's a little more neatly organized and a lot more accessible than yours. You have it all up there, too, but some memories are so crowded out by others that you can't reach them anymore. I don't have that problem."

"A blessing, and a curse."

"It is if you have something you'd rather forget, which most of us do."

"I know it's hard, Decker."

He stared out the window at an endless sky, which, to him right now, seemed as big as his personal memory. "Life is hard for everybody, Alex. Anybody who says otherwise has just decided to ignore all the shit that comes with waking up every day and walking out the door."

She said, "So your way of coping is focusing entirely on your work?"

Decker glanced at her, his features inscrutable. "My way of coping is just finding the truth, Alex. If I can do that, then I can deal with everything else."

52

The farm looked like something out of *The Grapes of Wrath*, only with less dust and a modicum of water sources.

They pulled to a stop in front of the plank-sided house and got out. There was a dirty and ancient Jeep two-door parked in the front. They could see a barn in the distance, and corrals full of cows collected around a water trough and salt lick. There was also a paddock where some bow-backed horses nibbled grass. The overall operation looked neat and efficient.

The leaning mailbox at the end of the dirt road had said PURDY, so they knew they were in the right place.

Before they could reach the front steps, the screen door opened and a woman stood there, a Remington over-under shotgun in hand. She was in her mid-fifties, with long gray hair, a slender, wiry build, and a pair of piercing blue eyes. She had on faded dungarees, weathered boots, and a checkered shirt tucked into the pants. The belt holding them up was made of knotted leather. Her face was wrinkled and tanned. And full of suspicion.

"Who are you?" she demanded.

Jamison immediately took out her FBI creds and badge.

"FBI Special Agent Alex Jamison. My partner, Amos Decker. Are you Beverly Purdy?"

Instead of de-escalating the situation, this only caused the woman to raise the gun and point it directly at them, her finger near the trigger. "What the hell do you want? You tell me right now."

Decker stepped forward, putting himself between Jamison and the gun. "We wanted to talk to Ben, if he's here."

She snapped. "He's not. But why do you want to talk to him?"

"We're not with the Air Force, if that's what you're thinking. And we have no interest in whether he might be absent without leave. We just want to talk to him about his last posting, in London, North Dakota."

"Bullshit. You've come to arrest him."

"Why would we do that?"

"You just said. AWOL."

"We're investigating a series of murders in London."

"Ben didn't kill nobody."

"We're not suggesting he did. He was long gone before the killings took place. But he said something to someone back in London. We just wanted to ask him what he meant by that. We believe it might have ties to our investigation."

The woman slowly lowered the weapon. "He's not here, like I said."

"Was he here at some point?"

"He might'a been," she said guardedly.

"Do you know where we could find him?"

She shook her head. "Got no idea. Haven't heard from him in a while."

"And so you must be worried?" said Jamison, coming to stand next to Decker.

"I'm his ma, 'course I'm worried."

"Well, we're worried about him too, so maybe together we can find him."

"I . . . I don't know."

"I get that you're suspicious, Mrs. Purdy. So just to show our good faith, we'll leave now. But can I give you our contact information so he could call us if you do see him? All we want to do is talk to him, not arrest him. That's all." He pulled a card from his jacket pocket and held it out to her.

She looked at the paper warily, as though if she touched it she might feel pain. But, apparently now satisfied that they were not here to arrest her son, Purdy said, "Look, do you all want to come in? I just made some fresh coffee."

Decker glanced at Jamison and said, "Sounds good.

It was a long drive. And it's colder here than it was in North Dakota."

They followed her inside. The front room was dominated by heads of animals mounted on the wall.

Purdy caught Jamison gawking and said, "My husband and Ben were avid hunters. Most everybody in these parts are. But it's not just for show. We eat what we shoot."

She led them into a small, plain kitchen with pine cupboards and dark, swirl-patterned, laminated countertops. The floor was aged linoleum and the furnishings rustic. The curtains around the windows looked to be about fifty years old. The whole place seemed locked in time from around then.

She set the Remington in a gun rack on the wall and pointed to two chairs around the table. "Take a seat."

They sat while she got the coffee and cups together.

After she poured and handed out their drinks, she joined them at the table. She moved a stray hair out of her eyes and sipped her coffee, not meeting their curious gazes.

"We understand you live here alone?" said Decker.

The blue eyes flashed. "Who told you that? You been spying on me?" Her gaze darted to the shotgun. "What do you want? You tell me now."

"We already told you," replied Decker calmly. "To talk to your son."

"That's what you *said*," she retorted in a skeptical tone. "Doesn't mean it's true."

"It *is* true," said Jamison. "We just want to talk to him. We are not here to arrest him. That is not our concern. We have no jurisdiction over his military career."

"Feds are Feds," Purdy snapped.

"It may seem like it, but it doesn't actually work that way, at least not in our case," said Decker.

She finally calmed and said, "My husband died three years ago. I was hoping Ben would come back here and help me run the place. But that didn't happen."

Decker said, "You told us he might've been here. *Was* he here? Did he talk to you about what might have happened back there, that caused him to leave the way he did?"

Purdy fingered her coffee cup. "They . . . they moved everybody from that place. Meaning the Air Force, Ben, and the others."

"Right, a private security firm named Vector came in to run the facility," said Jamison.

"Don't know about that."

"What did he do there?" asked Decker.

"Technical stuff. Computers and the like." She snapped her fingers. "Radar, I think he said. But not anymore, I guess."

"Why do you say that?" asked Jamison.

"Like I just said, they reassigned Ben and the

others. I guess there's nobody left to do the radar and such. He trained for it, you know. He was good at his job. Real smart. Always has been."

"So he was upset about being transferred out?" asked Decker.

"Yeah."

"But surely he'd been reassigned before. I mean, you go where the military tells you to."

Purdy looked confused by this. "Well, that's right. He was in Nebraska for a while, then Colorado. Then he got transferred to North Dakota. So that's right."

"He never got upset about those transfers?" said Decker.

"No."

"But he did this time?"

"He . . . he called me one night, over a year ago. He said, 'Ma, they're moving us out. We're going to the East Coast somewhere.' I forget where he said, and then they were being reassigned to Colorado, I think. Least he was."

"But he didn't go?" said Decker.

She looked up at him nervously. "You sure you're not here to get him in trouble?"

"I give you my word. Did he ever say anything to you that showed he was troubled by something?"

"Not in so many words, no, but I could tell something *was* bothering him. When he would call, he didn't sound like himself."

"Did he know about the changes taking place at the installation?"

"No, he never mentioned anything like that to me."

"Did he ever mention a Colonel Mark Sumter?"

"No."

"Has he been back here since then?" asked Jamison.

"Once," she said, looking down at her long, weathered fingers. "About ten months ago. He'd lost weight, wouldn't meet my eye. I asked what was wrong. But all he said was he couldn't tell me without maybe getting me in trouble."

"Was he in uniform?"

"No, he didn't always come home dressed up. But he only had a backpack with him. Not big enough for his uniforms and all. I asked him where he was stationed. 'Out in Colorado?' I asked. But he just changed the subject. He said if anybody came looking for him, to just say I hadn't seen hide nor hair of him."

Decker said, "And *did* people come looking for him?"

She nodded. "The Air Force. Three times. Said he was AWOL. In a lot of trouble. When Ben come here that one time it was late at night, and he didn't stay long. He left the next morning at the crack of dawn. I told him about the Air Force folks. He said not to worry. I haven't seen him since," she added gravely, her voice breaking.

"Did anyone else ever come looking for him, besides the Air Force?" said Jamison.

Purdy took another sip of coffee before answering. "No, just them. Nobody else."

Jamison asked, "Did he have any close friends in North Dakota? Anyone he served with that he might have mentioned?"

"Not that he said, no."

"Did he ever mention anyone named Irene Cramer?" asked Decker.

Purdy thought about this but then shook her head. "Not that I recall, no. Who is she?"

"One of the people who was killed."

Purdy shook her head. "I worry myself sick that Ben's dead, too. He's never gone this long without calling me. What do you all think is going on at that place?"

"That's what we're trying to find out," said Decker. "Does Ben have a room here?"

"In the back."

"Is that where he slept the last time he was here?"

"Yes."

"Do you mind if we have a look?"

She rose and led them down the hall.

53

It was the faded room of a teenager from years ago. Old movie and music posters. Pictures of athletes from fifteen years past. A small gunmetal desk with a dusty PlayStation console and a pair of headphones. Some dog-eared Stephen King and Dean Koontz novels along with books of a technical nature were lined up on a small bookshelf. The bed was a twin and neatly made. The carpet was old and stained.

Decker and Jamison stood in the center of the small space and looked around, while Purdy remained in the doorway blinking away tears.

"I come in here sometimes and sit on his bed," she said, staring at it. "He's thirty now. Enlisted right out of high school. Time goes by so fast. Hard to believe. Seems like I just came home from the hospital with him."

"Did he have a computer?" asked Jamison.

"One of them laptops. But he took that with him. We don't get real good whatever-it's-called, out here."

"Internet connection? Broadband?" said Jamison.

"Yeah. He would always complain about that. But what can you do? Couldn't up and move the dang farm."

Decker opened the closet door and peered inside it. There were a few clothes on hangers. He went through the pockets. On the floor was a cardboard box. He pulled it out and set it on the bed. Inside were some books, magazines, and some loose printed pages. Decker looked at the books and magazines and ran his gaze over the pages. The books and magazines all dealt with technical subjects, mostly having to do with electronic communication applications. The loose pages were about various military installations in Maryland, Colorado, Arkansas, and California. Decker held them up. "Any idea why he was interested in these places?"

Purdy came forward and took the pages from him. "I don't know. Maybe he was thinking about asking for a transfer there."

"But they're not all Air Force installations."

Jamison said, "Or they could be from when he was thinking about enlisting years ago. He might not have settled on a service branch yet."

"No," said Decker, shaking his head. "There's a time stamp at the bottom right of the page. It shows when it was printed out."

Jamison looked at the dates. "About a year ago," she said, giving him a confused look.

"You mind if we take these?" he asked Purdy.

"No, help yourself."

They went back into the kitchen.

Purdy said, "Do you think I'll see my son again?"

"I wish I could give you a straight answer on that, ma'am. I can tell you that we'll do all in our power to find him."

She put a hand on Decker's arm. "Thank you for that."

They took their leave and drove off, with Purdy in the doorway of the little house staring forlornly after them.

"I can't imagine what she's going through," said Jamison. "Her only kid is missing and obviously involved in some dangerous things."

Decker wasn't listening. He was staring down at the pages he had taken, lost in thought.

Halfway through the trip it was well dark. They had just crossed back over into North Dakota when Jamison glanced in the rearview mirror. "Well, that's the first pair of headlights I've seen in a long time."

Decker looked in the side mirror and sat up straighter.

"Brace, Alex," he called out, right as the front of the vehicle trailing them plowed into the rear of theirs.

The collision slammed both of them back against their seats, momentarily stunning them.

Then Jamison went into action. She floored the gas, and the SUV leapt forward.

"Can you see anything?" she called out.

Decker turned around and looked at the head-lights a few feet behind them. "Yeah, and here they come again."

They were bucked forward once more with a second collision. Jamison was having to struggle mightily just to keep the truck on the road.

She said, "They have more horsepower than we do. I've got the pedal to the floor."

"Well, let's see if we can do something about that."

Decker undid his seat harness, climbed over the seats, and settled in the cargo area at the back. "Pop the window," he called out as he slid his Glock from its belt holster.

Jamison did so and Decker edged the glass further up.

He used the back of the cargo door as his fulcrum, aimed, and fired five shots into the driver's side of the windshield.

The vehicle immediately started to veer erratically to the left and right.

"Think I hit the driver," he yelled out. As he said this he ducked down. "Look out, Alex!"

Their SUV was strafed with machine-gun fire.

She bent low, cut the wheel hard to the left, and shot onto the wrong side of the road.

"Decker, Decker, you okay? Decker."

She glanced frantically in the rearview mirror. "Amos!"

His head poked up into view. "Okay, that was a little closer than I would have liked."

Their SUV started wobbling badly and Jamison said, "They hit our tires. I can't hold this speed."

Decker looked to the right. "Road coming up. Take it."

Jamison left rubber on the road as she drilled a ninety-degree turn onto another ribbon of asphalt heading south. She eased up on the gas because the SUV was fishtailing so badly. "They must have shredded our rear tires. Feels like we're riding on the rims."

"Just keep going."

He watched as the shot-up vehicle, now revealed as a Hummer, made the turn. And then he watched with a sickening feeling as another Hummer pulled in right behind the first one.

They had reinforcements and machine guns. This would not be a long or fair fight.

He looked toward the front of their SUV and saw what looked to be an abandoned farmhouse with broken corral fencing and a hay barn with rotted doors swinging off.

"Head for that barn," he told Jamison.

The SUV shot through the opening and she slammed on the brakes, bringing them to a stop right before they crashed into the opposite wall. They scrambled out of the SUV and took up position behind their vehicle.

Decker has already tried to call 911 for help, but there were no bars on his phone. Even if he had, it would probably take hours for even a single cop to show up out here.

Jamison had her gun pointed at the open doors. She glanced at Decker. "What now?"

He was eyeing the interior of the barn, and then his gaze went up. "High ground is the best."

They hustled to an old wooden ladder and clambered up to the hayloft, which was half full of thoroughly rotted straw.

Decker tested each floorboard with his weight before edging over to the hayloft doors and opening them just a crack.

Twin pairs of headlights were cutting through the darkness around the farmyard. The doors of the Hummer with the cracked windshield opened and four men climbed out. They wore all black, including ski masks, and carried automatic weapons. The doors of the second Hummer opened and three more men got out. In the blink of an eye they fanned out, and within seconds they had the barn surrounded.

Decker turned back to Jamison. "Well, our options seem limited."

"Yeah, as in zero," she replied grimly.

Decker reached into his pocket and pulled out the device Robie had given him.

Jamison noted this and said, "Little late for that."

"I was thinking the same thing but what do we have to lose now?"

The shots outside drew their attention back to the hayloft doors.

As they watched, the lead Hummer exploded and the detonation lifted the multiton vehicle straight up into the air before it slammed back down to earth, a collision that burst all four tires.

"What the hell?" began Jamison.

They dropped to the floor and slid backward as automatic gunfire started up again.

A few moments later Decker crawled forward and peered through the crack in the doors. He watched as two of the men in black were gunned down. Three more rushed from around the rear of the barn and took up position behind the destroyed Hummer.

They fired into the distance and received return fire.

Decker pointed his gun out the crack, took aim, and shot one of the men in the back. He fell to the dirt. The other men turned and fired at the barn.

Decker slammed the door shut, and he and Jamison took up cover behind a thick bale of rotted hay. Multiple rounds ripped through the wooden doors and into the straw.

There was more gunfire, another detonation. Screams, more gunfire, shouts. And then, the sound of a vehicle starting up.

Decker and Jamison crawled forward in time to

see the second Hummer racing back down the road. Soon, it had disappeared into the darkness.

Jamison looked at Decker and said breathlessly, "What the hell just happened?"

Before Decker could answer, the phone Robie had given him buzzed. He answered it.

Will Robie said, "You can come down now."

54

Robie and Reel were in the front seats and Jamison and Decker in the rear of Reel's SUV as they drove back to London. When Jamison and Decker had come out of the barn, they had been met by the pair along with a number of dead bodies.

Robie had introduced Jessica Reel to them. She had said nothing, only nodding curtly in their direction.

"How'd you know where we were?" asked Jamison.

Before Robie could answer, Decker held up the phone. "This has a tracking device."

Robie nodded. "We followed you to your destination. Then saw the Hummers on the return trip. It was a close call."

"I wish you didn't have to keep saving my life," said Decker quite frankly. "It's getting a little bit hairy."

"I can see that."

"What did you find out with Purdy's mother?" asked Reel as she steered the SUV.

"Ben Purdy was last there around ten months ago. The Air Force has been by looking for him a few times. No one else. We took some things from his room. They may be clues." He held up the printed pages.

Robie took them and looked the pages over. "A bunch of different military installations. What do you think he was looking for?"

"Facts about something that was important to him."

"You think this has to do with Vector taking over London AFS?" said Robie.

"If you asked me that yesterday I would have said maybe. But I don't think Purdy was aware it was going to become a prison."

"We thought you might have figured that out," said Robie.

"Purdy was transferred out before any of that happened. He was upset about the transfer, his mother said, but he didn't know the details of what was coming in to replace him and the others. Vector apparently wasn't on the scene yet, and without them around there weren't going to be any prisoners sent there."

Jamison said, "So it seems clear that the time bomb Purdy mentioned doesn't involve the prison."

"Little town for so many big things to be happening," commented Reel.

"Couldn't have said it better myself," remarked Jamison.

Robie said, "The guys we took care of back there looked just like the ones who tried to ambush me the other night."

"We figured you were involved in all that," said Decker.

Robie glanced at Reel. "But for my partner here, they would have had to send someone else to take my place."

Reel said, "We all do our part."

Robie continued, "They're clearly mercenaries. And there are a shitload of them out for hire. Anyone with enough money can have their pick of some very serious people."

"But again, why London, North Dakota, for all the attention?" said Jamison.

"Time bomb," said Decker as he glanced down at the printed pages Robie had handed back to him. "And apparently these folks want to make damn sure it goes off."

The knock came on Decker's door about an hour after they got back to London.

Considering what had happened to them, Decker answered the door with his Glock in hand.

It was Robie. "Got a minute?" he asked.

They sat in two chairs facing each other. Robie looked grim.

"I take it you have bad news," said Decker.

"They got to Beverly Purdy. She's dead."

Decker sat back and slowly absorbed this not-so-surprising news. What else could they do? They had no idea what Ben had told his mother, or him and Jamison. It was surprising that they hadn't killed her before. But then there was a simple answer to that.

"So when we went there we signed her death warrant?" said Decker. "They obviously followed us out there."

"I doubt it would have mattered," said Robie. "She was a loose end. They would have gotten to her at some point."

Decker stood and looked out the window into the darkness. "I'm a cop, Robie. And right now I feel like I'm in the middle of a James Bond film. I have no experience with shit like this."

Robie didn't respond right away, but when he did it was in a calm, judicious tone.

"The world hasn't gotten safer over time, Decker. It's just gotten more complicated. Humans are still in control and humans do bad things all the time. We had the Cold War with nukes, and now we have hot spots all over with people slaughtering other people and dictators rising up again because democracy seems stalemated and nothing gets done and people get fed up. But a dictator doesn't need *supporters*, he just needs *followers*. And the best way to make people follow, at least in the eyes of guys like that, is to give them no choice in the matter."

Decker sat back down. "Thanks for the geopolitical education, but it still doesn't get us where we need to go."

"Jessica Reel and I are here to help you. Our strengths are in protection, and in *removing* people in the most efficient way possible."

"I've seen your handiwork."

"Your strength is figuring things out. So any ideas? You said the prison thing is not the big deal here. And for what it's worth, our boss agrees with you."

"Does *he* have any ideas?" asked Decker.

"Not that he's shared. But from what I could gather, he has a strategy about the prison issue that's he's going to pull the trigger on. We'll let him handle that piece. You focus on the time bomb."

Decker eyed him skeptically. "You're not authorized to operate in this country."

"So the law says."

"Well, you seem to be *operating* okay."

Robie rose. "You should get some sleep."

"What I should do is start to figure this out."

55

Blue Man sat in a leather chair at a prestigious club within a stone's throw of the Capitol Building. Silent men in starched livery walked around carrying trays with expensive whiskeys and bowls of cheap nuts. The walls were paneled with luxurious wallpaper, and on them were hung portraits of old, grave men in suits. The carpet underfoot had several inches of give. The furnishings were old but originally expensive. Newspapers rustled alongside murmurings of educated, cultured voices and clinks of ice cubes in cocktail glasses as both business and government leaders made decisions that would have massive impact on millions of people, all without their knowledge or consent.

If one did not know better, it could have been 1920 rather than a century later.

Blue Man's gaze roamed the room. He nodded to those he liked and respected, and also to those he loathed and distrusted, but to whom some level of acknowledgment was required. It certainly said something that he had been in this business so long that the latter group far outnumbered the former.

His gaze finally alighted on the stout man who came into the room, carrying a folded newspaper and a glass half full of gin and tonic along with a self-important look.

Blue Man rose and approached him. "Patrick?" he said.

Patrick McIntosh, the gentleman who had met with Colonel Mark Sumter in that little house over a thousand miles from here, stared back at him, his features instantly wary.

"Roger, how are you?"

Blue Man's real name was Roger Walton. He had almost no occasion now to ever use it.

But this was one of those times.

"Not bad, not bad. You?"

"Things are going very well, thank you."

"Do you have a moment?" said Blue Man. "I've engaged a private room."

The smile that McIntosh had forced onto his lips retreated to a straight line one might employ after being sworn in to testify in front of a hostile congressional committee.

"A private room? Why the need for that?" He chuckled. "Am I going to get the third degree?"

"We've both been around long enough to know the answer to that," replied Blue Man genially and also largely unresponsively, as he placed a firm grip on McIntosh's elbow. "Oh, and Director Cassidy sends her best."

"So you've spoken with Rachel?" said McIntosh as Blue Man led him down a dark paneled corridor to a door that opened into a ten-by-ten windowless room with two upholstered chairs facing one another.

"She is my superior, after all."

"I meant had you spoken to her about *me*?"

"Not to sound like a cliché, but that would be classified." Blue Man tacked on a smile, which seemed to relieve McIntosh.

"I'm glad I'm no longer in the public sector. You should make the jump, Roger. A man with your experience and Rolodex. The money you could make."

"My needs are simple, my salary more than ample."

"I just bought an Italian villa in Tuscany. Sherry and I will spend the summers there."

"Congratulations. Please have a seat."

The men faced off in the chairs.

McIntosh laid his paper aside but did drain the rest of his gin.

"I've been traveling," said Blue Man.

"Oh really? Where? I hope somewhere nice. South of France? Rome? Sydney?"

"London."

"Oh, very nice."

"London, *North Dakota.*"

McIntosh set the empty glass down on a table next to his chair. To his credit, his hand remained sure and steady, noted Blue Man.

"Did you enjoy your time there, wherever that is? North Dakota, you said?"

"It was instructive. But surely your memory fails you?"

"Come again?"

Blue Man slid an envelope and a small digital recorder from his pocket. He took his time opening the envelope and slipped out a number of photos. "You look distinguished in these photos, Patrick. It was quite hot that night, if I recall. Your colleague, or more accurately your *coconspirator*, Colonel Mark Sumter, decided not to dress in uniform, it was so toasty. He opted for civilian clothes."

McIntosh glanced at the photos as Blue Man fanned them out but said nothing in reply.

Next, Blue Man set the recorder down and hit the start button. The conversation between McIntosh and Sumter wafted over the small room.

When it was finished, Blue Man shut off the machine and settled back in his chair.

"Well?"

"Well what?"

"Do you not feel that explanations are in order?"

"Not at all," said McIntosh offhandedly.

"I see. Well then, let me speak for a bit and see if

what I have to say prompts you to rethink that answer."

"I doubt that it will."

Blue Man said, "Guantanamo hasn't accepted any new prisoners since 2008. The current cost of the remaining prisoners there, all one hundred of them, is around one point three billion and change."

McIntosh picked a piece of lint off his sleeve. "Is it? My goodness. Hardly a bargain to house savages like that."

"Granted. But it is *authorized*."

McIntosh flicked away the piece of lint. "Are we done here yet? Because, frankly, I'm not following any of this."

"You're on the board of Vector Security."

"I know I am. A wonderful, patriotic company."

"With only one contract approved by the government. Namely, to operate the Douglas S. George Defense Complex, aka London Air Force Station."

"I hope it doesn't surprise you that I was already aware of that. Hence my visit there. I am a good board member after all."

"You're not only a board member. You also have a direct financial interest in the business of Vector."

"As board members so often do."

"The budget for the complex is six hundred and forty-four million, nine hundred and seventy-six thousand dollars per annum."

"It's expensive keeping us safe. Now, if you'll excuse me." McIntosh started to rise from his seat.

"Which means the cost of *each* of the ten prisoners currently housed there is over sixty-four million dollars. Hardly a bargain compared to Gitmo's thirteen million per pop."

McIntosh sat down. "*Prisoners?* What on earth are you talking about, Roger? Have you suffered a stroke or something?"

Blue Man took out additional photos that Robie had taken showing the men being wheeled off to ambulances. "I'm talking about these men."

"Could be anyone," said McIntosh, glancing at them. "Looks like some Air Force personnel in distress. As you said, it gets hot out there."

"They're not Air Force personnel, as you well know."

"You say, I say."

Blue Man's expression now hardened. "This back-and-forth grows wearisome, and you are not the only item on my agenda for today." He leaned forward. "Vector's COO and CFO also *say*. As does Colonel Sumter. They're ISIS, Taliban, and Al-Qaeda prisoners taken from the battlefields and smuggled into this country *without* the knowledge of government leadership."

McIntosh's eyelids rose a bit more fully, revealing his pale blue eyes. "You've . . . you've talked to Sumter?"

"We actually couldn't get him to *stop* talking once he saw the trouble he was in."

"I don't see it that way at all. And contrary to your observation, it *was* all approved with a nice little bow on top."

"What was approved a very long time ago and never revisited was the operation of London AFS as a PARCS radar array monitoring facility, which function it was performing up until about a year ago. Then its purpose dramatically shifted. It has the same quasi-pyramidal building as its cousin in Grand Forks and the same impressive surveillance system. However, since we already have one of those in North Dakota, and the one at Grand Forks is newer and better positioned, a spare was not really needed. But that's certainly not the first time the Pentagon has had redundancies and wasted money. So a complex out in the hinterlands with a duplicative purpose? You must have felt like a pot of gold had been dropped into your lap because that made it the perfect facility to house additional unauthorized prisoners who should never have been brought into this country. To torture them. And then dispose of them when they had told all they could or refused to do so, and then you would pass along this intelligence to others in government under the subterfuge that it had come through ordinary channels. The ambulances? They might as well have been meat wagons for the *bodies*. Which we are right now digging up, by the way, based on information provided to us."

McIntosh sat back. "I commend the speed with which you have moved on this, Roger. I really do."

"The federal government is like an aircraft carrier. It takes us a while to get going, but once we do, look out."

"Yes, indeed." McIntosh managed to tack on a smile, even as his skin grew as gray as the side of a naval vessel.

Blue Man next took out the photos Robie had given him of the people getting off the jet.

"I wondered why Vector was given the contract, since the capabilities of their people are not known to be in the PARCS space. But the VP of operations for Vector is well-known to me. He headed up security at Gitmo for six years. And here he is with two of his top lieutenants arriving at London AFS." Blue Man held up the photos for McIntosh to see. "He of course has also been arrested, and from what I understand he is already attempting to make a deal. The CFO and COO have already received blanket immunity in return for their testimony. It may well be that you're the odd man out on that, Patrick, which is why I saved you for last, if for no other reason than I don't like you and never have."

McIntosh made a hissing sound as he sucked on his tongue. "Why are you even involved in this? You are barred from operating in this country. I think you left me a hole to climb through."

"We are an intelligence agency tasked with protecting this country from enemies both foreign and domestic. We have worked in conjunction with the FBI this entire time. They are the lead agency on this, we merely their very willing helpmate. That type of arrangement occurs all the time and has been thoroughly vetted in the courts. Thus you will find that not only is there no hole for you to escape through, but that the roof over your head for your remaining time on this earth will be provided by the federal government."

"Roger, I think if we discussed this civilly—"

Blue Man spoke over him. "The long and the short of it is you are running a secret and unauthorized prison, using government funds that were meant to pay for a fully operational eye in the sky, with the result that you are charging the American taxpayer many times what it costs to house prisoners at Gitmo, which was an alarmingly high rate to begin with. In the last year your good CFO has calculated that, thus far, profits to Vector have exceeded nearly a half billion dollars, which is, by any standard, an outrageous margin of return. I trust you understand that Uncle Sam frowns on gouging like that. In fact, he frowns on it so much that there are multiple laws against it, all of which you have broken."

"We were doing good, Roger. The information we received and passed along—"

"—has not resulted in anything positive. Almost all of it has been proven erroneous and thus useless. The rest of it was already known through legitimate intelligence sources." He paused. "Let me be as clear as I possibly can be. This was not about helping this country. This was about lining your pocket. So please do not plead patriotism as your defense. You'll only embarrass yourself and make me even angrier than I already am."

As Blue Man had been speaking, McIntosh had sunk lower and lower in his very fine and very expensive chair.

Blue Man continued, "It speaks to the appallingly large and frustratingly complex footprint of the DoD that such a scheme could have worked in the first place, and that it's taken so long for the truth to come out. But with an overall budget of nearly a trillion dollars, thousands of facilities all over the globe, millions of employees and contractors, billions of square feet of space, and enough divisions and departments and programs that the right hand literally isn't even aware that there *is* a left hand, it wasn't that difficult to hide this sort of thing. The budget at London, though obscenely out of whack, doesn't even register as a blip on the Pentagon's overall spending. You, of course, had allies within the Air Force, the Pentagon, and the Congress to help you bury the truth—whom your

CFO has helpfully provided information about—including significant six- and seven-figure payoffs. My director has been fully briefed on this and has communicated this in writing to the director of the FBI and the IGs of the Air Force and the DoD. And lastly, again to be as transparent as possible, a warrant for your arrest is being issued as we speak."

Blue Man rose and smoothed out his dress shirt and tie. "Now I'm going to leave before I do or say something I might regret. However, I would suggest that you make plans to sell your vacation home in Italy. I don't see much opportunity for you to use it. And you might need the additional funds for legal fees. And please dissuade yourself from any thoughts of fleeing. As soon as you leave this room there will be multiple eyes on you, until your arrest warrant is executed. Thank you for your time." He pointed at the empty glass. "And you might want to get yourself another drink, Patrick. Good-bye. We will not be meeting again."

Blue Man closed the door behind him.

56

The Douglas S. George Defense Complex was buzzing.

As Decker and Jamison drove there in their new rental SUV, they saw the line of vehicles heading in and some heading out. A line of choppers was coming in and a small jet was taking off. They passed the oil rig nearest the facility, the All-American Energy Company, and found workers standing there staring at all the activity going on with their neighbor. They also spotted several members of the Brothers riding on farm equipment in their fields doing the very same thing.

They were here because Robie had called Decker and told him to come here as fast as possible.

Someone had obviously authorized their clearance into the facility because they were passed swiftly through after presenting their creds.

Robie and Reel came out to meet them as they pulled to a stop in front of the building where they had initially met with Colonel Mark Sumter.

They followed the pair down the hall and entered

a small room where Blue Man sat at the head of a small, battered conference table. He motioned for them to sit, then spent the next twenty or so minutes filling them in on recent developments including his confrontation with Patrick McIntosh back in Washington.

"Your agency is taking the lead on the law enforcement side, and the DOJ will of course deal with the prosecutions."

"So it *was* prisoners, as we suspected?" said Decker.

"Yes. Some in positions of power and who should have known better deemed it a worthy project to restart what was done at Abu Ghraib prison and other locations, despite the complete debacle that turned out to be. I am cheered by the fact that my agency had learned its lesson and was not party to a second go-round with this sort of thing."

"How many prisoners died?" asked Jamison.

"At least a dozen, if not more. Information is still coming in. It will take a while to dig through it all."

"The locals are certainly curious about what's going on here," said Jamison.

"It will all be hushed up in due time," said Blue Man. "This show of force is really for those out there who might have information. Or for those who are as yet unknown to us but are involved and will now panic and attempt to flee. Your director likened it to sending hunting dogs into the brush to flush out the quail."

"But the truth will come out?" said Jamison.

"Not in the press, no. It would cause more trouble than is warranted. People need to have faith in their government."

Decker said, "Well, maybe the government might want to consider earning that faith."

"I'm utterly in agreement with you. But now we must move on."

Decker gave him an appraising look. "This case is closed, but this was not the ticking time bomb. Purdy was gone before the prison became active. And I'm convinced this has to do with something that happened a long time ago."

"Which is why I requested your presence here, in addition to wanting to fill you in on what had happened here. How can we assist you?"

"I'm surprised that you're not packing up to go home," said Decker.

"Let me explain it this way. If an international presence exists on American soil for a purpose to do harm to America and its citizens, then we can very clearly justify our continued presence in this matter. I don't know about you, but I do not want a second 9/11 to happen because we got caught up in a bureaucratic tussle."

"Okay, I need to see Ben Purdy's service record."

"What do you hope to find in it?"

"A lead, because right now we don't have one."

★

Decker put down his third cup of coffee, glanced at the remains of a largely uneaten meal, and settled back in his chair in the hotel restaurant. He opened the email he'd just gotten on his phone and did likewise with the email's attachment.

It was Ben Purdy's service record. He had joined the Air Force straight out of high school and had spent the next dozen years in uniform. Decker went methodically through screen after screen. Purdy had covered a lot of ground in his career and had sought a great many educational and training opportunities that the Air Force had offered. He'd even attended conferences overseas in England, Germany, Qatar, and India. By all accounts he was a brilliant techie, though he had grown up in modest circumstances and had not been able to afford to go to college. He had risen to the rank of technical sergeant, which the document said was a very difficult rank to achieve, and Purdy had done it in record time. He had been on pace to make master sergeant when he had disappeared.

Decker sipped his coffee and then focused on actions that Purdy had taken in the last sixteen months, figuring that whatever ticking time bomb he had come across would have dated from more recent times. Purdy had briefly left London AFS during that time to take a class offered in DC on the latest types of communication technology available, and also what might be coming in the future. That made sense for a specialist like Purdy. After that, he had taken other offered courses in a variety of specialties, none of which could reasonably lead Decker to a ticking time bomb.

His phone buzzed. It was Bogart.

"Hey, Ross."

"Decker, I've heard about London AFS. Something big is going down and the Bureau is involved."

"I know. But it doesn't explain our case."

"Well, I dug up what I could on the military record of Bradley Unger Daniels."

"Anything of interest?"

"He served at London AFS from 1955 until 1987."

"I guess that makes sense. He had been an aviation navigator in the war, and he was into radar."

"Right, but the most interesting thing I found was that parts of his record were redacted and marked classified."

Decker sat up straighter. "He told us he couldn't talk about his time at London because it was classified. I thought he was just messing with us. But why would it be classified? Just because it was about looking for nukes during the Cold War?"

"I don't know, Decker. I can't get a straight answer from anyone."

"So a dead end?"

"I'm afraid so, unless you can think of another path forward."

"Well, that's my job."

Decker clicked off and stared down at Purdy's service record while he thought about Bogart's words.

He could see only one way forward.

He phoned Jamison.

"It's time we cracked 'BUD,'" he said.

57

Jamison and Decker arrived at Green Hills Nursing Home and were once more taken to the supervisor's office. Her face turned red when she saw them.

"You upset him greatly. I can't believe you're back."

Decker stared her down. "We're back because Brad Daniels is a key witness in a case that has national security interests. Now, if you won't let us see him, a whole army of Feds is going to come down on you and this facility like a ton of bricks. Your call."

The woman's hostile look quickly faded. "Are you serious?"

"We would not be here otherwise."

"All right, but please don't upset him again."

"All I can do is ask the questions I have to ask. If he gets upset, that's an answer in itself."

She led them to Daniels's room. The old man was sitting in the corner in his wheelchair, the cane clutched in his hands.

"Who is it?" he snapped as he heard them come in.

"Mr. Daniels, you have some visitors," said the woman.

"What visitors? It's not Christmas, is it?"

"I'll let them explain," she said sweetly. Then she fled the room.

Decker and Jamison came forward.

"Mr. Daniels?" he said.

The old man started. "It's you! I recognize your voice. Can't see no more, but I recognize voices. Get the hell out of here."

"You can either answer our questions, or other people will come here and ask them."

"I don't give a rat's ass. Get out!"

"Part of your military service record was redacted. Classified."

"Well, hell, I told you that."

"But you didn't say why."

"I can't, dumbass. That's sort of the point of it being *classified*."

"More people have been killed," said Decker. "Several more. Something big is being planned. We need you to help us understand what that could be."

"I only have your word for that and I don't believe you. You're not pulling the wool over my eyes. For all I know, you're spies."

"We can show you our credentials," offered Jamison.

"Can't see 'em. I told you that."

Decker sat on the edge of the bed. "Is there anything you *can* tell us about your time at London AFS?"

"No."

"We've been there. We've seen the radar array."

"So?"

"It's funny."

"What is?"

"They have an identical facility near Grand Forks, North Dakota."

A hint of a smile crept across Daniels's features. "Is that right?"

"But you knew that, didn't you?"

The smile vanished. "Who says?"

"It was discovered that the facility was being used for another purpose just recently. Not an eye in the sky, but something totally different."

"Who cares?"

"Your help could be vital to the national security interests of this country."

"Again, says you. You're not tricking me. I gave an oath."

"You've been out of uniform a long time."

"An oath is an oath. Take it to my grave. Just how it's done."

Decker looked at Jamison in frustration.

"Is there anything we can say to make you change your mind?" said Jamison.

"Yeah, you can get the president of the United

States of America to order me to give it up. Other than that, fuck off."

"You're the only one left from that time at London AFS."

"Last man standing," cackled Daniels.

"So you're the only one who can help us prevent something really bad from happening."

"It's lunch time. I can smell the onions. I'm going to the dining room."

He wheeled his chair forward, managed to ease it past the bed and wall, and then maneuvered it through the doorway.

"For a blind guy, he navigates pretty well," said Jamison.

"He's obviously not going to talk," said Decker.

Jamison said, "I'm surprised they haven't come here and killed him, too. I mean, look at poor Beverly Purdy."

"If Irene Cramer never gave him up, they probably would have no way of knowing."

"But if they followed us here? And found out we asked him questions? That's probably how Beverly Purdy died."

"Good point, Alex. I'll have some security put here to guard against that."

He got up to leave but then glanced at the nightstand. He picked up Daniels's ballcap.

Jamison joined him. "Shows the unit in the Air

Force he was assigned to," she said. "Lots of veterans have them."

"Right, but that's not all." Decker pointed to a series of metal pins that were attached to the hat. "Look at these."

"Places where he worked. Sort of like merit badges he earned," observed Jamison.

Decker ran his eye over all of them, until they held on one.

He shoved the hat into his pocket. "Let's get out of here before Daniels comes back and notices his hat is missing."

"He said he can't see."

"He said a lot of things. I don't believe any of them."

"So what's with the hat?"

"A clue. Maybe a really big one."

58

"USACC," said Decker.

They were driving back to London from the nursing home. Decker was holding the hat and looking at the pins. One in particular had drawn his focus.

"USACC? What does that stand for?"

Decker took out his phone and searched for the meaning. "United States Army Chemical Corps," he said.

"But Daniels was Air Force, not Army."

"He still has the pin. And that's not all." He unclipped several of the pins from the hat and held them up. "Beale Air Force Base, Rocky Mountain Arsenal, Camp Detrick, Pine Bluff, Arkansas. Some of them are Army, some Air Force. And Camp Detrick is in Maryland and now it's *Fort* Detrick."

"So he spent time at all of them?"

"Apparently enough time to earn a pin."

"What do they do at those places?"

"The question is what did they do when *Daniels* was in the military." He paused. "And there's something else. From his service record, I learned that

Purdy spent time at Beale and Rocky Mountain Arsenal."

"Okay, that's a definite connection."

"And that's not all. The printed pages we found in his closet of the military facilities? They're all places that Daniels has pins from."

"I would definitely call that a big clue," replied Jamison.

She saw Decker glancing in the side mirror. She did the same in the rearview. "I don't see anybody back there," she said.

"I was just checking, after last time."

They arrived back in London. Decker and Jamison went immediately to her hotel room, where Jamison logged on to her computer.

Decker had given her Daniels's hat with all of the pins, and she had searched each of them online.

Twenty minutes later she was finished and sat back. She glanced at Decker, her face pale and her expression one of slight panic. "They all have one common denominator from the time period that Daniels worked there."

Decker nodded. He had been looking and reading over her shoulder. "Back then all those facilities were involved in developing chemical and biological weapons of mass destruction."

"It apparently all began during World War II. We didn't have those types of weapons, but Germany did. So we started researching and developing them. Both the Army and the Air Force. The programs accelerated from the end of World War II through the Korean War and beyond. During that time the U.S. and the Soviet Union made enough of the stuff to kill everyone on earth. And that doesn't include nukes," said Jamison as she scrolled down the screen. "But then Nixon halted all such programs at the end of the sixties. All stores of such weapons were destroyed and the facilities that those programs operated were cleaned up and reassigned."

"Only maybe some of them weren't destroyed," said Decker. "And maybe there was a facility that worked on them that wasn't included in the list you just researched."

"Meaning London Air Force Station?"

Decker nodded. "I think it was originally built not for radar array but for production of biochemical weapons. Then the place was converted into a radar installation, even though it duplicated what the other one did near Grand Forks. Hell, maybe they added on to it at that point, to make it look like the other facility. You know, a pyramid with a golf ball on top."

"Until they started using it for a secret prison. What, do people just wait around to do something secret and illegal and then just plop it here?"

"You're talking about the government, Alex, so anything is possible."

"So is that the time bomb we're all sitting on here? WMDs?"

"It's a theory, but a good one. We just need to prove that it's true."

"And if it is true?"

"We need to find the WMDs."

"Oh, no sweat. We can wrap this all up by to-morrow."

When he didn't respond to her sarcasm she glanced up at him. He was clearly lost in thought.

"Are you thinking of some way to actually *do* that?"

"We'll need to alert Robie to what we found. Maybe they can get some people on it. But we have some angles to work, too."

"Beginning with what?"

"London Air Force Station."

"If they were making WMDs over there, I'm not sure I want to go there again."

"But we will anyway," replied Decker.

It was the next day. Jamison was driving, and Decker was staring out the window at yet another approaching storm.

"Dollar for your thoughts," said Jamison.

"Not sure they're worth that much."

"You seem down. I mean I can understand that, what with our line of work. But you always seem to be able to, I don't know, rise above it."

He turned to look at her. "Stan has been my brother-in-law for over two decades. I've spoken to him more here than I have in the last twenty years. Same with my sisters."

"Well, they lived a long way away. And siblings grow up and move on with their own lives."

"You have siblings. You keep in touch with them all."

"I'm the oldest. It sort of comes with the territory. And not to stereotype, but girls are a little better at that than guys. At least in my experience."

"Before what happened to me happened, I *did* keep in touch. I would call and even write letters, if you can believe that. Before Stan and Renee moved to California, I went to visit them in Colorado. I was still in college. They were pretty much still newlyweds. I helped Stan lay a brick patio in their backyard."

"That's really nice, Decker."

"I wasn't drafted after my senior year. I was a walk-on with the Browns, worked my tail off and made the team, really just as a special teams player. I was a good athlete. I was big enough and strong enough. But the NFL is a whole other level, the best of the best. I didn't have the speed or the other intangibles you needed to really be more than a journeyman. Then I was running down the field after the kickoff on opening day. And the next thing I woke up in a hospital. Both my sisters were there. I'd been in a coma for days. Renee was holding one of my hands and Diane the other. I didn't even notice them at first. I was looking at the weird colors on the monitor and the clock. And I thought I was losing my mind. Then I saw my sisters, and even though I knew they were my sisters, there was just something . . . gone. I felt nothing for them. I mean nothing."

He looked away.

Jamison, who had clearly been stunned by this candid outpouring from her partner, finally found her voice. "You'd been through a terrible trauma, Decker. And then you had some unexpected . . . challenges."

"A nice, polite way to describe it."

"But you've changed. Since the first time I met you in that courthouse back in Burlington. You're different."

"I know. And that's what scares the hell out of me."

He said nothing more, but just stared at the darkening skies like they would any minute starkly reveal his even darker future.

59

When they drove up to the front gate of the facility two men in suits approached them.

Jamison rolled down her window and showed her creds.

"Go right in," said one of the men. "You've been cleared through."

The gate opened and Jamison drove on.

"Robie's doing?" she said.

"When I called Robie and filled him in on what we had discovered, he said he was going to get the wheels turning for our visit here. And they were going to start making discreet inquiries about the chemical weapons piece."

They parked where they had last time and got out.

Jamison said, "So where do we begin?"

"Let's try the pyramid building first. Probably the closest I'll ever get to Egypt."

Another man stationed there and also wearing a suit, his eyes shielded by sunglasses though now the dark clouds fully covered the sky, let them inside.

They could see that the stone walls on the outside also constituted the interior walls.

The inside was enormous. In the center of the facility was, at least Decker assumed, the PARCS radar apparatus that Sumter had told them about. It looked somewhat like the enormous telescopes one would see in an observatory but with lots of other equipment surrounding it, including workstations lining the walls, with banks of darkened computers on them.

"Wow," said Jamison. "This looks like something you'd see in a weird science fiction film where they're plotting how to blow up the world."

"It might not be fiction," retorted Decker.

"Gee, thanks for that comforting thought."

Decker saw only one doorway set into the far wall. "Let's go see where that leads."

Multiple sets of stairs led to a lower level, where Robie had previously told them the prisoners had been kept.

They were cages more than prison cells, obviously improvised by the look of them.

"They probably just dumped these things in here once they decided to use this place as a jail," said Decker. "Doesn't look like a lot of thought went into it at all."

"Imprisoning and torture don't require a lot of thought. Just a lot of immoral people doing all the wrong things for all the wrong reasons," Jamison said forcefully.

"I can see you've given this some thought."

"In my previous life as a journalist I did a story on the subject. It wasn't pretty."

They both noted the blood and what looked like bodily waste on the floors of the cages. And the smell of urine was strong in the air.

"Despite how disgusting this all is, I take it we won't see any congressional hearings," said Jamison.

"They're going to bury it all like they told us," replied Decker. "And so long as the people behind it are punished, I'm okay with that. We have enough to deal with as a country without having this added to the pile."

"I suppose," said Jamison doubtfully. "But what about the truth coming out being the cornerstone of democracy?"

He glanced at her. "Your old journalist's antennae tingling for the truth to come out again?"

"But that's in the past. I follow orders now."

"No, it's not in the past, Alex. It's why we're here. To find the truth."

She smiled. "I knew I liked you for a very good reason."

"If they did work on chemical and biological weapons, it must have been down here somewhere." He eyed twin corridors that went off to the left and right.

"Do you think this place might be contaminated?" asked Jamison suddenly. "I mean some of that stuff can hang around a long time."

Decker stiffened. "I didn't really think about that. But people have been working here for decades. If the place had been contaminated, they would have shut it down. At least they should have."

"Let's hope you're right. I'm not as confident."

He led the way down the corridor on the right. After taking flights of steps down they reached a cavernous room nearly as large as the one containing the PARCS system above them.

"We went down several sets of long steps to get to this point," noted Jamison. "So this space must be well underground. A hundred feet or more."

Decker nodded in agreement as he gazed around. "Doesn't look like they used this when they were running the prison. And it smells moldy, too." He walked the perimeter of the room, examining the walls and floor. In one place the wall was lighter than the other sections. Decker looked this over and then kept moving.

He stopped abruptly and turned to Jamison. "Wait a minute. How did Ben Purdy even know that something like that had happened here? That there were chemical and biological weapons produced here."

"I don't know. But we saw the research he'd done on those pages." She tensed. "Wait a minute. What would prompt him to even *do* that research?"

"That's what I was talking about. And I think the answer is Brad Daniels."

"No, Daniels was the catalyst for *Cramer's* coming here. He had nothing to do with Purdy."

"Why do you think that?" asked Decker.

"Your cardinal rule: there are no coincidences."

"Well, for every rule there is an exception. In fact, I think he *did* learn about it from Brad Daniels."

"Based on what?" she asked.

Decker pulled out Daniels's hat and pointed to another pin on there.

Jamison examined it. "An anniversary event the Air Force held?"

"Two years ago, at Minot Air Force Base, right here in North Dakota."

"But how can we know they *both* attended, even with that pin on his hat?"

"I know they did, because it was noted in Purdy's service record that he attended that very same event."

"But we still can't be sure that they met there."

"Which is why I'm going to call the nursing home in Williston and have it out with Brad Daniels once and for all."

"Go easy on him, Decker. He's an old man."

"That 'old man' is tougher than just about any son of a bitch I've ever met," Decker groused.

"But he wouldn't tell us anything before. Why would he now?"

He held up the hat and smiled. "Because now I've got a bargaining chip."

60

"Mr. Daniels, it's Amos Decker with the FBI."

Decker held the phone away from his ear as the old man started screaming at him.

"You son of a bitch. You give me back my hat. You're a thief!"

"So you noticed it was gone? I take it your eyesight is better than you let on."

"If I were forty years younger, I'd kick your ass."

"But you're not, so let's make a deal, Mr. Daniels. You answer my questions and I guarantee that you'll get your hat back intact."

"What questions?" Daniels barked. "I told you I can't answer nothing. It's classified. Do you know what 'classified' means, moron?"

"What I'm going to ask you has nothing to do with classified information. I just want to ask if you met someone at the anniversary event you attended at Minot Air Force Base."

"How the hell did you know about that?" Daniels barked.

"You have a pin about it on your hat."

"A hat you *stole*. That's a felony."

"At most it's a misdemeanor. And like I said, you'll get your hat back. I promise."

"How do I know you'll keep your word?"

"Because, like you, I took an oath to serve this country. And that oath means a lot to me, like it did to you."

"Go on," said a suddenly calmer Daniels.

"Was there someone there you met named Ben Purdy, he was a sergeant with the Air Force?"

Daniels didn't answer right away. Finally, he said, "Is he dead, too?"

"No, but he is missing. So you did meet up with him?"

"What the hell is going on up there?"

"I'm trying to find that out. Did you mention to Purdy that the London facility was used to work on biological and chemical weapons?"

"That's classified, dammit. You said nothing you asked me would make me reveal classified information. You're a big, fat liar, you are."

"I know all about the program that went on up here and at other facilities around the country. Pine Bluff, Rocky Mountain Arsenal, Fort Detrick."

"Camp Detrick, least it was back then." He fell silent. "So, you been read in, I see."

"I have been. I have top secret security clearances."

"What does this have to do with anything?"

"I'm not sure. But it seems that a lot of people are interested in it enough to kill other people. So it wasn't a radar facility back then?"

"Not exactly."

"But you worked with radar and such. Why would they send you there if it involved working on chemical weapons? You had no expertise in that."

Decker heard a long sigh, and then Daniels said, "It was *supposed* to be a radar facility, so they had to have radar people stationed there. Otherwise, it would look funny. So I was one of those guys. You know, keeping up pretenses."

"Did you know that going in?"

"I didn't know anything. I went where I was told."

"Did you have anything to do with the work there?"

"Not really. Us radar guys learned pretty quick that something was up. I mean we weren't running a radar facility, for starters, and we had been sworn to secrecy, even beyond what you normally are. We had to sign papers and stuff. Now, we knew the commies were in a nuke race with us. But we also knew the Germans had been making chemical weapons during the Big One and we had to play catch-up. That wasn't a huge secret. So when we started seeing some of the stuff being brought into London? Well, I saw enough boxes marked with skulls and crossbones to know what was going on. And then they recruited us to do some stuff with what they were doing. I don't mean making the shit. But I'd seen some of the labs they had down there."

"You mean in the lower level of the pyramid building?" Decker asked.

"Yeah. They usually didn't want us down there. We mainly worked on security and keeping up the facility, stuff like that. But occasionally, as time went on, we were sent down there to do some tasks. And we had to put on masks and special suits and crap like that."

"Did you see any of the stuff that came out of there?"

"Yeah, we helped put it in these special storage rooms in these bombproof containers. Scared the crap out of me, I can tell you. They had warning signs all over the place: 'Highly toxic,' 'Do not touch,' 'Never take your masks and goggles off,' stuff like that. Even with that some of the guys got sick. I mean inadvertently. They never tested stuff on anybody, nothing like that. This is the good, old U.S. of A. We don't do that shit."

"Anything else?"

Daniels didn't answer.

"Mr. Daniels, anything else? It's important."

Daniels didn't respond and Decker decided to just let the silence linger. He wanted Daniels to feel the moment, to let him understand that something momentous was happening and he could be an integral part of it. If he would just open up.

Daniels said, "Then, sometime in the late sixties, it all went away. They closed up shop and then we started using the facility as a radar station. I got to do what I was trained to do. It was really exciting stuff. We were protecting our country from the commies."

"So they took all the 'stuff' away?"

"That's right."

"Now, can you tell me about your talk with Purdy, the young man you met at the event?"

"He was a nice young guy. Stationed where I had been. He had proper security clearances. We had a lot in common. We hit it off. We had a couple drinks even. Made me feel young again."

"And then what?"

"And then, well, I told him about some of the stuff that we had done up there."

"And he was interested?"

"Yeah, asked a million questions. I answered what I could."

"Did you ever tell him about Mary Rice?"

"No, I never did."

"How did you leave it with him?"

"I didn't leave it any way with him. If he followed up on any of it, I didn't know nothing about that." He paused. "You said he's missing. He was a right nice young fellow. Proud to serve his country. You think he's okay?"

"I'm hoping he is, Mr. Daniels. But in my business sometimes hope isn't good enough."

Decker filled Jamison in as they left the facility.

"So Ben Purdy did learn about the WMDs from the same source that Irene Cramer did—Brad Daniels."

"Yep," replied Decker. "But we still have a lot to figure out."

As they passed the land ringing the installation, Jamison pointed out a large John Deere combine that was kicking up dust in an adjacent field.

"Do you think the Brothers have anything to do with this?"

"I can't say one way or another," answered Decker.

Jamison pointed in the other direction. "At least that's a positive."

Decker looked in that direction where there was an operating oil rig. "What?"

"The pipe over there. No methane gas flare. They must be piping the gas out instead of wasting it, or maybe separating the bad stuff out like Stan was talking about."

"Will miracles never cease," replied Decker, smiling.

His phone buzzed the next instant.

Decker said, "Hey, Kelly, what's up?"

"Decker, we have a situation here," said Kelly, the strain quite clear in his voice.

"What situation?"

"Stuart McClellan has been found dead."

"Dead! How? Where?"

"In a car at one of his storage facilities. Looks like he committed suicide."

"Give me the address and we'll be there as fast as we can."

61

It was the perfect place to off yourself, thought Decker as they drove up to the old wooden building that was about the size of five large barns melded together. In a fenced-in area were remnants of what looked to be broken pieces of drilling equipment. Three police squad cars and Kelly's SUV were parked by the entrance.

Yellow police tape fluttered and crackled in the stiffening breeze that heralded the storm system marching on them.

Kelly met them outside and led them into the building. In the center of the sprawling space was a late-model black Cadillac sedan with its driver's-side door open. They eyed the hose running from the tailpipe to the rear passenger window, which was open a crack, allowing the hose to fit through.

Kelly pointed to the driver's-side door. "We opened the door to check the body." Decker and Jamison stepped forward.

Stuart McClellan lay across the front seat, his head on the console separating the front seats, with his feet on the floorboard. His eyes were closed, and his face was the trademark cherry red. Inhaling a tank full of exhaust fumes caused carbon monoxide atoms to piggyback on red blood cells, jettisoning oxygen atoms in the process. The cells traveled throughout the body but arrived at their destinations without the oxygen needed to keep the body functioning, result-ing in both death and the cherry-red color.

"He suffocated, clearly," noted Kelly.

Decker said, "Any signs of a struggle, defensive wounds, bruising to the body to show that he was knocked out and then placed here?"

"We haven't done a full exam of the body, but we've found nothing like that," said Kelly. "No obvi-ous wounds and no blood. We're going to dust for prints, of course, but we don't expect that to yield much. The guy obviously killed himself."

Jamison said, "There was no one else here? No security cameras to show any activity?"

"No and no," replied Kelly. "McClellan's had this place forever. But it's mostly a junkyard now. No one works out here anymore. And there are no security cameras because there's nothing of value. Hell, he probably wished someone had taken some of this junk."

"Did he leave a note?" asked Jamison.

"Not that we found, no, but a lot of suicides don't."

"Does Shane know?" asked Jamison.

"I've left a message. I'm sure I'll hear back."

"When's the last time someone saw McClellan?" asked Decker.

"He and Hugh Dawson were seen last night having dinner together at Maddie's. Couldn't believe that when I heard it. I mean, I don't think those two have even shared a civil word, much less a dinner."

"Well, McClellan owns the restaurant now. Or did," replied Jamison.

"Come again?" said a surprised Kelly.

"Might as well tell him," said Decker.

"Tell me what?" said Kelly.

Jamison said, "Dawson was selling all his businesses to McClellan, including the restaurant."

"The hell you say."

"They were probably there celebrating the deal closing," added Jamison.

Kelly looked stunned. "Why in the world would he do that? And how did you find out?"

"We happened upon them while they were meeting," said Jamison vaguely. "As to the reason for the sale, Dawson basically just wanted to cash in and get out. At least that's what he told us."

"And what about Caroline?"

"Her father said she'd be fine with it."

Kelly looked angry. "No way in hell she'll be *fine* about it. She's worked her ass off for all this. And Maddie's was her baby. This is going to kill her."

This outburst surprised Jamison, and her expression showed it. She said, "Uh, I know you said you were really tight with her growing up."

Kelly calmed, looking sheepish. "Look, any guy around here that wasn't in love with Caroline Dawson needed to have his head examined, and I was no exception."

"But that was high school," said Jamison.

Kelly glanced at her. "Sometimes time doesn't make a difference in how you feel about someone." He suddenly refocused. "But that's neither here nor there. So we got either a murder or a suicide here, and we need to figure out which it is."

Decker ran his gaze over the Caddy's interior. "Any signs that someone else was recently here? Tire marks? Another vehicle seen coming or going during the relevant times?"

"No, nothing like that. But considering everything that's happened so far, I think we need to go slow on this. Because while it sure looks like a suicide, for the life of me I can't imagine what his motive would be. The *facts* are that McClellan is rich as shit, just bought out his rival, and had this entire town in his pocket. Maybe a lifelong dream of his, for all I know. So right after completing that, and maybe, like Alex suggested, celebrating his triumph, he drives out here and sucks on a tailpipe to finish off the best day of his life? Tell me how that makes sense."

"I agree with you," said Decker.

"Who's doing the post?" asked Jamison.

"The guy who came up to do Walt's isn't available."

"Let me call someone in from the Bureau to do it," said Decker.

"I appreciate that."

Decker pulled a pair of latex gloves from his jacket pocket, slapped them on, and leaned into the Caddy. He felt one of the dead man's arms. "He's clearly in rigor. So roughly twelve hours or more. Ambient temp in here is average. But if he burned through a full tank of gas after he died, it might've gotten pretty hot in here."

"Definitely could have sped up the rigor initiation *and* body decomp," pointed out Jamison.

Kelly said, "That's going to be important because we need to establish alibis."

"So any idea where Hugh Dawson is?"

"You're thinking Hugh had something to do with this?"

"If he was the last person to see McClellan before he died, I have some questions to ask the man. And the sooner the better."

62

One phone call found Hugh Dawson at his home. Kelly, Decker, and Jamison arranged to meet him out there that night. They didn't tell him why.

The maid led them to his office, where he rose from behind his desk to greet them.

He looked anxiously at Kelly. "Is it true? Is Stuart really dead?"

"How'd you hear about that?" said Kelly imperturbably.

"Hell, it's all over. My maid told me. She heard it from her boyfriend who works for McClellan."

"It is true," said Decker.

"How'd he die?"

Decker said, "He was found dead in his car. Looks like carbon monoxide poisoning. The same way your wife died," he added, drawing sharp looks from both Jamison and Kelly.

Dawson plopped back down in his chair. "Holy Lord."

"We understand you had dinner with McClellan last night," said Kelly.

"That's right, at Maddie's."

"Did he pick the place?" asked Jamison.

"Uh . . ." He glanced at Kelly.

"I know about the deal," Kelly said.

"Okay. To answer your question, it *was* his idea. Now that he owns it."

"And have you told Caroline yet?" asked Kelly sternly.

"I'm going to meet with her and tell her."

"Can I ask why you sold out?" said Kelly. "Jamison said you told her you just wanted to cash out. Last time I was here you were upbeat about things. Buying properties. Caroline opened her restaurant and everything."

"I also talked about the downsides to fracking. And I'm just tired, Joe. Been doing this for nearly forty years."

"What are you going to do?" Kelly asked.

"Buying a place in France. Only a lot bigger than the one I had before. Got a guesthouse for Caroline large enough for the kiddies when they come along."

"I wouldn't count on that," said Kelly. "You basically sold out her life from under her."

"I don't see it that way," he said crossly.

"Then you're choosing not to see."

"I know you were very close growing up—hell, there was a time there when I thought you two would walk down the aisle. But this is none of your damn business."

"Okay, then let me get back to what *is* my business. When was the last time you saw McClellan?"

"When we left the restaurant."

"Give us the details."

"It was around eleven. He got in his car and I got in mine. I drove back here."

"Can anyone corroborate that?" asked Decker.

"No. Everybody here had gone home long before then. It was just me."

"So nobody can vouch for your whereabouts?" asked Kelly.

"Wait a minute. Are you implying—? Why the hell would I want to kill Stuart McClellan? He just paid me a great deal of money."

Jamison interjected, "We're just trying to learn about timelines and alibis, Mr. Dawson. It's all routine."

"Well it sure doesn't come across as routine. Where was Stuart found? At his place?"

"No," said Kelly.

"And you said it was carbon monoxide poisoning? Could it have been an accident? Like Maddie?"

Decker said, "No, it was clearly deliberate. Can you think of any reason why he would commit suicide?"

Dawson considered this for a few moments. "Not a single one. He stood to make a great deal more money now that he had combined his businesses with mine. He could merge the back-end offices, eliminate redundancies, and increase his cash flow. He was sitting pretty. So why would he kill himself?"

"Then it looks like murder," said Decker. "Unless we're missing something. Do you know why anyone would want to kill him?"

Dawson looked warily at him. "I don't like making accusations against anybody."

"Let's call them suggested persons of interest," said Decker. "It goes no further than this room. But if you have names we can check them out."

"Stuart was a hard-nosed businessman. He drove tough bargains. Left some with nothing."

"These people have names?" asked Jamison.

"None of them are still around here. And the one that I might have named has been dead about a year." He paused and looked uncertain.

"What?" said Decker quickly.

"Look, I like the boy fine. I really do. Fought for his country and all. But Stuart was merciless to him."

"You mean Shane?" said Kelly.

"I know you are buds."

"We were friends growing up. And we're still friends, but not as tight as before. Do you have anything more concrete than his abusing Shane?"

"Not really, no. But you asked and so that's what my answer is."

"And Shane would inherit his father's fortune, of course," said Jamison.

"As far as I know. You'd have to check with the

415

lawyers on that. Stuart could have made a will leaving it to anybody he wanted."

"But if he did that and Shane didn't know, he could still have a motive for murdering his father," pointed out Decker.

"I don't think I know anyone less in love with money and business than Shane," noted Kelly.

"Shane told us you and he weren't as close as you once were," noted Jamison. "And you just said the same thing."

"High school was high school. Then life came along. We went our separate ways. But I knew the guy back then, and that guy hasn't changed. Hell, he could have stayed here and sat on his ass and let his father pay him. But he joined the Army and risked his life for his country. He came back with medals and he never talks about any of it."

Dawson smiled. "You two were the best football players this town ever turned out."

"Decker played for the Cleveland Browns," said Jamison. "After starting for Ohio State."

"Wow," said Kelly. "That is damn impressive."

"Well, you're certainly big enough," said Dawson, eyeing Decker's huge frame.

"Yeah, if it were only about size I'd be in the hall of fame," noted Decker wryly. He looked at Kelly. "We still have to check it out."

"I know we do," said Kelly brusquely. "And I'll

keep an open mind, but I think that's the wrong tree to bark up."

"Well, if Shane has an alibi, then that will settle it," said Jamison.

Kelly eyed Dawson. "You might want to talk to your daughter sooner rather than later. You don't want her finding out about the sale from somebody else. That would not be good."

"You let me worry about that, Joe," snapped Dawson.

"So you're going to live in France with Caroline?"

"That's right."

Kelly smiled grimly. "And what, maybe she'll meet some Frenchman, fall in love, and have a bunch of kids?"

"That's up to her, not me."

"And if she doesn't want to go, will you give her a stake to start her own business?"

"I don't know. I . . . I'm not sure I'm ready to be separated from her. I lost her mother. I don't want to lose her."

"Well, be prepared to do just that," said Kelly.

"She can start another restaurant in France," said Dawson dismissively. "She was ready to move last time. What's the difference now?"

"Well, I guess you'll find out one way or another," said Kelly.

"What do you care?" demanded Dawson. "Don't tell me you're still in love with her?"

"It's not a crime to care about somebody, Hugh, even if they make decisions you don't agree with. Especially if they're family. But maybe you don't think that way. I mean, look at what happened to your son."

Dawson's face grew red. "You can just get the hell out of here."

"Don't worry, we were leaving anyway."

63

"Of all the dumb, shortsighted things to do," groused Kelly as they were driving back to town. "He expects his daughter, who he just sold down the river, to up and move to France with him and leave everything and everybody she's ever known behind."

"I agree that it's both presumptuous and really insensitive," said Jamison. She looked at Decker. "What do you think?"

"I was wondering whether Hugh Dawson could have been involved in McClellan's death."

"That wasn't what we were talking about," said Jamison.

"Well, it's what I want to talk about. But I don't see a motive."

Kelly said, "Shane probably has a motive, at least on paper. But he doesn't care about inheriting a fortune. And if he were going to kill his old man, he'd just shoot him."

"You'd be surprised how many people start to care when they're actually close to getting the money," noted Decker. "But money isn't the only reason to kill someone. I can imagine Stuart made Shane's life a hell on earth."

"But Stuart's always been like that with Shane. Why all of a sudden would it make him kill the guy?"

"That's what they pay us to figure out," retorted Decker. "Did you reach Shane? How'd he take the news?"

"I met with him before we went to see Hugh. Unless he's a world-class actor, he had nothing to do with it."

"Did he have any ideas about who might want to kill Stuart?"

"Not that he volunteered."

"Did he say what he was going to do?" asked Jamison.

"No. He walked out in a daze, really."

Jamison said, "Dawson got really upset with you at the end, when you mentioned his son, Junior."

"None of that was right. Junior should still be alive leading a good, full life. Instead he's six feet under because of that guy."

"Was it really that bad?" asked Jamison.

"It was worse."

Decker continued. "What I found curious was McClellan died by carbon monoxide poisoning."

"You mean like Caroline's mother," noted Jamison.

"Exactly. Tell me exactly what you saw at the scene of Maddie's death," said Decker, looking at Kelly.

Kelly took a few moments to marshal his thoughts. "The car had slid off the road. There was an embankment there. The snow was about three feet deep at that point. The vehicle was leaning at about a thirty-degree angle. The tailpipe had gotten pushed up against the embankment. It was partially bent, and snow and dirt had gotten lodged in there. Totally clogged."

"But why wouldn't she have gotten out of the car and checked?" asked Jamison. "She naturally would have wanted to see *how* she was stuck, so she could get free somehow."

"Exactly what I thought. And the answer was when she slid off the road sideways the brute force smashed her up against the window. She hit her head and was unconscious. There was a hematoma on the side of her head and a bit of blood and other trace on the window where she struck it."

"And the airbags didn't deploy?" asked Jamison.

"We checked that. Had an expert come in. He said in that situation the airbags probably would not have deployed. And it was an older model Jeep SUV. It didn't have side airbag curtains anyway. And the seat harness would not have necessarily prevented her from being thrown to the side. There were no other signs of anyone else being there, though the snowfall would have covered any traces. She had cash and credit cards in her purse, and still had her wedding ring and a pair of diamond studs on. So robbery wasn't a motive. And we could never find any reason for anyone to intentionally kill her. And, besides, how would anyone know she would have been out in the blizzard? She only went out because Alice Pritchard called her when she lost power. The autopsy came back with an accident as the manner of death and carbon monoxide poisoning as the cause."

"Who called overseas to tell them she'd died?" said Jamison.

"Actually, that was me. I was in charge of the investigation. Hardest call I've ever had to make. As soon as I told Caroline she started sobbing. I couldn't make out another word after that. And I felt bad because I couldn't do anything to help her. I just felt so helpless," Kelly said miserably.

They dropped him off at the police station and watched him go inside.

Jamison said somberly, "He's still very much in love with Caroline Dawson."

"Yes he is. And I wish him luck, but if I was Kelly, I wouldn't hold my breath. I don't think she's going to suddenly run into his arms."

As they pulled away, Jamison said, "But this may very well have nothing to do with why we're up here. Figuring out the time-bomb comment by Ben Purdy. That has to be our focus."

"Our focus is finding out who killed Irene Cramer."

"But isn't one connected to the other?"

"Not necessarily."

As they pulled in front of their hotel, Baker hailed them from the street.

Decker rolled down the passenger window and said, "Stan, what's up?"

"Was just coming to see you. That photo you gave me, of the dead woman?"

"Irene Cramer. What about it?"

"I asked around about anyone that might have, you know, *been* with her."

"And did you find anybody?"

"Three guys. All oil field workers."

"And?"

"And they all said that they hadn't had sex with her."

"So what *did* they do with her?" asked Jamison.

"She bought them food and drinks."

"That's interesting," said Jamison.

Decker said, "But it makes sense. Why get into bed with strangers if she could get the info she wanted by springing for food and booze? Be a lot easier for her."

"Boy, I hear you on that," said Jamison a bit too quickly. When Decker glanced at her she blushed and looked away.

Baker said, "As I was saying, she bought them food and drinks, and asked a lot of questions."

"Questions about what?"

"That Air Force installation."

"But why ask oil workers about a military base?"

"Beats the hell out of me. She might have talked to some of the guys who worked there before the Air Force pulled out. And I never saw any of the Vector guys come into town, so she might not have been able to ask them."

"What sort of questions did she ask?" Decker wanted to know.

"Anything suspicious they might have seen. Whether they knew the history of the facility. And she asked about the auctioning off of the land around the facility."

Decker nodded thoughtfully. "Now, that is interesting. Anything else?"

"That's about it. Hope it helps."

"Thanks, Stan."

Baker moved off and Decker rolled his window back up.

"*Did* that help?" asked Jamison, who had listened to the whole exchange.

"I don't know. I can understand her wanting to know about the military base and the land around it. I mean that's where Daniels worked, after all."

"But it's still puzzling," conceded Jamison.

"Everything about this damn case is puzzling."

64

Later that night Decker and Jamison were summoned once more to a meeting with Blue Man. Robie and Reel picked them up outside their hotel and drove them to a home about fifteen miles outside of town.

As they pulled up to the house Decker said, "Looks abandoned."

"That's what we like about this place," said Reel. "So many free spaces to meet."

"That's the *only* thing we like about this place," added Robie. "Otherwise, it's turning out to be more dangerous than the Middle East."

They were led inside, where Blue Man was sitting in a wooden-backed chair, dressed in a perfectly tailored suit and looking like he had just started his day.

"We have some things of interest to share," he began. "Patrick McIntosh and Mark Sumter are currently lawyering up, if only to enter guilty pleas."

"And Vector?"

"They *should* be permanently barred from future defense contracting, along with all their executives."

"But will that actually happen?"

"We'll see. Washington, DC, is full of successful second acts. But the uniforms involved in this are going to take a tumble. At least the ones who can't find a chair to sit in before the music stops will."

"Anything else?" asked Decker.

"For your purposes, something far more important. And ominous."

"Let's hear it."

"It may mean nothing, or it may mean everything, but we've been getting some curious chatter from the Middle East lately."

"What sort of chatter?"

"The sort that we do not like to get. We often get enhanced communication activity when something significant is going down. It happened before 9/11 but no one registered it. Now we take these occurrences very seriously."

"Is there any indication where it might be coming from?" asked Jamison.

"Not precisely. But from what we can tell, there is a nexus to *this* country."

"What does that mean?"

"Nothing good, I'm afraid."

"What can we do about it?" asked Jamison.

"We need to solve this thing faster rather than slower. Time is not on our side."

"You've said that before. And we're working as fast as we can."

"Then we must work faster."

Decker stared down at him. "Do you know what was going on at London, AFS *decades* ago? And it had nothing to do with radar or prisoners."

"Tell me."

"They were making biochemical weapons," said Jamison.

Blue Man nodded and said, "That was before my time, though I knew of the past military efforts in that regard. But those programs were ended and all stockpiles destroyed."

"Maybe nobody told the folks over at London."

"And this information came from . . . ?"

"An old man in a nursing home named Brad Daniels. He worked there back then. He saw things. And he knew both Ben Purdy and Irene Cramer. We placed a security guard at the facility to look after him."

"And Daniels told Cramer and Purdy about this past work?"

"Yes."

"And the relevance today?"

"If people who knew about it are dying, there must be some relevance. Otherwise, what's the point?"

"What do you think?"

"If the stockpiles weren't destroyed, where might they be?"

"We were at the facility and didn't see anything, but we didn't come close to searching the whole place," noted Jamison.

"Perhaps it would be a good idea to get a team in to more thoroughly go through it," said Blue Man. "As discreetly as possible."

"I think that would be a great idea," said Decker.

"Then we will make that happen. Now, Purdy was transferred out of the facility, so if the stockpile is still there, I wonder what he was going to do about it. It's not like he could have gone back to London AFS. And it also makes me wonder what Cramer's plan was. What could she possibly think she could do about a weapons stockpile at an Air Force facility? She couldn't go near the place."

"It doesn't make much sense," agreed Decker.

"But if this *is* connected to the increased chatter from the Middle East, then it makes sense to somebody," pointed out Jamison.

"Then those people must be here right now," said Decker.

Robie said, "The guys who came after me were a mix of folks. But they could have been hired by others. They looked the mercenary type. Same with the ones chasing you to that barn."

"Possibly," said Decker.

"If these people want the stockpiles, assuming

they actually exist, they must want to smuggle them out of the country," said Blue Man.

"Or use them here," said Decker.

"Which was my next comment," said Blue Man. "Any indication from this Daniels exactly what sort of biochem weapons we're talking about?"

"Only that they're classified and he'll take them to the grave," said Decker.

"But Decker," said Jamison, "remember Daniels said he told Purdy because Purdy was military and had security clearances. And he opened up to you more on the phone not just because you had his hat, but because you told him you had high-level security clearances." She glanced at Blue Man. "If you all were to talk to him, he might open up even more. I mean, you can clearly receive classified information."

Blue Man looked at Robie and Reel. "Attend to that. Right away."

"We can give you the details," said Jamison.

As they were dropping Decker and Jamison off back at the hotel Robie said to Decker, "While we're seeing this old guy, you all are on your own."

Jamison patted her holstered Glock and said, "We'll be careful."

"From what I've seen so far, you'll have to be more than careful," said Reel. "Good luck."

65

"Any activity?" said Reel, who drove while Robie rode shotgun on the way down to Williston.

"Nothing so far. If we picked up a tail, they're good."

"Well, so far, they have been."

"How much further?"

"Twenty clicks."

"Read the service record on Bradley Daniels," said Robie. "Sounds like a real patriot. Purple, Bronze, DFC, and the Airman's Medal. Well over a hundred bombing missions in the European and Pacific Theaters. Shot down twice. Sat in a life raft with three other crew members for a month in the Pacific before they got picked up by a Navy destroyer. Then got right back in the saddle."

"Like you said, a real patriot."

Robie glanced in the side view and saw what he had seen for the last hour: nothing. And he wasn't pleased by that. None of this felt right to him.

It was well after eleven by the time they got to the nursing home and past visiting hours, but their federal badges intimidated the night supervisor so much, he led them directly to Daniels's room and then fled.

The old man was fast asleep in his bed. The light was off in his room, and Robie debated whether to turn it on. He finally opted not to.

They drew near the bed, one on each side.

"Mr. Daniels?" Reel said gently, before touching the man's shoulder.

He started and his eyes opened, then closed, then opened and stayed that way.

"Who the hell are you?" he said, blinking rapidly and sitting up slightly.

Robie and Reel held out their creds and official badges. "We're with the intel community," said Robie.

"Turn on a damn light so I can see."

Reel turned on the overhead light and Daniels scrutinized the badges and cred packs.

"We were told you couldn't see very well," said Robie.

"Yeah, well, I let people think that for my own reasons."

"Okay."

"These look real," he finally said, handing them back.

"That's because they are."

"What do you want with me?"

"London AFS?" said Reel.

Daniels lay back on his pillow. "I already talked to

431

the Feds. That big fellow. FBI. He took my hat, the son of a bitch."

Reel reached into her jacket pocket, pulled out the hat, and handed it to him. "And he asked us to return it."

Daniels looked pleased by this and said, "Well, at least he's a man of his word."

Robie said, "Ben Purdy? You told him more than you told Decker. We've been ordered here to get the rest of the story."

"Why?"

"It's become relevant again, sir," said Reel.

"You don't have to call me sir."

"I do it out of respect. Purple, Bronze, Distinguished Flying Cross, Airman's Medal? You more than earned it."

Daniels blinked again and his eyes grew watery. "Everybody I served with is long since dead. My wife's dead, so are my kids. Nobody left 'cept my grandkids and their kids, and they got their own lives. Sucks being old and alone. I just sit in here rotting away, waiting for the end."

Reel glanced at Robie and said to Daniels, "You should be at a VA facility. You'd find a lot more in common with the folks there than you probably do here."

Daniels looked excited. "You can make that happen?"

Robie said, "If that's what you want, sir."

They helped Daniels to sit up straighter.

"What do you want to know?"

"What exactly did you tell Ben Purdy?"

"I told him the truth. Everything."

"Which was?" said Reel.

The power in the facility went out, every room, every inch.

Panicked cries were heard all over the nursing home.

Robie's and Reel's weapons came out. Reel covered the door and Robie closed the window curtains, after gently pressing Daniels flat onto the bed and whispering into his ear. "Stay right there and don't move."

Daniels gave one curt nod and then froze.

The sounds of footsteps could be heard rushing along the hall. Reel poked her head out and saw nurses and other personnel running around. The night supervisor raced up to the door and said, "We don't know what happened. Everything just went black. And our backup generator didn't kick on. And . . . and two big trucks just pulled up in front."

"Call the cops, do it now. Tell them you have a mass shooting event going down."

"We do?"

"You do. Go!"

He ran off, looking terrified.

Reel looked at Robie. "Two big trucks?"

"Who are they?" whispered Daniels from his bed.

"We got this, sir," said Reel. She eyed the wheelchair and then looked at Robie. "This room is Ground Zero. They have to know."

He nodded. They slipped over to the bed, gently lifted Daniels up, and placed him in the wheelchair. Robie pushed it while Reel led the way.

They reached the doorway; Reel poked her head out and gave the all clear. They turned and moved quickly to the left, away from the front doors.

Reel slipped another pistol out of her second holster. Both guns had laser scopes. She had already put on a pair of NV optics, as had Robie. The darkness to both of them was now represented as daylight. The problem was, their opponents would no doubt have the same technology.

Robie pushed the wheelchair with one hand and held his pistol in the other. They disappeared down the hallway.

Thirty seconds later the doors to the nursing home were forced open. A barrage of armed men did not storm in. There was a whizzing sound as the motorized stainless steel robot rolled along on tubeless tires. Its laser eye swept across the hall, comparing what it was seeing with the building layout stored in its database.

It turned right and accelerated. There it ran into the off-duty police officer that Decker had engaged to look after Daniels. His pistol was pointed at the robot, his flashlight beam reflecting off the thing's metal sides.

"What the hell?" the man exclaimed.

He started to lower his weapon as the laser eye ran over him and held on the weapon. The next moment the guard looked down at his chest where a dart was now sticking out. His eyes rolled back in his head and he fell to the floor.

The robot whirled on, neatly navigating around the fallen man.

It reached Daniels's room. The laser hit all four corners of the room and then drew and held on the empty bed. The robot rolled forward and a tiny probe extended from its front side. This probe hit the sheets and ran its tiny metallic head over it.

Information flashed back to the sensor pack in the robot's brain and confirmation was made. The probe receded but did not fully return to the cavity from which it had emerged. The robot turned and headed back out as the probe swiveled from side to side, drawing in myriad *scents* in its path, as it searched for only one, that of Brad Daniels.

It turned right and left and then stopped at a closed door. The probe twitched, like the nose on a scent hound, and a red light illuminated on the front of the robot's steel wall. The robot retreated about a foot, a portal opened on the front of it, and stabilizers shot out from its sides and gripped the floor, like a construction crane would employ to keep upright and balanced.

The next moment the round fired from the portal smashed into the door and the force of the impact caused it to topple inward.

Through the smoke emerged Reel. She saw the robot, her gaze ran over its contours, she raised her weapon and placed three incendiary rounds with explosive kickers right into the thing's hide, with one round impacting the machine's laser eye.

The laser eye went out, the rounds performed as they were engineered, and the robot disappeared behind a thick cloud of smoke.

Reel heard the alarming screech of a timer and threw herself back into the room, right as the robot's failsafe counter hit zero.

The blast collapsed the walls of the room Reel had leapt back into.

When the smoke cleared, sirens could be heard.

The two big trucks that had been parked in front of the nursing home, and from which the attack robot had been launched, were long gone.

Inside the room, a coughing and sputtering Robie and Reel slowly rose from the remains of the shattered room. They were alive only because they had taken cover behind a large metal storage unit standing against one wall.

As they gazed around, their collective eyes caught and held on Daniels. He was still in his wheelchair, but he hung limply to the side. His head was bleeding, and his breaths were shallow. A section of the ceiling had fallen on him.

Reel raced over to him and felt for his pulse. "Really weak."

Robie cleared the debris away and pushed him out of the room and down the hall, toward the front entrance. Reel was right next to him.

"If he dies—" she began.

"—then we've lost," Robie finished for her.

66

"He's in a coma," said Robie. "They don't know if he's going to make it. But he's a tough old bird. My money's on him."

It was the following evening and he was sitting in the back seat of Jamison's SUV. Decker was in the passenger seat. Reel had gone to stay with Daniels at the hospital.

"A robot?" said Jamison. "They sent a freaking robot?"

"A killing machine," said Robie. "Didn't expect to see it at a nursing home in North Dakota."

"So we don't know what he told Purdy," said Decker.

"He was just about to tell us when everything went to hell."

"We keep swinging and missing," said Decker. "And we're getting down to our last outs." A text appeared on his phone and he looked down at it.

"The ME just completed the post on McClellan, and he has some interesting findings."

"Let's go hear what they are," said Jamison.

Robie opened the truck door and climbed out. "I'd like to remain in the background. Loop me in later."

Twenty minutes after leaving Robie they stared down at the naked body of Stuart McClellan. Joe Kelly had joined them at the funeral home. McClellan had been professionally sliced and diced by an ME provided by the FBI. Tom Reynolds was a stern-looking gent in his late fifties with a military haircut, and his manner was no-nonsense. But there was a twinkle in his eyes that perhaps evinced the *interesting* development he had mentioned in his text.

"What do you have?" said Decker.

"Death was certainly by carbon monoxide poisoning. Tissue samples presented classic microscopic hemorrhaging and dead tissue throughout. Congestion and swelling of the brain, spleen, liver, and kidneys. The skin is obviously flushed, another classic sign, and the blood was a cherry red, a further telltale sign."

"So it was suicide then?" said Kelly.

"No, it's not," said Decker, as he closely eyed Reynolds. "Something that straightforward would not have prompted you to text me about some 'interesting findings.'"

"Correct," said Reynolds. "Do you know what TTX is?"

Kelly shook his head but Decker said, "Tetrodo-toxin. It's a powerful neurotoxin."

Reynolds nodded. "Nasty stuff. It stops nerve con-duction between the brain and body by, in part, shutting down sodium channels. A tiny bit paralyzes the muscles needed to breathe and the heart to keep pumping blood. It's lethal whether ingested, inhaled, or absorbed into the skin, like through a cut. Takes about six hours to fully take effect. Once it stops the diaphragm, you're dead. It's one of the deadliest sub-stances on the planet. Only seen it one other time in my career, on the other side of the world."

"And yet here it shows up in London, North Dakota," said Decker.

"How did you find it?" asked Jamison.

Reynolds led them over to a highly complex-looking device. "I always bring this baby with me. Never know when it might come in handy. There were certain puzzling elements that I saw in the brain, the diaphragm, and the heart that made me suspi-cious, made me think that something neurological was going on that could not be explained away simply by the carbon monoxide. They were slight, but I have enough experience for warning bells to go off. So I ran a test on some urine in the body. And there it was, clear as day."

"Where the hell does someone get this TTX?" said Kelly.

"It's found in marine life," replied Reynolds.

"Most principally in the puffer fish. The puffer fish is a Japanese delicacy. Most TTX deaths are accidental and take place because of improperly prepared puffer fish. If the organs containing the toxin are damaged or not completely removed, that dish might be the last one you ever eat. Me, I'd stick with chicken nuggets. They'll eventually kill you, but it'll take decades." He grinned.

Decker did not smile back. "Was it ingested, inhaled, or absorbed?" he said.

"If I had to make an educated guess, I'd say ingested."

"So it might have been in something he drank?"

"Yes."

"But why poison a guy and then kill him with carbon monoxide?" asked Kelly.

"To incapacitate him and get him into the car," replied Jamison. "That way it looks like a suicide." She looked at the machine that Reynolds had used to find the poison. "And without that, we'd probably never have known. Walt Southern for sure would never have found it."

"And a murder would have been missed," added Decker. He glanced at Reynolds. "You said you'd handled a case of TTX before. Where was that, exactly?"

"The vic was found in a hotel room in Brisbane."

"Brisbane, Australia?"

"Puffer fish are found in those waters, and those in Asia. They're not indigenous to American waters."

They thanked Reynolds and walked back outside.

"Australia," said Decker again, looking thoughtful.

"What about it?" said Kelly.

"Hugh Dawson lives there part of the year, right? During the winters here?"

Kelly looked taken aback. "Okay but we already went over this. What would the motive be? He just made a ton of money off McClellan."

"I don't know what the motive might be. I'm just saying he had the means and the opportunity. And I don't like coincidences. And here we have a big one."

Jamison said, "Namely, a very rare poison that is found in fish in waters off Australia and a person here who lives there part of the time."

"And the opportunity comes from the fact that he was one of the last people to see McClellan alive and he has no alibi for the time he was killed," added Decker.

"But you'd think he'd have tried to come up with an alibi," remarked Kelly. "I mean, the TOD on carbon monoxide poisoning is never going to be to the minute. He could have stuck the guy in the car and then gone someplace where there were other people to see him."

"But he probably assumed it would never be seen

as anything other than a suicide," countered Decker. "So why bother with an alibi?"

Kelly didn't look convinced by this, but he said, "Look, I know this toxin stuff casts a whole new light on things. There has to be more to it than suicide, I'll agree with you on that. So you want to go talk to Hugh again?"

"Yeah, and right now would be a good time."

"And what about Shane?" asked Decker.

"We checked his alibi. At all relevant times he was out of town getting fracking supplies a good five hours from here. People where he was confirmed it. I told you he had nothing to do with it."

"Well, that's something," said Decker.

"Joe!"

They turned to see Caroline Dawson striding toward them, a fierce look on her features.

"Oh boy, she does not look happy," said the detective nervously.

She reached them and she stood face-to-face with Kelly. "You son of a bitch."

"What did I do?" he said, taking a step back.

"My father sold out to McClellan, everything. And you knew all about it. And you didn't tell me? I thought we were friends."

"Caroline, look, we, I mean, you have to understand—" He looked desperately at Decker for help.

Decker said, "We were the ones to find out, and then we told Joe."

Caroline didn't take her eyes off Kelly. "So you *did* know? Just say it, you did know?"

"Yes, I did."

"And Maddie's, too? That's gone as well?"

"Yes. Look, I was going to tell you but your father said—"

"Thanks for nothing." She slapped him, turned, and strode off.

Kelly rubbed his cheek where she had hit him. "Did I mention that she has a temper?"

"Boy, I would not want to be her father," said Jamison.

"Speaking of, let's go talk to him right now," said Decker. "There might be nothing left of him by the time Caroline finishes with him. We need to beat her to it."

67

On the drive out, Decker asked Kelly, "What made Shane come back here?"

Kelly eyed him. "This was his hometown."

"I understand that he was close to his mother but she had died by then, correct?"

"She had, yeah."

"And he didn't really care for his father. So why come back here and work for the guy?"

"Why don't you ask him?"

"Because I'm asking you. You're his friend."

"What does it matter why he came back?"

"Right now everything matters."

Kelly sat up straighter and stared out the window. "Shane never talked about the war with me. I only found out from other guys he served with. There were a couple that visited him here. We all went out, had some drinks, ate a bunch of red meat, and watched some football. Guy stuff, you know."

"And what did they say?" asked Jamison.

"That Shane was really brave. That he was a good

leader. That he cared about his guys more than he cared about himself. He was a Ranger, you know."

"No, I didn't know that," said Jamison.

"Yeah. He was a sergeant when he came out. He could have stayed in and worked his way up higher, I guess. But he didn't."

"Maybe he wanted to see someone here," said Decker suggestively.

Kelly continued to look out the window. "If you're thinking of Caroline, I won't disagree with you."

"But it seems unrequited," said Jamison.

"Even though their dads are both rich, they're from two different worlds. Shane is a 'beer and shoot a deer' kind of guy. Caroline could be plopped in the middle of Paris and do just fine." He paused and rubbed at his cheek. "The truth is she left us both in the dust a long time ago."

"But that doesn't mean a guy has to give up trying," said Decker.

"No, it doesn't," said Kelly slowly. "But as the years go by, it is an effort with diminishing returns."

Decker wondered if Kelly was just talking about Shane or himself.

"Okay, that does not look good. It's like Hal Parker's place all over again."

Jamison said this as they pulled into the front of Dawson's house. The door was standing wide open.

They hustled up to the porch.

Kelly peered inside the doorway and called out, "Hugh? Everything okay?"

There was no answer.

Kelly said, "At this time of the night all the hired help has long since gone home."

He pulled his gun and rushed inside. They drew their weapons and followed him in.

"Hugh!" cried out Kelly. "Hugh, you here? Everything okay? Answer me!"

They moved slowly down the hallway, taking time to clear each room before they passed by it.

They heard nothing and saw no one.

They finally reached the door to Dawson's office. It wasn't open, but Kelly tried the doorknob and found it unlocked. He tapped on the door. "Hugh, it's Joe Kelly."

There was no answer.

He turned the knob and slowly pushed open the door.

They all looked into the room, their gazes moving from one section to the next until they stopped at the desk.

"Holy shit!" exclaimed Kelly.

"Oh my God," echoed Jamison.

Decker said nothing. He gingerly moved toward the desk, avoiding the obvious debris on the floor, and stared down at Hugh Dawson, or what was left of him.

The room had now taken on an electric blue

shade for Decker as the pall of death cascaded all over the room.

I guess that sensation is going to continue to come and go, he thought.

It had been a particularly violent death.

The man was slumped in his chair with most of his head gone. The desk, chair, floor, and walls were covered with blood and bits of the deceased man.

Kelly and Jamison joined him, taking care not to impact the crime scene.

Decker ran his gaze down the weapon that had done this level of damage. The Remington side-by-side lay on the desk. It had been perched on top of a pile of books and then secured using masking tape. The muzzle was angled up and pointed at the dead man. Decker noted the line of string running from the triggers around the butt of the weapon and then back to where Dawson sat. There it dropped off the edge of the desk and into the kneehole. The man had apparently used the twine to pull the triggers, ending his life, without a doubt.

Decker examined blood and bits on the floor in front of the desk and on the sides.

Kelly shook his head. "I can't believe this. First Stuart dead, and now Hugh?"

Jamison managed to maneuver herself close enough to the desk to see a piece of paper lying there. It was covered with blood and other matter.

"It's a suicide note," she said in a hushed voice.

"What does it say?" asked Decker.

"It says he killed himself because he felt guilty for murdering Stuart McClellan."

None of them said anything for a long moment as this revelation sank in.

"Does he give a reason for murdering the guy?" asked Kelly, who was standing behind her.

"No. Just that he admits it and felt badly afterward."

They heard footsteps behind them.

They all turned to see Caroline Dawson rush into the room.

She looked around and then saw them by the desk. Her gaze reached her father's body and then moved to his destroyed face. Every muscle in her body tensed, she turned deathly pale, stopped moving forward, and screamed hysterically. A moment later she tottered to the side and collapsed to the floor unconscious, hitting her head on the side of the chair on the way down.

And she didn't move after that.

68

Kelly said, "Caroline is going to be fine. They've checked her out. No internal bleeding, but she is concussed. They're just keeping her for observation. But it could have been a lot worse. She hit her head really hard when she fell."

He finished the cup of weak coffee he'd bought from the hospital café, tossed it in the trash, and sat down next to Jamison in the visitors room. Decker was leaning against the wall.

Kelly said, "We've showed the note to several of Dawson's associates. They said it looked like his handwriting."

"I guess it's probably legit, then," said Jamison.

"So he blew his head off from guilt," muttered Kelly. "I never would have believed he had anything to do with McClellan's murder."

"Maybe Caroline will have some ideas about that."

"I doubt she knew this was coming. You saw her reaction."

"No, I meant whether she knew why her father would want to kill McClellan."

"Right. Look, the guys have been business rivals for years, that's no secret. But that's all it was: business. And why now? After they closed this big deal?"

"That's the sixty-four-thousand-dollar question," said Decker.

"Well, I've got to do the paperwork on this back at the station," said Kelly.

"And we'll go back out to the crime scene," replied Decker.

A moment later Liz Southern walked in looking breathless and distressed. She had on pale blue slacks, a dark brown blouse, and flat shoes. Her hair was tied up in a bun.

"Is Hugh really dead?"

"I'm afraid so."

"But how?"

"Looks like suicide," replied Kelly. "He left a note."

Southern looked gobsmacked. "Why would Hugh kill himself?"

"We have to figure that out."

"Why are you here?" asked Decker. "And how did you know about Hugh?"

Kelly said, "I called her and told her what had happened."

"Where is Caroline?" said Southern. "Is she going to be all right?"

Kelly said, "She's in room two-oh-three. She's going to be fine," he added when Southern looked concerned.

451

"Can I go and sit with her? I can't imagine what she must be going through."

"I see no reason why you can't. She probably needs someone with her. In fact, that's why I called you."

"Thanks." She hurried off.

After Kelly left, Jamison said, "Caroline is going to need more than a friend to see her through this. Seeing your father with his head missing? She's going to need therapy."

"And lots of it," noted Decker.

They left the hospital and drove back out to Dawson's house. Two cops were there on duty. One of the patrolmen told Decker and Jamison that a forensic tech was inside.

They put on booties and gloves and entered the house.

Dawson had not been moved. The tech was still taking pictures.

"Messy," said the young man, who had identified himself as Ryan Leakey.

"Shotgun blasts to the head usually are," commented Jamison drily.

Decker walked around the perimeter of the room, taking it all in.

"Reynolds has already been by," said Jamison, looking at her phone. "He just texted me a prelim on the time of death. Based on body temp, he died about an hour before we got here."

Decker nodded. "That's important. It's a tight enough time frame to eliminate people from the suspect list." He moved closer to the corpse and examined the end of the string dangling in front of the dead man. "You got pics of the desk yet?" he asked Leakey.

"Just one set."

"Do multiple sets, including one from directly above. From as high a point as you can."

"I got a ladder in my van outside."

"Go get it."

Decker came around to the back of the desk and looked over the shoulder of the dead man. He eyed the weapon, the twine, and the position of the body. It all fit together, he had to admit.

"See anything of interest?" asked Jamison.

"Yeah, a dead guy with no head and it's too early for Halloween."

Decker looked down at the twine, then squatted and studied the desk. He leaned in for a better look.

He straightened and looked at the doorway as Leakey came in carrying a ten-foot ladder. Decker held it for him while Leakey climbed up it and took the pictures.

"Measure the twine, too," said Decker.

"The twine?" said the tech.

"Yeah, the twine. I want to know *exactly* how long it is."

Jamison said, "Decker, what's going on? What are you thinking?"

"I'm not sure. Yet."

When the tech was done with the photos and the measurements, Decker crossed the room and sat in the same chair he had used when they had come to visit Dawson that first time. Jamison came to stand next to him.

"Looks pretty straightforward, I guess," she said.

"Yeah, except it's always the straightforward ones that end up going sideways on you. And I still don't see how this gets us to the ticking time bomb."

"I've been telling you that for a while now," Jamison pointed out.

When Decker didn't respond she added, "Well, at least we don't have to ferret out the cause and manner of death on this one."

"Don't we?" replied Decker, staring resolutely at the dead man.

69

"Caroline, why did you go out to your dad's house?" asked Jamison.

It was the following day, and she and Decker were in the woman's hospital room where the woman was lying in the bed, groggy and pale.

Liz Southern sat silently in a chair across from her, gazing at her friend sympathetically.

Caroline gazed up at Jamison and Decker, who hovered over her.

"W-what?"

"Why were you at your dad's house?"

Caroline closed her eyes and fell asleep.

Southern said, "Let's step outside. She needs her rest. I think she was more concussed than they originally thought."

Out in the hall Decker looked at Southern. "Hugh Dawson told us you and Caroline had become good friends, sort of like sisters?"

Southern smiled. "I would be quite the older sister, but yes, we have become friends." Her features turned somber. "When I heard about what happened I couldn't believe it. The nurse told me they gave her some meds to help her rest. She didn't sleep all that much last night, apparently. They said she's probably in shock after what happened to Hugh."

"Did you talk to her?" asked Decker.

Southern nodded. "Just for a few minutes. Off and on."

"Okay, then you know more than we do. What did she tell you?"

"From what I could understand, she went there to have it out with her father over some business issues. She didn't tell me what they were."

"That's right, you don't know," said Jamison.

"Don't know what?"

"Hugh Dawson sold out to Stuart McClellan."

Southern gaped. "'Sold out'? What does that mean?"

"He sold his business, all his properties, to McClellan."

"Everything, including Maddie's?" Southern looked even more stunned.

"Yes," said Jamison. "Including Maddie's."

Southern shook her head. "So I guess that explains why she was going out there. That would have been devastating for her." She paused. "So Stuart kills himself and then Hugh does, too?"

"McClellan may not have been a suicide," said Jamison.

"You mean someone murdered him?"

Decker interjected, "What else did Caroline tell you?"

"She wasn't making a whole lot of sense, but she did tell me that Hugh had betrayed her trust, only I didn't know what she meant until now."

"What else?" asked Jamison.

Southern's features turned grim. "She told me she walked into his office ready to have it out with him and then she saw him . . . dead. She started to become hysterical at that point. I went and got a nurse, and she gave her the medication."

At that moment Shane hurried up to them, looking wildly around.

"What the hell is going on? I just got back to town. Joe texted and said Caroline was in the hospital but didn't say why."

Jamison said, "She's going to be fine, Shane. But she's had a shock. Her father's dead."

Shane whirled around to look at Jamison. "Dead! What are you talking about?"

"He was found dead in his home last night. It looks like he killed himself."

"Where's Caroline? I need to see her."

"She's asleep."

"I still need to see her."

They went back into the room. Shane hurried over to the bed and looked down at Caroline. "You're . . . you're sure she's going to be okay?"

"Yes," said Southern. "She had a concussion and just needs to rest."

He backed away from the bed as Caroline stirred in her sleep and said in a lower voice, "Why would my dad kill himself?"

Decker glanced at Jamison before asking Shane, "Did you know your father and Hugh Dawson were doing a deal together?"

Shane glanced at Southern before plopping down in a chair. "Yeah, I knew they were doing some deal, but no details. He probably didn't trust me with the information. And I knew they had been meeting on the sly. But I didn't know it was for the whole business."

"Did it surprise you?" said Jamison. "That your dad was buying Dawson out?"

"Hugh Dawson has been sick of this place for a long time, and who can blame him? All you got are companies digging the land up to get the oil and gas. And you got all these people coming here who don't give a crap about this place. They just want to make their pile and go back to where they came from when it's all gone."

Southern protested, "That's not really true anymore, Shane. There are more families coming here and putting roots down."

He waved this off. "It'll always be a mining town. And when everything's sucked out, what then? You really think people are going to stick around here?"

Decker said, "So Dawson wanted to get out? You know that for a fact?"

"When Maddie was alive they were fixing to go to France. All of them, Caroline too."

"But then Maddie died," said Jamison.

Shane nodded. "And Hugh built his big house. But I could tell the man's heart wasn't in it."

"So he might have wanted to sell out?"

"Yeah, and my old man would be the only one with the money to buy him out. And it would help his business. Hell, he'd pay his workers to get the oil and gas out, and they'd pay him all that money back in rent and food and whatnot."

"Like the old company coal-mining towns," observed Decker.

"Right."

Decker said, "I want you to take a few deep breaths, Shane."

"Why?"

"Because I have something to tell you that will be upsetting."

"Hell, Decker, I've seen my buddies blown to pieces in Iraq and Afghanistan, okay?"

"Okay. So do you have any idea why Dawson would leave a suicide note saying that he killed your father?"

The blood slowly drained from Shane's face. "Hugh said he killed my dad."

459

"We found a note that said that. And there is some forensic evidence pointing to his having done so."

"What kind of evidence?" asked Southern quickly.

"We can't get into that," replied Decker.

Shane rose on wobbly legs. "He killed my old man?"

"At least that's what the note said," said Jamison.

"You sure he wrote it?"

"Several people identified it as his handwriting."

"Son of a bitch." He turned and looked at Caroline. In a low voice he added, "Does . . . does she know about this?"

Decker shook his head. "No, she doesn't." He paused and sized Shane up. "Of course with your father dead, you're a very wealthy man." He glanced at Caroline. "And she's a very rich woman."

Shane glanced at him. "*If* my old man left me anything."

"So you haven't seen his will?"

"Never had a reason to."

"Not into money?" said Decker. "With all that you could live in grand style."

"Never been one much for style," said Shane. And with that he went over to the bed, bent down, kissed Caroline on the forehead, and walked out.

Southern watched him go with a sad expression. "I've known him since he was a baby," she said. "Him and Joe. Watched them grow up together with Caroline."

"We understand they were pretty tight," said Decker.

"Inseparable was more like it. This was before Hugh and Stuart were all supercompetitive with their businesses. The kids could just be kids. Caroline was like a sister with her two protective brothers, least she was back then."

"What about her actual brother?" asked Jamison.

"Junior was always quiet and kept to himself. He was uncomfortable around his family, especially his father. Caroline, Joe, and Shane would roughhouse, but not Junior."

"I guess later, when he came out?" prompted Jamison.

Southern's lips pursed. "Caroline and his mom stood by him, that was for sure. But Hugh was especially brutal."

"That's what Kelly told us."

"Hugh wanted sons like him—strong, aggressive, kick-ass, none of the things Junior was."

"So did he see Kelly and Shane as sort of his sons?" asked Jamison.

"That's very perceptive of you because, in a way, he did, yes. He went to all the football games. Junior was the drum major of the marching band at school. He could play pretty much any musical instrument. But did his daddy acknowledge any of that? No. He just cheered on Joe and Shane scoring touchdowns."

"And when they got older?"

461

"Hugh and Stuart were at each other's throats by then. Caroline got sent off to college to learn what she needed to learn to inherit the business. Joe became a cop, as you know. Shane joined the Army right out of high school. So like that, everything changed. The gang went their separate ways."

"Kelly was the only one left here," said Jamison.

"Yeah. I'd see him around town. He looked like a lost pup." She smiled sadly. "I felt badly for him. His two best friends, gone like that. Then Caroline graduated and came back. After that Shane returned home. But it was never the same. Then Maddie died. That nearly destroyed Hugh. I didn't much care for the man, but I have to give him credit where it's due: he loved his wife."

"You seem to have definite opinions of all of them," noted Decker.

Southern gazed at him. "And that's what they are, my opinions. You can accept them or not."

Jamison glanced over at the sleeping Caroline. "And what about Caroline? Kelly and Hugh had a discussion about her. Kelly thought her father wanted Caroline to move to France with him, to find a man there to marry, and have a big family."

"Hell, I thought she might stay right here and marry Joe, or Shane. But that never happened. If you want my two cents, I think her seeing how her father treated her brother just wrecked her. The names he would call his own son, right out in public. The ridicule. It was like watching a TV show from the sixties or something. So cruel, so mean." She shook her head. "So to answer your question, I don't know if she'll ever find someone. I hope she does. She deserves to be happy."

"Daddy's perfect little girl," said Decker.

"What?"

"I told Caroline before that that's what I think her dad saw in her. She said there was no such thing."

"Well," said Southern. "I think she's right about that."

70

"So Dawson killed his rival and then shot himself. At least that part of the case is closed."

After Jamison said this she glanced at her partner. She was driving them back to the hotel.

"Decker, did you hear me?"

Decker didn't comment.

"And once again this has nothing to do with the ticking time bomb," she added. "We're still at square zero there."

"Not quite."

"What do you mean?" she shot back. "Are you holding out on me? I hate when you do that. I *am* your partner. I bet Robie doesn't hold out on Jessica Reel."

"I'm *not* holding out on you. I'm just thinking."

"Of what?"

Decker closed his eyes and downloaded a memory. "Speaking of the ticking time bomb, remember what she told us Cramer said? 'To maybe not grow our own food'?"

"Wait a minute, who said that?"

"Judith White. Cramer advised her not to grow food on her land. That's what she told us when we interviewed her."

"That's right, she did," Jamison said. "Wait a minute, their farm is right next to the Air Force facility. Are you thinking . . . ?"

Decker didn't answer right away because another memory came to him. It was something Daniels had said. And it was perhaps even more ominous than Cramer's comment.

"Let's drive out to the Brothers' place again."

"Why?"

"Just humor me, Alex."

"Okay, but you don't make it easy," she snapped.

"Since when have I ever been easy?"

"Well, you could make an effort every once in a while."

Jamison cut a sharp U-turn and headed off in the opposite direction.

Forty minutes later they pulled to a stop in front of the metal farm gate that was the main entrance to the Brothers' Colony. The gate was now closed.

Jamison put the SUV in park and said, "Okay, now what?"

Decker got out and started to look around. Jamison followed him.

"What are we looking for?"

He stared across the acres of farmland. "They've been here a while, right? The Brothers, I mean."

"You know they have."

"I mean at this location."

Jamison looked uncertain. "Well, from the looks of things they've been here a few years. It would take at least that long to build all this up to what we're seeing today."

Decker continued to watch as twin John Deere tractors moved slowly across a field far in the distance. Beyond that was the Air Force station.

"I think you're right about that."

"But why is the amount of time they've been here important?"

"It's just a theory," he said absently.

"Can you explain your theory," she said curtly.

He didn't answer. Decker headed back to the SUV, and she followed, not looking happy.

"This can't be right," he said, stopping at the vehicle's passenger door.

"What can't be?"

"If it were on the Air Force property," he began, but now Jamison saw what he was getting at and leapt ahead of him.

"The biochemical weapons. No one could get to them if they were on the Air Force property. Meaning they must be on the land they *auctioned* off."

"Right. But I don't see how they could be on the Brothers' land. I mean how could anyone hoping to get to the WMDs go there without them knowing?" He paused and his confused look deepened. "But why else would Cramer have mentioned to Judith White not to eat the crops they were growing there."

"Meaning she thought if the weapons were buried they might have leached out and contaminated the soil?"

"Exactly."

Realization grew across Jamison's features. "But, Decker, part of the auctioned land was leased. The Brothers don't control it."

He shot her a look. "The frackers. Come on!"

They ran to the SUV and jumped in.

After they had driven for a bit, Jamison pulled off next to the land occupied by the All-American Energy Company drilling site.

"Got your binoculars?" Decker asked.

She pulled the optics from the console and handed them across.

Decker focused the binoculars and surveyed the site. Then he looked in the distance at the adjacent Air Force station, and the ground in between.

After about a minute she said, "See anything interesting?"

"It's more what I'm *not* seeing."

"What?" she said.

"There's nobody working the site. It's empty. I wonder if they've finished fracking it?"

"Let me see."

She slowly surveyed the property and then lowered the binoculars. "But if they've finished fracking, why isn't there a gas flare on the vent pipe sticking up over there? Remember, I noticed that before and you called it a miracle. And I don't see any rig pumping the oil up like the other sites have, either."

"We need to ask an expert. And I know just the person."

71

They skidded to a stop at the oil rig that Stan Baker was staging and jumped out of the SUV.

They hustled up to the trailer. Decker didn't bother knocking, he just burst in with Jamison right behind.

Baker was seated in front of the computer terminals. He whirled around to stare at them. "Hey, what are you two doing here?"

"The All-American Energy Company?" said Decker.

"What about them?"

"There's nobody working the site."

"What do you mean?"

"There's nobody there. No trucks, no people, no activity."

"Decker thought they might have finished fracking the site, but we couldn't be sure," said Jamison. "So we came to see you, since you're the expert."

Baker shook his head. "They couldn't have finished fracking that well. They haven't been there long enough. They haven't even been drilling that long, so they couldn't have gotten down all that far."

"Stan, how come McClellan didn't get the rights to that parcel of land? He's got most all the other ones around here."

"I heard scuttlebutt that All-American kept bidding the price up to where it got crazy. Like two or three times what it was worth. I guess McClellan just thought those boys didn't know what the hell they were doing."

"I think they knew exactly what they were doing," said Decker ominously.

Jamison said, "And they have one of those vent pipes like we've seen around, but there's no lit flare coming off it."

"A vent pipe!" Baker looked puzzled. "No way they could be having gas coming up at this stage."

Decker suddenly flinched. "How far *could* they have gone down by now?"

"If I had to guess, I'd say no more than a couple hundred feet."

"That's what I was afraid you might say."

"Afraid? Why?"

Decker looked at Jamison. "I think we just found our ticking time bomb."

When they reached the fenced-in area at the All-American Energy Company, Decker jumped out of the SUV and tried to open the gate. It was locked.

He climbed back into the vehicle.

"Ram it, Alex," he ordered.

"Are you—"

"Just do it. We're out of time."

Baker, who was in the back seat, curled his fingers around his armrest and looked nervously at his brother-in-law.

Jamison gunned the motor, put it in drive, and slammed her foot down on the gas pedal. The big SUV leapt forward and smashed through the gates.

They leapt out, with Decker leading the way to the trailer. The door was locked.

"Decker, we don't have a warrant," said Jamison.

"To hell with a warrant, Alex."

He pulled his gun and shot the lock off. He kicked open the door, and they plunged inside. It was set up much like Baker's trailer, but there was only one computer monitor on the desk with what looked to be live data covering it.

Decker looked at the screen and said, "Stan, can you make sense of this?"

Baker sat down in the chair and started studying the graphs and other information flowing over the monitor's face.

"No, I can't, because it doesn't make a bit of sense," he said.

"What doesn't?" said Decker.

"Well, for starters, I was right. They've only drilled down about two hundred feet. At about the hundred-and-fifty-foot mark they've started to go horizontally at about a forty-five-degree angle." He used the mouse to manipulate the screen. Another image flickered up.

"And what is that thing?"

They all stared at where he was pointing.

It was represented on the screen as large and black. "They've got imaging sensors in the hole, obviously. And that sucker is showing up."

"How big do you reckon that is?" asked Decker.

"If I had to thumbnail it, based on the scales I'm used to, I'd say it's about fifty feet square."

"So about the size of an average house?"

"About, yeah. Wait, you don't think there's a house down there?"

"No. But it's a big space and you have to wonder what's in it. And the All-American Energy Company is obviously curious because, from the screen, it looks like they've drilled right into it." He indicated a spot on the screen. "Do you see where it shows one of the walls being pierced?"

"Decker!" exclaimed Jamison. "The biochem weapons!"

"The what?" barked Baker.

"I think we found them," said Decker. "And so did they." He glanced out the window of the trailer. "And why do I think that whatever is down there is an airborne weapon? And that right this minute it's being brought to the surface through that pipe?"

"Holy shit," said Baker.

"Stan, how do we stop that from happening? As fast as possible?"

Baker ran outside and they followed. He rushed over to the drill site and stopped dead. "That's odd as hell. They've got the vent pipe directly attached to the drill hole."

Decker barked, "It's not odd if that's how they're bringing this shit to the surface. It'll cover the whole area, maybe the whole state."

"But how are they bringing it up here?" said Jamison. "It's not like oil, and the pressure makes it move up into the pipe and to the surface like Stan described to us."

"Do you hear that?" said Baker.

"What?" said Decker.

"That low hum from somewhere. If I had to guess they've got some sort of vacuum system built into their equipment. That must be how they're bringing whatever is down there up here. They're creating a suction line."

"Can we turn it off?" said Decker.

Baker shook his head. "Take too long to find it and figure out how to do it. And if the suction has already been deployed, it might not matter if we turn it off. It'll be like a siphon hose into a gas tank."

Jamison exclaimed, "But if they stored that shit down there all those decades ago, won't it be like in bottles or some other containers and on shelves or even in some sort of secure vault? It's not like gas sitting in a tank that'll just be free to come up once a suction is started."

Baker snapped his fingers. "But it might if they sent a detonator down there first and blew everything up. That would smash whatever containers they're in and also create pressure vacuums within that bunker. Once pierced, the stuff, if it is airborne, would seek the point of least resistance to get out. And that would be this pipe. At least we have to assume it would be."

Baker quickly examined the roughly twelve-foot-tall pipe and then pulled out his phone.

"Rick, this is Stan. I need a concrete pumper at the All-American Energy Company site. Yeah, I know that's not our job. Just do it and tell them to move their ass. We got a pumper all loaded and ready to go over there. I want it here in ten minutes. Five would be better. Do it!"

"Guys!"

Jamison had gone back into the trailer and now appeared in the doorway.

They ran back inside. She was pointing to the screen. "Isn't that the pressure indicator you showed us back at your trailer, Stan?"

"Yeah," said Baker.

"Well it just spiked."

"What does that mean?" said Decker anxiously.

Baker said, "It means whatever the hell is down there is coming up here. And fast."

"Oh, shit!" Jamison exclaimed.

"Come on!" yelled Baker.

They all ran back outside and Baker started searching the worksite area.

"What are we looking for?" cried out Jamison.

"Something to cap that pipe."

"Can't we just bang the shit out of the end of the pipe and close it up that way?" said Decker.

"It's twelve feet off the ground, Amos, and do you see anything here to bang it with? And if you're right about the crap down there it has to be airtight."

"A piece of metal," suggested Jamison.

"You're talking a lot of pressure in that pipe, including all the air that's been trapped in that bunker. Unless it's welded on we can't count on a metal cap holding, and we don't have time to weld it or thread it."

They all looked frantically around.

"There!" shouted Baker.

It was a hose attached to a thousand-gallon barrel of water.

He grabbed the hose and ran the end of it over to the vent pipe. He flipped a box over and stood on it. "Alex, take the hose and get on my shoulders. Amos, there's a hand crank on that water tank. Once Alex gets the hose in the pipe, pump like your life depends on it."

"Well, it does," Decker muttered, getting in position.

Alex took the hose. Baker bent down, and she climbed onto his broad shoulders. She settled in as he stood up straight. The top of the pipe was still a foot above her outstretched hands, but she worked the hose up and then managed to get the end pointed into the wide pipe.

"Go, Amos!" shouted Baker unnecessarily, because Decker was already pumping like mad. A few seconds later water started coursing through the hose and into the pipe.

"Are you sure this will work?" said Jamison.

"Water is heavier than air. So it should buy us some time until the concrete pumper truck gets here."

"How will we know if it's worked?" Jamison called out.

"We won't be dead," retorted Decker, breathing hard and furiously turning the hand crank.

And it did apparently work, because they didn't die.

The pumper truck showed up a few minutes later, and Baker directed the stunned men to fill the pipe with concrete.

After that, Decker, Jamison, and Baker slumped to the ground.

Decker looked at his brother-in-law. "You're a genius, Stan. You should get a medal."

Jamison put a shaky hand on Baker's shoulder. "I second that. A really big one."

Decker let out a long breath. "Well, we stopped the time bomb. Now we just have to figure out who set it off and why."

72

"So you figured all that out from Cramer's comment about not eating stuff grown on that land?" said Jamison.

They were driving back to town.

Decker had called Robie and brought him up to speed. Robie had told him they were calling in the DoD and the Department of Homeland Security to take over the situation.

"Not just that. It was also something that Brad Daniels said," said Decker.

"Which was what?"

"He expressed surprise and maybe fear when we told him about the activity going on at the land the Air Force had sold. He said, 'They're drilling on that land?'"

"I don't remember him even saying that," said Jamison.

"Well, that's sort of my department, to recall stuff like that. But he lied to us. They didn't get rid of that stockpile."

"Maybe he thought they had."

"No, he wouldn't have been concerned about them drilling on the land unless he *knew* that stuff was down there."

Jamison nodded. "Yeah, I guess that does makes sense. I suppose he didn't trust us with the information."

"And then there was an off-color section of wall in the lower level of the radar building. I think there was a door there that was later walled up. And why have a door more than a hundred feet belowground?"

"You'd only do that if there were a tunnel to be accessed through it."

"Exactly," said Decker.

"But why in the hell would the government sell off that land with those weapons buried there? That's what I don't get."

"The easiest answer would be the folks in charge today had no idea it was even there."

"But wouldn't there be records of it?" said Jamison.

"If so, they might be buried as deep as that crap was. But I think what happened was the Air Force continued to do work on biochem weapons even after the order came down to stop. Or else they didn't want to destroy what they had worked so long to make. So they, or some rogues working there, decided to bury the shit. Maybe they thought it could come in useful down the road. Or they didn't want anyone to know what they were doing, or what they had come up with. But they had to put it some-where that they thought was safe. Back then nobody ever imagined they'd be fracking up here."

Jamison said, "And Daniels was the only one left who knew the truth? I can understand his telling Purdy. He was in the Air Force and had security clearances and all. But why would he tell Irene Cramer? Hell, he wouldn't even tell us at first."

Decker said, "Cramer's mother was a spy. Maybe the daughter learned some interview techniques from her mother. She could have taken her time, asked innocuous questions at first. Maybe she noticed Daniels's hat like I did. Maybe she researched him after he let something slip. She was a PT person. He liked her, she probably made him feel comfortable. She could have spent months working on him until she got most of the story from him. But she didn't get all of it, which led her to come here and start asking questions. The fact that she was trying to meet oil field hands and not people from the military facil-ity should have been a clue. She probably found out it was on the land *around* the installation, but she just didn't know exactly where."

"But still, you would have thought Daniels would have been more careful."

"He's an old guy, Alex. I'm not saying he's not sharp, because he is. But he wasn't going to be on his guard now to the extent he was all those years ago. And he probably never thought she would ever do anything with that information. He couldn't have known about Cramer's past, or who her mother was."

"So, a perfect storm," said Jamison.

"That's right."

"So then who killed Cramer? The people behind All-American?"

"They would be the ones with a motive. Same for Parker and Ames. They had learned things and had to be eliminated. And Purdy might be in that mix as well."

"And maybe Cramer had some evidence, which she swallowed, and they cut her open to get it back. And they blackmailed Walt Southern to mess with the post reports."

"It all fits together," agreed Decker. "In fact, it's the only thing that makes sense."

"So whoever is behind this has some serious money."

"And the sort of firepower they've brought to this area isn't cheap either, like Robie said."

"But what would be the reason to release bio-chem weapons in a remote area like this? I mean, I get that it would be terrible to happen anywhere. But to do the most damage, you'd set the stuff off in a large city where millions of people and billions of dollars of property could be impacted."

"Well, it might have been impossible to dig the bunker up without anyone knowing. And if they did succeed in digging it up, how were they going to safely open that crypt and collect the stuff inside? And then transport it out of here without anyone knowing?"

"But still."

"And you forget that while there aren't millions of people here, there are billions of dollars' worth of property in North Dakota."

Jamison said, "Of course, the oil and gas. It could have made this place uninhabitable and contaminate the oil and gas fields for centuries."

"That's right."

When they got back to the hotel Jamison pulled the SUV to the curb and said, "What now?"

"I don't know about you, but I'm going to take a shower. Maybe none of that stuff got out of the pipe, but maybe some of it did. Who knows? I'm going to call Stan and tell him to do the same thing."

Jamison's eyes widened. "Right. I think I'm going to take a shower, too. And go through a couple bars of soap."

They were about to climb out of the SUV when Jessica Reel appeared at the driver's-side glass and said, "You need to come with me."

"Why?"

"Decontamination."

"Do you know what was down there?" said Jamison anxiously.

"Not definitively, but the speculation mandates that you two go in for decon and testing."

"My brother-in-law—" began Decker.

"We've already picked him up. And the men from the pumper truck." She pointed down the street. "We have a van over there. Get in the back and put on the suits that are in there."

"Wait a minute—are you saying we're contagious?"

"I'm saying we don't know. We'll take charge of your SUV. It needs to be tested, too. So leave the keys." She moved back and pointed to the van.

They climbed into the back of the van and put on the hazmat suits that had been laid out for them. They even had their own closed-loop air pack systems.

"Okay, this is scary," said Jamison, through her face mask. "Do you really think we're contaminated?"

"I guess we'll find out soon enough," said Decker. "But we better not be."

"Well, yeah, duh."

"No, I mean we have murders to solve."

73

It was the next day and every known test had been run on them, Baker, and the other men and their vehicles before they'd finally been given the all clear. Whatever was in the pipe, first the water and then the concrete had stopped it from escaping. A federal hazmat response team was currently at the site, walling it off and using sophisticated detection technology to assess the situation.

Jamison and Decker were in a small conference room at their hotel. Robie, Reel, and Blue Man sat across from them.

Blue Man said, "You are to be commended. What you did saved a lot of lives."

"The target had to be the oil and gas," said Decker.

"Which explains the chatter we were getting from the Middle East," said Blue Man.

"Meaning the threat came from there," said Jamison.

"We believe so, and it would make sense from a geoeconomic perspective. Fracking in North Dakota helped in a very large way to make this country mostly energy independent," stated Blue Man. "That is good for us, and that is very bad for every other petroleum-producing nation, including those who are members of OPEC, especially the Saudis. We still import oil from them, just not nearly as much as we used to."

"So what exactly was down there in the ground?" asked Jamison. "No one's told us."

"That's because we don't know for certain. But since I learned of your discovery, I have been in touch with some high-level contacts from the DoD and informed them of the situation here. With some prodding from my superiors, they, in turn, did some deep digging within certain old records."

"With what result?" asked Jamison.

"It seems that decades ago certain elements within the Air Force community might not have followed the presidential directive to discontinue all work on such weapons and destroy the stockpiles that did exist. Work on one project may have continued. The results of that work may well have been what ended up in that bunker."

"There's no maybe about it," said Decker. "It did."

"Any idea what that project was?" asked Jamison.

"We can't be sure until they get into that bunker and examine the contents. That will take some time. In addition to the concrete that was poured down that pipe, they will be using vapor seals, pressure chamber technology, and other protocols to ensure that what is in the pipe and bunker remains there until it can be permanently dealt with. The problem is that if an explosive was used in piercing the bunker, some of the contents may have escaped already into the surrounding earth. The response team understands that and is using every tool they have to contain it until a complete study is conducted and a full-scale remediation plan can be implemented."

Jamison persisted, "Don't you have some idea after talking to those people?"

"I have come to learn that back then the Air Force, as an alternative to the deployment of nuclear weapons, was very keenly working on developing 'synthetic' airborne weapons, including ricin, anthrax, sarin, a substance today known as compound 1080, and an *inhalable* form of the world's most lethal poison, botulinum. If I had to guess, I would say that the medium used was some type of laboratory-crafted *spore*. I say that only because I was aware of a similar project being undertaken by the Soviets during the Cold War."

"Wonderful how really smart people spend so much time trying to kill each other," commented a clearly disgusted Jamison.

"Yes, well, anyway, it was intended that these weapons would be deployed from aircraft—making the Air Force the perfect medium to deploy them, of course. I have also learned that the intent back then was to devise these toxins in such a way that once released they would linger in the ground for centuries, in the same way that radiation from a nuclear explosion would. Years later, if you happened to walk along and disturb such toxins on the ground and then inhaled them, you could be dead within hours or even minutes without ever knowing what had killed you. And I was told that one of the other goals was to make some or all of these poisons, once inhaled, capable of being transmitted through the air from one living thing to another. In other words, they wanted to make a synthetic plague that was actually far deadlier than the original version."

"That is absolutely horrible," said Jamison.

"But effective, if mass death over a long period of time is your goal," pointed out Blue Man. "It's no wonder they eventually buried it in that bunker. They probably didn't know how to destroy these weapons safely. You couldn't burn them or blow them up without risk that some of the airborne contaminants would escape. And once they did, they could be there a long time waiting to kill the unsuspecting. And with prevailing wind patterns, storms, and unsuspecting, contaminated people moving here and there, it could have affected a far larger area than simply North Dakota. It would have been truly catastrophic and beyond this country's capability to adequately respond." He smiled at the pair. "But you two and your brother-in-law managed to stop it."

"My brother-in-law deserves the credit there," said Decker.

"Decker," admonished Jamison, "if you hadn't figured it out, Stan would have had no chance to stop it."

"I think there's enough credit to go around," noted Blue Man. He looked expectantly at Decker. "Now, it's one thing to stop such a plot. It's quite another to catch those who did it."

Decker said, "We're talking deep pockets. The mercenaries they've used aren't cheap, and neither was paying for the land and all the equipment to do what they almost succeeded in doing."

"We're making inquiries, but I'm afraid it will be a long and involved process and it may well be that no definitive answer comes from it. And even if we do determine who was responsible, our options may be limited in how to respond."

"That's bullshit," said Jamison.

Blue Man smiled demurely. "And it's also the nature of geopolitics. For better or worse, some of the players undoubtedly behind this are countries we need in other areas to keep the world relatively stable."

"So they'll get a pass?" said Jamison. "If there are no consequences, what will stop them from trying again?"

"I didn't say there would be no consequences," said Blue Man. "But there may be no *public* consequences."

"So a cover-up?" exclaimed Jamison.

"And since I know you were a journalist, every molecule of your nature rises up in protest at the very thought of such a thing. And I can't say that you're wrong. I can only say that the matter is complicated and not everyone in power believes in transparency. Or if they do, it's *their* version of it."

Jamison shook her head in resignation but said nothing.

Decker said, "We still have the matter of finding out who killed Irene Cramer and Pamela Ames, and abducted Hal Parker. And who probably killed Ben Purdy and *did* murder his mother."

Jamison added, "And who was also blackmailing Walt Southern. It has to be the same people behind the biochemical weapons scheme."

"It could be that someone local was working with foreign elements to bring this plot about," said Robie.

"I think that's exactly what happened," said Decker. "Now we just have to find out who the *local* is."

74

Decker, Baker, and Jamison were having dinner at the OK Corral Saloon that evening.

"Don't think I've been poked and prodded that much since I was in boot camp," said Baker as he sipped on a bottle of beer.

"Well, it could have been a lot worse," noted Jamison. "We could be in a morgue."

Baker nodded. "So do they know what's down there? Saw a big crew poring over the place until they put up these screens to block the sight lines."

"Let's just say it was some serious shit from the past that never should have been put down there in the first place," said Jamison.

Baker shook his head. "Damn military playing God like always. I mean, when are they gonna learn?"

"Don't hold your breath," said Decker. "I suppose you heard about Hugh Dawson?"

Baker nodded, looking sad. "I tried to visit Caroline at the hospital, but they said she was still medicated and asleep. How's she doing?"

"It's going to take time," said Jamison. "She's been through a lot."

"Shane lost his father, but it wasn't the same situation," noted Decker. "Although we've learned Hugh was no saint."

"Considering Hugh Dawson killed McClellan, I think they both have it pretty bad," Jamison countered.

"What the hell are you talking about?" exclaimed Baker.

Decker quickly explained what had happened.

Baker sipped his beer, a thoughtful expression on his face. "Guess it shows you money can't buy happiness. I mean those two were rolling in it, and now they're both dead and won't enjoy a penny of it."

Decker looked up as the door opened and in walked Kelly, Shane, Liz Southern, and, surprisingly, a tired-looking Caroline Dawson.

"Look who's all together again," commented Jamison.

"The sister and her two honorary brothers," added Decker.

"Brothers who would rather be something else, you mean," countered Jamison.

Kelly spotted them and led the others over to their table.

Baker stood and reached a hand out to Dawson. "I tried to see you at the hospital, but you were asleep, Caroline. I'm so sorry about, well, everything."

"Thank you, Stan, that's very kind of you," she said, her voice low and unnaturally slow.

To Decker, her unfocused eyes and feeble manner showed that she was not yet fully recovered from her ordeal.

Jamison, noting this, said, "Are you sure you should be out? You look like you should still be in the hospital."

Southern said, "I told her that until I was hoarse, but she wouldn't listen."

Dawson said, "I didn't want to stay there anymore. I was feeling claustrophobic."

Shane interjected, "The docs said it was okay. She just needs to take it easy."

"Do you want us to drive you to your condo?" asked Jamison.

Dawson said, "No, I'm going to go up to my room here, and—"

Kelly said quickly, "You want me to come with you?"

"Or I can," added Shane.

"No. I'll be fine, thanks, guys." She looked at Southern. "Thanks for coming to stay with me at the hospital, Liz. I'll give you a call tomorrow."

"Sleep well," said Southern kindly.

She headed off as they all watched. Then Shane, Southern, and Kelly sat down at the table.

"She doesn't look good," said Baker.

"Well, she's been through hell and back," said Southern defensively.

"Shane has, too," pointed out Kelly. "Lost his dad and all." He glanced at Shane. "And considering *how* he died."

Shane shrugged at this and motioned to the waitress and ordered the same beer Decker was drinking. "It's not like my old man thought much of me. But he didn't deserve to die like that, either." He eyed Decker. "You really think Hugh killed him?"

Jamison answered, "I don't know why he would write a suicide note saying he did if he didn't."

Shane looked at Kelly. "What do you think, Joe?"

Kelly stared down at his hands. "You know those guys have been at each other for years. Maybe Hugh just reached the last straw. Sell out to McClellan and then make sure he could never enjoy the fruits of it?"

"But then he kills himself so he could never enjoy his fortune, either?" said Jamison in a doubting tone.

"Guilt can make people do crazy things," said Kelly. "But I know, none of it makes much sense."

After his beer came, Shane took a sip and eyed Decker. "Something big went down over near the Brothers' Colony. Lots of people and trucks and they put up a shield around it. You know anything about that?"

"I saw that too when I was driving by there," said Southern.

"What do you know about the All-American Energy Company?" Decker asked Shane.

"Seen them around. Never talked to them. Drove by their rig from time to time."

Kelly said, "We've been totally shut out of what's going on over there, Decker. I know enough to know that those are Feds swarming the place. You have to know something."

"Not that I can share." He looked at Shane. "You really don't know if your father left you anything? I get that you're not into money and business, but still. Most people would want to know."

Shane finished his beer and glared at Decker. "Look, I went to war, okay? I nearly got killed a bunch'a times over there, so I never thought I'd out-live my dad. What the hell did it matter to me about whether he was leaving me his money? Money that he got by digging shit out of the ground. Money that I don't want or need."

"What will you do then?" asked Southern.

"Got my farm. I got some of my own money saved. If my old man did leave something to me, maybe I'll donate it. Know a lot of vets who can't even rub two dimes together."

"That's good of you, Shane," commented Jamison.

"And Caroline?" asked Decker.

"What about her?" said Shane sharply.

"I'm assuming she inherited from her father."

"I would imagine so. Hugh doted on her."

"Did you know her brother well?" asked Jamison.

Shane slowly nodded, his features turning sad. "Junior was a great guy. Gentle and funny. Had a big heart. We were friends. He didn't deserve what happened to him."

"We understand that he was gay," said Jamison.

"Yeah, so?" said Shane.

"And his father didn't understand that?"

"His father made his life a living hell. It's why he killed himself."

"Caroline said it was an overdose," said Jamison.

Kelly said, "He didn't leave a note. He left a recording. It was . . . it was pretty damn sad."

"You heard it?"

"I was one of the cops investigating the case, so yeah, I did. I kept a copy of it, in fact. Haven't listened to it since. I'm not ashamed to say I cried when I heard it."

"It must've hit Caroline and her mother particularly hard," said Jamison as Southern nodded.

Kelly shrugged. "It did. I think it would've driven a lasting wedge between her and her father, but then Maddie died and those two were the only ones left. I'm not saying she didn't still care for her father, but . . . it was complicated."

"She told us sort of the same thing," noted Jamison.

Decker's phone buzzed. He took it out and looked at a series of photos and reports that had just been delivered in an email. As his gaze ran over them, Decker tensed, and then realization spread over his features.

Jamison noticed this and whispered, "What is it?"

Decker's gaze drifted up the stairs, where Dawson had gone. He rose.

Jamison said, "Where are you going?"

"*We're* going to see Caroline."

Southern said, "Let me go with you. I think I might be of some help. She is still very vulnerable."

Decker looked at Jamison, who nodded.

"Okay, but whatever you hear up there you don't share with anyone."

"Understood."

Kelly said, "I hope that doesn't include me! I *am* investigating this case."

"We'll fill you in," Jamison assured him.

They rose and headed up the stairs, leaving a troubled-looking Kelly and Shane staring after them.

75

The space above the bar was a series of rooms. One was a large open area that probably served as an event space. Chairs were stacked against the wall along with folding tables. Piles of linen napkins and table-cloths were on a long buffet set against one wall. Decker, Jamison, and Southern walked through this space to a bar area that was a replica of the one below, only much smaller. Decker spotted a spool of twine sitting on one table. He scooped it up and put it in his jacket pocket.

"What's that for?" asked Jamison.

"You'll see."

Next they passed through an open doorway, turned left, and ran into the only other door there.

Decker stepped up to it and knocked.

"Caroline, it's Decker and Jamison, we'd like to talk to you."

"Please go away. I don't feel well."

"Caroline," said Southern. "I'm here too. I really think you should talk to them."

"I'm too tired. I'm going to bed."

Southern looked helplessly at Decker.

"Your father didn't kill himself," Decker called out through the door, drawing a surprised look from Jamison. "He was murdered."

Now they could hear footsteps. The door opened and there was Dawson, barefoot and her eyes welling with tears. But the look on her face was one of anger. "What the hell are you talking about? He killed himself. We all saw it."

"Can we come in?" asked Decker.

For a split second she looked like she might slam the door in their faces. But then her expression softened and she stepped back.

Jamison sat in a chair and Decker stood while Dawson curled up on the bed. Southern hovered near her, looking anxiously at her friend.

"What are you talking about?" demanded Dawson.

Decker took out his phone. "I just got these pictures and reports from the forensic tech who worked your father's crime scene. They tell a very different story than suicide."

"How?"

In answer Decker took out the spool of twine and rolled out a length of it about a foot longer than he was tall and held it up.

"Twine?" said Dawson, looking confused.

"I had the tech measure the twine that was found at the scene. It was seven feet, four inches long. That's about the length of this section of twine."

"So?"

"So why would he use a length of twine that long? From the triggers to the gun stock and back to his hand was about forty-three inches. He had to wrap it around the stock to pull the triggers the right way to discharge it. Then he wraps it once around his hand, that's maybe a few inches. What's the other three feet or so for?"

"I . . . I don't know. Maybe he just cut off a long length without measuring it. The rest was just extra. So that proves nothing."

"No, *all* of that length was actually needed."

"What do you mean?"

"A mark made by the twine was found around your father's wrist, and another trace of it through one of the handles on the desk drawer. I also had the tech take pics from overhead, to show the top of the desk."

"Why did you do that?" asked Caroline.

"Blood spatters can be worth a thousand words and a thousand convictions. Blood and other organic matter were everywhere, except the photos I just got reveal a long, thin line that ran across the top of the desk. A thin line that was not impacted by the blood spatters."

"What does that mean?"

"It means that Decker is right," said Southern, who had been following Decker's words closely. "Someone killed your father."

Decker explained, "When the shotgun went off, the twine that was used to pull the triggers was on top of the desk and pulled taut. It prevented blood and other detritus from colliding with the desk along that line. It's a thin trail, to be sure, but it's clearly there." He passed her the phone with the photo on it.

"I don't understand," said Dawson, staring down at the picture.

"Someone took the twine, wrapped it around the shotgun's triggers and gunstock after securing it to the desk, ran the line around your father's wrist, through the desk drawer handle, and then over the top of the desk where the person probably squatted on the floor, well below the top of the desk and out of harm's way. Then he pulled the twine and fired the shotgun from that position, killing your father. That would account for all of the forensic evidence that we found."

"But my father was a big, strong man. He wouldn't have—"

Decker interrupted. "He was undoubtedly unconscious. If he was drugged, the autopsy will show that. If he was struck across the face, the shotgun blast would have removed any evidence of such a blow."

"So you're really saying he was murdered?" she said in disbelief.

"I believe so."

"Did he leave a note?"

"That's right, you couldn't know that," said Decker.

Jamison said, "It said that he had killed Stuart McClellan and was committing suicide because he felt guilt about that."

"Do you have the note?"

Jamison brought a screen up on her phone. "Here's a photo of it."

Dawson looked at it closely. "That looks like my dad's handwriting and signature. I've seen it often enough. If someone did forge that, they were really good."

Decker said, "We had several people who were familiar with your dad's handwriting say the same thing, but that's not really a confirmation. We're having the handwriting analyzed by an expert. I think they will find that it's a clever forgery."

"But why would someone go to all that trouble?"

"It may tie into Stuart McClellan's murder. And even though I think the suicide note claiming responsibility for McClellan's death is fake, there *is* some evidence of your father being involved in Stuart's death. And he could have been, only I don't think he killed himself over it. Those are two separate issues."

"What sort of evidence?"

"I can't say right now."

Dawson handed the phone back. "But why would my father want to kill Stuart?"

"Can you think of any reason?" asked Decker.

Dawson composed herself and sat back on the bed. "No. I mean they were business rivals, but not really. They needed each other. And Stuart just paid a lot of cash to my dad."

Decker looked disappointed but then Southern stirred. "Look, I have no proof of any of this, but . . ." she began.

"Anything you tell us will be more than what we have now," said Decker.

She looked nervously at Dawson. "Your mother's death?"

"What about it?" said Dawson.

Southern glanced at Decker before turning back to Dawson. "Everybody said it was an accident. But your mother was born and raised here. She'd been out in blizzards before. Why didn't she get out of the car to check around it when it went off the road? She would have seen the tailpipe was full of snow. I told Walt the same thing when it happened. He agreed with me, though he could find nothing suspicious in the postmortem."

"There was an indication she might have been knocked unconscious by the impact," noted Jamison.

Southern shook her head stubbornly. "I don't believe that, I really don't. And I don't think you do either, Caroline. Everyone who grew up around here is used to driving in bad conditions." She gazed directly at Caroline. "And the Jeep she was in was tried and true, wasn't it?"

Dawson nodded. "She'd had it for years."

"Are you suggesting that Stuart McClellan had reason to kill Caroline's mother?" said Decker. "Why?"

"This is all speculation on my part."

"Let's hear it."

She looked at Dawson. "You all were planning to leave the country and move to France."

"Right, so? What did that have to do with Stuart?" asked Dawson.

"I think that Stuart McClellan was in love with your mother."

Jamison and Decker exchanged glances. She said, "We never heard about that before."

"Neither have I," said Dawson, looking bewildered.

Southern looked nervous, but she plunged ahead. "Katherine McClellan and your mom were friends, despite their husbands not being on good terms. In that way, Stuart and your mom spent time together. Now, I knew both women, but I was especially close to Katherine. I can tell you that before she died Katherine believed her husband was infatuated with Maddie."

"My God," said a stunned Dawson.

"I know this is hard for you," said Southern, her eyes growing misty.

"Why didn't you ever mention this before, Liz?"

"I didn't want to upset you. And I couldn't prove anything. But now with everything that's happened . . ." She paused and looked at Decker in distress. "But maybe I should just shut up now."

"I don't think you can now," said Decker.

Southern put a hand on Dawson's shoulder. "Caroline? What do you want me to do?"

"I . . . I need you to finish telling us, Liz."

Southern nodded and took a few moments to compose her thoughts. "Some people's love can be wonderful, but when it's not reciprocated, it can turn to something else. Something that is hateful and destructive."

"So are you saying that Maddie Dawson knew of Stuart's infatuation and, what, cut him off at the knees?" said Decker.

"I think that's exactly what happened. And a man like Stuart would not take rejection well."

"I can see that," said Jamison.

A moment of silence passed before Decker said, "So that would be his motive to kill her? In retaliation for being spurned?"

"Kill her rather than lose her," amended Southern.

"And Hugh Dawson?" asked Jamison.

"If Katherine noticed Stuart's attraction to Maddie, I can't help but believe he did, too. And if he thought Stuart had anything to do with her death . . . ?"

"But why kill him now?" said Jamison.

Southern shrugged. "He had sold out to him. I

doubt he was going to be staying here. This might have been his last chance."

Jamison said, "He *did* mention moving away to France. He told us he hoped Caroline would come with him."

Dawson glanced uncertainly at Southern and then at Decker. "I feel like my entire world has turned upside down."

"I can understand that," said Decker.

"What are you going to do now?" asked Southern.

"Find a killer," said Decker. "It's the only reason we're here."

76

"So any thoughts on how to catch the killer?" asked Jamison.

They were in her room at the hotel. Decker hadn't spoken a word since they had left the saloon.

Decker didn't answer right away. "Let's get back to basics: motive, means, and opportunity."

"Well, Caroline had the motive to kill her father. She stands to inherit, and she was also furious with him for selling out. But she didn't have the opportunity. We saw her in town around the time Dawson was killed. So she's ruled out. Now, Shane, I guess, could have a motive to kill his father, because he stands to inherit, but he also has an alibi for the time McClellan was killed. The exotic toxin came from a place Hugh frequented. I doubt anyone else around here visits Australia on a regular basis. And even though you think Dawson didn't kill himself, that doesn't mean he didn't kill McClellan. From what Liz Southern told us tonight, he might have had a motive if he thought McClellan had killed his wife. He wanted revenge."

Without a word, Decker got up and walked to the door.

A stunned Jamison said, "Where are you going?"

"For a walk."

"Why?"

"I need to think. Something here just doesn't make sense."

After he left, Jamison slumped back on her bed in obvious frustration, put a pillow over her face, and screamed into it.

It was chilly and windy, and Decker stuffed his hands into his pockets as he walked along the dark and mostly empty streets of London. The most difficult thing about this case was there were too many angles to adequately grab even one for long. They had been entirely reactive, instead of proactive. Every time he felt he was gaining traction, another event would force them into an entirely new direction. Part of that was happenstance, he was sure. And he was also certain that part of it was intentional.

He entered the OK Corral Saloon once more, took a seat at the bar, and ordered a beer. When it came he cradled it, closed his eyes for a few moments, and went over everything in his head.

Irene Cramer was dead.

Pamela Ames was dead.

Hal Parker had been taken.

Beverly Purdy was dead.

Walt Southern had killed himself.

Brad Daniels was nearly killed.

Stuart McClellan was dead.

Hugh Dawson was dead.

And a host of foreign mercenaries were no longer living, largely thanks to Robie and Reel, but others still might be around.

However, Decker did not consider the secret prison to be connected to the above events. That was encapsulated and solved and the appropriate parties punished.

But clearly the All-American Energy Company and the bunker full of toxic chemical and biological weapons were connected. And the responsible parties had not been fully accounted for and punished.

Another question really nagged at him. How had these mercenary types even learned about the secret bunker with the weapons? Brad Daniels would surely have mentioned any foreign-looking folks coming to visit him and asking strange questions.

So by process of elimination they could have learned about it one of two ways: from Ben Purdy or Irene Cramer. Then they could have bought the land where the bunker was buried from the Brothers, started the drilling operation, and gone from there.

But Cramer had been killed, and it seemed obvious to Decker that Purdy was dead, too. So had they learned about the bunker, or parts thereof, from each of them? So that each of them had to later die?

Then Decker considered a question he never had before.

Did Purdy and Cramer know each other? Were they working together to figure this out? And had they gotten discovered, and then were killed?

And what had Cramer swallowed that they needed to so desperately get back that they cut open her belly and intestines looking for it?

All good questions. And he had not a single answer to any of them.

And by this point in the investigation, he should have had at least one answer.

He opened his eyes and drank his beer, sullenly looking over the bar area as he did so.

He was growing weary of this town, because it would not give up the secrets it was holding. And his "infallible" memory was not providing much help, either.

A man sat down next to Decker.

When Decker glanced over, he was staring at Will Robie.

The man was quietly dressed in jeans, an oversized sweatshirt, and worn boots. A John Deere baseball cap sat on his head. If he was armed, Decker saw no bulge. Maybe that was the reason for the bulky sweatshirt.

Robie ordered a beer and waited for it to come as he continually scanned the room and everyone there.

"You look pensive," Robie said.

"That's because I am. Did you find what was in that bunker?"

"We're officially not in the loop. DoD and Homeland Security are all over it. But unofficially, I can tell you that they haven't yet. 'Slow and steady' is the rule for that. You were right about the tunnel. They broke through the wall and found it. They put additional countermeasures on top of the cement your friend poured into the pipe, to ensure that stuff will never get to the surface. They're probably going to have to build another bunker around the original vault before they're comfortable opening it up and seeing exactly what's inside."

"Anything else?" asked Decker.

"We did some digging on the All-American Energy Company. Turns out there are international layers to it, which puts it squarely in my agency's wheelhouse."

"International how?"

Robie said, "It's a shell, owned by another shell incorporated in Bermuda that is, in turn, owned by another shell we ran to ground in London. After that, the trail vanished."

"And with North Dakota fracking off-line, what would that do to this country's energy independence?"

"It wouldn't help it. And the price of certain types of crude and even natural gas would have spiked."

"So that helps other energy-producing countries," said Decker.

"The Middle East, Russia, Canada, Venezuela."

"I don't see the Canadians behind this. And Venezuela is imploding right now."

"So either the sheiks or Putin then," opined Robie.

"Or maybe both," said Decker. "The world has produced some strange bedfellows lately, and Russia has made inroads into that part of the world, for sure. But they had to have local operatives here, to get the lay of the land, do the deal to get the property, and set up the whole thing while at the same time keeping under the radar."

Robie took a swallow of his beer. "I think that makes a lot of sense. So how do you get to the finish line?"

"We keep digging. It's all we can do."

"Ben Purdy was digging and it cost him. And his mother."

"Yes, it did," said Decker. "But I've still been wondering how Purdy——" He stopped and set his beer down.

"What is it?" When Decker didn't answer, Robie said more urgently, "Decker!"

Decker looked at him. "Shit, I've been looking at this thing totally bass-ackwards."

"How so?"

"We gotta go."

"Go where?" asked Robie.

"To Hal Parker's place."

77

On the drive out in Robie's vehicle, Decker said, "I just assumed that Purdy had been told the story of the bunker by Brad Daniels and then started doing some digging, ran into the wrong people, and that sealed his fate."

"Well, we've all been thinking that."

"But that doesn't mean we're right."

"Lay out your theory for me," said Robie.

"You said that Brad Daniels told you he divulged everything to Purdy."

"That's right. I don't think he held anything back. He was about to do the same for us when we got attacked."

Decker said, "Okay, let's look at the situation fully and not piecemeal. Purdy's a veteran member of the Air Force, trained and experienced."

"Right."

"And he's attending a military event where he's just been told by someone who used to work at the very same installation decades ago that there's the possibility of a bunker full of biochemical weapons buried on land belonging to the Air Force. That is a clear and present danger to everyone in the area. A real national security risk if ever there was one. Agreed?"

"Agreed."

"Okay, if you were in Purdy's position, with his experience, and you had learned all of that, what would you do?"

"I would report it to my superior officer and let them worry about it. It's just common sense and also how someone like Purdy would naturally react."

"*Exactly*. But also think about this. I doubt that Daniels told Irene Cramer everything he told Purdy. So with Purdy there would have been no need to dig into anything. He already knew all he needed to know. He just reports it and the Air Force looks into it. His job is done. If he's proved right, he gets a medal and maybe a promotion. He doesn't have to be involved anymore."

"Well, he might have been afraid of retaliation within the Air Force if he did let all this come out."

"Why? Brad Daniels is well into his nineties. I seriously doubt there's anyone left in the Air Force who had anything to do with this. And even if he were afraid of retaliation there are whistleblower laws to protect someone with the sort of information Purdy possessed. He could have communicated what he knew safely through that channel."

"So what are you saying, Decker?"

"You'll see."

They arrived at Hal Parker's home, and Decker led Robie inside. He went over to the wall of pictures he had seen on his previous visit here and pointed to one.

"Recognize him?"

Robie's jaw slackened. "That's Ben Purdy."

"He knew Parker. He obviously hunted with him. I remembered at the Purdy ranch in Montana that they had animal heads mounted on the wall. Beverly Purdy said her husband and son were avid hunters."

"So you think there's some connection with Purdy and Parker. He *did* find the body of Irene Cramer."

"I do."

"So what *is* your theory?"

Decker seemed startled by this query. "My theory is that Purdy didn't report what he knew to his superiors because he saw certain personal advantages in concealing it. And he wanted to take full advantage of them."

"What exactly do you mean by 'taking full advantage'?"

"His service record showed that he was a really smart guy. He'd been promoted frequently and had received a lot of commendations. He went overseas frequently to attend conferences and other meetings, and was always educating himself. Among other places, he went to Qatar and Jordan."

Robie ruminated on this before answering. "So you mean he might have met some folks there who would be very interested in destroying the fracking industry in North Dakota?"

"Yes. And they would no doubt pay him enormous sums of money and also provide all the manpower he would need."

"And his mother?"

"Yeah, they killed his mother. Whether he was involved in that decision or not, I don't know. But a brilliant kid stuck in the middle of nowhere who'll top out at maybe master sergeant after another ten years of service? He might have aimed higher. He might have aimed high enough to have committed treason against his own country in return for a fortune and a change of address. Which would also explain him going AWOL."

"And the research you found at his mother's house? If Daniels had told him everything, why would he need to do that?"

"If I were him and I had a grand scheme that would involve dealing with some very serious and dangerous people, I would want to verify everything. I wouldn't accept the word of a ninety-something-year-old guy living in a nursing home. He needed to make certain, not blindly accept what might be the skewed memories of an old man."

"So he was responsible for killing Cramer and

515

Ames, and"—he pointed to the photo—"kidnapping Parker?"

An uncertain Decker shook his head. "That's far from clear, Robie. As I said, Purdy knew a lot more than Cramer did. She came up here to dig for information. She knew it had something to do with the oil fields around the Air Force station, and she knew whatever it was, was in the ground and dangerous. That's why she made that comment to Judith White about not eating the food they grew there. But that was all she knew. I think she wanted to expose this whole thing to make the U.S. government look bad in retaliation for what it had done to her mother. But why would Purdy need her? What could she possibly tell him that he didn't already know? And we've been able to show no connection between them."

"But if Cramer came up here to dig into the situation she might have run into Purdy. He couldn't let her tell anyone what she knew. It would ruin his plan. He would have every reason to kill her."

"And what did she swallow that he needed to get back?"

"Something that would expose the plan."

Decker nodded but didn't look convinced. "I guess it's possible. But it doesn't explain what happened to Parker and Ames."

"So, what now?" said Robie.

"We need to find Purdy. That's the only way to know for sure."

"If he was behind this, won't he be long gone by now?"

"Maybe and maybe not."

"And if you're wrong and he's not behind this?"

"Then he's probably dead."

They left the house, and a moment later everything went dark for both of them.

78

Robie's eyes fluttered open and then closed. He moved not a muscle, seeming to remain remarkably still. He was actually testing the strength of the restraints around his hands and ankles. He sniffed the air and got a lungful of noxious smells in return. Next, he listened. For anyone, anything, any type of nearby threat. Finally, he opened his eyes and shifted his gaze from one spot to the next, taking it all in.

He was in a room with no windows and no door. This puzzled Robie, but only for an instant. He angled his gaze upward and saw the ladder leading to what looked to be a trapdoor in the ceiling. He lifted his arms, until he felt the resistance. The same with his legs. He looked down, and in the dim light provided by the sole overhead bulb, he observed the chains around his limbs that were attached to a thick iron ring set in the floor. They had shackled his hands in front of him, which was the only positive development that Robie could see.

He shifted his weight to the right and saw the hulking figure of Amos Decker lying a foot from him. Decker, too, was shackled, and his chains were also inserted into the same floor ring.

Decker was also awake and staring at him. "Not good," he said softly.

Robie gave one curt nod in agreement. They had taken both his pistols. He could feel their absence. He was sure they had taken Decker's gun as well. "They got the jump on us."

"Any idea where we might be?" asked Decker.

Robie once more looked around. "Underground. Air is musty with an overlay of petroleum products. No windows, ceiling trap door. I'd say maybe an old underground storage facility for an abandoned oil well."

Decker nodded and looked around. He managed to sit up and planted his back against the wall. Robie did the same. The pair were shoulder to shoulder looking down at the thick chains that stood in the way of their freedom.

"Feel like I got hit by a truck," said Decker. "But I can't remember anything of what happened. And that's saying something for me."

"They probably deployed the same concoction I used on the woman at the Air Force facility. Incapacitation agent blended with an amnesiac component. We remember nothing that might have happened, who we might have seen, or how they got us here, although that wouldn't be much, because the spray works pretty much instantly."

"So do you have a plan to get us out of here?"

"Working on it." Robie tested the chains once again. Solid, no cracks, not an imperfection or weak spot he could see. The floor ring was about two inches in width. An elephant wouldn't have been able to defeat it. The steel plate it was a part of was securely bolted to the floor. He eyed the door in the ceiling. "That's our only way out. I wonder if they wired it, just in case?"

"Well, I don't see us getting that far, so what does it matter?"

Robie didn't answer him. He reached down, lifted his sweatshirt, and unbuckled his belt.

"Don't tell me you have some sort of acid in there to melt our chains," said Decker, eyeing him incredulously. "I think I saw that on TV."

Robie had removed a Velcro backing from the inside of his belt and plucked out two slender pieces of metal that had been hidden there. "Just lock picks. And this isn't a TV show."

He went to work on his shackles and soon had himself and Decker free.

Robie next eyed the ladder and the door in the ceiling. "Just stay here while I check it out." He gripped the ladder and began to climb. As Robie neared the door he ran his gaze over the frame, looking for stray wires, a power pack, or anything else that would give away some sort of booby trap. Seeing none, he gingerly pushed against the wood. It didn't budge.

"Locked," he said. "No surprise there."

He came back down and looked around the room. In an old bucket were four long iron spikes. He slipped them through his belt, took off his boot, and uncovered a cavity in the heel.

Decker saw a small blob of what looked like Play-Doh. "C-Four?"

"Semtex, but it does the same thing," replied Robie as he removed something else from the cavity and worked away combining the two elements. When that was done, he clambered back up the ladder, pressed the Semtex against the door, uncovered two wires he had pressed into the blob and twined their ends around one another. He quickly retreated and grabbed Decker, and they backed away as far as possible from the door.

Ten seconds later the explosive detonated, blowing the ceiling door out of the way. Their escape path was now exposed.

But Robie didn't rush forward. He kept a hand on Decker's shoulder. Decker could see the intensity on the other man's face as he waited, listening and watching.

"Okay, let's move."

Robie scrambled up the ladder first, with Decker following more slowly. Robie eased his head above the rim of the doorway and looked around. He jumped clear of the opening and helped Decker through. They were in what looked like a long passageway made of dirt and rock with steel beams overhead and posts set in the dirt at regular intervals. Fluorescent lights overhead provided feeble illumination.

"Which way?" said Decker.

Robie looked in both directions, took a sniff of the air, examined the dirt on either side of the doorway, and said, "Footprints and airflow only come from that way," he said, pointing to their right.

He took the spikes out of his belt and held two in each hand. They poked out between his fingers like an animal's claws.

"If anyone's here, that explosion will have alerted them," said Decker.

"I'm actually counting on that," said Robie.

A hundred feet later, Robie grabbed Decker and thrust him into the shadows right next to the wall. Robie reached up and pulled the wires from the light directly above them. This part of the passageway became far darker.

Someone was coming fast.

A few moments later a trio of men burst into view; all three were armed. They ran in a column formation.

Right as they passed, Robie struck with the spikes. He stabbed one man in the neck, spun around, and sunk two spikes into the second man's gut, thrusting the spikes upward to his diaphragm. Both men went down, and neither would get back up.

The other man turned and pointed his sub gun at Robie. He never fired, because Decker fell on top of him. His nearly three hundred pounds pinned the man flat to the ground, and his sub gun tumbled from his hands.

Robie picked up the weapon and looked at the other two men. One was dead, the other was gurgling his last few breaths. Robie waited until he expired and said to Decker, "Let him up."

Decker slowly rose off the man. Robie said, "Who are you?"

The man sat on his haunches and shook his head. He was around forty and his dark, curly hair was shot through with gray.

"Where are we?" said Robie.

Another shake of the head.

"Why did you kidnap us?"

This time the man didn't even bother to shake his head. He just sat there and stared at Robie for a moment before lifting his hand to his mouth.

Robie leapt forward but the man had already swallowed something.

He started convulsing, then foam seeped out of his mouth, and he fell sideways. He took a few tortured breaths and then his body relaxed.

Decker bent over him and checked his pulse. There was none.

"That was a fast poison," he said.

"Sort of the point," replied Robie.

Decker picked up one of the sub guns, and they kept going in the same direction.

There was a doorway up ahead.

Robie fingered the sub gun and looked at Decker.

"Count of three. You go left, I go right."

Decker nodded.

"One . . . two . . . three."

They burst into the room, Robie's gun covering the right half of the space and Decker's the left.

Dead center of the room stood Ben Purdy.

He wasn't alone.

He was holding a gun to the other person's head.

And that person was Alex Jamison.

79

"You guys are really something," said Purdy, shaking his head. "I seem to have run out of men to take you on."

"If you let her go, we all walk away from this," said Decker.

"That won't be happening," said Purdy matter-of-factly. "You destroyed everything I've been working on."

"You want to talk about it?" said Decker.

"No, I want to kill all three of you. But first, put down your weapons, or she gets an unwanted hole in the head. Do it now," he added in a calm, measured voice. "I don't have anything left to lose."

Robie and Decker laid their weapons down and stepped away from them.

"I'm surprised you came back here," said Decker.

"Well, considering the people who were going to pay me shitloads of money are now not going to stop looking for me until I'm good and dead, I figured they might have thought the same thing. I convinced my remaining team members of that philosophy, but you've taken care of them, so I'm the last man standing." He pushed the gun against Jamison's head. "And I had to stay and repay you for all you've done to ruin my life. In fact, that's my only focus in life right now."

"I take it you followed us to Hal Parker's?" said Decker.

"We've definitely been keeping eyes on you. My men heard you inside arriving at the truth behind what I did. I'm surprised you didn't figure it out sooner. After that, well, I thought it best to bring you here. In fact, if I show photos of you three dead, my employers might just cut me some slack. It's worth a shot anyway."

"How'd you get all those guys into the country?" asked Robie.

"How else? Right over the little old Canadian border. It was easy." He eyed Decker. "They found the bunker, didn't they?"

Decker nodded.

"Was the stuff as potent as Daniels told me it was?"

"Apparently so. You do realize that 'stuff' would have killed millions of people."

Purdy shook his head dismissively. "No, Daniels told me it would remain localized. It was heavy enough to where it couldn't remain airborne in a concentrated pattern to be distributed by wind currents over large distances. It would max out at about a hundred miles in all directions."

"Still really bad."

"Bullshit. You want to know something?"

"What?"

"That's why the Air Force put the kibosh on the program, Daniels told me. Because it *couldn't* kill *enough* people. There's your goody-good U.S. of A. The shit they do, you wouldn't believe. And you think I'm a bad guy?"

"I don't think, I *know* you are," replied Decker.

"Yeah, well, distributing the stuff here was certainly enough to put the stop on the fracking industry."

"And that's what you were really being paid for," said Decker.

"An amount of money that was truly beyond belief."

"Even if it stayed local, it would have killed a lot of people," Decker pointed out.

"Every plan has collateral damage. The Pentagon builds that into every scenario. What's the civilian death count going to be? How many kiddies will bite the bullet? Price of doing the business of war. There's nothing innocent about that. We're just like everybody else."

"No, we're not. And I didn't realize you were at war with your own country," commented Robie.

Purdy eyed him. "I was just a grunt. All I ever would be. But I had brains and ambition. Which led me to this point. The risks I took. All the work. For nothing." In his anger, he tightened his grip on Jamison, causing her to cry out in pain.

"Ticking time bomb?" said Decker. "You mentioned that to a guy in the bar. That's how we got on to you. Only back then we thought you were a good guy."

Purdy grimaced. "I had just found out all the stuff and hadn't decided what to do about it yet. And I was drunk at the time. Finding out that you're sitting on a possible Armageddon will cause you to drink. I regretted it the moment I said it, but I didn't even remember who I said it to."

Decker said, "With your smarts you could have gone to Silicon Valley and made a lot more than Uncle Sam was paying you."

"They couldn't pay me what these guys were, not if I busted my ass for a million years. I could have made the *Forbes* list. I'm not kidding."

"And who *was* paying you?" asked Robie.

"People that even if you knew who they were you couldn't touch."

"Why's that?"

Purdy grinned. "Because they're valuable and trusted allies of ours, that's why. We'd never expose them for what they really are. Don't you read the newspapers? We're suckers. We know they're bad but we do nothing. And you want to know why? Oil! It makes me sick."

"So did the collateral damage calculation include your mother?" queried Decker.

Purdy's expression turned grim. "That was *your* fault, not mine. You went there to question her, my partners got nervous, and they took care of that end. I wasn't happy about it, but I had no choice. Just so you know, I was going to buy her a nice place, take care of her. But what did she have really to live for? You saw her place. It was shitsville in the middle of nowhere. Wherever she is, I think she's better off."

Both Jamison and Decker flinched at this cruel comment.

Robie said, "And who gave you the right to make that decision for her?"

"I gave myself the right!" Purdy snapped.

"Can you answer a question?" said Decker.

"What?"

"Did you kill Irene Cramer, Hal Parker, and Pamela Ames?"

Purdy looked genuinely confused. "I know Hal. I hunted with him. I didn't know he was dead."

"Well, we're not sure he is. But he is missing. And the others?"

"I've never heard of—what were the names again?"

"Irene Cramer and Pamela Ames."

He shook his head. "I had nothing to do with whatever happened to them."

"Okay, so where does that leave us?" said Decker.

"With the three of you dead and me not. I couldn't believe you dropped your weapons. That was a mistake."

Decker glanced at Jamison. But she wasn't looking at Decker. She seemed to be looking past him, when she suddenly slumped downward as though unconscious, causing Purdy to reach forward and grab at her.

The next moment Decker felt something fly past his ear.

The spike embedded several inches deep in Purdy's eye socket. He screamed from the impact and shock, dropped his gun, and staggered back. Then he went into convulsions and fell to the floor, where he continued to gyrate and pull at the spike for a few more seconds before his clutching hands fell away and he grew still.

Robie came to stand over him as Decker helped Jamison up. Then Robie reached down, pulled the spike free, and threw it on the floor. "What a prick," he said quietly.

He looked back at Decker and Jamison. "Nice pickup on my signal, Jamison."

"Nice throwing with that spike," she replied breathlessly.

"You guys ready to get out of here?"

"That would be a hell yes," said Decker.

It was still dark outside, though in the horizon could be seen the first few streaks of dawn.

The building they had been in appeared indeed to

be an abandoned storage facility of some kind, with rusted equipment parked behind a leaning ten-foot-high chain-link fence.

They had found their guns and phones, along with the keys to the SUV parked out here.

Robie drove them back to town in the SUV.

"I'll get some people out to where they took us to scrub it of the bodies," said Robie.

"So Purdy did all this for the cash," said Jamison. "And sacrificed his own mother in the process. What a piece of work."

"How'd they snatch you?" asked Decker.

"I went out to get in the SUV, and the next thing I know I woke up on the floor." She glanced at Robie. "What Purdy said about the people behind this suffering the consequences. It mirrored what your boss said."

"Yeah," said Robie.

"Is that really how it's going to go down?" she asked.

"Probably."

"And that doesn't piss you off?"

"Every molecule in my body."

"And you're just going to let it happen?"

Robie eyed her in the mirror. "I didn't say that, did I? But that's for another day. And you can't tell anyone about finding Purdy and what happened back there. That will do this country no good and might unleash some nightmare scenarios that are far better avoided."

Decker and Jamison exchanged glances. He said, "That's a tough favor to ask, Robie."

"And I wouldn't be asking unless it were really important. Because it is."

Finally, Decker and Jamison nodded in agreement.

"Well, at least this nightmare is over, right, Decker?" said Jamison.

"It's not over yet," he replied.

"What? Why not?"

"Because Irene Cramer, Pamela Ames, Hal Parker, Stuart McClellan, and Maddie and Hugh Dawson deserve justice. And it hasn't happened yet. And I'm not leaving North Dakota until they get it."

80

The next day after breakfast Decker got a cup of coffee from the hotel restaurant and carried it up to his room, sat on his bed, sipped on the drink, and thought about, well, everything.

But that only seemed to make the muddle worse.

He finally took out his wallet and slipped out the photo of his wife and daughter. He gazed at Molly's young face, her crinkled smile, her plump cheeks, and he saw a bit of himself and a lot of her mother in there. He closed his eyes and just imagined being with them again. Holding hands, giving kisses and hugs, simply going for a walk, helping Molly to learn how to ride a bike, gripping Cassie's hand and giving encouragement as their daughter was born.

He opened his eyes after this cleansing moment. As his wife and daughter receded into his memories, they both seemed to be speaking to him, telling him something.

You can do this.

Whether it was his imagination or something else, Decker really didn't care.

You're a detective—start acting like it.

He settled back and refocused. Something had been burning in Decker's gut for a long time now and he'd really done nothing about it. He had, instead, just followed blithely along a traditional investigative path.

Okay, let's go blank slate, square one. First rule, you don't trust anybody. Second related rule, you suspect everybody until something comes along to definitively remove that suspicion.

He truly believed that the key to this whole thing had not started a week ago, or a month ago, or even a year ago. The bunker piece might have dated from then because up until that point, Ben Purdy could not have known that some of the deadliest substances on earth were buried in the North Dakota soil. But something really important to the current case had started even before that.

As he focused on certain possibilities, Decker's memory file popped down from his cloud and settled front and center in his thoughts. In this memory, he saw the woman walk to the stairs and head up.

Decker grabbed his jacket and headed out.

Finally, finally, he might be getting somewhere.

The OK Corral Saloon was not yet open when Decker burst in.

Employees were unstacking chairs from the tops of

tables and wiping down the walnut bar, counting glasses, sorting inventory, and unloading dishwashers.

"We don't open until noon," one of them said to Decker. "The door should have been locked."

Decker strode forward, held up his FBI credentials, and said, "I need to go up there." He pointed to the staircase that led to the second floor.

"You can't," said the man, who was in his twenties, scrawny, with pimply cheeks and a ragged goatee.

"Why not?"

"Because we're closed, like I just told you!"

Decker stuck his creds right in the guy's face. "This says otherwise."

The man looked around at the others, who had stopped what they were doing and were staring at this face-off.

"Why?"

"Caroline Dawson keeps a room up there."

"So?"

"So I need to see it. Now."

"I have to call somebody."

"The only person *I'll* be calling will be the police, if you don't let me up there."

The guy's Adam's apple was bobbing up and down and he looked desperately around for some support from his fellow workers.

To a person, they all turned away from him and commenced performing their tasks again.

"Okay," said the guy. "But you need a key."

"Where is it?"

He grinned triumphantly. "Ms. Dawson keeps it."

"No problem," said Decker as he headed up the stairs.

"Hey!"

Decker doubled his speed.

He reached a closed door that was apparently the sole entrance to the space up here. It had been open the previous time. He tried the knob, but now it was locked.

He took out a small leather kit. Inside were two pick tools. He only needed one to do the job, since the lock was not a deadbolt.

He pushed the door open and went through. He quickly moved through the event space and bar area, turned left, and came face-to-face with the only other door here.

This lock took both his pick tools. And when that didn't work, his shoulder did the trick.

When the lock burst and the heavy door swung inward, Decker found himself looking at the nicely appointed bedroom that he had been in once before while meeting with Caroline Dawson. Four-poster bed, an enormous armoire, a couple of nightstands, and an attached bathroom. He hadn't seen that on his previous visit. He poked his head in and saw a toilet, a bidet, a double granite-topped vanity, and a marble walk-in shower with a rainfall showerhead.

Decker slowly took it all in, until his gaze fell upon

the armoire. He walked over and opened the door. It was full of women's clothing, some costume jewelry, and many pairs of shoes. He searched through it all but found nothing particularly useful.

He closed the door and took out his tac light. He shone it under all the furniture before coming to the bed. That was where he struck gold, in the crevice between the bed frame and the box springs. No one would notice unless they'd been looking closely.

His fingers gripped the tiny object and examined it closely. He had seen it before. Right in the bar downstairs. He pocketed it and went back down.

The same man confronted him at the bottom.

"I've called the cops," he blurted out.

"Give them my best," said Decker as he walked past him and out the door.

81

Decker's long legs carried him swiftly to the funeral home. On the way he had called Jamison and told her to join him after filling her in on his discovery.

The funeral home parking lot held two long black hearses and a limo for transporting the family to the cemetery. There was also a late-model Mustang convertible, with its top up, parked near the side door. The license plate read: HEAVN.

Jamison joined him at the front door. "What are you going to do?"

"Cut through the crap," he replied.

They entered the front doors and were confronted by the same young man they had previously dealt with here.

"Oh, it's you again."

"Where is Mrs. Southern?"

"She's currently occupied."

"Not good enough," said Jamison, holding out her badge. "Be more specific."

"She's . . . she's working on a client."

"Where?" said Decker.

"You can't go back there."

"Watch me."

He strode off with Jamison in tow.

The young man cried out, "I'm calling the cops."

"Good," said Decker.

They heard noises and followed them to their source. It was a door to a room on a hallway they had not been down before.

Decker gripped the knob and glanced at Jamison, who nodded. He pushed the door open, and they strode in.

Liz Southern looked up from what she was doing, which apparently was preparing her husband's body for his funeral. He lay naked on a table before her. On a rolling cart lay all the tools and cosmetics she was employing to do her task.

"What the hell are you doing here?" she snapped, jumping up. "How did you get back here?"

"We need to talk to you," said Decker.

"I'm going to have both of you—"

She stopped when Decker held it up. The item he'd found under the bed.

"You've probably been looking for this," he said.

She froze, her hand halfway to the phone sitting on a counter. She turned, seemingly mesmerized by what he was holding, and held her hand out for it.

She had almost reached it when Decker pulled it back.

"Jade earring. You were wearing a pair when I first met you at the bar. Buddhist temples. Very nice."

"Where did you find it?" she asked quietly, slumping down on the stool she had been perched on when they had come in.

Decker glanced at Walt Southern's body. "I'm not shy about these things, but still. Can you cover him up?"

Southern hastily draped a sheet over her husband's remains.

"Surprised you're the one doing that," he commented.

"Someone had to do it," she explained, her gaze downcast. "I want him . . . I want him to look . . . presentable."

"It must be very hard," said Jamison sympathetically.

"Right now everything is hard," Southern shot back. She glanced at Decker. "And apparently it's about to get even harder."

"To answer your question, I found it under the bed in the room Caroline Dawson keeps at the OK Corral Saloon. The same one I saw you heading up to that night. And I have it on good authority that Caroline Dawson spent that night there as well. She said she went up there with a headache, but that apparently wasn't true. You could obviously confirm that for us."

"I don't feel the need or desire to confirm anything."

"You and Caroline are a couple?" said Decker.

"I really don't know what you're getting at," said Southern dully.

"You told us your husband was being blackmailed because he was seeing another woman. If the truth had come out it would have ruined him. Well, we checked on that story. And we could find no evidence of any such affair."

Southern looked uncertain. "That's not possible. I know that he was having an affair."

"And I'm telling you he wasn't. Which means you lied."

Southern looked stricken at Decker's words. She took a moment to compose herself. "Okay, you're right, he wasn't having an affair. I did lie about that."

"Then how exactly was he being blackmailed? And we need the truth this time, Liz."

She let out a long, resigned sigh. "He was stealing."

"Stealing what?" asked Jamison.

"Personal effects that people were supposed to be buried with. Watches, rings, other jewelry. He'd put them on the bodies for the viewing and the funeral service, but right before the casket was sealed, he'd take them off. Who would know, right? It wasn't like they were going to dig the person up or check. And if they were cremated, there was no way to ever check. Then he would take trips out of town or even the state to sell them. He made quite a lot of money doing that."

"Why did he do that?" asked Jamison.

Southern looked at Decker. "Remember when we first met I told you that during bad times when people couldn't pay us for our services they'd try to barter?"

"Yes."

"Well, Walt got desperate. I think he convinced himself that he was simply just getting paid for services rendered by the very people he was providing the service to."

"That doesn't make it legal, or right," Jamison pointed out.

"Desperate people do desperate things," retorted Southern.

"And you knew?" asked Decker.

"I suspected. Right before he killed himself we had a big argument. You see, I knew that one of our clients had been dressed in her diamond engagement ring. It was at least four carats. Exquisite. Walt closed up the casket after the service, right before the body was loaded into the hearse to be taken to the cemetery. Then I couldn't find one of my tools that I used to touch up the body before the viewing. I remembered that I had used it to work on her. I opened the casket and found it. It had slid down to the side of the body. That's when I noticed that the ring was gone. After the service was over, I confronted him about it. He was furious. He said I was nuts. I thought he might hit me."

"So that explains his note," said Jamison. "That he was sorry and hated himself."

"I suppose it does, yes."

"And someone else must've found out," said Jamison. "And blackmailed him."

"How did the blackmail start?" asked Decker.

"He received an anonymous message just about the time that Irene Cramer's body was found."

"He showed it to you?"

"Yes. He was both angry and scared."

"What did it say?"

"Basically, it threatened exposure unless Walt did what they asked him to do."

"Fudge the post results?" said Jamison.

"Yes. Particularly about the slicing of the stomach and intestines. To tell the truth, I was surprised that he had even mentioned it in his report. But he really did care about doing a good job, I'll give him that."

"How did you know they weren't bluffing about knowing about his thefts?"

"Those 'business' trips he took? They had photos of him pawning the items he'd stolen. Business records, payment receipts."

"Any idea who it was?"

Southern shook her head.

"Why did he tell you about the blackmail?"

"I guess he needed my support on this to make sure it all went okay. I mean, I was part of the business, too. Our whole life is tied up in this place. If it went under we'd have nothing. And Walt said if he was caught he'd say I knew all about it. That I would go to jail, too. I was so scared. So I just went along with everything."

"Have the blackmailers been in touch with you since Walt killed himself?" asked Decker.

"No. Why would they contact me?"

"I don't know, but they might. And let us know if they do." He paused. "So what do you plan to do now?"

"I don't know. My head is filled with so much stuff now it's hard to think straight. I have to keep the business going, for one thing."

"Can you manage that?"

"Walt was certified in doing postmortems, which I'm not. But I am a trained and certified mortician. I can do embalming, cosmetics, cremation, everything you need to take care of people properly at the end."

"Will you eventually leave here?" asked Jamison. "I mean, you could build a business somewhere else."

"Caroline would have to agree. I don't want to go without her. I really do care for her. And, yes, we are a couple."

"But she was seeing my brother-in-law. You saw them together at the OK Corral."

Southern smiled grimly. "She was merely keeping up *heterosexual* appearances."

"That must've been hard to keep secret in a town this small."

"We worked at it. We were very careful."

"Not so careful if you met up in the bedroom above the bar," Decker pointed out.

"We did that very infrequently. Besides, all the people at the bar were drunk and the staff was too busy to notice. And we were friends. Everyone knew that. They just didn't realize what close 'friends' we were. And we'd leave out the back only very late at night. Most of the time we would go out to my parents' old farmhouse to be together. I thought about selling the place. Walt wanted me to. My father fought in Vietnam. He brought back a lot of curiosities from there that might be quite valuable. Plus a lot of weapons. He was quite the gun guy. But it made for a private place for Caroline and me. So I'm glad I kept it."

"Is that your car in the parking lot?" asked Decker. "'Heaven'?"

"Yes." She smiled.

"What?" asked Decker.

"Remember I talked about barter? Well, the tires on the Mustang came from Hal Parker in payment for us burying his wife."

"I guess people do what they have to do."

"Will this have to come out, I mean, Caroline and me?"

"Lots of gay people live their lives openly and freely now," said Jamison.

"Yes, but not here, I think."

"Look," said Decker, "we can't guarantee anything. We're trying to solve a series of crimes. We have to go where the evidence takes us."

"I guess I can understand that. Will you be talking to Caroline, too?"

"Probably."

"Can you tell her that I didn't tell you about us? That you figured it out?"

"If it's important to you," said Jamison.

"It is. Very important."

"I can see that," said Decker quietly.

82

Decker made a brief stop at the police station to look at an old report. Then he and Jamison drove to the offices of Dawson Enterprises, located in a building in downtown London.

"Why are we here?" Jamison asked.

"To learn stuff we don't know," replied Decker cryptically.

They were taken to the office of the firm's CFO. His name was Abner Crutchfield, a small, dapper man in his late fifties with resolute features and a deep voice. He was dressed in an open-collared shirt, slacks, and polished tasseled loafers.

"Terrible business with Mr. Dawson and Mr. McClellan," he began. "I guess you're working on their cases."

"We are," said Decker. "We're looking for motives, and we'd like to know about the business deal that they concluded right before their deaths."

"All right. I'll certainly tell you what I can," said Crutchfield cautiously.

Decker glanced at Jamison before saying, "I was

surprised that Dawson would sell out. He was in the midst of a buying spree, or so I've been told. Even sold his daughter's restaurant out from under her."

"Yes, yes, that surprised many of us here."

"Was it a large amount that McClellan paid?"

"I can't get into specific numbers, but it was into the nine figures."

"Wow," said Jamison.

"Yes, indeed," commented Crutchfield. "Quite a fortune."

"When did you first learn that McClellan was going to buy him out?" asked Jamison.

"About two months ago. We worked on the deal ever since then in absolute secrecy. And finally closed it. All the docs were signed, sealed, and delivered. Money already wired out and ownership transferred. So McClellan really owns the whole town now." He paused and looked embarrassed. "I mean he did."

"So now his son will own the town?" said Jamison.

"I'm not privy to that information. I know Mr. McClellan's CFO quite well, though, and he never mentioned that the father had cut the son out, so I assume that Shane will inherit."

"He doesn't seem to care that much about business," noted Decker.

"I know that's the general rule of thought around here. But can I give you my opinion?"

"Please do."

"I've known Shane since he was a little boy. He

adored his mother and she loved him, but Stuart was totally wrapped up in business. He showed very little affection to either of them."

"Go on," prompted Decker.

"Shane was very popular in high school. Very athletic."

"He said he and Joe Kelly made a potent QB-receiver combo."

Crutchfield smiled warmly. "That's right. They were always together, those three, including Caroline, I mean. In fact, Joe was the Homecoming King and Caroline was the Homecoming Queen at junior prom. And then senior year it was Caroline and Shane as Queen and King."

"We didn't know that," said Decker.

"But then they graduated. Caroline went to college and Shane went off to war. Joe joined the police force. Then Shane came home. His mother had died. He joined the business, reluctantly, I think. His father never gave him any praise, never an ounce of encouragement. Just the opposite, in fact. But—and this is based on what my CFO friend at McClellan's told me—Shane is actually very smart and detail oriented. I think you would have to be to survive a war. He actually did good work. And now with his father off his back, I think he will run the company very well. That's my two cents, anyway."

"And it was a very helpful two cents," said Decker.

"One more question: Did Caroline know that her father was selling out?"

Crutchfield's expression changed. "That isn't an easy question to answer."

"Just whatever you can tell us."

"Over the last year or so I've sensed some uneasiness between the two of them. Nothing too serious. But Mr. Dawson came to me one day and said he believed that Caroline was growing weary of London. That's when he began reaching out to McClellan's camp."

"Did he say why he felt that way?" asked Decker.

"No. And I didn't press him on it. That was his own business, not mine. The deal went rather quickly after that."

"Maddie's Restaurant?" said Decker. "A tribute to her mother?"

"Yes. She and her mother were very close. Do you know about Junior Dawson?"

Jamison said, "We know he killed himself."

"Yes, years ago, after coming out as gay to his parents." He shook his head sadly. "It was very tragic."

"His father didn't care for that 'alternative' lifestyle, I guess," said Jamison.

"Caroline loved her brother but had a real problem with her father because of the way he treated Junior, especially in public. And Maddie felt the same as Caroline. It drove a wedge between him and his wife, for sure. In fact, if she hadn't died in that tragic accident, I'm not sure they would still be together."

"But they were moving to France at the time," said Decker.

"Yes, well, all I can say is that wherever they went, I'm not sure they would have stayed together."

"Did you ever notice that Stuart McClellan might have been infatuated with Maddie Dawson?" asked Decker.

"Stuart? Well, I didn't know him all that well. But my take on that man was that the only person he was infatuated with was himself."

They left Crutchfield's office and headed back to the SUV. Along the way, Decker said quietly, "You know, Alex, sometimes the cases that seem the most complex are the most simple."

"I would *never* call this case simple."

"Oh, but it is, *very* simple. We were the ones making it complicated. But we had help there, from some unusual sources."

"Meaning?"

"Meaning we got played big-time. Now it's our turn."

83

Later, Decker and Jamison walked into Joe Kelly's office at the police station.

He looked at them. "Where have you two been lately? I've had some thoughts on Ben Purdy and where he might be."

"Forget about Purdy," said Decker. "We need a search warrant and we need it now."

"For who and what?"

Decker told him and Kelly's eyes widened at the answer. "Can you tell me why?" he asked.

"I can tell you enough to get the judge to issue the warrant. For the rest, I'd much prefer to show you."

Later that evening, with a warrant in hand, they drove over to a large, well-kept house on the periphery of downtown London and knocked on the door.

"The car isn't in the driveway," said Decker.

"She may not be home," said Kelly.

"Well, the warrant allows us to enter," said Jamison.

Decker picked the front door lock and they went inside.

He didn't head for the bedrooms upstairs. Instead he made a beeline for the laundry room. Hanging there on a peg was a bag marked "dry cleaning."

He rummaged through it and pulled out the slacks and blouse. "We're very lucky they haven't been cleaned yet."

Later, from a closet shelf, he snagged a pair of pumps off a shelf and checked the size. He nodded to himself.

Kelly said, "Now can you tell me what this is about?"

"As soon as we get these clothes analyzed, you'll know about as much as me."

Late that night Decker sat in the SUV in downtown London with Jamison in the passenger seat.

Jamison was shaking her head in disbelief. "It's still mind-boggling," she said.

He glanced at her. "You ready to do this?"

She touched her Glock. "Ready."

The drive out took about an hour. They stopped well short of the property and made the rest of their way on foot. There was one vehicle parked out front. They recognized it. Decker went over to the car and looked at the tires, then hit the treads with his light.

"What are you looking for?" asked Jamison.

"Exactly what I found."

The one-story farmhouse was old and badly in need of repair, but it was isolated, without another house in sight.

With Decker leading, they made their way to the barn first. The doors were unlocked. They stepped through and looked around with the aid of Decker's tac light. Flies and mosquitoes were buzzing around, and they had to continually swat them away.

They finally spotted a door set against one wall that had an open padlock on it.

They stepped through and looked around at the straw floor.

Jamison swiped at her face where bugs were swirling. "Yuck. I think I swallowed one."

Decker seemed unbothered by the insects. He knelt down and ran his light over the straw on the floor. "Looks like some blood there. We can get it checked later."

"You think this was where Irene Cramer's body was kept?"

"It would allow bugs in but no animals, so it's a safe bet. And there would be no one around to hear her scream."

"That's certainly true," said Jamison.

They searched another outbuilding that was behind the barn. Inside was a vehicle covered by a tarp. When Decker lifted it, a small Honda was revealed. "It must be Irene Cramer's car," said Jamison.

Before Decker could respond they heard the car approaching.

As they watched from out of sight, the yellow Porsche SUV pulled up to the front of the farmhouse. Caroline Dawson got out and walked up to the door and into the farmhouse.

"Okay, that's an unexpected development," said Decker.

"So what do we do?"

"We go and do what we came here to do."

Decker and Jamison crept up to the front door, and Decker whipped it open.

Standing in the front room were Caroline and Liz Southern.

"What the hell?" exclaimed Southern. "What are you doing here?"

Dawson turned around and looked at them blankly.

Decker noted the suitcase on the floor next to Southern.

"Going somewhere?"

Dawson said, "We're going to Canada for a few days."

"Just a few days?" said Decker, looking at Southern.

"Yes, Liz thought it would be a good idea to get away."

"We know about you and Liz," said Jamison.

Dawson looked taken aback. "What are you talking about. We're just—"

Southern interjected, "What we are is none of your business. And what are you doing here?"

Decker pointed his gun at them. "We came for the truth, Liz. I think it's time."

84

Southern placed herself between Dawson and Decker. "You can't come in here and threaten us. I'm calling the police."

"Not to worry, I already called them" was Decker's surprising reply.

A moment later there was a noise from outside. "And there they are. Keep them covered," Decker said to Jamison.

He went to the door and opened it. "Come on in."

A few moments later Joe Kelly walked through the doorway. He looked at Decker questioningly. "Why'd you want me to come out here?" But when he saw Southern and Dawson, he said, "I saw the Porsche outside. What is going on?"

Decker said, "I thought you'd like to be in on the end of this case."

Kelly looked even more confused. "What do they have to do with any of it?"

"You mean what does *she* have to do with it. Well, for starters, Liz killed Maddie Dawson *and* Alice Pritchard."

Kelly exclaimed, "What? No, that can't be right. It was an accident."

Southern snapped, "I had no cause to kill Maddie or Alice."

"You love Caroline, and you didn't want her to move to France. I don't know how you managed it, but you did."

Dawson cried out, "What the hell are you talking about?" She shot Southern a glance. "Liz, what is he talking about?"

"I wish I knew, Caroline. These allegations are ludicrous."

"And, Caroline, with your mother gone, and your brother already dead, Liz only had your father to worry about. But then Liz had another problem."

"What?" snapped Southern.

"Someone found out about your relationship with Caroline."

"Your relationship?" said a shocked-looking Kelly.

Dawson shot Kelly a glance. "Yes, Joe. Liz and I have been together."

Kelly gaped but said nothing.

"But your father didn't know?" said Decker.

"It was none of his business. I did want to be open about my sexuality, but Liz thought we should keep it secret."

"But you said someone found out. Who?" asked Kelly.

"Irene Cramer," replied Decker.

"What are you talking about? How?" said Kelly, his gaze holding on Dawson.

"Liz told me that she and Caroline would sometimes hook up in the apartment above the bar. She and Caroline would leave very late at night, after the bar had closed, and go out the rear entrance. I'm betting that Cramer—who kept late hours, as we know—saw them together. And Cramer lived for a while at Dawson Towers, where Caroline has a condo. Cramer probably saw them there, too."

Jamison said, "And that might be the reason Cramer moved. Liz might have threatened her."

Dawson glanced sharply at Southern. "That woman at the condo building who saw us together? That was Irene Cramer? She never told us her name."

"Maybe it was, so what?" said Southern.

Dawson looked at Decker. "We were sharing a kiss in the doorway of my condo when, I guess, this Cramer person came by. She apologized for intruding. It was no big deal." She looked at Southern again. "I mean, it *was* no big deal, Liz."

"I don't think Cramer had a problem with it. I think the problem was all Liz's."

"What do you mean?" said Dawson.

Decker continued. "Cramer had gotten a note that had disturbed her. That's what Alex was referring to: a threat from Liz. She was planning to leave town. But before she could get away Cramer was abducted. And she was held out in the barn here. But she must've gotten free and found something incriminating and swallowed it." He turned to Southern. "But you saw her do that because you knew you had to get it back." He stopped and eyed both her and Dawson's hands where sat the pinky rings he had seen on each of them before. However, he was seeing them for the first time *together*.

"Your rings are identical. You two exchanged them, right?"

Dawson rubbed at the ring. "Liz got them both. There are inscriptions inside each."

"An inscription inside them that would identify you as being a couple?"

"Something like that," said a perplexed Dawson, while Southern remained quiet.

"If so, Liz *had* to get that back. And performing an autopsy on Cramer would have been easy for you, Liz, since your hubby did it for a living, and you no doubt picked up a lot of the techniques and knowledge. You also told us you were a licensed mortician. You can embalm bodies."

Dawson had taken a step away from Southern. "Liz, this is crazy. You couldn't do anything like that."

"You really cut her open?" said a disgusted Kelly.

Southern still said nothing. Her cool gaze remained on Decker.

"And you're responsible for Walt's death, too," said Decker.

"He shot himself," said Southern quietly. "We all know that."

"I believe you were telling the truth about his stealing. But you found out a lot sooner than you told us you had. And you used that against him."

"Then why didn't he point the finger at me?" retorted Southern.

"Because he didn't know it was you. All he got were anonymous letters. The threat of losing his business and going to prison was enough to get him to go along with the scheme. I doubt he ever suspected you of being involved in killing Cramer. And his note was entirely sincere. He did feel guilt and he did hate himself for what he'd done."

"This is all speculation."

"No, it's not. Now, next up are Hal Parker and Pamela Ames."

"Why would Liz do anything to them?" said Dawson.

"Irene Cramer was a tall woman, about a hundred and thirty pounds or so. She was found in the middle of nowhere. You couldn't carry her all the way there, Liz. So you *drove* the body there. After you killed her you kept her in the barn to screw up the time of death, and then you dumped her in a place where you knew a wolf was prowling around. The animal would be attracted to a dead body by the scent. You might have been hoping that the wolf would get to the body and tear it apart, further hiding what you did to get back the object Cramer swallowed. But the body hadn't been there all that long before Parker showed up. The condition of the body told us that. I guess you didn't know he was even in the area. You didn't figure on that complication. And in addition to finding the body, he found something else, didn't he?"

"Tire tracks," answered Jamison.

Decker nodded. "Ones he knew very well because, as you told us, he gave those tires to you in exchange for your doing his wife's funeral service. The rain would have washed the tracks away, but not before Parker saw them. Did he threaten to expose you?"

Southern put her hands in her pockets and said nothing.

"And Pamela Ames?" asked Kelly.

"She knew Cramer from the Colony. It would make sense that she would ask Cramer for help when she left there. Hell, for all I know, Cramer might have encouraged her to leave. So if Cramer mentioned to Ames that she had seen Liz and Caroline in an intimate embrace? And then she turns up dead?" Decker turned to Caroline. "Ames needed money to get out of town. Did she try to get some from you?"

"No, she never contacted me."

He turned to Southern. "How about you? Or was she going to go to the police with her suspicions? Either way, you had to get rid of her and Parker. I think the clothes you dressed her in came from your own closet. Your clothes size is the same as the ones found on Ames. And your shoe size, too. I checked."

"Liz?" said Dawson nervously.

Decker said, "That only left Hugh Dawson."

"What did my father have to do with anything? And why would Liz hurt him?"

"For the money, of course," answered Jamison.

"The money?"

"Your *inheritance*," said Decker. He looked at Southern. "You wanted Caroline *and* her fortune. But there was no way you were getting that if Hugh found out about you two. That's why you wanted to keep it secret. You knew what happened to Junior. You needed Hugh gone. So you fed us a bullshit story about Stuart McClellan lusting after Maddie Dawson and your theory that he had killed her. And that her husband suspected and picked now to exact his revenge. The puffer fish toxin was a neat touch. If we check the records, I think it will show that you obtained it somehow. Once he ingested that, it would have been easy for you to drive him out to where he was found and set up the carbon monoxide death trap."

"But why kill Stuart?" asked Kelly.

"To give a motive for Hugh to kill himself," replied Decker.

"But what about his suicide note?" said Dawson. "People said it was his handwriting."

"We had an expert examine it. It was forged. By Liz. She'd known Hugh a long time. She's probably seen many examples of his handwriting."

"You have no proof, Decker," said Southern. "Not a shred of it. But I have proof, of being slandered by you."

"Well, in addition to Cramer's car in your out-building, here's some evidence that will knock your socks off."

He pulled an evidence pack from his jacket pocket. Inside was a blouse. "We got a warrant to search your house in town. We found this and your slacks in your dry cleaning bag. This is the blouse you wore to the hospital when you came to check on Caroline, the same day her father was killed. You really should have gotten it cleaned right away."

Southern looked nervously at the blouse, while Dawson looked on in confusion.

Decker said, "Caroline, I explained to you already my theory of how your father was murdered using the extra-long twine. Well, I had the FBI medical examiner analyze this blouse today. Do you know what he found?" When she didn't answer, Decker said, "Your father's blood. Perfect match." He paused to let this sink in with the woman before glancing at Southern. "Even if you were a forensics expert, there's never a way to really perfectly predict how blood and DNA spatters are going to fall with a shotgun in play, even if you were kneeling on the other side of the desk. You probably didn't even notice the drops hit you. But the bottom line is, there is no way that trace would have been on your blouse unless you had been in the room when the shotgun was fired, Liz. So there's your proof."

"My God, Liz," said Kelly, shaking his head in disbelief.

Caroline looked at the other woman. "My father, Liz. You did that to my father."

Southern's expression turned contemptuous. "A man who would have loathed you if he knew you had been with me. And look what he did to your dear brother. So was it really that big a loss?"

"I . . . I can't believe you're even saying that. You killed him!"

Southern shook her head, smiled, and said, "But, Decker, you're not quite as smart as you think you are."

"How's that?" he asked.

"My neighbor told me about your visit to my house. And how you came out carrying some of my clothes."

Decker looked warily at her.

"It's why I told you we needed to get away to Canada, Caroline," said Southern. "I thought Decker might be showing up soon." She looked at Decker. "Remember when I told you my dad fought in Vietnam, and brought back some curiosities?"

"What about it?" said Decker.

"Here's one of them." Southern withdrew her hand from her pocket. In it was a grenade.

"No, Liz, don't!" screamed Dawson.

Southern pulled the pin and threw it at Decker.

85

Decker grabbed Jamison and yanked her from the room and out onto the front porch.

The blast blew out the front windows, and the front wall partially collapsed on them, but it had also taken the brunt of the explosion, leaving them bruised but not seriously injured.

They staggered up and looked around.

"Where's Kelly?" shouted Jamison.

They pushed through the debris and went back inside the house to find the front room demolished.

They saw Kelly climbing out a broken window at the rear of the room. He was all bloody and one of his arms was dangling by his side.

"Kelly, wait," called out Decker.

But the man disappeared from view.

"Where are Liz and Caroline?" cried out Jamison.

Decker ran to the shattered window and looked outside. "I can't see anything, but their cars are out front. It's the only way out."

They clambered over the debris and ran out of the house.

No one was near the vehicles parked in front.

"What the hell!" exclaimed Decker. "Where did they go?"

They heard an engine start up. A few moments later, Cramer's Honda raced from the outbuilding. They ran toward it even as it bore down on them.

At the last possible second, Decker went one way and Jamison the other.

Then shots were fired. Decker looked up from the ground to see Kelly standing in the middle of the one road leading out, his left arm dangling uselessly next to his torso and the other curled around his service pistol, which he was emptying into the car's front windshield on the driver's side.

"Kelly, look out," screamed Jamison.

The car lurched to the right and appeared ready to miss Kelly, but then it straightened out and continued to bear down on him.

Kelly launched himself sideways, a second too late, as the edge of the right bumper clipped his leg and sent him flying.

He landed hard in a heap twenty feet away and didn't move.

The Honda, cracked windshield and all, stopped, backed up, and turned. Now it was heading right toward Decker. He stood and aimed his pistol.

Jamison did the same.

Before either of them could fire, a heavy round hit the car dead center of the front grille and it exploded.

The Honda was lifted off the ground before slamming back down to the dirt.

Before Decker could move, a man came to stand next to him, his long gun in hand.

Robie said, "You okay?"

Decker nodded.

Jessica Reel appeared and helped Jamison up. "Nothing broken?" she said.

"I'm good," replied Jamison before seeing Kelly writhing in pain on the ground. She hustled over to him and cried out, "Call 911. Hurry!"

Decker pulled out his phone but Reel barked, "Ambulance is already coming. One minute away. We figured it might be needed when you told us to be here tonight as backup."

Decker, Robie, and Reel stared at the Honda. It was no longer mobile, so they weren't worried about it coming at them. But no one had gotten out of the vehicle, either.

Both Robie's rifle and Reel's pistol were pointed at the car.

Decker called out, "Liz, come out of the car. Now!"

Seconds passed and then the passenger door opened. Southern climbed out with a gun pressed against Dawson's head.

When Robie and Reel started to move forward, Decker called out, "Wait. Just . . . wait."

The two women moved in front of the Honda.

"Put the gun down, now," barked Robie. Both his and Reel's weapons were pointed directly at Southern's head.

"Don't think so," said Southern. "Now, you're going to let us pass, we're getting in Caroline's Porsche, and then we're getting the hell out of this godforsaken place."

"Liz, please," said Dawson. "Let me go."

"It's going to be okay, Caroline. Just trust me. You've always trusted me. I would never do anything to hurt you."

"You're holding a gun to her head," Decker pointed out.

"Well, you sort of forced my hand on that."

Dawson looked over at where Jamison was kneeling next to Kelly. "I hope Joe is all right. I tried to stop Liz from hitting him."

"You should have known better, Caroline. But that's okay. I'll be strong for both of us. I'll take care of you."

"Put the gun down, Liz," said Decker, watching her every movement, while Robie and Reel did likewise. "You are not leaving here."

"Well, then we have a very big problem, because I have no intention of going to prison."

"Did you really have to kill Cramer?" said Decker.

"I kidnapped her and brought her here. I had the idea that I could get some money from Caroline to make her go away and leave us alone."

"She moved from Dawson Towers and was planning to leave town. I don't think she was doing anything to try to hurt the two of you. I think you're paranoid and you read way too much into the situation."

"You couldn't be more wrong, Decker. My love for Caroline is absolute. But there are others, so many others, who will do anything to keep us apart. Caroline understands that. She knows I had to do what I did."

Dawson flinched at this but remained slient.

"How did Cramer end up dead and butchered, then?" asked Decker grimly.

"I was taking her some food when she broke free. There was a struggle. My ring came off. And . . . Cramer just swallowed it. I couldn't believe she did that. So . . . I stabbed her and then dumped the body. I never expected the FBI to come here and investigate."

"You didn't know about Cramer's past," said Decker.

"And then Hal Parker appeared one day and threatened me. You were right about the tires. He had taken photos. He wanted money."

"What about Ames?"

"At the same time she came around and started asking questions. About Cramer. She seemed to know about me and Liz. Ames knew Cramer from the Colony. I thought she might have told Ames what she had seen. I got scared. If Hugh found out, he'd cut Caroline out of the money."

"So it was just about the money then?" said Dawson bitterly.

"I loved you," shouted Southern, tears spilling down her cheeks. "Like I have never loved anyone ever. I was looking forward to spending the rest of my life with you."

"Liz, you were very special to me. So kind and supportive. But . . . killing people and saying you did it for me? That's . . . you can't do that. It's wrong. You know that."

Southern tightened her grip around Dawson's throat. "I loved you. That's why I did it. It was all for you! You!"

"Okay, put the gun down now, Liz," said a nervous Decker as Southern grew more and more out of control.

She shook her head. "That won't be happening, Decker."

"Why not?"

"Caroline and I were meant to be together. And nothing will stop that from happening."

Southern took a deep breath. Her gaze grew rigid and her expression determined. Her finger slipped to the trigger. "We will be together. If not in this life, then the next."

Decker shouted, "Don't!"

The shot rang out.

It was like a frozen instant in time. No one moved, no one breathed.

The round passed right through Southern's head and out the back. She stood there, dead, for less than a second. And then she toppled to the dirt.

Dawson screamed and ran toward them.

They all looked around to see the source of the shot.

From a hundred yards behind them, Shane rose from a prone position on the ground, his rifle and scope in hand.

"I was a sniper in the Army," he said quietly.

Robie looked at Southern's body.

"And a good one," he said.

86

"They say you're going to make a pretty full recovery," said Jamison.

She and Decker were looking down at Joe Kelly, who was lying in a hospital bed.

He had undergone surgery for a broken arm, leg, and hip, and the removal of some grenade shrapnel.

He looked up at them with a weary, troubled expression.

"I . . . I still can't believe it about Liz."

"It saved her a lifetime in prison," said Jamison.

Decker kept his gaze on Kelly. "What are you going to do now?"

"What else? Soon as I get all healed up, going back to being a cop."

"You might have other options," said a voice.

They all turned to see Shane walk in the door.

He came to stand next to the bed.

Kelly looked up at him, his eyes growing watery. "I was hoping you'd come by."

Shane put a hand on Kelly's shoulder. "You've been through hell and back, Joe."

"We both have, Shane."

"And we'll get through it, together."

"You never said why you were out at Liz's that night," said Decker.

"I was out driving. Saw Caroline pass by. Decided to follow her. I hadn't talked to her alone for a while. I just wanted to see how she was doing. Then she got to Liz's and all hell broke loose. I grabbed my rifle. When you shouted 'Don't!' I took the shot." He shook his head, and his expression was one of misery. "Took shots like that a lot overseas. Never thought I'd have to do it here. I knew Liz . . . I liked her."

Jamison said, "What did you mean by 'other options'?"

"I'm a rich dude," said Shane, now grinning weakly. "Need somebody to help me run the business. Too much for just me."

"Hell, I'm not a businessman, Shane," said Kelly.

"Anybody can learn to be a businessman. Look at me." His tone became more serious. "The thing is, Joe, I trust you. That matters more to me than you know."

Kelly shook his head. "High school was a long time ago. Haven't thrown a touchdown pass to you in over a decade."

"And so maybe it's time we reconnected," said Shane. "And maybe now would be a good time to do it."

"So you'll keep running the businesses?" said Jamison.

"The town needs it. Hell, I need it."

"What about the restaurant?" asked Kelly. "What about Maddie's?"

"I've got some ideas about that," said another voice.

They turned to see Dawson walk into the room. Her haunted look and unsteady gait indicated that she had not fully recovered from her ordeal.

She came to stand next to Shane.

"You saved my life."

His voice trembled when he replied, "I couldn't let that woman shoot you."

She kissed him on the cheek and touched Kelly's hand. "How are you, Joe?"

"Better now," he said, though his smile didn't reach his eyes.

She seemed to read his mind. "I'm the same Caroline, you know. Well, maybe not exactly the same. I feel like I've grown more in the last few days than I have in all the years before that."

Shane said, "I feel the same."

Kelly nodded in agreement, then said, "You mentioned you had some ideas?"

Dawson perched on the side of the bed and took one of Shane's hands and one of Kelly's in each of hers. "This is our home. My dad wanted to move to France, but I never did. We grew up here. We've seen so many changes." She paused. "And now so many people have died. Stuart, my dad, Walt, Liz, and all the others."

Kelly said, "And something big went down over at the military base and at the drilling site, but Decker can't tell us what."

"My point is," said Dawson, "that this town really needs us right now. Shane now owns pretty much everything. But the future of London depends on the investments and the decisions made now. We're sort of at a crossroads. While the busts seem to be behind us, the world's not going to live on oil forever. We need to do it right. Because doing it wrong is not an option."

Shane said, "I came here in part to get Joe to help me run it. I just thought you were going to leave, Caroline, or else I would have asked you too."

"Well, I'm not, I'm staying. For a lot of reasons." She drew a long breath. "So I was thinking that we could work together to keep everything going. See, I'm betting on London, North Dakota, making the transition from just an oil town to a place where people want to live. And, well, I hope you feel the same."

Shane said, "I never wanted any part of my dad's business. But now that it's mine to run, I'm thinking a lot differently. I know about fracking, but you know about everything else, Caroline. So working

577

together seems like a great idea." He looked at Kelly. "You in?"

Kelly squeezed Dawson's hand. "Well, considering I might not be able to pass the physical to qualify as a cop again, and that you two were always my best friends, it's a pretty easy decision."

Dawson hugged first Kelly, then Shane. All three of them had fresh tears in their eyes.

"And we wish you the best of luck," said Jamison, while Decker nodded.

Kelly said, "I hope I never need the FBI again, but if I do, I hope to hell they send you."

Shane said, "Goes double for me."

Dawson gave Jamison and Decker hugs. "Thank you, for everything."

As Decker left with Jamison, he turned around to see three lifelong friends plotting how to change their little piece of the world for the better. Or at least the little part of it represented by London, North Dakota.

Blue Man had a government jet sent to take Decker and Jamison and Robie and Reel back to DC.

After the plane took off from the runway at the Air Force installation in London, Robie eyed Decker, who was sitting in his seat, obviously lost in thought.

"You did good, Decker," he said. "Saved a lot of lives."

"We *all* did good," said Jamison. "And we wouldn't be here but for you two."

Decker said nothing to this. He just stared at the seatback.

"And Brad Daniels recovered and is living at a VA hospital," said Robie. "Hear he's loving telling stories from the past."

As the plane leveled out, Robie got two beers from the bar up front, sat next to Decker, and handed him one. Reel and Jamison got up from their seats and sat at a table in the back with coffees.

Robie took a sip of his beer and looked out the window. "The folks Purdy was working with have been identified. Appropriate back channels have been opened to bring the hammer down on them and to make sure some people are punished. There *will* be consequences."

"Right," said Decker absently.

"No, there *will* be consequences. And Jess and I are going to be the tips of that spear. We volunteered."

Decker eyed him closely. "That makes me feel better," he said quite sincerely.

Robie glanced at him. "You know, every time I finish a mission I take a walk down by Memorial Bridge in DC late at night."

"Why do you do that?" asked Decker, suddenly interested.

"Don't know. Why does anyone do anything?"

"To think, maybe?"

"Maybe. A little quiet time before . . ."

". . . going back to work?"

"Yeah."

Decker drained half his beer. "Maybe that's all we have."

"Meaning work?"

"Meaning, what else?" answered Decker.

"You're good at what you do."

"So are you."

"And I used to think that was enough," said Robie.

Decker shot him a glance. "And now you don't?"

"And now . . . *maybe* I don't." He paused and stared at his drink. "I read your file."

"I didn't have the opportunity to read yours."

"I've never been married, Decker, never had kids. That would be tough for anyone. I'm sorry that happened to you."

Decker didn't respond; he shifted his gaze to look out the window, where it was dark.

"They're getting ready to enter the bunker," said Robie. "And clean out all the crap."

"Good to know."

"It's not a bad thing for people to do from time to time. Clean out the crap."

This caused Decker to look at the man. "You never struck me as being a philosopher."

"Is that what you call it?"

"I don't know. First thing that popped into my head."

"I guess I can see that."

"People often feel the need to give me advice," said Decker, a bite to his words.

Robie nodded slowly. "I felt the same way, until I realized I had never followed any of that advice, and then suddenly I was in a place I didn't want to be."

"And are you out of that place now?"

"Not even close. But just think where I'd be if I hadn't even considered other possibilities." A few moments of quiet passed before Robie rose and said, "I'll leave you to it."

He headed to the front of the jet.

Decker called after him. "Going to Memorial Bridge after we land?"

"Always." He glanced back. "Everyone needs a . . . place, right?"

87

Nearly three hours later, the jet touched down in DC and rolled to a stop. After deplaning, the four said their good-byes.

Jamison shook Robie's and Reel's hands. "I hope this isn't the last time we see you."

"Be careful what you wish for," said Reel, her eyes twinkling. "We usually only show up when the world is about to end."

"Well, if it is, I wouldn't mind you having our backs."

Decker shook Reel's hand, then turned to Robie and said, "Enjoy your Memorial Bridge time."

"And you enjoy wherever you end up going for your 'quiet time.'"

As Decker and Jamison were heading to the terminal, she said, "I don't think I ever want to go back to North Dakota."

"Hey, don't hold it against the state. And Kelly, Shane, and Caroline will have it in tip-top shape in no time."

She glanced at him. "But I still don't understand how you could call this case simple. Look at everything you figured out, everything you said back at Liz's place."

"But the critical part that allowed me to grab the end of the chain and run with it? That was simple."

"What do you mean?"

"Greed, Alex, one of the oldest motives in the book. It explains everything Liz did."

"I think there's one more thing to add to that, Decker."

"What's that?" he said, looking at her in surprise.

"Maybe the *oldest* motive in the book to hurt someone else."

"Which is?"

"Love," she said simply. "Liz's twisted, terrible love for Caroline. But love all the same."

Decker let out a long sigh and nodded. "I think that's the most insightful thing either one of us has said during this case, Alex."

"High praise coming from you," she said.

As they entered the terminal Decker said, "Um, my sister invited me to visit her and the kids out in California in a couple of weeks. Stan's flying out, too."

"That's great, Decker. Are you going to go?"

"I haven't made up my mind."

She looked at him closely. "Well, I think you should. And I mean it. After everything that just happened, a little family time might do you wonders. I know I'm going to visit my family. I need some hugs and kisses."

Decker said, "I know that, Alex. I *did* have a family, you know."

"You *still* have a family, *Amos,*" she shot back.

They took a cab to the condo they shared in southeast DC.

When they got there, Jamison took a shower, changed into sweats, dropped into bed, and fell right asleep.

Decker put his coat back on and went for a walk down near the Anacostia River.

On the other side of town, he figured, Will Robie would be making his way about now to Memorial Bridge and the Potomac to do his brooding.

Decker took a seat on a bench and looked out at the dark flowing waters and the lights beyond.

Now what? as Robie had implied.

He took out his phone and called his sister.

Renee answered on the second ring. "My God, Amos, Stan called and told me some of what happened. It's a miracle you're all still alive."

"Yeah, I guess it is."

"I suppose this sort of thing happens to you a lot."

"Maybe more than most. Look, about coming to see you and the kids?"

"Rest assured, we'll give you your own space. No suffocating you with love and affection on my watch," she added in a lighthearted tone. When she next spoke, her voice, though, had lost its frivolity. "Will . . . will you come?"

He didn't answer right away. "I'm not sure, Renee. I'll have to let you know."

"O-okay." Her tone of disappointment bounded over the ether and hit Decker as hard as anyone ever had on the football field.

"There's just a lot going on."

"I know. And, Amos, regardless of whether you come or not?"

"Yeah?"

"You will always be loved, little brother."

"I'm not sure I deserve that, Renee."

"Well, I think you've *earned* it. And coming from your sister, I hope you know how big a deal that is."

She clicked off and he rose and started walking. Perhaps in search of *his* Memorial Bridge. Perhaps in search of something . . . anything *else*. And terrified that he would never be able to find it, because maybe it did not exist for someone like him.

He took out the photo of Cassie and Molly and studied it under the moonlight.

Time did not heal all wounds for him. It barely touched them, in fact. It was like pouring iodine on a cancerous tumor.

I don't miss you less and less. I miss you more and more. And I'm so sorry there's absolutely nothing I can do about it.

585

Decker put the photo away and started to walk on, but then stopped.

In his mind's eye were the images of his wife and daughter.

He just stood there, frozen for a few moments. They seemed to be talking to him, somehow communicating something he already knew, but simply refused to acknowledge.

And then Jamison's last words came back to him. *You still have a family.*

Decker slowly reached into his pocket, took out his phone, and punched in the number.

"Renee?"

"Amos, what's wrong?"

"I just wanted to tell you that . . . that I'll be there."

Acknowledgments

To Michelle, here comes Amos Decker again. I know you like the big guy.

To Michael Pietsch, for your continued support.

To Ben Sevier, Elizabeth Kulhanek, Jonathan Valuckas, Matthew Ballast, Beth deGuzman, Anthony Goff, Rena Kornbluh, Karen Kosztolnyik, Brian McLendon, Albert Tang, Andy Dodds, Ivy Cheng, Joseph Benincase, Andrew Duncan, Morgan Swift, Bob Castillo, Laura Eisenhard, Sean Ford, Kristen Lemire, Briana Loewen, Mark Long, Thomas Louie, Rachael Kelly, Kirsiah McNamara, Nita Basu, Lisa Cahn, Megan Fitzpatrick, Michele McGonigle, Alison Lazarus, Barry Broadhead, Martha Bucci, Rick Cobban, Ali Cutrone, Raylan Davis, Tracy Dowd, Jean Griffin, Elizabeth Blue Guess, Julie Hernandez, Erica Hohos, Linda Jamison, John Leary, John Lefler, Rachel Hairston, Suzanne Marx, Christopher Murphy, Rob Philpott, Barbara Slavin, Karen Torres, Mary Urban, Jeff Shay, Carla Stockalper, and everyone at Grand Central Publishing, for being a great team.

David Baldacci

To Aaron and Arleen Priest, Lucy Childs, Lisa Erbach Vance, Frances Jalet-Miller, John Richmond, and Juliana Nador, for all you do, and it's a lot.

To Mitch Hoffman, for once more pushing me to do better!

To Anthony Forbes Watson, Jeremy Trevathan, Trisha Jackson, Alex Saunders, Laura Sherlock, Sara Lloyd, Claire Evans, Sarah Arratoon, Stuart Dwyer, Jonathan Atkins, Anna Bond, Leanne Williams, Natalie Young, Stacey Hamilton, Laura Ricchetti, Charlotte Williams, and Neil Lang at Pan Macmillan, for such a great tour last year and allowing me to dress up in my kilt. 2020 is looking great!

To Praveen Naidoo and the wonderful team at Pan Macmillan in Australia.

To Caspian Dennis and Sandy Violette, for doing what you do so well!

And to Kristen White and Michelle Butler, for helping me in so many ways!

Author's Note

The idea for this story came from three things I learned about North Dakota. First, the Stanley R. Mickelsen Safeguard Complex is an Air Force eye-in-the-sky installation near Grand Forks, North Dakota. Second, the Air Force auctioned off some of the adjacent land in 2012. Third, the auction was won by a sect of Anabaptist Hutterites, who established a community there.

Then I created my own Air Force installation, which I set on the opposite side of North Dakota, amid all the fracking operations, and the plot took off from there.

Hope you enjoyed the story.

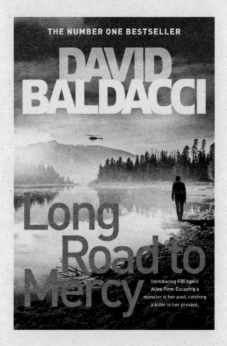

OUT NOW

A Minute to Midnight

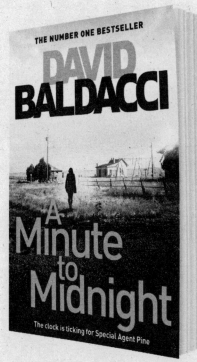

Special Agent Atlee Pine's quest for the truth about what happened to her sister Mercy continues in *A Minute to Midnight*.

OUT NOW

Redemption

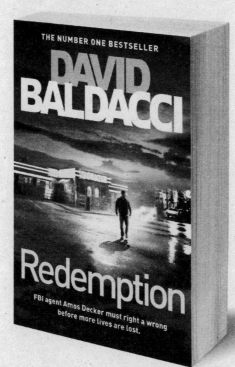

FBI consultant Amos Decker discovers that he
may have made a fatal mistake when he was a
rookie homicide detective. Back in his home town,
he's now compelled to discover the truth . . .

One Good Deed

Murder and family secrets, a touch of romance and
deeply felt revenge – with the twist of all twists –
make up the ingredients of this gripping page-turner
for all those who love mystery, crime, Raymond
Chandler and Agatha Christie from one of the world's
favourite thriller writers, David Baldacci.

Daylight

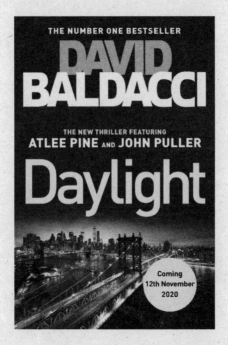

The gripping third title in the FBI special agent Atlee Pine series. Joining forces with old friend and military investigator John Puller, Atlee continues the search for her sister and in the process exposes corruption at the highest levels of government.

Vega Jane and the Secrets of Sorcery is the first title in the thrilling fantasy adventure series for children by bestselling master storyteller David Baldacci, and is illustrated throughout by Tomislav Tomić.

Full of monsters, magic, danger and mystery, this new edition, previously published as *The Finisher*, launches in January 2021.

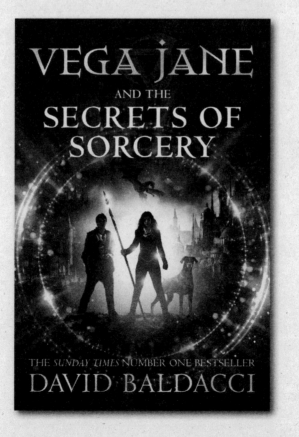